New York Times bestselling author **Christine Feehan** has had over thirty novels published and has thrilled legions of fans with her seductive Dark Carpathian tales. She has received numerous honours throughout her career, including being a nominee for the Romance Writers of America RITA and receiving a Career Achievement Award from *Romantic Times*, and has been published in multiple languages.

Visit Christine Feehan online:

www.christinefeehan.com
www.facebook.com/christinefeehanauthor
@AuthorCFeehan

Praise for Christine Feehan:

'After Bram Stoker, Anne Rice and Joss Whedon, Feehan is the person most credited with popularizing the neck gripper'
Time magazine

'The queen of paranormal romance'
USA Today

'Feehan has a knack for bringing vampiric Carpathians to vivid, virile life in her Dark Carpathian novels'
Publishers Weekly

'The amazingly prolific author's ability to create captivating and adrenaline-raising worlds is unsurpassed'
Romantic Times

CHRISTINE
FEEHAN

Lightning Game

A GHOSTWALKER NOVEL

PIATKUS

PIATKUS

First published in the US in 2021 by Berkley,
An imprint of Penguin Random House LLC
First published in Great Britain in 2021 by Piatkus
This edition published in 2021 by Piatkus

1 3 5 7 9 10 8 6 4 2

A CIP catalogue record for this book
is available from the British Library.

ISBN: 978-0-349-42836-9

Printed and bound in Great Britain by Clays Ltd, Elcograf S.p.A.

Papers used by Piatkus are from well-managed forests
and other responsible sources.

MIX
Paper from
responsible sources
FSC® C104740

Piatkus
An imprint of
Little, Brown Book Group
Carmelite House
50 Victoria Embankment
London EC4Y 0DZ

An Hachette UK Company
www.hachette.co.uk

www.littlebrown.co.uk

For Kylie Wurst,
who shares my love of research, experiments and all things
unique and different in this world! Hope you love this one.

FOR MY READERS

Be sure to go to christinefeehan.com/members/ to sign up for my private book announcement list and download the free ebook of *Dark Desserts*. Join my community and get firsthand news, enter the book discussions, ask your questions and chat with me. Please feel free to email me at Christine@christinefeehan.com. I would love to hear from you.

ACKNOWLEDGMENTS

As in any book, there are so many people to thank: Brian, for putting up with me during power hours on Skype so I can get the books written. Domini, for always editing, no matter how many times I ask her to go over the same book before we send it for additional editing. Every single time I FaceTime you, no matter what time of day it is, there you are working, and you stop what you're doing to talk books with me when I'm so frustrated. Thank you a million times over! Denise, for staying up nights and letting me write while she does the brunt of the business I never want to do. I can't thank you enough for working tirelessly to keep the machine going even when I have no clue what I'm doing and you're endlessly patient and talk me through it. Sheila, my go-to woman, who will figure it out when we're hanging by our fingernails. Renee, for making me laugh no matter what is going on.

THE GHOSTWALKER
SYMBOL DETAILS

SIGNIFIES
shadow

SIGNIFIES
protection against evil forces

SIGNIFIES
the Greek letter psi, which is used by parapsychology researchers to signify ESP or other psychic abilities

SIGNIFIES
qualities of a knight—loyalty, generosity, courage and honor

SIGNIFIES
shadow knights who protect against evil forces using psychic powers, courage and honor

nox noctis est nostri

THE GHOSTWALKER CREED

We are the GhostWalkers, we live in the shadows
The sea, the earth, and the air are our domain
No fallen comrade will be left behind
We are loyalty and honor bound
We are invisible to our enemies
and we destroy them where we find them
We believe in justice and we protect our country
and those unable to protect themselves
What goes unseen, unheard and unknown are GhostWalkers
There is honor in the shadows and it is us
We move in complete silence whether in jungle or desert
We walk among our enemy unseen and unheard
Striking without sound and scatter to the winds
before they have knowledge of our existence
We gather information and wait with endless patience
for that perfect moment to deliver swift justice
We are both merciful and merciless
We are relentless and implacable in our resolve
We are the GhostWalkers and the night is ours

1

Rubin Campo stood in front of the small cabin made of mostly broken lumber his brothers and father had dragged or cut from the trees in the forest and pieced together. No one had lived there in years, but he and Diego came back every year and fixed the place up. He had no idea why. Some compulsion buried deep in them that pulled them back, he supposed.

They'd been born there. The cabin hadn't been so large then. At the time it had been one room. His two older brothers and father had begun expanding it as the family grew in size. Eventually, there were nine children. Had their father not died when his horse stepped in a hole and fell, rolling on him, breaking his father's neck, there most likely would have been more children.

They had lived off the land and were distrustful of outsiders. He'd learned hunting, fishing and trapping at a very early age. By the time he was three, he had learned to shoot. Every bullet counted. None could be wasted. It mattered little what age he was—if he pulled a trigger, he was expected to bring home something to put in the cooking pot.

"Someone's been moving around the property," Diego said, coming up behind him. "Tracks everywhere. Been coming here for a while."

"Stripping the place," Rubin guessed. He'd noticed the tracks as well.

The community was a very closed one. They didn't let outsiders in, and everyone within several miles of their land knew the brothers returned to their property. They were doctors, and they came back and treated the sick. The people were so distrustful of government and everyone else, they refused to go to the nearest towns for medical aid, relying on homeopathic treatments. Rubin and Diego returning, two of their own, were welcome. No one would steal from them. Whoever was taking things from their cabin had to be an outsider, yet the tracks indicated that the person was coming and going on a regular basis.

"Maybe," Diego mused.

Rubin didn't know why it bothered him that someone would take anything from the old cabin. It wasn't like they lived there or needed the things they'd left. People were poor. He remembered being hungry all the time. Real hunger, not knowing when his next meal was coming or even if it was coming. He knew exactly how that felt.

Rubin was ten months older than Diego, and they'd been seven years old when their father had died, leaving their mother with nine children and only the land to sustain them. Their two oldest brothers, at fourteen and fifteen, had gone off looking for work, hoping to bring in money, but they had never returned. Rubin and Diego never learned what happened to them.

The two boys, as young as they were, began to hunt, fish and trap to put food on the table for the family. The girls helped by gathering plants and roots and growing as much as they could to help provide. Out hunting rabbits, the boys discovered a spring up above their cabin. Both were already showing astonishing promise of their genius abilities in spite of their lack of formal education. By the time they were eight, they figured out how to use gravity to bring that water to their cabin, and for the first time, they had running water in the house.

They were nine years old when Mary left to marry a man on the farm closest to theirs: Mathew Sawyer. There were few choices for men or women to find anyone where they lived, but he was a good man. She was barely of age and she died in childbirth nine months later. Their mother didn't smile much after that, no matter how many times the boys or their sisters tried to coax her.

Rubin reached back and rubbed at the knots in his neck. "I swear, every time I come to this place, I think it will be my last, but I can't stop." He turned away from the cabin. "It's really beautiful up here. I need the isolation of it. I love the swamp in Louisiana and our team, everyone there, but sometimes . . ." He trailed off.

Sometimes he needed space. He had gifts—psychic gifts that were rare. He belonged to an elite and covert military team called GhostWalkers. All of them had psychic gifts. His entire team. It was just that his gift or one of his gifts happened to be extremely rare, and so they protected him. They shielded him so that any enemy would never find out that he had such an ability. As far as they knew, only two people in the world had the gift of being a psychic surgeon. He was one of the two. The team tended to hover until sometimes he felt he couldn't breathe.

Diego sent him a small grin. He got what Rubin meant without a huge explanation. "There's nothing like the fireflies in the spring, is there?"

Rubin referred to the fireflies as lightning bugs, and he always looked forward to dusk. The setting of the sun brought that first note in the beautiful melody, as the fireflies rose up to dance in harmony along the edges of the grass. He used to sit with his sisters and whisper to them of fairies and fey creatures, telling them stories he made up to entertain them. He knew Diego listened just as raptly as his sisters did.

The lightning bugs represented peace to him. Magic. Their world was one of survival and grim reality. But in the spring, when the fireflies came out at the setting of the sun to dance and provide their spellbinding performance, Rubin took his sisters outside and would sit with them in spite of his mother's forbidding silence. He would spin tales for them to go along with the glowing dips and spins of the fairy-like lightning bugs.

A traveling man had once told stories to them when he had stopped by, trying to get their mother to purchase cloth from him. They had no money. They made their own clothes from hand-me-downs. Most were too small or too big because they traded with other families from farms. Rubin and Diego had kept a rifle on the man the entire time he was near them. He never saw it. They concealed their weapons under a blanket. Rubin had followed him off the property while Diego had gone up into the trees to cover Rubin. Rubin hadn't liked the man, but he liked the stories.

"I miss the lightning bugs when we're in the swamp," Rubin conceded. His throat closed at the memories welling up. His sisters. Lucy, Jayne and the twins, Ruby and Star. They would sit so still when he told them stories, rapt attention on their faces.

Rubin and Diego were ten when they managed to find a way to get in the old mining shaft, found the equipment and stripped it. They figured out how to make a generator after taking apart the one at the mine. It was the first time their mother ever had hot water and electricity. That winter was a good one. They were able to keep food on the table. Their mother didn't smile, but she participated a bit in the conversations.

That next summer, four men hiked the Appalachian Trail and camped just past their land. Lucy, their twelve-year-old sister, had gone night-fishing with eight-year-old Jayne. It wasn't uncommon for them to be gone most of the night, but when they didn't come home in the morning, Rubin and Diego went looking for them. They found Lucy's body half in and half out of the stream, her clothes ripped off her and blood under her fingernails. Little Jayne lay beside her, drooling, clothes torn, head bleeding from where someone had struck her a terrible blow. She screamed and screamed when she saw her brothers, not making any sense at all.

Rubin carried Jayne home while Diego carried Lucy's body. They left both to be looked after by their mother and Ruby and Star, the thirteen-year-old twins, while they collected their rifles and went back to look for tracks. They caught up with the four men the second night. The men had camped up by a little waterfall and were laughing and talking like they didn't have a care in the world. The boys each chose a target, took careful aim and shot them through the heart. Two shots. Two kills. Just like they'd been taught from the time they were toddlers. They couldn't afford to waste ammunition.

The other two men took to cover, hiding. Scared. It didn't matter. They were varmints. And they were being hunted by experts. They might be boys, but they were elite trackers already. They both could call on animals to hunt with them, usually raptors. They knew

5

the land. This was their world, and they were merciless when they had to be. By early the next morning, the other two men were dead as well.

They didn't bother to bury or hide the bodies. The men had gone off trail. The boys had no respect for them, so as far as they were concerned, the vultures could have them. They were many miles from their run-down cabin, and by the time someone did find the bodies—if they did—there would be no tracks leading back to them.

Rubin glanced down at the tracks around his cabin. They were recent. The grass was barely pressed down, as if either the person going in and out of their home didn't weigh much or enough time had passed that the grass was beginning to stand again. He'd let his brother figure it out. Diego was amazing at tracking.

"You going inside?" Diego's southern accent had deepened as it often did when they returned to their roots.

"I'm thinking on it," Rubin said. "It was a long trip and I'm tired, but if I go inside and the place is a mess, I'll be upset and won't be able to settle for the night." He wouldn't anyway. There were too many memories crowding in. It always happened that way when they came back. He was always conflicted when he first came home. Always. How could he not be? They'd lost so much.

The flu hit the winter they turned thirteen. Ruby, Jayne and their mother all came down with it. Rubin had never felt so helpless in his life. He tried to nurse them back to health. He tried every potion and herbal medicine he knew to cure them. Nothing seemed to work. He couldn't bring down their fevers. They buried Jayne first. Three days later, Ruby died. Their mother was down for six weeks. She never spoke a single word after that. She sat in a chair and rocked back and forth, humming songs and refusing to eat or acknowledge any of them no matter how much Star tried to coax her.

The winter they turned fourteen was a bad one and they had no choice but to go out hunting, often long distances, or starve. When they returned from one particularly long hunt, Star was sobbing. Their mother's body swung from a rope hung from the center beam of the miserable little cabin. Star was inconsolable, certain their mother's death was her fault. She'd fallen asleep for just a few minutes. It was left to Rubin and Diego to cut their mother down and bury her alongside her husband and children in the graveyard behind the cabin, a nearly impossible task in the hard, frozen ground.

They woke the next morning to find a note from their sister explaining she couldn't stay. She was sorry and hoped they would forgive her, but she was going to the nuns in the neighboring town a good distance away. Rubin and Diego were alarmed. The snow and ice were bad and the distance too far. None of the family had good winter gear. She was dead by the time they found her, frozen in a small crevice near the stream where Lucy and Jayne had been attacked. It took them three days to dig a hole deep enough to bury Star in the family graveyard.

The graveyard was still behind the house. They planted wildflowers over the graves and kept it nice each year they returned. They also worked on the cabin, improving it just a little, knowing they would return to help those who distrusted doctors and refused to go anywhere near cities or towns and outsiders but would trust one of their own.

"You going inside or just going to stand there with your hand on the door?" Diego prompted him again.

"I'm contemplating." Rubin gave him a look. Sometimes being ten months older meant he could be bossy, not that Diego ever acknowledged anyone was his boss. He preferred to think they were twins and therefore the same age.

Diego flashed a little cocky grin. "If you keep contemplating, we're both going to have white beards by the time you make up your mind whether to open the door."

"Did it ever occur to you this could be a trap? Someone might have a grenade strapped to the doorknob, and if I turn it and walk inside, that's the end of both of us? We've got a few enemies. I could be saving your life."

"I don't make enemies. No one ever knows I exist. I'm a ghost," Diego pointed out.

That was true enough, Rubin had to concede. In a forest, or just about anywhere really, Diego was difficult to spot. He was one of the best, and once set on an enemy, he would find them. Animals and birds aided him. He was silent and deadly. Diego appeared mild-mannered, but he truly was a dangerous man.

"Still, step aside. I might have to be the one to open the door. I can't take chances that the brain in our family gets blown up. I'd have to file all kinds of reports, and I do hate paperwork. Not to mention Ezekiel would be really pissed."

Ezekiel Fortunes. The man who had ultimately saved their lives. They owed him everything. The two boys had waited until spring before they packed what little they had and hiked to the railway, hopping the train leading out of the mountains. They rode the rails for days, staying hidden, until they got off in a big city thinking they could find work. It was a terrible mistake, one of the worst they'd ever made. There were no jobs. Now they had no home and no forest to hunt or trap in. No stream to fish in.

Everyone they loved was dead. No one knew they even existed. Not a single person cared whether they lived or died. And then they ran into Ezekiel Fortunes. He wasn't much older than they were, but he knew the streets of Detroit. He had two younger brothers he protected, but he was still willing to take them on as long as they followed his rules.

They believed in Ezekiel so much they ended up following him into the military and ultimately into the GhostWalker program. And yeah, he'd be pissed if they got blown up because they were so careless they didn't look for a grenade when they knew someone had been in their cabin.

"There's no grenade," Rubin admitted. "I'd feel it." He could too. He could disrupt electronics with the energy in his body and he could feel traps fairly easily.

He'd been enhanced, just as all GhostWalkers had, both psychically and physically. They'd all signed on for the psychic enhancements, but they had been tricked into the physical enhancements. There was no going back. Dr. Peter Whitney had performed the surgeries on all of them, changing their DNA, giving them different traits and abilities, making them into something they were never meant to be.

The first team Whitney had experimented on was "flawed." Many suffered all kinds of physical problems and needed "anchors" to work outside of their environments without the continual assault from the outside world on their unprotected brains. There were four teams, and Whitney had improved his soldiers with each team. No one realized that prior to working on the soldiers he had performed hundreds of experiments on orphaned girls, believing them to be useless and, in his mind, giving them a higher purpose—serving their country.

Rubin opened the door to the cabin, bracing himself for the flood of memories before walking inside. The cabin should have been dirty. Dusty at the very least. Instead, not only was it immaculate, but someone had fixed it up, repairing the sink that he'd been telling himself he would get to the last two visits. The wood around it had rotted. He was going to replace it but never had enough time. Someone had not only done so, but the job was impeccable.

Rubin turned to look at his brother, not knowing how to feel about someone invading their cabin and actually working on it. No one had ever done anything to the Campo cabin other than a Campo. He stepped into the middle of the room and took a long, slow look around, taking in everything. His brother took his back, doing the same. It was a familiar position, but they were looking at a very unfamiliar cabin.

Their cabin didn't even smell the same. Coral honeysuckle was rare to find in the mountains and yet the cabin definitely held the subtle fragrance, mixed strangely enough with the scent of daffodils. His mother called them jonquils. All along the neighboring holler where they grew freely, they referred to them as Easter lilies. There was no hint of a musty smell at all. The loft held a new mattress. He could tell because it didn't stink of the usual rodents that had burrowed their way inside the foam. A sleeping bag covered the top of the mattress.

Someone hadn't been taking things from their cabin. Someone was *living* there. That someone was female. There were no flowers, but that fragrance told both men the occupant was a woman.

"I'll get rid of any sign outside that we were anywhere near the place," Diego said.

Rubin nodded. He was uneasy. When he was uneasy, it usually meant something was very wrong. "Be careful, Diego. I've got a bad feeling."

"I've got the same bad feeling. Stay away from the windows."

Rubin didn't need the warning. He waited until his brother had slipped outside. Once Diego was out of the cabin, he felt better. He had never seen anyone who could match his brother's ability in the forest. At least he knew Diego would be safe. He crouched low, squatting, the way his father had taught him, relieving pressure on his spine while he studied the interior of the cabin, inspecting every corner.

The floors were spotless. There was a handwoven rug at the foot of the ladder leading to the loft where the bed was. Four years earlier, they had roughed in a shower and toilet. It had been very rough. They had been used to an outhouse and an outdoor shower when they came to the mountains. The shower was still open, but it was much nicer. The floor of the shower had been set in smooth, polished stones over the plastic around the drain they'd roughed in. They had packed in a brand-new porcelain toilet when they came that year and it was spotless.

The kitchen sink was immaculate. The small gas stove had been thoroughly cleaned. That had been brought up only last year. Ordinarily, they made do with a small grill they kept in the shed around back. The woman who was living in their cabin believed in cleanliness. She hadn't made things worse, but she had made changes to the kitchen and the bathroom, and even fixed the ladder going to the loft.

Rubin glanced up at the ceiling. They were planning on reroofing this trip. There had been water damage and they hadn't been able to do more than patch the roof before they had to leave last time. There were no water marks on the ceiling. The wood had been replaced. That wood had been there since he was born. Even with water stains, his father and brothers had hauled that wood from the forest, trimmed it, notched it and put it in place. It had lasted all these years. An outsider had taken it down and replaced it. It didn't matter that she'd done a damn good job. That was part of his family legacy—all he and Diego had left other than the graveyard behind the cabin.

At least she hadn't touched the two rocking chairs their father had carved so long ago. Diego and Rubin had kept them in pristine condition. Each year they'd returned, they'd polished the wood and treated it so no insects would bore into it and ruin it. The seats were wide and very comfortable. The armrests were the perfect height. Had anyone stolen or harmed those rocking chairs, he might have considered hunting them down and shooting them. He definitely would have hunted the thieves to retrieve the chairs.

In the dresser built into the wall going out to the mud porch—that had been the practical place to store extra clothing when they had no indoor shower—he found two pairs of jeans in the second drawer. They were a small size. Three tank tops, all dark colors, and three others in light colors. Four T-shirts in dark colors. Socks. Two sweaters. A puffy vest. The top drawer held leggings and a tank only.

She didn't have much in the way of clothing. Not summer gear. Not winter gear. What the hell was she doing up here? He was planning on asking her. She hadn't brought her own tools. She was clearly using their tools right out of the shed.

He spotted the backpack pushed inside the pantry where they normally stored potatoes. It was darkest there. He pulled it out, unzipped it and began pulling out the contents. She didn't have much there either. A pair of running shoes. A first-aid kit, but it was pretty sparse. Lightweight flashlight and batteries. Knife in a leather scabbard, this one lethal looking. Pocket knife that she should have had on her if she was running around in the woods.

On the bed was a sketch pad, charcoal drawing pencils and colored pencils. She was a good artist. Lots of flowering plants. He knew all of them. Knew where they were located. Most were quite a bit off the beaten path. She could easily get lost if she was off chasing flowers and mushrooms, lacy ferns and shrubbery through the forest, especially if she wasn't native to the area. Most were medicinal plants. She obviously knew something about homeo-pathic medicine.

Where the hell was she? The sun was long past setting. He was beginning to feel a little worried about her, which was stupid since he didn't know her and she'd been trespassing. He inhaled again, the scent of coral honeysuckle filling his lungs. It was a beautiful flower, one rare for the mountains. *Extremely* rare. He wondered if she was a transplant just like that flower, rare like the fragrance permeating his cabin.

For some reason he couldn't quite identify, he was beginning to lay claim to the woman. Maybe because she was in his cabin and that fragrance was filling his senses. He was essentially a loner. He preferred it that way. He and Diego always stayed close to each other, and they stayed close to the Fortunes brothers, but in terms of letting people know who he was, that just didn't happen.

He was intelligent enough to know he'd suffered too much loss early in his life. He didn't believe anyone would stay, so he locked his emotions away and he fiercely protected Diego, just as his brother fiercely protected him. Still, for all that, that scent was wreaking havoc with his senses and his protective instincts.

The flutelike notes of the nightingale added to the sounds sur-rounding the cabin. Rubin listened to the rich ballad, the male crooning to a female. The sky had turned a variety of dark purples and deep blues long after the sun had disappeared, leaving the sky to the moon. Diego, in the form of that nightingale, had warned Rubin he was about to have company. Diego had perfected the art of singing like any bird he'd heard at a very young age, so much so that he could draw them to him.

Rubin moved into position in the middle of the cabin, waiting for his brother to tell him if she was coming to the front door or the back. The song started again just a few moments later, the male clearly persuading his potential ladylove to accept him. The notes doubled up if one listened closely, which meant his transplant was coming in through the back door. Not surprising if she'd been traipsing through the woods.

She could easily be a potential enemy sent by any number of foreign nations anxious to acquire a GhostWalker. She could also have been sent by Whitney. He wanted his soldiers back, particularly the ones with special talents. He often pitted his supersoldiers against the GhostWalkers to see which of his experiments would live through the battles.

Rubin slid into the shadows and went still. He'd learned years earlier to disappear there. The back door opened and a slight silhouette came through. The door closed and she crouched down to unlace her hiking boots. Putting the boots neatly aside, she tossed her socks into a small basket and then hung her jacket on a hook by the door. Pulling her shirt over her head, she tossed that into the same basket along with her bra. Stripping off her jeans and panties, those went into the basket and she stepped into the shower.

Rubin was inherently a gentleman. It wasn't that he wasn't interested enough to want to look at the female body given the opportunity, but he wouldn't take undue advantage, especially in this circumstance. This woman was out in the middle of nowhere, alone, and would be terrified as a rule, confronted by two men—except for one thing. Most GhostWalkers recognized the energy of another GhostWalker. Rubin recognized her energy immediately.

It was impossible that it was a coincidence that a female Ghost-Walker just happened to be in his cabin in the Appalachian Mountains, camping out. Whitney had sent her. And if Whitney had sent her, she was his enemy. She was there to distract or kill him. Either way, there were more coming. It was no secret that he returned to his home to treat those refusing to trust outsiders. Both

Diego and Rubin came sometimes twice a year. She was living in the cabin for a reason, and that reason was to get to them.

Rubin considered whether or not to confront her while she was shampooing her hair. She hadn't turned on lights. Or lit candles. The night hadn't completely fallen, so it wasn't completely dark yet, but still, most people, when they were alone, preferred to have lights. A GhostWalker wouldn't necessarily need lights. Whitney's experiments often included animal DNA, so many of them could easily see in the dark.

He studied her body while she conditioned her hair. She was fit. Really fit. Feminine, but without a doubt, muscles moved beneath that flawless skin. Her hair was nearly white it was so blond, and the color was natural because the tiny curls at the junction between her legs were just as white as the wealth of hair on her head.

He found himself fascinated with the way her body moved, a display of feminine power, of beautiful lines and movement, almost like a dancer, yet clearly that of a fighter. She was deceptively delicate, so when she was wearing clothes, no one would ever see that beneath she would be deadly, a true assassin coiled to strike.

The water went off, and she stepped out of the stall and wrapped a towel around her body. He let her get into the center of the room, away from all potential weapons. She had toweled off the blond pixie cut framing her face, now a shade or two darker from the dampness of the water than it had been when she'd entered the shower.

"I think you might want to just stop right there and stay very still. My brother has you covered dead center from the window, and he doesn't miss, which I'm certain you know." Rubin kept his voice low. Smooth. "No, don't turn around. Stay facing that window."

Diego would be able to see her without a problem. Whitney had made certain of that.

"Start with your name. You must have one."

"Of course I have a name. It's Jonquille. Are you Rubin? Or Diego?"

"Diego is the one with the rifle pointed right between your eyes. I'm Rubin. We aren't going to be playing any games with you. This isn't a coincidence that you're here. I know you're a GhostWalker. I can feel your energy. You know I am. So let's just cut to the chase. When is the team going to arrive and how many should we be expecting?"

"There is no team. I came here looking for you. I studied everything about you I could find. There was no way to get anywhere near you in Louisiana. Your team was always around you. In any case, it was too dangerous for me and everyone else. So I came here and just waited. I knew you'd come, although you're early."

He couldn't detect a lie in her voice, but some GhostWalkers were adept at lying convincingly. "Why would you study everything about me and then stalk me?"

"I do sound like a stalker, don't I?"

For the first time nerves crept into her voice. Before, she had just sounded excited. Not even upset that she was naked beneath the towel and he'd caught her in a vulnerable position. Just excited.

"That's not how I meant it. I saw you speak at a conference on lightning. It was brilliant. You were brilliant. I know you're a hotshot doctor and all, and mostly you go to medical conferences, but you have an interest in lightning and you seem to have insights most so-called qualified people don't."

She talked so fast, her words tumbled over one another. Again, she started to turn.

"Don't." He reminded her sharply. "Diego will shoot you without hesitation."

"Can't you just tell him to put down his rifle for a minute so we can talk? If you don't believe me, he can pick it back up again."

He wanted to smile at the sheer exasperation in her voice. "No, I'm afraid we can't do that just yet. Keep talking."

He found it interesting that she wasn't in the least impressed with his being a "hotshot" doctor. He had a profound interest in all things lightning. He had written papers on it. Talked theories. Discussed ways to harness it. Uses for it. He had come up with ways to redirect natural lightning bolts in order to reduce damage to personal property everywhere. It could prevent loss of life. Part of coming home was to test his ability to redirect lightning strikes. Up in the mountains, away from everyone, he would ensure no one was around to get hurt. No one knew about his intentions other than a very select few.

The uses for a potential military weapon didn't sit right with him, but the potential use for good in so many other areas was huge. Already the military was looking at harnessing lightning in different forms for weapons. He couldn't stop that, but he could continue with his experiments with the consent of Major General Tennessee Milton, the direct commander of GhostWalker Team Four. He knew he would have to cooperate with those looking to weaponize lightning as well, but he'd looked at those experiments and realized it was too late to ever go back from them.

"What makes you so interested in lightning?"

"I'm one of Whitney's first experiments. One of his first orphans. I escaped from his compound and managed to get away on my own and stay hidden under the radar. He had a microchip on me, but it didn't work. I have too much electrical current building up in me at times, and it short-circuited. I know you're on his fourth team, the one he considers perfection. You get to be perfect because he started years ago with orphan girls. Infants. He experimented on us. He has laboratories all over and female orphans to experiment on. Once he believed he knew what he was doing, he transferred those experiments onto his first team of soldiers."

Rubin was well aware of what she was telling him. It was the truth. Whitney had more than one laboratory. He had many backers, although most didn't know—or didn't care—about the young girls he'd experimented on before he psychically enhanced his first team of soldiers. He had also, without their consent, physically enhanced them using animal DNA. The first team of GhostWalkers had many problems. They were good at their jobs, but they still had problems.

"I'm one of those very flawed experiments," Jonquille confessed. A little shiver went through her body. "It isn't safe for anyone to be around me for very long. Not ever. I've read everything I can about lightning. No one seems to really know how it works. I started taking chances, sneaking into the conferences on lightning and the various uses. I stayed away from everyone until I could tell I was drawing too much energy and then I'd leave. I'm a trained Ghost-Walker soldier. That was one thing Whitney did do for us. We were very well trained and we all speak multiple languages. I also went to med school. He wanted us to be productive. It wasn't difficult to get into the conferences."

Rubin couldn't help but be interested. Either she was the best liar in the world or she was telling the absolute truth. She also had an extremely interesting and well-rounded education for one of Whitney's orphans.

"You stay right there. Don't move. Diego has that rifle on you. I'm getting your clothes. I'm not taking chances you might have a weapon stashed. That would get you killed."

"Fine, just hurry, please. Tank top and there's a pair of leggings

I wear in the evenings. Can you grab those for me? Top drawer. After hiking all day, I like to be comfortable."

He resisted smiling. She still had that little bit of eagerness in her voice, as if she was so happy she'd finally connected with him, that she didn't really care that his brother had a gun aimed directly between her eyes. If she had done any research on him—and being a GhostWalker, most likely she was able to find out what others couldn't—she had to know Diego really didn't miss.

He wanted to tell his brother to stand down, but he couldn't take chances. She smelled good. Really, really good. The subtle fragrance of coral honeysuckle was alive and well, drifting through the cabin, filling his lungs with every breath he drew in. He found it intoxicating—and distracting. That was unprecedented.

He pulled the one pair of leggings out of the drawer along with a shorter tank top, both very soft. He could see why she preferred to wear them at night. The garments would cling to her body, and he didn't need any more of a distraction, nor did he need Diego to be looking at the clear outline of breasts and bottom in her clingy nightwear. He added the one long sweater she had. She could wear that as well. The woman could do with some modesty. So far, she hadn't shown any.

"I'm going to hand you your clothes. You're going to have to get dressed right there."

"Oh, for Pete's sake. This is ridiculous."

"You're the one who invaded our home. You had to know the chance you were taking. You're lucky we didn't just shoot you as you came up the trail. Coming at you over your right shoulder."

He tossed her the shirt first. Clutching the towel with one hand, she caught the tank with the other and pulled it over her head, keeping the towel in place. She was very coordinated. Very. She caught it without looking. Even when she had to switch hands, it was done so smoothly and fast, pulling the tank down without removing the towel.

"Pants coming over left shoulder." He wanted to see if she was trained equally on both sides. She was. She had no problem snagging the leggings out of the air without seeing them, then dragging them on. Only then did she fold the towel.

"I've got a sweater for you to wear."

"Are you going to call off your brother?"

"You're going to put on the sweater and then sit in the rocker. I already checked it for weapons. I checked your leggings and tank as well."

"What could I have been hiding in these leggings or my tank?"

"Don't be obtuse. A garrote. You probably stashed any number of weapons around the cabin." He lifted his hand to the window and made a short circle to tell Diego to come inside. "Put the sweater on, Jonquille."

Obediently, she caught the sweater and slipped into it. He did his best not to notice the way her breasts moved enticingly beneath the tank. He knew her body was going to be a distraction beneath that thin, clingy shirt. Her hair was beginning to dry, going light even there in the gathering dark of the cabin. She flounced over to the rocker and curled up into it. She looked smaller than ever in it.

Rubin and Diego were both a quarter of an inch shy of six feet. Their family was not made up of small people. Jonquille may have been diminutive in size, but she didn't *feel* that way to him. She might look deceptively delicate with clothes on, but he'd seen the muscles running like steel beneath her skin. She'd been confronted alone, far from any help, completely vulnerable, by two male GhostWalkers—and she knew what that meant—yet she didn't flinch from the danger. She was lethal and had her own secrets,

20

there was no doubt about that. For the first time in his life, Rubin was seriously interested in knowing more about a woman.

The door to the cabin opened, and Diego entered. His gaze slid over their guest and then jumped to Rubin's face. *She's a Ghost-Walker.* It was an accusation. They were quite capable of speaking telepathically to each other. Diego was a strong telepath, capable of building bridges for those weaker on the team.

Yes, she is.

You should have told me immediately. She's most likely bait.

I don't think so.

You don't get to take chances with your life. Diego was obviously irritated with him. That happened very seldom. He stalked to the small crisper. After dumping the duffel bag on the floor, he began to shove their supplies into the drawer.

I was making certain I wasn't taking chances with yours.

Throughout the entire conversation, Rubin didn't take his gaze from Jonquille. She regarded the brothers carefully, a small frown on her face. Her large blue eyes jumped back and forth between the two of them. Finally, she sighed.

"Here's the thing. Whitney's first experiments were very, very flawed. I'm one of those. Women can get moody. Temperamental. Let's say stormy under the right conditions. Like the weather changing. Dark clouds overhead. Pissed off."

"Spit it out," Diego said, his tone mild.

Rubin raised his gaze to his brother's. *I don't know what's going on here, but I'm already feeling protective of her.* It was a warning as well as a hope that Diego would protect her as well.

Yeah, I figured as much. That's got to be a Whitney thing if it's happening this fast, you know that, right? Another thing to be suspicious about. Diego sounded resigned.

Rubin was already well aware that Whitney had a penchant for "pairing" his experiments. He often used pheromones to cause attraction between the two he wanted paired. Rubin had seen the results of those pairings. Whitney had definitely caused a physical attraction, but he hadn't counted on an emotional one. There was no controlling that side of things. Whitney didn't feel real emotion, so he couldn't comprehend it.

Whitney certainly didn't understand the closeness or the loyalty the GhostWalker teams developed among one another. He had no idea of the protectiveness they could feel toward their women and children or even one another.

"Jonquille?" Rubin prompted.

She gripped the arm of the rocker with one hand, and her thigh with the other, the first sign of real tension she'd shown since Rubin had made himself known. "Whitney had this notion when I was about four that it would be a great idea to use lightning against our enemies. He's always wanted to use weather rather than soldiers, so no loss of life to us, but he could ruin their food sources and destroy their satellites, or use a series of devastating direct strikes against military installations. Several of us were used in related experiments, all considered failures. I am his lightning failure."

Rubin was gripped by the utter sorrow in her voice. His heart actually jumped in his chest. A human lightning bolt? He leaned toward her. That was impossible. But was it? If Whitney had really paired them, he would be a logical match. He was a master of electrical control.

Is it possible? Diego asked. *'Cause this doesn't feel like a lie.*

I don't know.

"Are you saying that when a storm brews you can actually direct lightning? Not only direct lightning from the storm but produce it?" Rubin asked.

He had to work to keep his voice mild. He didn't want to sound in any way like Whitney had to have sounded when she had been a child and the cold-blooded man had tested her over and over. Suppressing excitement wasn't easy. There was no one like her in the world that he'd ever heard of, if what she said was true. A human lightning bolt?

"I can't direct lightning. That was the problem. And disappointment. Just produce it."

But he could direct it. Jonquille was the weapon. Rubin was the trigger. He met his brother's gaze over her head. Whitney had definitely paired them.

2

Jonquille didn't take her eyes from Rubin. He was either going to believe her or he wasn't. He was her last hope for any kind of a life. "Do you think you can help me? Can you find a way to undo what he did to me?" She hated that her voice was thin and weak.

She wasn't a weak person. She had depended on herself because she had to. She didn't dare be around others. Even Whitney had gotten to the point that he was afraid to be around her. As she'd grown up, her ability to control her talent had gotten worse, not better. Her body had drawn so much energy from others that she could barely contain the electrical charges.

"What do you mean by helping you?" Diego asked.

He had busied himself preparing food. It smelled delicious. She was hungry after hiking all day in search of flowers and mushrooms to sketch. It was nice that someone else was cooking, although he hadn't specifically said he was going to offer her food. She just took it for granted she'd be included for dinner.

She lowered her lashes. That didn't sound good. What did he think she meant? She'd just confessed to being a human lightning bolt. "I was hoping your brother might be able to make me normal." It took effort to keep sarcasm from her tone. She didn't enunciate as if he were two and couldn't possibly understand her, although the desire was there. She had the feeling that wouldn't win her any points with Rubin. The brothers appeared to be close.

"What's normal in the GhostWalker world?" Rubin asked gently. "None of us are normal. Whitney experimented on all of us."

She resisted rolling her eyes. Instead, she pushed the hem of the sleeve of her sweater into her mouth and bit down to keep from calling him on his far-too-obvious shit. He was the elite. Team Four. Pararescue. The holy grail of GhostWalkers. Word was, they were perfection. They could do no wrong. They didn't get brain bleeds. They didn't accidentally set the world on fire or slam lightning bolts into laboratories.

She attracted electrical energy from everything around her. The moment she entered the cabin, she should have known she wasn't alone. She should have known Diego was close by when she *approached* the cabin. Neither brother gave off enough electrical energy to cause the least bit of alarm. She always knew when another GhostWalker was close. At least she *thought* she knew. She relied on her warning system. Now she was very concerned that all this time she had been wrong and she couldn't identify other Ghost-Walkers. That would be a disaster for her.

Jonquille had managed to escape from Whitney and had been on the run ever since. She was extremely good in the wilderness. She'd excelled in her training as a soldier, particularly in isolated situations. She could blend into her surroundings easily. She could be still for hours if necessary. Had she kept to the mountains and forests, she would have stayed safe, but she wanted to find a way to undo the enhancements Whitney had amplified in her. The only way she could do that was to understand what was happening to her body in relationship to the electromagnetic fields around her. That meant consulting with experts.

She hadn't just studied lightning in the hopes of finding a way to undo Whitney's experiment that way. She'd also gone the medical research way, using fake IDs and going into labs late at night, using computers, covering her tracks but trying to find out exactly what Whitney had done in order to reverse the damage. She'd boldly become a research assistant to one of the leading experts in the field studying lightning, helping to provide for his every need as he developed his theories. She'd covered her bases, and so far she hadn't been able to find a way to reverse the process.

"You can say no one is normal, but you can interact with others," she pointed out. "I've seen you. You have the luxury of being a doctor and helping patients. You could have a relationship if you wanted. A family. It's your choice whether to have a wife or children. I don't have those choices. Several of the women raised with me didn't have those choices."

"Why don't you have a choice, Jonquille?" Rubin asked, his voice as gentle as ever.

She considered showing him. Right there in the room. She could feel the heightened electrical charge moving through her. She wasn't drawing it from him or his brother. Their combined energy was still too low to be a magnet for her body to feed off of. Her hair moved of its own accord, a subtle wave, but one she recognized as a dangerous warning.

Diego turned toward her alertly. "I wouldn't do anything silly. I might be cooking, but the moment you threaten my brother, you're dead."

The moment she struck in the close confines of the cabin, they were all dead. "I could leave." She made the offer because it was beginning to look as if that was her only option.

"There's no need for this," Rubin said. "We're talking. You were telling me why you don't have a choice, Jonquille."

"I think that's rather obvious, Rubin."

She had liked him. At the conferences, she liked his personality. His calmness. He came off as a gentle man. He spoke with authority, and everyone, even the most expert there, deferred to him, and yet he didn't have an ego that she could perceive. He presented his findings on the ability to redirect lightning to save crops and reduce damage to populated areas. At the military conference she'd attended, he was able to speak with authority on how lightning could be used to direct strikes on enemy bases. He had extensive knowledge of the uses being harnessed or potentially harnessed as weapons.

Never once did she detect a change in his vanity as others treated him with such deference. If anything, he didn't like the spotlight. He had come to each conference to absorb as much as he had to share. She thought of him as a good man. Jonquille was also very honest with herself, and she thought he was a very attractive man. The more she watched him, the more she considered him appealing. Everything about him attracted her. In the end, that was why she decided to take the chance and ask him for help. Clearly, that wasn't her best idea.

"It isn't obvious to me," Rubin persisted.

Jonquille forced down her rising temper. That low, gentle voice hadn't changed in the least. His brother had the same soft voice, but the threat came off him in waves. There was no threat emanating from Rubin at all. None. Nor did he put up any defenses. She had been honest with them.

She'd been born with an abundance of electrical magnetic

27

fields, far more than what were in the human body. Whitney had enhanced her further, giving her the DNA of animals as he did other soldiers, but mostly trying to construct a human lightning weapon he could use against other countries. He had failed, and like all his failures, it had angered him considerably. He never believed the fault was his—rather, the failure fell squarely on his test subject. She had suffered quite a bit at his hands while he tried to force her to "work" correctly.

"I can't be in the company of humans. They give off too much energy. My body draws that energy to me like a magnet, especially if they're upset and throwing off a tremendous amount. If there's bad weather, that just compounds the problem." She shrugged, trying to look casual.

She realized Rubin wasn't any less alert than his brother, or even any less threatening to her. Diego was protective of Rubin. Extremely protective in a way that raised a little warning flag in the back of her mind. She filed things away to take out later and examine. She always had. That was the way she had managed to collect information Whitney otherwise would never have given her.

Diego and Rubin were extremely close. They looked after each other, and clearly, they both were dangerous, lethal men, capable of taking care of themselves. She had no doubt that Rubin would protect Diego with his life. She had to go very carefully and figure out the dynamic between the brothers, because there was something here she didn't understand. Diego was acting more defensive toward his brother than the circumstances warranted. Not with her confined to a chair in the center of the room and both men watching her like a hawk.

Rubin was patient, waiting her out. She was going to have to come up with more of an answer. "When I was growing up in Whitney's compound, as I got older, into my teens, and it got harder and harder to control the electrical energy, I was put in complete isolation to study or work. I realized, after a while, that although I didn't like being alone, it did allow me to maintain easier."

Whitney had used a Faraday shield around her room to block the electromagnetic fields and keep her from pulling the energy from other girls or the guards. He'd also developed clothing, which she took with her and wore when she went into any public place, such as the conferences. The long, dark hoodie in particular was her best help. Having that, she could get as far from others as possible and make herself small. The electrical charges would find her, but very slowly because the mesh couldn't cover every inch of her skin. But it gave her time.

"What kinds of things were triggering you when you were young?" Rubin asked.

That voice of his was mild. Not in the least interrogating. Almost as if they were sharing an intellectual conversation. A part of her hoped he was asking because if he had the answers, he might be able to figure out how to reverse the process.

"The training had become pretty brutal. Whitney wanted each of us to use the psychic abilities he had enhanced us with. We trained with weapons and in hand-to-hand combat as well as studied regularly as students. That wasn't bad. We enjoyed that part. But once he would take us into what our handlers called field training, it got pretty brutal."

Her heart began to beat too fast and there was no calming it down. She took a slow, deep breath, trying to cover it. These men were both enhanced with animal DNA. Essentially, they were predators, just like she was, and they could hear the heartbeat of prey. Her lips had gone dry as memories crowded in. She tried hard to slam the doors on those years when Whitney pitted each of them against teams of his supersoldiers. At times it was a couple of soldiers. Other times it was a full team. Always those times were life or death. You survived or you didn't.

She knew she didn't have it the worst. Some of the other girls were forced to practice their skills on one another, literally bringing another girl to the brink of death. Whitney was merciless. It was all in the name of science. They should be happy to die for their country. To kill for their country. They were patriots, weren't they? He drilled it into them that they were worth nothing other than as experiments to be used over and over until they were used up.

She was a healer, and he had allowed her to study medicine. To go to medical school, or at least study within the compound, and that spared her quite a bit of the terrors some of the others endured. Certainly not all. And not his anger when she didn't perform well in the field.

Jonquille fell silent. She didn't owe them an explanation. She wasn't about to tell them anything else. She'd given up too much already because she'd broken into their cabin, and it was justified that they thought she might be sent by Whitney, or as a distraction so Whitney's team could sneak up on the cabin and capture or kill them.

"Have you tried controlling the way your body draws energy to you? Have you ever been able to keep it from happening?"

She shook her head. "No. The electricity begins to build up when I'm around others whether I like it or not. My core temperature rises. It begins to go all over the place. Hot and cold throughout my body. Feet cold. Head hot. My hair becomes static all over my body, and everything around me becomes that way as well. I try to stay out in the open and away from anything that can catch fire or be harmed. Over the years, I've gotten to know my limitations. That was how I was able to go to the lectures. I would stay a good distance from everyone, and if my body began to draw too much energy, I'd leave. When I was a little kid, it wasn't bad, but the teenage years were pretty horrendous."

"Are you ever burned?" Diego asked.

That surprised her. There was a hint of compassion in his voice. Just a touch.

"When I try to direct it, or shield anyone or anything. My fingertips are singed or blistered, but I'm immune to the temperatures, and they're blistering, of course. I don't really feel it, and my skin heals immediately."

"Under what circumstances did you try to shield someone?" Rubin asked.

She remained silent, her gaze meeting his, telling him to go to hell with her eyes. She wasn't about to answer that question. If he wanted to take out the gun he had concealed in his left boot and shoot her, she was all right with that. They stared at each other for what seemed like an eternity.

"Can you explain about when you tried to direct the blast?" Rubin asked. He didn't seem in the least upset that she had chosen not to answer him.

"I told you, I can't direct the blast. Whitney was determined to have a weapon. He was certain one could learn to direct a lightning bolt. I'm twenty-four years old. I was the youngest in the compound that I know of. So, he had that idea all those years ago. I don't know if he was the one to really bring this idea to the military's attention, but that's a long time ago to begin work on what had to seem far-fetched to most people at that time. Who would ever think one could harness lightning and use it as a weapon? Or direct it away from populated areas?"

"What happened when you tried?" Rubin persisted.

She couldn't meet his eyes. Whitney had set up targets at first and wanted her to hit them. She hadn't been able to do what he wanted. Lightning wasn't a precision weapon, at least not with her at the helm. He had gotten so angry with her that he scattered human beings throughout the field. Tall ones, wearing metal. Standing in water. Two of the girls were her friends, whom he was upset with because they hadn't met his expectations. Each person was in jeopardy.

If Jonquille didn't direct her strike exactly where it was supposed to go, and the lightning bolt behaved naturally, someone would die. She knew from experience that Whitney wouldn't be satisfied with one death. He would be furious and demand she try again and, sometimes, again and again. He wouldn't yell. He would look at her as if she were a great disappointment, and he would stand there until she did what he said. If she refused, he would direct one of his soldiers to shoot one of those in the field. Inevitably, the soldiers chose a girl.

She attracted lightning. It came to her. The lead stroke always found her. She couldn't send it somewhere else. She didn't work that way. She was the magnet on the ground. It didn't matter how high a target was, how tempting. The lead from the cloud would seek her out wherever she was. She couldn't make it go somewhere else.

Jonquille didn't realize there were tears in her eyes until her vision blurred. She looked away from Rubin, blinking rapidly, slamming the door closed on those memories. She wouldn't look back. There was no sense in it. She wasn't going back there. No matter how many teams of soldiers Whitney sent after her, she wouldn't go back. Very few could match her skills in the woods. She didn't need accuracy with her lightning strikes. She was a skilled soldier. She was a marksman. A sniper. Every bit as good with a knife. She could live off the land if need be.

"There's no need to tell us," Rubin said. "I've heard many stories about Whitney and his insane experiments. Several of my fellow teammates are married to women who escaped from one of his laboratories. They didn't believe they had choices either, Jonquille. That's why I asked you. I wasn't trying to be sarcastic or make you relive a painful past."

She managed to get herself under control, pulling in enough air to recover quickly. Growing up in Whitney's compound, one learned fast not to show weakness.

"One of my teammates is married to a woman who has the venom of a blue-ringed octopus in her. If she calls up that venom when she feels threatened or excited, she can kill. Another has three little girls who all have venom sacs and when they bite, they can kill. They're babies, and all babies cut teeth. Another GhostWalker— not one of my teammates, but on another team—is married to a woman who has difficulties with the buildup of fire. These are problems, but they aren't insurmountable."

Dahlia. He had to be talking about Dahlia. She had grown up with a girl who couldn't control fire. Jonquille pressed her lips together. She wouldn't ask. She wouldn't show interest. If he was fishing, and a part of her was certain he was, she wasn't going to take the bait.

"I took a risk going to the conferences because I knew the more information I had, the more likely I was to discover a way to help myself," Jonquille declared, determined to get back on track. "I'd attended several over the last couple of years. You were the only one who made any sense at all. Your ideas were more advanced, and you actually sounded as if you believed you could direct and manipulate lightning. Perhaps use it for your purposes. If you could do that, I thought it was possible you might have ideas on how to undo what Whitney did to me."

Rubin looked at her for a long time. "Whitney has a lot to answer for, doesn't he? He took advantage of infant girls. Of soldiers. Of the government who believed in him. Of those who still do. He's a brilliant man, and he surrounds himself with other brilliant and unscrupulous scientists. He can't do these experiments alone. He has other like-minded men and women eager to carry out his ideas. It isn't just that he has money—and he has billions—he also has others covering for him. People very high up. For all we know, the president is sanctioning what he does."

Her stomach twisted into hard knots. She didn't want to hear what he was saying, but she couldn't help it. She'd thought along the same lines. There was no hope. He was telling her no matter what, Whitney was a force that couldn't be stopped. What he'd done was so far advanced . . .

Rubin kept going. "Not one soldier thought when we volunteered for psychic enhancement that he would also mess with our DNA. Who knew he would arbitrarily decide to give us the sight of an eagle or the setae of a lizard? Any of the thousands of enhancements he decided his soldiers might need to make us better in water or in sand or in the mountains, as long as we were hunting the enemy? When he did those physical enhancements, he made us more aggressive. I'm sure you saw those results in his private army."

Jonquille nodded. She had. She didn't know what his newer soldiers were like, but the first versions, the ones with the rejected psych evaluations, had proven they'd been rejected for a reason.

"Every single one of us across the board wanted Whitney to reverse his DNA experiments. We had asked for the psychic enhancements, so we couldn't very well bellyache about what we got, even though those weren't what we expected either. But the DNA enhancements have been difficult to live with. I imagine it isn't any different with you?"

She knew he was fishing again. Asking if Whitney had experimented on her as well, enhancing her DNA. She figured it didn't matter if he knew. He was fourth generation. By now, those soldiers had to know what Whitney had been up to with the orphans he'd experimented on. The longer he'd had the girls in his possession, the more he'd done to them. She could admit it to Rubin and his brother, but they wouldn't know how she was enhanced—what exactly Whitney had done to her.

Jonquille nodded. "Yes. In order to make his perfect soldiers, he had to do his experiments over and over to make certain nothing went wrong when he tried them on all of you." She kept the bitterness from her voice with effort.

Whitney did love his soldiers. It mattered little if the women were imperfect and his supersoldiers were imperfect. He ran tests on soldiers in the military to see if they could join the elite Ghost-Walker program, but they had to score very high in so many areas and most flunked out in the psychological division.

Whitney offered those failures another program—his. They could "die." Receive full military honors and their families, their benefits. He would then pay them ridiculous amounts of money to work for him. He would enhance them and they would be every bit as good as the elite GhostWalkers they had applied for. What he didn't tell them was they would burn out very fast. He would send them to be tested against the female soldiers he'd created, with their venomous bites or other deadly enhancements, promising the soldiers they could then be paired in his breeding program with the woman of their choice. He often sent them against the Ghost-Walker teams to be tested as well. They lived very short lives.

"Whitney does have a flawed way of thinking," Rubin conceded without rancor. "He has his breeding program now, forcing the women he still holds captive into it, expecting them to give him

35

babies, yet having no respect for what they can provide. That doesn't even make sense."

Jonquille was very glad she had escaped before Whitney could pair her with someone in the program.

"You're saying the things he does can't be reversed." She just put it out there, watching his face.

She studied Rubin. He didn't give much away on his very handsome face. He looked a little sad. A little regretful. Those dark eyes of his didn't blink, reminding her even more of a predator and less of a man. She was susceptible to him in many ways. His voice. His looks. His brain. She had to be careful not to let her guard down. He wasn't the gentle man he appeared to be. It was important to always remember that. He'd all but warned her.

The bottom line was, he wasn't going to help her. She heard it in his voice. Maybe he couldn't. Maybe there was no way to help her. She'd run out of options. All that work tracking him down for nothing. She'd known. That really wasn't why she was here, but when she saw him, she'd suddenly had hope. She wasn't going to cry. She'd given too many tears to Whitney's messed-up experiments already. She didn't have any left to give.

She took a deep breath, letting it out slowly. "All right, then. I'm sorry I invaded your space. It was just an idea. My last one, actually, but you sounded promising." She looked around the cabin. "This has been one of the nicer places I've stayed."

Rubin frowned. "You're moving on just a little too fast."

He was reading her body language and everything said she was getting ready to run. She couldn't help it. Maybe she should have tried to hide her intentions better. She knew he'd tried to be very careful of every word he said, but it hadn't mattered. She was intelligent and she knew what he meant. At least he hadn't tried to lie to her. That wouldn't have worked either.

"I'm not certain what you mean." She tried to sound neutral, but knew it was impossible to keep her body language from screaming that she wanted out of there.

"We might not be able to undo everything Whitney did as far as enhancements go, but between the three of us, we should be able to figure out ways to ease the situation."

She shook her head. "I can't stay in one place too long. I picked up a tail a few months back, after that last convention where you gave a talk on the uses of managing lightning strikes."

She pulled the edge of her sweater out of her mouth, suddenly aware of what she was doing. It was a bad habit and one she thought she'd overcome a long time ago. "I spent too much time at those conferences trying to learn everything I could. In doing so, I probably attracted too much notice. I was careful not to ask questions or call attention to myself, but . . ." She trailed off.

She's ready to run, Diego. Everything in her is in a hurry to leave. I can feel her anxiety. I'm just as anxious for her to stay. If we're really paired together, why isn't she fighting to find reasons to stay? Would Whitney have paired only me? Not her? I heard that on occasion he will pair the woman with a man but not the man. Would he do the opposite?

Her looks alone would have garnered attention. Rubin found himself really studying her. There was something ethereal about her. Her skin. Her hair. Even her eyes. She almost glowed from the inside out. Her hair was just that little bit *too* blond. Her eyes weren't just blue, they were cornflower blue with interesting silver irises now that he had the opportunity to look closer. Outer silver rings as well as inner silver. She would definitely draw attention, especially if she attended more than one conference. It wouldn't matter if she stayed quiet or if she tried to stay in a corner somewhere, her energy was too strong, drawing others toward her like a magnet.

That was essentially what she was—a magnet for electrical charges. Human beings reacted to electric fields, even to sensing the fields, much like animals did. Living cells moved along electric fields when healing wounds. The human body had at least one sensor mechanism for detecting an electrical field and was certain to have many more.

I don't know. She's skittish, that's for certain, but she's too cool with the two of us as her enemies, Rubin. She has to be very dangerous to be so confident in herself.

"Stop looking at me like that," Jonquille snapped, and dropped both feet to the floor. She wanted to run away and hide from that inspection. She'd spent her childhood under a microscope.

Rubin, tall and good-looking on the podium, delivering a speech that made the most sense of anything she'd heard, had given her hope. She'd actually, for the first time in her life, been attracted to a man. She put it down to what she considered his genius and giving her a real sense of hope. Being in the small room with him gave her claustrophobia. She hadn't spent time with others in a very long time. She'd had fantasies about this man, and it was a rude awakening to have him look at her as if she were a science experiment—the way Whitney had.

"Stay still," Rubin ordered in the same mild voice. "I'm figuring this out. The human body certainly produces electromagnetic fields. In organs. In cells. In varying degrees. Your body clearly produced those fields in much higher amounts, and then Whitney in his usual godlike manner boosted those amounts to an alarming rate. How your body keeps from overheating is another mystery altogether, but that is something else to figure out. Right now, at the very basic level, what we're dealing with is an electromagnetic field. Do you always need a gathering storm to conduct lightning?"

His tone, that same dispassionate, calm tone coming out of this handsome man, upset her beyond comprehension. He had thick dark hair that could use a cut, spilling onto his forehead, accenting his very dark eyes. His shoulders were wide, his body toward the lean side, but all muscle. She'd been attracted to him from the first moment she'd laid eyes on him at the conference, and she'd never been able to get him out of her mind. It was strange that she didn't feel the same way about his brother when they looked almost identical. She could tell them apart easily and always would be able to.

Rubin's energy was low-key, which was a good thing. Sometimes when people were angry or violent, or just overly excited, her body absorbed their electrical energy rapidly. Unfortunately, she seemed to feed off a variety of different types of energy, siphoning off dark tendencies and fear as well as flat-out rage. Neither Diego nor Rubin gave off enough energy to even detect it, let alone absorb it. That was good so she could be in their company, but bad if she wanted to know they were around.

"Jonquille?" Rubin's dark eyes met hers. "Do you need a storm to conduct lightning?"

"You've indicated that you can't help me," she said, "so there really isn't much point to these questions."

The way his eyes remained on hers made it impossible to look away. Her stomach did a strange little flip. She felt, rather than saw, Diego turn to look at her over his shoulder. Apparently he didn't like the way she refused to answer his brother.

"I'd like to understand what he did to you. How it works." Rubin's dark eyes were velvet soft, fathomless, an endless pool one could get trapped in.

She shrugged her shoulders. She made every attempt to look as if it didn't matter that he couldn't help her. That he hadn't shattered her with his casual denial or his treating her like she was a science project.

"I'm sure you understand that after years of being Whitney's experiment, I'm over having anyone even consider me in that light. I'm really sorry for invading your space. I wouldn't mind something to eat if you have enough. In the meantime, I can pack fast and be out of here tonight. I'm used to traveling."

Rubin shook his head. "You didn't finish telling us about who you thought might be following you."

"Whitney? You must have escaped his laboratory," Diego guessed. "He doesn't like his girls to get away from him. You had to be one from the first group with Lily, Dahlia and Flame, right? They're all married now."

Jonquille didn't react to the news. That was twice they'd referred to Dahlia. She wasn't certain if they were trying to trick her or not, but she wasn't going to give anything away. Maybe she shouldn't stay for dinner. She could go a day or two without food. She'd certainly done so in the past. She could use her hunting and fishing skills once she put distance between them.

"I have no idea who might be following me, but I don't think it's Whitney. His supersoldiers have never been very patient. I've given these men the slip a few times, and they always work out my back trail, and the next thing I know, they find me. I knew I wouldn't have too much time here before they worked it out."

"Your best guess?"

"We aren't the only government with insane scientists who want to use weather for weapons. I backtracked and laid up on a hillside a couple of months back just to get a look at them. They're carrying weapons I've never seen before. I was privy to some of the top secret military weapons we have, but these guys . . ." She shook her head. "I didn't want to tangle with them. I laid down partial tracks that would be extremely difficult to work out, so very believable. They would have to spend time unraveling that trail before they lost it completely."

There was confidence in her voice because she was confident. She knew she'd been careless around Rubin's cabin for her own reasons, but there was no going into those reasons with either one of them. There were no tracks leading to the cabin, and none of the locals had seen her.

"High-tech weapons," Diego mused. "And you were privy to top secret weapons but had never seen these before."

"Whitney always had the latest in weapons. He had an entire department dedicated to thinking up weapons. So yes, I've seen a lot of new designs, but nothing like what they have. I speak several languages. These men all spoke English, but they also had a code they were using that was only theirs." She frowned. "Unique. Only to them, I'd guess."

She watched as Diego and Rubin looked at each other for a long moment. Diego didn't look happy. Rubin's expression gave nothing away.

"You're very good in the woods to be able to mislead a team like that," Rubin said.

She shrugged, wary all over again. "Whitney wanted each of us to be able to handle ourselves in any environment." That had to be common knowledge, especially if it was true that some of the girls that had broken free from Whitney had actually married Ghost-Walkers from the teams. "We trained for all situations."

She was particularly skilled in the mountains and woods. She had an affinity with animals and she was never lost or turned around. She could be absolutely still for as long as she had to be and blend in with whatever terrain she was in. She was small enough to use animal trails to navigate unseen, leaving no trail.

"You sound like an asset to me," Diego observed. "Stay for a while and help me protect my fancy-ass-doctor brother while he sees all his patients." He deftly shoved food onto three plates. Although he didn't look at Jonquille, there was one note in his voice that implied he might really need the help to protect his brother should there be trouble.

What are you doing? Rubin demanded.

You want her to stay, don't you? You're not going to get her to do that with your serious lack of charm. She's ready to run.

Why would she want to run? I don't get this. She should want to stay if she's paired with me.

Seriously, Rubin? Diego sighed in exasperation. He nearly slammed the dishes onto the table, glaring at his brother. *You did everything but pull out a microscope. You may as well have been Whitney. I have to be the charming brother now.*

You try to charm her and I'm going to shoot you. Rubin held out his hand to Jonquille. He didn't like the way she was looking at him, her gaze speculative. She was intelligent and quick.

"Pay no attention to Diego. If those men show up, looking to acquire you, I'm perfectly capable of helping to keep them off you."

You've got her thinking something might be wrong with me, Diego, that I can't defend myself.

Now you're a mystery. Women like mysteries. Diego groaned deliberately. "He's not civilized. He spends most of his life tramping around in the swamp, avoiding everyone so he doesn't have to speak to them."

Jonquille flashed a tentative smile. "I'm not very civilized either. I spend most of my time hiking in the woods, looking for plants to sketch."

She took Rubin's hand and allowed him to pull her out of the rocking chair. The moment her hand was in his, he realized maybe it wasn't such a good idea to touch her skin. He expected her hands to feel rough from being outside so much, but instead, her skin, next to his, felt soft. Up close, her subtle fragrance of coral honeysuckle and mountain daffodils surrounded him, filling his lungs until he felt as if he were drowning in her.

She looked up at him through a veil of thick lashes. Her lashes were long but so light-colored they appeared silver, with the tips almost bluish. The silver circles surrounding the deep blue of her eyes had thickened, giving her eyes a uniquely rare and extraordinarily beautiful appearance.

Rubin couldn't tell whether or not her taking his hand meant she was willing to stay or that she was just hungry. He pulled out the chair for her, reluctant to give up her hand, but knowing if he made excuses to hold it, he'd look strange.

She isn't reacting to me the way I am to her. He was disappointed. *Maybe we really aren't paired, Diego, and I'm just very attracted to her.*

Diego heaved a sigh and Rubin shot him a quick, quelling look. Diego was a good cook. They both were. They'd had to be in order to survive.

"You have skills," Jonquille observed. "I haven't had real food in a while."

Rubin noticed she ate slowly and very sparingly. They'd brought beef with them. They usually hunted once they were on the land, but first they'd deplete the supplies they'd brought. It was clear Jonquille really did have survival skills. She knew the correct way to eat after going light for a while. Her gaze flicked to Rubin's face a few times, but she didn't ask questions.

"You any good with a gun?" Diego asked.

"Whitney trained all of us as soldiers from the time we were very young. I'm very good with a gun. Just about any weapon." She shrugged easily.

"How good?" Diego persisted.

"I don't miss what I'm aiming at," Jonquille stated matter-of-factly.

Rubin believed her. He liked that she was confident. That she was cool sitting at the table with the two of them. She'd been in their cabin. She knew they'd grown up there. She had to know they didn't miss either.

"I feel compelled to point out to you, if that team of mercenaries is hunting me because I was at the conference on harnessing lightning too many times, Rubin, you speak at the conferences. Not only do you speak, but you're practically revered. If I decided this was a perfect place to look for you, wouldn't they think so as well? I would think your knowledge would be much more valuable to them than someone like me. What do I have to contribute? They don't even know."

"What do they know about you?" Diego asked. "Why would they suddenly choose to follow you? Not only follow you, but keep after you?"

She was silent for so long Rubin realized she wasn't going to answer. He sent her a small smile. She had learned to use silence as a weapon, just as they had.

"First it was the electricity, the buildup around you, that brought you to their attention, wasn't it?" He guessed. "They couldn't help but feel it."

Her gaze jumped to his face. She nodded and pushed potatoes around on her plate. "There's no way to control it when so many people are together. I try to stay out of the way, off by myself, but if the crowd gets too excited, or especially if the debate starts raging, then if I don't leave fast enough, the electromagnetic field can be alarming very quickly. It's hard to tear myself away when the material is so fascinating."

44

"The changes in your body would happen subtly at first, right? The static electricity. The power would be difficult to contain." Rubin forced himself to keep his voice very mellow, as if he were simply stating facts. Deep inside, he felt real excitement, the kind he hadn't felt in a long, long while. He wanted to see her like that.

"Yes," she admitted. "Unfortunately, that's what happened. In a dark room, my hair and skin can be a beacon. That isn't all that can happen. When the electrical current is moving through me, sometimes the charges can be seen circling my skin or hair as well. It can look something like the little lightning bugs dancing around in the grass here at sunset. I hide it behind clothing, but when it's becoming too strong, it can be difficult."

She didn't look at either of them but took a small bite of the potatoes she'd been pushing around and chewed as if it were her life's work.

"I imagine there could be sound," Rubin said.

She nodded. "If the buildup is bad enough. I usually get out before it's that bad."

"Someone from this team saw this phenomenon?" Diego asked.

"Maybe. Probably." She shrugged. "They could have as I was slipping out the door."

"But that wasn't the worst of it, was it?" Rubin asked quietly. He didn't look at her. He concentrated on eating. He wanted to see her face. Instead, he chose to feel her. She was first-generation Ghost-Walker. It was difficult for her to hide her emotions when they were heightened. She gave off far too much energy to be able to be successful if she wanted to escape his scrutiny.

3

"Diego, the food was absolutely delicious, but I'm not used to eating very much, nor am I used to spending time in the company of others. I'll just step outside for a few minutes. If you'll excuse me." Jonquille sent both of them a vague smile and was on her feet, pushing back her chair.

You pushed her too hard, Rubin.

I think I got that. She's going to run.

She won't go without her things. They're here inside, Diego pointed out as he watched her go out the door.

She doesn't have enough weapons or clothes in here. No rifle. If she's that good of a shot, she's got a rifle. Where the hell is it? Rubin asked. *She's got a stash somewhere else.*

Rubin pushed back his own chair. "Leave the dishes for me. I'll go do damage control."

"Don't let her shove a knife in your gut," Diego advised. "Although you might deserve it if you keep interrogating her."

Rubin followed Jonquille out into the gathering darkness. She stood at the edge of the tree line, nearly blending into the woods. Had he not had superior night vision, he doubted he would have seen her. As he stepped outside, she turned her head to look his way and he caught the sheen of silver in her eyes. His heart contracted. He hoped she wasn't close to tears, because if she was, he'd done that. She looked on the verge of flight, a wild thing, unable to make up her mind whether to stay or flee into the woods, where she could escape him. He continued walking right to her, using the same easy, steady, nonthreatening pace.

"I love the night," he confessed. "The peace of it."

There was a slight breeze moving through the trees, just enough to ruffle the leaves and produce a music he recalled from his childhood. Enough to send her unique fragrance to him.

"Did you know that you have this incredible scent on your skin? I've never smelled anything like it. I noticed it immediately, when I first entered the cabin. It isn't a perfume. It's not your shampoo. It's not even your soap. It's really you. It's very subtle and incredibly alluring, not that I want to sound like some crazy mountain man who's been alone too long." He tried not to fixate on her mouth when her lips suddenly curved into a smile.

"I smelled alluring? Rubin, I had been traipsing around in the woods all day."

"Nevertheless. It's a combination of coral honeysuckle and wild daffodils. Just barely there. I doubt if anyone else notices it. I didn't ask Diego. Maybe I should have."

"Maybe you shouldn't." There was amusement in her voice.

She didn't look as ready to run as she had a few moments earlier, and Rubin wasn't certain why. He was socially inept. He was considered brilliant in a lot of ways, but he kept to himself. He certainly wasn't a ladies' man.

He sent her a grin. "Maybe you're right. I'm sorry for sounding like I was treating you like an experiment. Anything to do with lightning, I get excited about. It interests me. I have a few gifts of my own that were enhanced by Whitney. I was asking you questions because one of those enhancements has to do with electrical energy."

He heaved a sigh. "I actually came up here because I get tired of the way everyone watches out for me. Stands over me, eyes on me all the time. I imagine you felt similar, way worse, in Whitney's laboratory. At least I have freedom. I shouldn't have started in on you."

He pushed a hand through his hair, trying to find his way with her. Trying to be honest. "I'm not good with women. I don't usually . . ." He trailed off. "It's just that I find you very attractive and I didn't quite know what to do with that, so I fell back on what was most comfortable for me . . . science. I apologize, Jonquille."

Her silvery-blue gaze drifted over his face in slow scrutiny as if checking to see if he was telling the truth. His gut clenched. There was something very otherworldly about the color of her eyes. The electrical charge in him bumped against the electrical charge in her over and over and then moved away just as it would in a thundercloud. He felt the buildup between them more as a sexual jolt each time and wondered if she was experiencing the same strange phenomenon.

He waved his hand, dismissing the subject. "Let's not talk about Whitney or his experiments for a while. I came up here to get away from everything to do with him."

She looked around her. "It is beautiful here."

"Very remote. Not too many people could live here. Or understand the people who do choose to live here," Rubin said. He swept his hand toward the cabin. He was beginning to feel a little desperate to find a way to get around the electrical charge building between them. He could feel the air growing heavier with it. "Did you discover the graveyard behind the house?"

"It's covered over in the most beautiful wildflowers," Jonquille said. "I weeded. I could tell it was a family plot."

"Nearly our entire family is buried there. It started with both sets of grandparents. Then my father. My two older brothers aren't in it because they disappeared, hiked out to find work, but they never returned, so we knew they were dead. If they weren't dead, they would have come back to help. The rest of the graves are my sisters and mother. Diego and I buried them, one by one, before we left for Detroit to find work. We were kids when we left. Fourteen."

He was giving her something of himself. Something real. He knew her life; it was only fair that she knew something of his. He hoped she realized it was difficult for him. He and Diego didn't share much about themselves.

Again, those silvery-blue eyes of hers moved over him. This time he saw a little glow in them as if it were impossible to contain the brightness in her.

"You're a brilliant man, Rubin. I stalked you like a groupie. Followed you to three different conferences where you were speaking. I had to dress in dark clothing made from a special Faraday mesh. That blocked all electromagnetic fields from escaping or getting to me. I had to cover my hair and skin. At one of them, you were presenting the same material, but I wanted to hear the sound of your voice. You're an incredibly charismatic man. I remember thinking you had everything. Looks, brains, your voice. You were fourth-generation GhostWalker, so even that was perfection. I should have known better than to judge anyone like that, let alone someone Whitney had access to."

She sounded thoroughly ashamed of herself. He was just happy she thought all those things about him. He sent her a quick grin. "You think I'm brilliant?" Of course she'd found a way to cover herself. A Faraday cage essentially made into clothing. Clearly, the covering hadn't contained the electromagnetic buildup completely, but certainly contained it enough to get her through the conferences for the most part. She was smart. Highly intelligent. He liked that.

"You know you are."

"And charismatic?"

She gave him a faint smile. "You know you are," she repeated.

"You like the sound of my voice *and* my looks?"

"Now you're just pushing it." She heaved an exaggerated sigh and rolled her eyes. "But yes, since you need affirmation, I do rather love the sound of your voice, and you're impossibly good-looking."

His smile widened. "Let me just tell my brother. He needs to know someone finds me attractive. He gets all the attention from the women."

She thinks I'm brilliant, handsome and charismatic and that I have a great voice. Just so you know. She hasn't mentioned how I smell yet.

You smell like a goat.

"He says I smell like a goat."

Jonquille burst out laughing. A real laugh. His body reacted to the sound. She wasn't loud, in fact her laughter was very soft, but it moved through his body the same way the electrical charges had.

"I can assure you that you do not smell like a goat. You have your own unique scent. In fact, I was upset with myself that I wasn't aware of you when I first entered the cabin. Ordinarily, I have a very good sense of smell, thanks to our mutual enemy Whitney. It's very . . ." She trailed off and looked away from him. "Suffice it to say, you do *not* smell like a goat. Your brother just wishes you did."

He laughed. "We used to get into arguments over songs. I would listen to every song that had lyrics to do with storms. Thunder. Lightning. I'd learn the words and the beat. It drove Diego up the walls."

"You did?" She stopped right on the small dirt path and turned to him. "I did the same thing. I think I know every song about lightning there is."

At last, something to connect them. It was silly, but it was something to make her relax in his company. They walked for the next ten minutes slowly, shooting off names of songs they each knew that had the lyrics containing the word "lightning" in them, each trying to stump the other. Rubin was older than she was and certain he would stump her first, but she knew every song he tested her with.

It was Jonquille who bested him with a band from the UK. She sang a few lines and tapped out the beat over and over on her thigh as she sang the refrain. When he couldn't name it, she was declared the winner, and he insisted she sing the entire song. He was fascinated with the way she tapped on her thigh as she sang, clearly typing her own code of the song with the pads of her fingers. It was fascinating and a little sexy.

He indicated the small pathway leading deeper into the woods, the one that led to the spring they'd developed behind the house. It was a pretty walk. He wanted her to feel comfortable. Night sounds always brought him peace. The katydids in the trees were rubbing their wings together like violins to give them their continual tunes. The crickets accompanied them without missing a beat. Frogs chimed in, a chorus of various types, tree frogs and frogs sitting down by the stream calling back and forth to one another. He could identify each of them and whether or not they were male or female.

He waited until they were halfway to the spring. "I've been thinking about our conversation on smells. A lot about it, actually. You're not going to get away with that. I told you what you smell like. It's only fair that you tell me what I smell like, even if it's worse than a goat."

She walked a few steps, color seeping up her neck into her cheeks. She gave him a faint smile. "When the needles of a red spruce are crushed, they give off a faint orangey scent. It's really nice combined with the actual scent of the spruce itself. You smell like a combination of that, leather and earth. Very subtle."

He walked a few more steps with her, aware she didn't make a sound when she moved along the trail. There were leaves and twigs underfoot, but the way she placed her feet, she didn't snap them.

"Did you train in the swamps?" He glanced at her, needing to see her expression.

"We trained in all environments. I know that you make your home base near Stennis in Louisiana. I did my research. If I couldn't connect with you here, I considered going there, but it was too risky, so I decided against it. I would have waited until next year if you hadn't shown up. I'm patient. I don't really have any other choice."

There was something off. A note in her voice that told him most of what she said was the truth. *Most.* Not all. "These people following you, do you think you could have stayed ahead of them for another year?"

"I was moving, making my way here. They had a trail to follow. I would have lost them and then found a place, very remote, where I could have lived off the land until next year. I do think they'll come here, though, Rubin. It's probably best if you get back to your team. I can wait here and then lead them away."

There it was again. That note of pure confidence.

"Why would you want to do that? It doesn't make any sense, Jonquille. Sooner or later they'll catch up to you. I'm a complete stranger. Why sacrifice yourself for me?"

They had arrived at the original spring they'd used. The land had changed over the years, and the little creek had shifted. It was now merged with the stream. Since the last time he'd been up there to see it, the creek had widened, climbing out of the original margins to expand by another six inches on either side. It had deepened as well. The water was clear, rushing over rocks in places and then leaves and debris were trapped, spinning in a wild frenzy in a pool at the bottom of a series of rocks.

Jonquille found a flat boulder to sit on. Clouds shifted across the stars and moon, one moment covering them and the next allowing them to shine. "How long do you think a person can realistically live alone, Rubin?" She dipped her fingers into the stream. "I can't do this forever. I'm not going back to Whitney and I'm sure as hell not going to help a foreign government or a terrorist cell or whoever those men represent."

Rubin remained silent, listening to the sounds of the night. There was peace there, just like in the swamp. He often went into the swamp just to hear the sounds of the insects and night creatures, so he could feel this same kind of solace. "Often, even when surrounded by others, one can be intensely lonely, Jonquille."

Her feathery lashes lifted quickly, her gaze colliding with his. "How could someone like you possibly be lonely, Rubin?"

He found another flat rock a few feet from her. "Diego and I were lucky when we hit Detroit. Ezekiel Fortunes found us. He was a kid a little older than we were, and he knew the streets. He had two younger brothers he took care of. He made us go to school, and we all worked together to stay safe and eat. We pooled money and eventually joined the Air Force. We just followed Zeke wherever he went. He believed in education and insisted we keep learning, so we did. He has a way of persuading you." He sent her a little grin.

"I take that to mean if you don't agree he finds a way to make certain you do."

"He's handy with his fists. On the other hand, that man would die for you. None of us really went against him. We followed him into every program he went into, including the GhostWalker program. Fortunately, all of us had some small psychic talent that allowed us in."

He looked down at his hands. "I love the swamp—everything about it—and eventually, I'd like to make my permanent home there, but I want a partner. A woman of my own. It's difficult for someone like me to envision who that would be. The others know what they're looking for. Me, I think about this." He gestured toward the woods and stream. "How to encompass the old with the new. My interests and my gifts. The things I know I need with the balance I think a woman might need."

She didn't respond. She just kept looking at him with those blue eyes of hers. The energy in her body seemed to have dissipated. He knew his body had drawn it from hers. She had to be aware of it, but he doubted if she'd guessed what that meant yet.

"Our team is close-knit. Each of them has a distinctly different personality, but I like them all. Wyatt is one of my team members, and his grandmother, Nonny, owns the property where most of us stayed in the beginning. Now several have bought up the properties around hers, Diego and I included. But Nonny simply accepted all of us as if we were family. It didn't matter what kind of animal or insect or reptile DNA we had, she just accepted us. We eat together. We laugh and talk like one big family. Still, I'm ashamed to admit, I feel lonely."

There was something about the steadiness of her gaze that made Rubin just a little uncomfortable, as if she had laser vision and could see inside him to where the weight of his talent sometimes crushed him.

"It's more than that."

The way she said it, so completely confident that she knew—*knew*—what he meant, had his head jerking up. Had him staring at her speculatively. If Whitney had paired them, at least on Rubin's side, given him an attraction for her, then her blood type would be the same as his. That way, if either were wounded, they could save the other. But more than that, their enhancements complemented each other. He was positive his ability to control electrical energy would be able to aid in the control of her talent. Her DNA most likely matched closely with his.

Whitney had known, from the original testing, that Rubin had psychic gifts that could be used for healing. He had enhanced those gifts. He had no idea what those results had been, only that Rubin was very good with the wounded soldiers his team rescued in combat situations. He was a gifted doctor, a surgeon, and he seemed to perform miracles in the hottest war zones. Whitney was satisfied with his work, probably proud. He had no idea of his true gift or he'd be moving heaven and hell to reacquire him.

If Rubin had the ability to heal, what about the woman Whitney would select to partner with him? For all his failings, Whitney had a way of choosing a woman that worked for a pairing. Rubin had seen it happen over and over. Not only were the man and woman attracted physically, but they actually fell in love. They bonded emotionally and became a strong, unbreakable family unit. That unit fit perfectly into the team. Whitney had a lot of faults, but his psychic ability seemed to be choosing the correct pair whether he wanted it that way or not.

"Jonquille, I don't just have one psychic talent. None of us seems to be that way. I don't know if it was the way Whitney enhanced us, or we had them all along, but I certainly have more than one. Some are stronger than others. When I filled out the questionnaire asking me about what kinds of 'instincts' I had, I put down healing, or taking care of injuries in other people or even animals. Do you have any ability along those same lines?"

Jonquille dipped her fingers in the stream again, letting the water run around them, making pathways as if each were a mini dam. She stared down at the silvery sheen of running water moving so fast, spinning and dancing in the bed of rocks. She seemed fascinated, but she sighed softly, and he knew she was considering whether to give him an answer.

"I have some ability, yes. Mostly, I've used it on animals. I don't have a lot of contact with humans. When I was in Whitney's laboratory, I did use it on the other girls there, after he did his horrible experiments. Sometimes I used it on the soldiers, though never when he was around or in sight of his cameras. I was careful that no one really knew it was me helping them. I didn't want him to know."

Even as a child, she'd recognized the danger of allowing Whitney to have too much information on her. Other children had made the mistake of thinking if they cooperated, they would incur his favor. He only experimented more.

A dread began to build in Rubin. His talent—psychic surgeon—the one that as far as he was aware only one other person possessed, was kept entirely secret by his team. He was guarded everywhere he went, and he despised that. He didn't like that other team members and his own brother would put his life before their own. Especially Diego. He couldn't take the thought of losing his last family member. He didn't want Jonquille to have the same burden.

"You were given training as a medic, Jonquille?" Again, he tried to be casual, as if they were just conversing and his heart weren't pounding and his mouth hadn't gone dry.

He was always calm in every situation. He had survived that way. That was how he and Diego had managed to do all the things they had done as young children and teens. They never panicked. They were calm and worked the problem. But the thought of Jonquille alone in the wilderness, a vulnerable target with the weight of a talent so heavy as being a psychic surgeon, was abhorrent and a little terrifying to him.

"Yes. I was given training first as an EMT, then as a doctor. I retain what I read very easily, and we had small private classes for the most part. I interned at small hospitals where he could control the environment. I never found the work difficult, only trying to balance the electrical energy so many people in emergency situations gave off with my body being a magnet for it. I wore certain clothing that helped. Eventually, I couldn't handle it and couldn't go to the hospital to work. I had to do simulated situations. That was much harder because Whitney was annoyed beyond description. He called me his greatest failure every chance he got. I think he was truly embarrassed that he had to pull me out of the program. The backlash kept getting worse. That's when he began to set up the field training in lightning management all over again."

"Did you ever use your talent to perform a healing on someone with major injuries, someone who needed surgery but wouldn't make it to the hospital if you didn't help them right there?"

Her lashes lifted again, and her eyes looked directly into his. "These questions are beginning to sound like an interrogation again, Rubin. They're very specific. Would you mind telling me where you're going with them? I'm beginning to feel very uncomfortable."

"That's because my brother is out there with a rifle and scope," Rubin said.

"I'm very aware of that," Jonquille said. "He followed you. He's been outside watching me the entire time. I made sure to give him a good target so he doesn't get trigger-happy."

He could definitely fall in love with her. She was so cool under fire. She hadn't let on in any way that she'd known Diego had followed him out and was up in the crotch of a tree with a sniper's scope making certain Rubin was safe. Knowing a sniper of great skill was watching her intently didn't seem to bother her enough to show concern. She exuded that much confidence.

"I'm trying to determine whether you have the same talents I have." That was honest enough without giving too much away.

She sent him a faint smile. "You're concerned that Whitney may have paired us the way he likes to do when he's playing god. He does like his little games."

"That's exactly what I think he's done. In spite of his genuine insanity, he does have a gift for pairing couples that can indisputably make a good match, physically and emotionally. They fit and they end up loving each other. He pairs them because he thinks they'll make a good team as soldiers in the field, but he never considers the emotional bond that builds between them. What do you think, Jonquille? Do you believe there's a possibility that he put us together?"

She dipped her head to one side and her wild blond hair spilled in an unruly riot of waves to her chin. "There isn't a doubt in my mind, Rubin, not if you're attracted to me. You've got brains and you're gorgeous. Why would you look at someone who can't get out of the woods and be around anyone? You mentioned how my skin smells. No one else would notice. Your brother didn't and he was sitting close at the same table. I'm afraid Whitney did, the bastard, and I'm sorry about that. That's one more burden for you to carry."

That didn't tell him anything about whether or not she felt the same way. She was careful to keep her emotions to herself. He didn't want that. He wanted to know everything there was to know about her. At the same time, he couldn't give her anything back, and there was no fairness in that. He was in the military, in a top secret program. He didn't have the luxury of talking about what he was or what he did.

"You aren't a burden to me, Jonquille, not unless you decide I'm not worth sticking around and taking a chance on." He just put it out there. Tossed it out like he wasn't saying the most ridiculous thing in the world. He hadn't thought about it or discussed it with his brother. The offer just came flying out. He was pragmatic. He wasn't a man who would go out on dates like Diego might. If this woman was paired with him, then why should he fight fate? Why shouldn't they just accept what was in store for them and begin to build a relationship? He wanted that. He wanted the chance to get to know her. To have her get to know him. The only way for that to happen was if she stayed.

Her gaze went electric blue again. He loved the blue of her eyes, but now that he'd seen that silvery-blue sheen, he thought that was just as beautiful, if not more so.

"I could never be with a man like you, Rubin." Her voice had gone soft and gentle. "I can't ever be in public. You go to these big medical conferences and the ones on lightning for weapons as well as manipulating lighting for the purposes of keeping the strikes from hitting anything important. You need a match that can be an asset to you. That will never be me, as much as I wish it were."

He heard the very real ring of sadness. "You can't know that.

You have no idea what two people can do together. We haven't even begun to talk about our gifts and how they might complement one another. To just dismiss a pairing when every single other pairing has been dead-on would be a major mistake. That heaviness I feel weighing me down, I feel it in you. We're both intelligent. We have no idea what we can think of or do together unless we at least give things a try."

Jonquille glanced into the woods. The clouds had turned a darker shade of gray at the bottom, leaving their fluffier tops lighter so they appeared almost as if they had an ombré effect. As the clouds floated across the sky, driven by the slight breeze, they blocked the light of the stars and moon completely, turning the woods and stream into an ominous, dark, shadowy underworld. She didn't flinch away from it or appear to be spooked by the sudden change.

Rubin studied her face as she contemplated how to answer him. She never seemed to feel she had to answer right away. She wasn't pushed into anything. She turned things over in her mind before she decided what to trust him with.

Around them, the trees began to moan as the wind picked up. Branches rubbed together to make the mournful sound. The frogs and katydids changed their tunes, singing a chorus to match the desolate notes the trees produced.

Get her to go inside, where it's warmer, Rubin.

She doesn't feel as threatened out here, even knowing you're holding a sniper's rifle on her. I'm trying to get her to admit she's been paired with me. She isn't a threat. Go inside and stay warm. We'll be in as soon as we can.

That's not going to happen in this lifetime.

Rubin sighed. He'd known that was going to be Diego's answer. Most of the time he didn't bother to answer at all.

"There's no doubt that he paired us, Rubin. I feel an almost overwhelming attraction to you, and that doesn't come easily to me. I'm certain we have many of the same psychic traits. In any case, those I don't have, you would complement, and vice versa. That seems to be how it works. I've never actually seen a couple in person, but I've seen them when they've been online and Whitney managed to get a recording when they were unaware."

He flashed her a grin. "At least you're willing to admit you're attracted to me."

"I think that was pretty clear when I didn't shoot you for watching me shower."

"You didn't shoot me because my brother had you dead to rights, just like he does now."

She gave him her sassy smile. "There is that, although I did consider whether or not I could hit the floor before he got the shot off. I didn't want to risk it. He has a bit of a reputation. And don't let the admission of my finding you attractive go to your head or make you think Whitney did that to me. Any woman with eyes would find you attractive."

He remained silent while she frowned, thinking over what she'd said. She laughed, those little bells skipping over the water in the sound he'd heard before when she realized what she'd said. He did like the sound of her laughter.

Her eyebrows drew together and for a moment she looked as if she was pouting. "That didn't come out right."

He laughed, genuine laughter, something he couldn't remember doing in a long time. "I thought it came out exactly right."

"You would. To answer your question, yes, I believe in his great narcissistic, godlike way, Whitney decided we were a perfect match."

"You must be very good at healing, then, because I am," Rubin confessed. "Not just because I'm a doctor." He waited several heartbeats. "I didn't have the necessary skills to heal when I was a kid. I was in survival mode, trying to put food on the table. Trying to keep the family alive." He gestured in the general direction of the family graveyard. "You can see, I wasn't good at it."

"Rubin." His name came out a gentle reprimand. "Why do you come back if it hurts so much?"

"To check in with my family even though they're gone," he answered without hesitation. "To make sure those living in the mountains have some medical attention when they otherwise wouldn't. And because this place calls to me. A part of me will always call it home, no matter where I settle."

She gave him a smile that made his heart contract. "You're a good man, Rubin. If Whitney had to pick a man for me, I'm grateful it was you."

Rubin studied her face. She was actually quite good at keeping that little pixie face from giving too much away.

"He likes flowers. Whitney. He really likes flowers. He grows them. He would know that Jonquille spelled without the extra 'L' and 'E' added is 'daffodil' or 'Easter lily' here in the Appalachian Mountains, where you were born. Of course, he had no way of knowing that when he named me . . . I don't think. Who knows what his talent is like?"

"Let's go back inside, Jonquille. It turns cold fast. You managed to grab your boots but you're not really dressed very warm."

She slid off the boulder and gave a last look at the stream. "This is a magical place. I know the winters are harsh and it can be a hard life, but I would have tried to stay here if I didn't have those men following me."

He didn't like that she would have tried to winter in the cabin alone. Even with the two of them, Diego and him, if one had fallen ill or broken a bone, it would have been dangerous.

"You know that wouldn't have been the best of ideas." He got to his feet, towering over her, conscious of the difference in their heights.

"I would have hunted for food and stored as much as I could have. Then collected edible roots and plants and stored those as well. I could have made it work."

"Too dangerous and you know it," he repeated.

"What do you think I've been doing all this time?"

"What would happen if a group of males caught you alone out here and they weren't in the mood to be nice?" The image of his sister's dead body floating in the stream rose up to haunt him. He shut it down immediately.

"I suppose I'd have to kill them." She shrugged. "I wouldn't like doing it, Rubin, but I would if I had to, if things got nasty." Again, she exhibited supreme confidence.

He let her lead the way, if for no other reason than to give his brother a break. "You seem to think you wouldn't have any problem taking on a group of men and coming out the victor."

"As a rule, I get a sense when I'm in over my head very fast. I did right away with you. Then I became aware of your brother and knew it was game over until I could figure out an advantage. You two don't make it easy."

"That's good to know. I'm curious as to how you think you can gain the advantage when there are several men, Jonquille."

She threw him a quick, secretive smile over her shoulder. "If I told you, that would take away my advantage, wouldn't it? What if I have to escape and do both you and your brother in? You knew I was going to take off and you came after me anyway."

"I had no choice." He thought he had a good argument for defense.

"There's always a choice."

He laughed. "I believe I said those exact words to you. That isn't very fair to throw my own platitudes back in my face."

"Why didn't you have a choice?"

"Because you're my woman and I couldn't very well let my one shot at happiness go running off into the woods never to be seen again. I'd already realized you were good, maybe even as good as Diego, at not leaving a trace behind. If that was the case, I wasn't taking chances on losing out."

She shot him another look over her shoulder, this time rolling her eyes at him. "I think mountain men are a little insane."

He laughed again. "So I've heard."

Jonquille was smooth on the trail, navigating it as if she'd been doing so from the time she was a toddler. She didn't seem to look at the ground, but navigated by memory or feel. He wasn't certain which.

What are you doing, Rubin? She's a big question mark. Your exact match suddenly appearing out of nowhere and camping out in our cabin. How convenient. You aren't thinking with your brain, and as long as I've known you, that's never happened before. It's too dangerous to have her around. You just asked a cougar to come play house with you.

I believe she's quite a bit younger than I am, Diego.

This isn't a joke. I need to know what you're doing.

I think she's a psychic surgeon. If I'm right, that makes three of us in the entire world. And possibly a fourth if Paul's match is one as well. If what she says is the truth, she has to be protected. If it isn't, we have to get her free of Whitney.

What we have to do is protect you, Rubin. If this is a setup, then we have to get you out of here. We can decide what to do about her when you're safe. Once I know you're good, I can scout around and look for signs of a team. They can't be too far away. They wouldn't leave her, especially if she's with Whitney. He never trusts the women, even if he puts a virus in them.

Rubin sighed. Ahead of him, Jonquille laughed softly and glanced back at him over her shoulder. "The two of you really do spend a lot of time arguing telepathically."

"That just started recently."

She turned back toward the cabin, picking up the pace. "You can't blame him for being suspicious. You have to be just a little bit, Rubin. To tell you the truth, I'm a little uneasy with all these revelations."

"Why? You came looking for me."

She was silent again. They were out at the edge of the trees when she halted, as if it was automatic to do so. She studied the cabin and the expanse of ground between them and the structure. "I did come looking for you. I went to all those conventions and listened to the speakers. No one resonated with me. Not one person seemed as if they could help me. Looking back, why is that? Many of them are considered the top experts in the field, and yet not one of them made me think they could help me. Only you."

She fell silent again, listening to the night, letting the insects and night creatures alert her to intruders. She inhaled, using all her senses in an effort to detect an enemy. Rubin did the same. It was automatic for him. For Diego. Evidently, it was for Jonquille as well.

"Doesn't that make you just a little bit suspicious? I didn't think about it at the time. I didn't think about your voice getting under my skin. Or the fact that the one time I got close to you, I could actually pick your scent distinctly out of the group of the men you were with and yet I'd never smelled your scent before. Those are red flags, Rubin. Huge red flags."

A memory surfaced. A brief moment when he was surrounded,

so many others talking to him at once, pressing close, all eager to make their points with him. A fragrance drifted to him out of nowhere—wild coral honeysuckle, so faint as to almost not be there, mixed with daffodils. He remembered it was so distracting his head had come up alertly and he had looked toward the side exit door, but there seemed to be a sea of faces looking at him, and then the elusive scent was gone.

He knew they were red flags. He didn't want to see them because he didn't want to miss out on a partner. He indicated it was safe to go back to the cabin. "No one is around. Let's go back inside. We can hash this out where it's warmer."

"I just think it's better if I leave."

She crossed into the open, moving cautiously. She stayed a distance from him, irritating him. Her hair was light, and she had nothing covering it. He had dark hair and was much harder to spot. Anger swept through him, and with it, realization. She was deliberating presenting a target, the way Diego would in order to protect him.

Jonquille wanted to leave. She was trying to find a way to maneuver them into having her leave when it would actually be safer for her to stay with them. If he didn't believe she was the bait for Whitney's team to recover him, or for a terrorist cell or a foreign government, then what would be her motivation? Why was Jonquille really there? Had she honestly come in order to ask him to help her?

She had almost reached the back door of the cabin when she stumbled. It was the last thing he'd expected. She crouched down to fix her shoelace as if it had come untied, allowing him to get ahead of her. Rubin had never had much of a temper. He was easygoing, always had been, but the way his team, and especially his brother, insisted on protecting him because they considered his talent so valuable annoyed him. Now she was doing it. He didn't be-lieve for one moment anyone was in the cabin. He would know. He would feel it. She was protecting his back. He wasn't a swearing man, but it was enough to make him want to become one. His team. His brother. The woman that should be his.

He'd been upset for weeks. Months. His entire team had been watching him closely, but his brother especially. Rubin had an-nounced abruptly that he needed to go to the mountains and see patients there. It wasn't exactly time yet, but he had to get away.

They weren't scheduled to come to the mountains for another month. Diego and Rubin had decided to go early to hunt and fish. To work on the property. Rubin had needed alone time before he saw to the people he would normally check on. They weren't two weeks early. They were *four* weeks early because Rubin thought he was going out of his mind.

4

Rubin strode into the cabin, his senses automatically flaring out to ensure for himself they were alone. He knew they were. He had the sinking feeling he knew why Jonquille had come to the cabin and what she planned to do there. It wasn't happening.

Rubin? Diego was cautious.

Diego had to feel that slow burn building to a raging fire. Rubin rarely got angry. He wasn't that kind of man, but when it did happen, as was often the case with quiet men, he was a volcano, capable of taking down a house and everything else in the vicinity when his temper did erupt.

I've had it. Just get in here.

Diego didn't argue or respond. His brother knew him too well. Rubin removed his boots and set them aside in the mudroom. Beside him, Jonquille cast little anxious glances at him while she did the same. Rubin didn't even try to stop the dark, smothering tension from pervading the room. It moved like an ominous cloud, spreading throughout the open rooms, filling every corner from floor to ceiling.

Diego came in the front door, his gaze flicking from Rubin to Jonquille and back. He set his rifle down and took his boots off as well before coming all the way inside. He didn't say anything to either of them. He simply put his rifle away, handling it with care, the way he always did.

Rubin noted that the dishes were done. Diego had done them before taking up his rifle and following them outside.

"Sit down, Jonquille," Rubin advised when she looked toward the sink where her duffel bag was. "Right there, in that rocker where you were before. I'm done with the half-truths you were telling us."

She hesitated, her gaze flicking toward the mudroom, where she'd just taken off her hiking boots. There was no doubt in his mind that she had more than one bag stashed in the forest so she could grab and go. She didn't need anything in the cabin.

"Sit. I'm not messing around with this anymore. I'm pissed as hell and you do not want to make me any angrier. Either one of you." He included his brother in that, daring Diego to say one more word against or about her.

Diego raised an eyebrow but remained silent. He knew Rubin better than anyone else. He wasn't about to tangle with his brother when Rubin was in this mood. Apparently Jonquille had a good sense of self-preservation. She walked across the room, looking for all the world like a small fairy, one of the lightning bugs that danced and entertained at dusk and then mysteriously disappeared. That wasn't happening.

The cabin was dark. No one had bothered to light candles or the gas lanterns, or even turn on the electrical lights. It was easy to see that Rubin's energy, usually so low, was pouring off him in waves, rushing to feed the magnetic hunger in Jonquille's body. Her skin had taken on a glow. Her hair seemed even whiter than usual. Her blue eyes had gone more silvery blue than that deep cornflower blue. Little forks of energy moved around her in blazing streaks of electricity, and the static buildup in the room heightened.

"Did you think I wouldn't figure out why you came here, Jonquille? What you were planning? It's not happening."

Fury rode him so hard he could barely contain it. His voice shook with it. The walls trembled, contracted and expanded as if alive. As if breathing. For a moment the floor trembled as if an earthquake threatened.

"Sit down, Diego. I don't need you pacing around."

Diego didn't object to his order as he ordinarily might. He simply chose the rocker beside Jonquille, whether to protect her or restrain her, Rubin couldn't tell.

"Answer me, Jonquille," Rubin hissed.

"You're a brilliant man, Rubin," Jonquille conceded. "I knew I didn't have much time before you started figuring things out. I tried to get away before you did. I'd hoped I could get into the forest and disappear."

Diego stirred as if he might say something, ask a question, but Rubin silenced him with a glare. He could barely breathe, he was so angry. Angry at himself. At Jonquille. At his team. At Diego. Mostly at Whitney.

"I wondered for a long time why Mama just gave up when she still had the rest of us left alive. I wondered for a long time, Diego."

Diego nodded. "I wondered too. Never could get over that. The sight of her like that." He glanced at Jonquille and then away, clearly not wanting to discuss their mother's suicide in front of an outsider.

Rubin didn't think of Jonquille as an outsider. Strangely, she was part of him, but he had no idea how to convince his brother of that when he couldn't explain it to himself or to her. She was the reason he was trying to tell his brother how he felt. What it was coming to for him.

"She had gifts. Psychic gifts. We got them from somewhere. They didn't just appear out of nowhere. She went to the neighbors when they were ill or giving birth. Remember? Sometimes people would come from far away just to see her. She had to be a healer. But she couldn't save her children or her husband. That weighed on her until she couldn't bear it anymore."

Diego's dark gaze jumped to him, intelligence there. Recognizing all the trips to the swamps when Rubin had gone alone after their missions. When more and more the laughter had faded and there were no more smiles, not even around Wyatt's little girls— and the three mischievous triplets could make anyone smile.

"Rubin," Diego began cautiously.

"All those boys, Diego," Rubin said. "Those kids. No matter what I do, I can't save them all. I think about their families. Their mothers, what I would have to say to them if I was facing them and they were asking me why I couldn't save their son when I saved the one next to him. Holding their hands, looking into their eyes."

There was anguish in his heart. In his voice. The weight of those soldiers he lost pressing down on him, haunting him until he couldn't sleep and couldn't find a way to make it right in his mind.

"Imagine having a gift like Mama's. Like mine. Having such a powerful gift and never being able to use it. You're compelled to use it, but you can't. You have the knowledge and even the medical training, but you can't. That would be the epitome of living in hell. Worse than Mama's hell. My hell."

Rubin turned his dark eyes on Jonquille. She shook her head and refused to look at him.

"You did go to the conferences to see if someone could help you. But you're too good, too careful to get caught. No one saw you. You wore that mesh clothing that concealed you. You saw them. You caught them watching me, didn't you, Jonquille? You knew I was in trouble. You decided, like my team, like my brother, that I was more important than you."

He didn't even try to keep the bitterness out of his voice. He detested the way everyone became his bodyguard, his shield, throwing up a protective safeguard around him whether he wanted it or not. He had made it clear over and over that he certainly didn't want it, but his wishes never changed anything.

She inclined her head. Just barely.

"You knew they would be coming here, so you took it upon yourself to get set so you could kill them, didn't you?"

Jonquille glanced at Diego and again her nod was barely perceptible.

"And then you planned to suicide, didn't you?"

She pressed her lips together, her gaze shifting away from his. She looked at the floor. "If they didn't kill me, I would have, yes." Her voice was very low. "I have no future, Rubin. You do. There's no help for me. The things Whitney did to me make it impossible for me to have human contact. I can't live like this anymore. I thought I could take out the team trying to acquire you, at least do something before I died. But then you had to come early. You were here so fast and I didn't expect to be so . . ." She broke off, shaking her head, looking at her hands.

There was silence after her confession. Rubin could barely think. He forced air in and out of his lungs, letting the night sounds and the air remove the anger from his system. Part of his temper had been fear. Jonquille was the woman meant for him and she had been about to sacrifice her life for him. He would have lost

72

her like he'd lost everyone else. One by one. It was why he held so tight to Diego. To Ezekiel, Mordichai and Malichai, his foster family. He wasn't about to lose them.

"We're going to come up with a different plan, one that involves you living. Staying with me. With us. Finding a way to make it work. I don't want to hear any negative crap from either of you. We're going to do this. So, unless you can come up with solutions, don't bother to say anything. I'm already pissed about the lies, Jonquille."

Jonquille leaned toward Diego. "Is he always like that?"

Diego nodded. "You may as well get used to it. He doesn't get pissed often, but when he does, he's like a freight train and just mows down everything in his path. Just go along with him, there's no other way. No use fighting him. How many in this team coming after him? How close behind you are they?"

"I made certain they got wind that you and Rubin were coming here but early. Like in the next couple of weeks. I didn't think you'd be even close to coming yet. There are a lot of soldiers and they have heavy equipment with them, which slows them down. I caught a glimpse of it on one of the roads the last place I camped. One is clearly the leader and he hangs back and gives all the orders. They have new weapons. I got up on them several times, although they guard those weapons pretty carefully. They're getting more and more careless though."

Diego was quiet a moment, turning that over. "How good are they in the woods?"

"They're not bad. Nothing to write home about. I can follow their tracks easily. The bad news is, they have access to a drone. The leader likes to put that drone in the air all the time. The good news is, here in the mountains, any stranger is instantly noticed. I haven't seen any indication that they're here yet. If they are, they haven't found a way to move around under the radar, and that's slowing them down. They wouldn't just want to kill everyone because you would instantly pick up on that."

That was true. Strangers never went unnoticed. Rubin was a little shocked that Jonquille hadn't been spotted. That was part of the reason he had been so certain she was every bit as good as Diego in the woods. If she wasn't, someone would have known she was using the Campo cabin, and they would have left signs for Rubin and Diego to warn them.

"Maybe the best plan would be to see the patients ahead of time while we decide where we're going to meet this team, Diego," Rubin said. "If we see the patients, that gives us the freedom to leave and lead them away from here. We don't want any civilians to get hurt. They can't take anyone hostage that way."

"Or we could skip seeing patients altogether," Diego suggested. "Head back to Louisiana and call in members of the team to meet up with us to escort us in."

"I'm not skipping seeing my patients if I have the time," Rubin said. "There aren't that many and they count on me. We're early. I can get started tomorrow morning. Jonquille, have you seen these men in action?"

"Not the men. Just the weapons. They're pretty badass. Scary badass. A couple of the weapons could tear up the mountain."

"What would a lightning strike hitting precisely on the weapon do to it?"

She sighed. "Don't start. I told you I can't direct lightning bolts."

"You can't. I can," Rubin admitted.

Her gaze jumped to his. "You can? How? That's impossible." But her voice didn't sound as if she believed it was impossible. She was interested—even excited, but trying not to be. "Whitney really did pair us, didn't he?"

"Yes."

"If Whitney really paired you," Diego said, "then this team of terrorists or whoever they are aren't the only ones who are going to be coming after you. Whitney likes to test his pairs. He's done it every single time. He has to know you've gone to the conferences on using lightning as a weapon, Jonquille. Even if he can't put a virus or a tracker in you, he would know that's your only hope. In order to be a match for Rubin, you have to be equally intelligent, which means you'd seek out answers. You'd go to those conferences. He'd have someone watching. He most likely even knows about this terrorist cell hunting Rubin."

Jonquille scowled. "So much for being intelligent. I should have thought of that. All I was thinking about was trying to figure out how to live with other human beings and use my ability to heal. He knew I could heal, but not to what extent. He thought of that as a smaller gift. He didn't know what a burning compulsion it can be. He did let me go to med school because he thought I would be an asset to the women soldiers he'd trained. He liked the idea. I excelled and he liked that even more. Of course he didn't let on to me, but one of the other girls, Flame, would hack into his files and read his notes on us. He'd encrypt them, but she got really good at reading them."

"Flame." Rubin repeated the name.

"Iris. He called her Iris. We called her Flame. She was always in trouble. He gave her cancer. He told her it was for the good of mankind." There was bitterness in Jonquille's voice now. "Flame was defiant, and Whitney hated her for it."

"She's alive. She's married to Wyatt Fontenot's older brother. Everyone calls him Gator. Gator's a member of Team One. He's crazy about that woman. Lily worked on her cancer and has hopefully put it in remission for good. You'll get a chance to see her when we're free and clear from all this."

Like before, when Rubin talked of the other girls, Jonquille instantly shut down. She was clearly willing to risk herself, but not any of the others.

"You have to trust someone eventually, honey," he said.

"That's not so easy. I don't know you. Either of you. Diego would prefer to shoot me and get it over with. I don't know exactly what you want from me yet."

"Diego has always been bloodthirsty," Rubin acknowledged. "He can't help himself. He pretends it's to protect me."

"It is to protect you," Diego defended.

"You just like to show off the fact that you have skills with your rifle." Rubin turned his attention to Jonquille. "There's a lot of competition on the teams. A lot of really good shots. Diego is used to being the best, and all of a sudden he's got several as good . . ."

"Not as good," Diego corrected. "They might be in the ballpark, but they aren't as good."

"As good," Rubin continued. "And he wants to practice all the time. If he has live targets, he thinks he'll do even better."

Jonquille laughed. "You two. You're both insane. I don't believe Diego just shoots people indiscriminately, as much as he would have liked to have gotten rid of me."

"Rubin keeps saying you're as good as I am in the woods," Diego pointed out. "That's a good enough reason."

"It's the truth. I'm probably better," Jonquille said.

Diego snorted. "Not on your life."

Jonquille sobered, the smile fading. "If you really want to talk about trust, Rubin, then let's get practical. We need to know if Whitney has sent a team coming this way. We also need to know how close this other team is as well. You're insisting on meeting with your patients. I agree with Diego on this one: I think you should give it a pass, but I also know that pull that just won't let you go, so I understand that you have to see them."

"What are you thinking?" Rubin asked.

Rubin, Diego cautioned.

Hear her out. I know she came up here with those intentions.

Why not take the team out before they got up here?

Because she already figured out that Whitney probably sent a team as well and she was hoping to pit them against each other.

Diego was silent for a minute. *Yeah. I didn't see that one coming.*

Jonquille sighed. "Do the two of you ever get tired of arguing? I could just go into the other room or step outside if you don't want to speak telepathically."

Diego glanced at Rubin sharply. "She knows?"

"She knows. You're probably not very good at it."

"I'm good at it. You're the one not guarding your thoughts around her."

Jonquille got up and went over to the countertop where the berry cobbler was sitting out. She scooped some into a bowl, got a spoon and returned to the rocker.

Both men frowned at her as she began eating very slowly, obviously savoring every bite. She looked up, arching one eyebrow at them. "What? I thought I might as well enjoy dessert while the two of you put on your little act. You don't usually fight. That's easy enough to see. I don't know why you are now. If you're insisting on seeing your patients, Rubin, you don't need either of us to do that."

She licked the spoon and then took another slow bite, as if contemplating, before she continued. "Diego and I can either go together to find how close the team of whoever they are is, or we can split up and one of us searches for them while the other looks for signs of Whitney's men. Presumably, Whitney will send his best mountain men after us."

Diego frowned, thinking it over. "You might be right, Jonquille. That might be the best way to handle it. Even if you were rude enough to get yourself dessert and not any for me, I have to say, you have a decent enough plan." He got up and scooped himself up a much larger helping of the cobbler, and sat down with an air of satisfaction.

Rubin studied their two faces and then shook his head. "Seriously? You think I'm going to fall for that? Nicely played, the two enemies falling together into some sort of uneasy alliance, but I'm not buying it for one minute. You're not leaving me here safe and sound, looking out for my patients, while the two of you go off hunting the enemy together. Do you think I'm an idiot?"

He got up and just took the rest of the cobbler, not bothering with a bowl. "When we go hunting, I'll be hunting with you. We're sticking together. This doesn't bode well for our future, Jonquille."

"I was planning on taking seconds," Jonquille said, indicating the cobbler with her spoon. "I took a very modest first helping."

"You don't deserve a second helping for conspiring against your future husband with my brother," Rubin informed her.

Jonquille rolled her eyes. "I don't have a future husband. In case you hadn't noticed, I'm a human lightning rod. Kissing me might be a little dangerous."

Diego groaned. "You just had to go and issue that particular challenge, didn't you?"

Rubin immediately turned his dark eyes on her, looking at her mouth with intense scrutiny. She had a beautiful mouth. That lower lip was especially intriguing. Jonquille drew herself back into the rocking chair as if she could make herself smaller, and held up the spoon as if to ward him off.

"You wouldn't dare."

"You were the one who didn't think it was possible. I assure you, not only is it possible, it's going to happen, and very soon. In fact, you have berries on your lower lip and I'm thinking I might have to lick them off in another minute."

"You might end up lit up like the Fourth of July if you try it," she pointed out, sounding a little faint.

Diego groaned again. "Haven't you learned *anything*? He thrives on challenges. Don't say that to him. Just wave him off or something. It's bad enough that he figured out you were trying to protect him. Now he's going to be watching you like a hawk. Since he lumped me into your conspiracy, he'll be doing the same to me. I won't get away with anything."

"Do you *ever* make sense?" Jonquille asked. "Because I'm pretty sure nothing that just came out of your mouth made any sense at all." She watched Rubin eating the cobbler. "Are you really going to eat all that by yourself?"

"Yes," Rubin said.

"No," Diego said.

"You both suck," Jonquille complained. "There was a reason I never went around people. I thought it was because I was a human lightning bolt. Now I know it's because people are annoying."

"Face it, woman," Diego said. "We make you laugh. You find us hilarious."

"I did until Rubin decided to eat all the cobbler."

"I'll share it with you if you kiss me."

"I have to *kiss* you in order to get more cobbler? I made it."

"In the interest of science and to prove I'm right," Rubin said. "This cobbler is extra delicious. You are my future wife as well, and wives need to kiss their husbands. Those are all good reasons to decide once and for all whether or not we can kiss."

"If we try it and you burn up, is Diego going to shoot me?"

"Depends on whether or not you agree to share that cobbler with me," Diego said. "Maybe I should hold it while you two try the kissing thing."

Jonquille studied his innocent features. "Not a chance. You don't touch that cobbler."

"Last chance, honey. Make up your mind," Rubin prompted.

"If I kiss you, I'm not agreeing in any way that you're my future husband. That's just going too far. It would be for science and the cobbler."

"I'm your future husband," Rubin said complacently. "I expect when I kiss you, we'll light up the night. Come over here." He put the cobbler on the small table beside his chair and beckoned with one finger.

Jonquille hesitated. Diego gave an exaggerated sigh and held out his hand for her empty dish. "Just go. You know you're going to, and it would be a shame if he ate all the cobbler. He would too. He's not nearly as nice as he pretends to be."

Jonquille slid off the rocker and padded on bare feet across the short distance to Rubin. She looked startled when he stood up, towering over her. Very gently, he framed her face with both palms, looking down into her eyes. Rubin found her eyes sexy, ethereal, intriguing. She seemed mysterious, like the fairies who moved between worlds in the stories he told his sisters.

He leaned his head down slowly, giving her plenty of time to pull away from him. The last thing he wanted to do was frighten her. Jonquille didn't seem to be the kind of woman who scared easily. She might not reduce him to ash with a lightning bolt, but she could stab him through the heart with any one of the weapons she had on her. Her eyes searched his, and then her lashes lowered as he continued to lower his head.

He brushed a kiss across along the corner of her mouth and licked off the berry on the sweet curve of her lower lip. He lingered there, rubbing gently, coaxing with his lips on hers. Sparks flew, lighting up her skin. His. Arcing between them just as he'd predicted. His energy found and fed the little forks of jagged energy building in her body. He slid his tongue along the seam of her lips, coaxing. Teasing. She didn't comply at first, so he used his teeth to nip at her lower lip.

She gasped and he swept in, feeling the building flames, pure fire burning between them. It was just the way he knew it would be. Her body leaned into his and a blaze rushed through his veins. Vaguely, behind his eyelids, he saw a flash of light and heard a sizzle of electricity, but the thunder in his ears drowned out everything but the wealth of flames rising in her like the tide. Her body, against his, was red hot. Fiery hot.

Electricity sparked over his skin. Over hers. A maelstrom of charging electrons poured down his throat. Down hers. Ice and fire bumping together, going apart, raging, the friction producing that flash-fire so intense the world faded away.

Something crept stealthily behind them, setting off a prickling of awareness. Rubin gently kissed Jonquille's velvet-soft lips one last time. He half turned, his hand sliding into his shirt. As Diego's hand inched toward the bowl sitting on the table beside the chair, Rubin's hand flicked out and a knife embedded deep into the tabletop between Diego's thumb and finger.

"I wouldn't touch that bowl if I were you. The next one won't miss," Rubin advised.

"What is the matter with you?" Diego demanded, removing his hand from harm's way. "When you're kissing a girl, you're supposed to be completely engaged, not looking with eyes in the back of your head at what anyone else in the room is doing. I was in stealth mode."

Jonquille pressed her forehead against Rubin's sternum, muffling her laughter with her hand. "Stealth mode?"

"That's what triggered my radar, his supposed stealth mode." Rubin caught up the bowl of cobbler, giving his brother a glaring reprimand. "She kissed me. She deserves the cobbler."

"Is that what you call a kiss? The two of you set the cabin on fire. You could have set the entire forest on fire if you'd been outside."

"Then you should have known the cobbler belonged to her, you thief," Rubin reprimanded sternly.

Diego put his hand over his heart. "I'm sorry, Jonquille. You do deserve the cobbler after subjecting yourself to kissing the dragon, but I couldn't resist how good the cobbler was. I don't suppose you made a second one?"

There was a mournful, hopeful note in his voice that made Rubin roll his eyes. "He practices sounding like that, Jonquille. He thinks the women will find him irresistible."

"Does it work?" Jonquille took the offered cobbler and sat in the rocker across from Rubin's chair.

"You tell me," Diego challenged.

She contemplated it over a spoonful of berries, then nodded her head. "I'd have to say yes. He's very charming, Rubin. He hits all the right notes with his voice. He has that face, perfectly gorgeous. Those eyes. Very mysterious. Yeah, he's probably a huge hit with women."

Diego flashed Rubin a grin. "There you have it, big brother. I told you. Your problem is you never listen to me. You don't bother talking. You actually have to talk."

"He does all right," Jonquille said. "And he can kiss. Talking versus kissing. I'll take kissing over talking any day."

"I've never had complaints in that department," Diego said.

Jonquille licked at the spoon, eyeing him over the top of it. "We only have your word to go on."

"That's all you're ever going to have, Jonquille," Rubin interrupted. "If you want more kisses, you can look this way. He's trying to get you to share the cobbler. I'm warning you, Diego, you try kissing my woman, I'm shooting you."

"You can't shoot me, I'm your brother."

"I can shoot you, I just can't kill you. I'm a doctor. And I have certain extraordinary gifts when it comes to healing. So does Jonquille. Between the two of us we could keep you alive." Rubin steepled his fingers and regarded Diego. "Jonquille probably needs the practice."

"She can't practice on me. You never did answer, woman—did you make more than one cobbler?"

"No, but I can make another one. They're easy enough to make."

"I'll take first watch tonight," Rubin said casually. "I'm not very tired. Jonquille, you may as well keep the loft and Diego can sleep down here. He can have the second shift. I'll wake him in four hours and then he'll wake you."

Diego nodded. "That sounds good. I'm beat, I'm not going to lie about it. I think I'm getting old. We covered a lot of ground today to make it to the cabin before dusk."

"That was a priority?" Jonquille asked.

"It's my favorite time of day," Rubin admitted. "The fireflies come out."

Her face lit up. "I love that so much. I sit outside and watch them every evening. I know it sounds silly, but it feels like they bring the setting of the sun. I feel a kinship with them. You call them fireflies. I think of them as lightning bugs. They appear and dance along the edges of the grass in this beautiful, musical display. I tell myself it's just for me. Some nights it makes me cry watching, it is that beautiful."

Rubin studied her face as she lifted her hand self-consciously to her hair, shoving back the wayward strands. Her eyes had settled back to the deeper blue, but he could still see the rings of silver circling the darker color. She handed the bowl of unfinished cobbler to Diego and drew up her knees, as if she'd given too much of herself away and felt too vulnerable.

"When I was a kid, I would sit outside and tell my sisters stories about the lightning bugs. I'd tell them they were fairies and were magic. I don't know how I made up such crazy tales for them, but they used to beg me for new ones all the time. I got the idea from hearing a traveling salesman telling stories. That started my imagination going. The girls would come outside with me and I'd want to transport them somewhere magical for just a little while."

"He did a great job too," Diego said. "I'd sit and listen. I'd pretend I wasn't, because I was a boy and boys weren't supposed to listen to stories about fairies and magic, but they were so fascinating. Mama had to have heard them, but she never said he had to stop. Magic would have been considered sinful and of the devil. He would have gotten a beating with a belt or worse if Daddy was alive, telling stories like that, but Mama never stopped him. She just pretended she didn't hear."

Rubin nodded. "She knew all of us needed something good, something bright. It was the only thing I could think of to give the girls. They were older for the most part, but they needed something to hang on to. We had some pretty rough times back then."

Jonquille rubbed her chin on the top of her knees. "I wonder how many people those little lightning bugs have helped when they come out and dance like that, bringing in the evening. There's a kind of peace that settles on the land itself and that helps settle into the people, or at least it does into me when I watch them."

Rubin smiled at her. "We are a good match, Jonquille. I feel exactly the same way."

Her gaze jumped to his face, her eyes enormous. "You have to stop thinking we're a match." In the dark room, her eyes seemed to glow.

"I feel compelled to point out," Diego interjected, "you didn't even char him. He didn't spontaneously combust. He didn't burst into flames, which was a bit of a disappointment. There was some electrical charge, which was cool, and the cabin did light up, but no shocking results as you'd hoped."

Jonquille nearly fell out of the rocking chair, she turned on Diego so fast. "Hoped? You thought I hoped I'd fry him?"

"At the very least. All in the name of science, of course."

She burst out laughing. "You're outrageous. I think I really should try kissing you, all in the name of science. Rubin does have some electrical energy that seems to react with mine, but I don't think you do. It might be much more interesting to see what would happen . . ."

"What would happen would be the wrath of hell coming down on you," Rubin said. "You might not want to admit we're a match, but you know we are. I'm not the kind of man to have my woman running around with other men. I don't share well with others."

Jonquille regarded him for a long time with her large blue eyes. She gave a little shake of her head. "I don't suppose I would like it very much if you were kissing a bunch of other women. Whitney might actually know what he's doing. Do you think he paired Diego with a woman who prefers swinging?"

Diego choked. "Swinging? How would you even know about

something like that? Rubin? Did you hear her? She shouldn't even know what swinging is. And my woman is not going to like swinging."

"You want to kiss multiple women," Jonquille pointed out. "If you enjoy kissing many women, I imagine your partner must enjoy kissing multiple men. Wouldn't that follow?"

"No, it would most certainly *not*," Diego declared.

"Why wouldn't it? I don't understand," Jonquille said, sounding innocent. Maybe a little too innocent, Rubin thought, but he wasn't going to help his brother out.

"Well, because," Diego said. He ran water in the bowl, rinsing it out. "It just doesn't work that way. If she's intended for me, she doesn't kiss other men."

"So she's happy to share her man with other women?" Jonquille asked, frowning. "What kind of woman enjoys that, but doesn't get to share herself with other men? I must be odd because if my man wanted me to share him with other women, I would think it fair that I get to have other men as well."

"You're giving me a headache, Jonquille," Diego complained. "Go to bed so I don't have to listen to your nonsense anymore."

"I'll take away your headache. I was teasing you," she said immediately. "But really, you shouldn't have a double standard. If you're going to go around kissing lots of women, you'd better expect that your woman has been doing the same with other men."

"I'm fine with that," he said. "I just don't want to hear about it."

"Good." Jonquille sent Rubin a small little grin, then stood up and touched Diego's temple with the tips of her fingers very briefly before turning away from them to head to the bathroom.

"Is it gone?" Rubin asked.

"Immediately. You were right about her being a strong healer." *Do you really think she's a psychic surgeon?*

I think there's a very good possibility. She wouldn't tell me if I asked her, which I didn't. She might not even know what it is. We're being cautious with her.

I'm being cautious with her, Diego corrected. *You went all in.*

Rubin didn't respond. He hadn't exactly gone all in. He was still being careful. He had his brother to protect. Had it been only his life, things would have gone differently, but there was Diego and he wasn't about to risk another grave behind the house.

Jonquille emerged and started for the ladder. Rubin called to her and when she turned, he beckoned to her. She walked very hesitantly to him. He pointed to the spot between his legs.

She moistened her lips and took the necessary step to put herself there. "What?"

"My woman kisses me before she goes to bed." He made it a declaration.

"She does?"

"Most certainly she does."

She stood there for a long moment, deciding, and then she put both hands on his shoulders, leaned forward and brushed her lips across his. His heart did a funny shift in his chest. She pulled back immediately, lashes covering the silvery blue, and then she climbed up to the loft.

"Good night, Jonquille."

"Good night, Rubin."

"Someone could say good night to me," Diego groused.

Rubin laughed. "I'm heading out for the first watch. I'll wake you in four hours."

5

Jonquille thought she wouldn't fall asleep with two men in the same house—virtually in the same room with her—but she did. Both men were incredibly silent sleepers. Rubin had taken first watch, patrolling around the cabin for the first few hours and then waking his brother. She was vaguely aware of Rubin coming in and Diego leaving, but there was no whisper of sound to give them away, only that slight heightened energy she felt when they spoke telepathically to each other. She had gone right back to sleep until Diego had awakened her for her shift.

She loved the early morning hours just as the sun was coming up. She had a small backpack with her, water and her sketch pad. Being as light on her feet as she was made traveling through the woods very easy. Patrolling through the woods, she was silent enough that she never bothered the wildlife or insects. This time of the morning she often came across both the night hunters and feeders as well as the early morning animals and birds. There was so much diversity, and all very close to the Campo cabin.

Jonquille knew it was because the brothers didn't live there year-round. They encouraged their properties to grow naturally and took care to manage the wildlife and forest in the best possible way. Animals that hadn't been there in years were returning— cautiously, but they had come back. Because they came back, the ecosystem was thriving, improving the conditions of the surrounding woods.

Walking slowly and without making a sound, she could enjoy the songs of the birds, one of her favorite things. She loved all the different early morning melodies mixed with the night birds calling out to one another before they began or ended their hunt for food. Inevitably, she came to the point overlooking the stream. She didn't go near it, because that was where the animals drank. The overlook was the best place to observe them.

Jonquille settled into a small depression above the stream and waited in silence. It was still relatively dark, although the sky was beginning to be streaked with gray. She could tell a storm was brewing just by the way her body reacted, but it was still a distance away. The stream sparkled at times as the moon shifted through the slow-moving clouds. Something about the way the water looked like diamonds and then would go almost black coupled with the drone of the early morning insects and mournful notes of the male frogs as they gave up calling for their ladyloves made her smile.

Suddenly, a chilling shriek, sounding all too like a child's cry, cut through the night and then faded away. She rarely allowed the doors to her childhood to unlock. Perhaps just talking with Rubin had cracked open the door enough to allow another recollection to slide out. In any case, that cry, she was certain, had been a bobcat, which brought another memory to the forefront of her mind.

She was younger than the other girls and very, very small. Even they treated her like a little doll. Her diminutive size tended to annoy Whitney. He was aware, even then, when she was three, that energy collected in her body. But she was so small, he didn't think it was enough to do the things he wanted, like draw lightning to her. She needed to be tall so that when he put her out in a field, she would attract the lightning. He ignored her for the most part, telling the nurses to find a way to make her grow.

She heard the muted cry of one of the girls down the hall and knew immediately it was Iris. None of the other girls called her Iris. She was always Flame. She defied Whitney at every turn and he despised her. He experimented on her and told her she should be happy to suffer for science. He repeatedly gave her a form of cancer and then put it in remission to see if it could be done. He couldn't care less whether she lived or died. To him, she wasn't human. She was a laboratory experiment. It didn't matter how often she got sick or her hair fell out. It only mattered to him if he was successful in stopping the cancer.

There were cameras in the hallway. Eyes on them at all times. Guards were stationed, although the guards were usually bored and detested watching a bunch of little girls they thought harmless, especially one vomiting in her room. Some of the guards felt sorry for her and would sneak in to try to help her. Others were indifferent. Some moved down the hall to avoid hearing her.

Jonquille covered her distinctly blond hair. It wasn't even blond. It was white. Just as Flame's hair was bright red, Jonquille's was as platinum as could be. Due to her looks, the guards called her "freaky" looking. The other girls were protective over her. Jonquille did her best not to cry at the hurtful things the men said, because they said the things to all the girls and seemed to hold them in contempt the way Whitney did. She wanted to be like Flame.

Being so small, she could secret herself in the tiniest cracks, or the smallest vents. She'd found that out when she was barely a year and a half. Now, she took off the grate and pulled herself up into the small hole, sliding into the pipe that connected her room to Flame's. The pipe was extremely narrow and she had to round her shoulders and push with her toes and fingers, but she did so, no problem.

She had tiny hairs or setae embedded in her palms and fingers as well as in the soles of her feet and toes, so tiny no one could see them. She never told the other girls because the hairs embarrassed her when she realized they didn't have them. The setae allowed her to climb straight up the walls and across the ceiling, which she did often when she was alone. She enjoyed climbing and practiced over and over, but never when anyone might see her.

Instinctively, she hid everything she could do from Whitney as well. She didn't trust him. She didn't trust the guards and was careful to stay out of their way. She was so small, they often overlooked her, which allowed her to see and overhear things she might not have heard if they'd known she was listening. Fortunately, even at three, she had above-average intelligence. What she didn't understand, she asked one of the older girls she trusted to explain to her.

Whitney didn't like the girls, and his dislike of them spilled over to the guards. He really didn't like Flame and another girl, Thorn. He thought they were the worst and he intended to get rid of them one way or another, but not before he got his money's worth out of them. Jonquille wasn't certain what that meant, but she knew it wasn't a good thing.

Jonquille used the setae on her hands to pull her way through the vent as fast as possible while still remaining silent, not making a whisper of sound. Whitney had a way of recording them, his cameras and audio equipment very sensitive.

Flame writhed on the bed, occasionally leaning over to violently vomit into a wastepaper basket located on the floor to the side of the bed. She clutched a wet cloth in her hand and would wipe at her mouth afterward and then lie back down. There were beads of sweat on her forehead, and her thin shirt was twisted and looked damp and uncomfortable on her body. Her hair, normally a bright red, was dark, soaked with sweat.

Two soldiers whispered to each other, one almost pushing the other toward the door. "I'll take care of this little brat, Jerry. She's mostly faking. I've seen her do this before. She can make herself get sick. She does it to make everyone feel sorry for her."

The other guard had his hand over his mouth. "I don't think so, Vern. She looks really sick to me. I've just never been good with this. It reeks in here. We should at least open the window." He made a move to do so, but Vern blocked him.

"I'll do it. You go on out before you hurl, man. I don't want to clean up your mess. Just go down the hall and drink some water. Get some air. I'll cover for you. Take fifteen."

Jonquille had always been able to hear false notes in voices, and there was something wrong with Vern's solicitation. He wasn't in the least concerned with Jerry. Vern had "bad" energy, and it was coming at her in waves. He was excited in a bad way. He wanted Jerry gone. Jerry was genuinely concerned for Flame, but felt sick and wanted to get away. His energy was low. Jonquille watched through the grille as he turned his head away and staggered out the door. Vern stood in the door frame until Jerry had gone all the way down the hall and then he stepped fully into the room, closed the door and slowly turned to face Flame.

Flame was sick again, leaning over the bed, vomiting, mostly bile, not looking at the guard, but Jonquille could see the man's face. He looked as evil as he felt. She had no idea what he wanted, but she was certain it wasn't something good. Flame was completely incapable of protecting herself. She was far too sick. Jonquille didn't understand what this man would do to her, as sick as she was, but she knew she was the only one who could stop him.

The guard stepped up to the side of the bed as Flame once more took the wet cloth and wiped at her face.

"It's just you and me, you little brat. You're going to be real quiet. No screaming, you hear me? If you aren't, I'm going to hurt you like you've never been hurt."

Flame didn't respond at all. She fell back against the pillows, her face dotted with beads of sweat. She didn't seem to have heard him.

The soldier slapped her hard. "You little bitch. Don't you ignore me when I'm talking to you. You can fool your nurses into being sorry for you, but you can't fool me."

Flame's head rolled to the side with the vicious slap, and her breath burst out in a long, ragged rush of air. Her gaze jumped to Jerry's face as he caught her hair in his fist and dragged her head up so she was forced to look at him.

"Yeah, kid, you see me now. You're going to cooperate and you're going to keep your mouth shut. You keep silent or I'm going to sneak into all the rooms and slit your little friends' throats one by one. I'll tell them you sent me. Understand? Nod your head if we have an understanding."

Jonquille had already loosened the grate. She allowed it to drop sideways slowly, so that the entire metal plate dangled sideways from one screw. She could pull it back easily from the little wire she had attached to it from one of the many trips she'd made earlier. The room was shadowy, not completely dark, but dim enough from the single light they'd left Flame to recover alone from her bouts of sickness from the chemo drugs. Those shadows suited Jonquille. She was able to slip out of the vent and, using the setae on her hands and feet, climb up the wall and over the ceiling until she was behind the guard.

He dropped Flame's hair and moved to the foot of the bed, unfastening his belt as he did. "You might not like this so much, but it's going to feel real good for me. Whitney doesn't need sex, doesn't even think about it, but someone like me, I gotta have it. You were running around the compound with all that hair, jumping rope right in front of us. Flirting with us."

Flame shook her head in protest, holding up nine fingers, trying to mouth her age to the guard. He ignored her, catching at her ankles and yanking her down to the edge of the bed.

"Makes no difference to me how old you are. You're all the same, right?" He opened his cargo pants and took out his heavy erection, one hand circling the base while the other went to grasp her panties.

Jonquille slid down the wall behind him and crept close. His energy was sizzling now with excitement, building the charges in her body. She was a mere shadow and he was so excited, his entire attention centered on what he was about to do, that he didn't notice they weren't alone until she deliberately reached up to the wrist where he had wrapped his fist around his eager cock.

Jonquille had only one real chance and she took it. The enemy was so wrapped up in the sensations of his body he didn't notice her sliding into position beside him. He barely noticed when she put her hand over his wrist. Her fingers were so small that she was able to position them exactly over his pulse and that artery she needed that would take the burst of energy straight to his heart when she released it. It would really be his energy as well. In a sense he would be aiding in his own death.

Flame saw her when the guard didn't. Her eyes went wide in shock and she even shook her head, afraid that the evil guard would hurt or kill Jonquille as well. Jonquille ignored her, took a deep breath and pressed down with all her might, pouring her strength and will into her fingertips, right into that pulse point. The moment the guard was aware of her and his adrenaline spiked, she met the charge with her own so the two merged into a blast much like a jolt of lightning—or an electrical surge. She jumped back as the guard went down hard, landing on his butt, clutching his chest.

"Jonquille." Flame whispered her name. "What did you do?"

Jonquille knew she didn't have much time. She skirted around the dying guard and climbed onto the bed. "I came to help you. You're so sick and I can't stand it."

Flame shook her head. "You have to get out of here before someone sees you. No one can ever know that you were here tonight. Never tell anyone, not even one of the other girls. Do you understand me? I mean it. Whitney can never know you did this."

Jonquille already knew that. She ignored Flame's fierce protection of her. They all treated her like she was a baby or didn't have a brain. She was smart. Smarter than some of the way older girls, but she wasn't going to point that out to them and hurt their feelings. She put her palms over Flame's body and immediately felt the difference in her cells.

Her breath hissed out of her. Whitney had introduced a different kind of cancer. This wasn't going to be healed with the chemotherapy he was using. He was making her suffer needlessly. Did he know it? Jonquille could only surmise he did. She began to fix what she could. It was a slow process, and the cancer had spread.

Flame suddenly caught at her and shook her, dragging her back to the awful-smelling room. It reeked of vomit, urine and death. Jonquille was terribly weak. So much so that she collapsed on the bed, feeling as if she couldn't move, couldn't lift her arms. Flame had tears running down her face.

"Baby, listen to me. I'm too weak to get you to the vent. You have to do it now. I know you feel like you can't move, but you don't have a choice. They can't find you in here. Get to the vent and pull the grille up. Go, Jonquille. Hurry. *Go*." Flame poured command into her voice.

Jonquille rolled off the bed to the floor and continued rolling until she was at the wall where the grille hung down. She forced one arm over her head and pulled with the setae. Fortunately, it didn't require strength to use setae to climb. She managed to make it up to the vent and slide inside feetfirst, pulling the grate closed behind her so she could twist the screw into place. She laid her head down and waited.

It didn't take long for Jerry to return. Flame must have been aware of his measured tread coming down the hall toward the room and she'd forced Jonquille to halt her healing session. Jerry flung open the door and took a step inside, and the expression on his face went straight to comprehension and horror as he took in the sight of Flame at the end of the bed with her torn panties and Vern on the floor with his cargo pants open and his genitals exposed.

Swearing, Jerry rushed to Flame. "Did he hurt you? I shouldn't have left you. Did he hurt you? I swear to God, I didn't know what he was going to do." He had a phone out. "I need a nurse in here now. Send Colleen."

Colleen was the one nurse the girls all liked. She was the most compassionate. She tried the hardest to be kind, no matter how much Whitney wanted the adults to distance themselves from the girls. They knew she wouldn't last long—the nice ones never did. Whitney wouldn't tolerate them once he realized they would help the girls. He was afraid they would get too close and might help them escape or give too much of the outside world to them.

"We need a doctor. It looks like Vern suffered a heart attack. He's dead." Jerry's voice was cold when he added the last. He put his phone away and went to the bathroom to get another wet cloth for Flame. "I'd cover you up, honey, but I want Colleen to see exactly what that bastard was trying to do to you, just in case someone accuses you of killing him. They seem to think you girls can kill anyone."

Colleen came running in, skidding to a halt as she took in the scene, one hand going to her throat, the other reaching toward Flame. "Baby. Did he touch you? Did that horrible man touch you?" She moved around Jerry, reaching for the sheet only to discover it was damp. "This is a disgrace. She should never have been left like this. My God, these people are animals."

"Shh, Colleen," Jerry cautioned. "This place has ears and eyes everywhere. Can you take pictures and then clean her up? I'll take pictures of him. We can exchange them so they can't destroy them. She didn't kill him. There isn't any way. She's too damned weak. I never should have left her alone with him. I've never been good with puke. I have this stupid reaction." He sounded ashamed as he took out his cell and crouched down, taking a series of photographs of Vern.

Even though she was so exhausted, Jonquille liked the guard. She liked his energy. He was angry. He was really angry, but she still liked his energy a lot. She liked the way his energy merged with Colleen's vitality and the way there was a protective drive to the energy he surrounded Flame with. That was when she learned

97

men could be many things. Before, they were all bad or evil. Jerry taught her men were much, much more.

Soon, Flame's room was overrun with people, and Jonquille dozed as they surrounded Vern to examine him, a doctor pronouncing him dead of a heart attack. Whitney demanded an autopsy immediately and the body was removed. Whitney remained impassive as Flame was examined to ensure she hadn't been raped by Vern before he had his heart attack, even though she assured them several times she hadn't been.

She was questioned repeatedly by the military police Whitney brought in. Jerry was questioned separately. Through it all, Whitney directed Colleen to sponge wash Flame, braid her hair and change her bedding as if he cared about her. A clean waste bucket was brought in. Windows were opened in the room so a cool breeze took the scent of vomit out. Fans were brought in to take the temperature down. Whitney paced up and down, all the while his sharp eyes looking at the floor and ceiling, examining the walls for any signs that Flame might not have been alone.

Once the others had left the room and only Jerry and Colleen remained at his command, Whitney pinned Flame with the eyes of a dead fish. That was the way Jonquille saw him. A dead fish.

"Which one of the girls came here tonight?"

"No one was here."

"They always come. It isn't in your best interest to lie, or theirs. I don't care about a dead guard. Especially one that would rape a child. I am not going to punish one of the girls for saving you from him. I give you my word on that, Iris."

"There wasn't time for one of them to come," Flame replied. "They wouldn't sneak in when the guards were here. They wait."

That much was true. They always waited. Jonquille would have waited. She hadn't because Vern was truly evil. She couldn't wait, not when the energy he had been throwing off had been so disgusting it made her feel sick.

Whitney stared at Flame for a long time and then his breath hissed out in a long rush of annoyance. "The cameras on this floor never work. Do you know why that is?"

Flame looked genuinely surprised because she was. She shook her head. "No."

Whitney studied her for what seemed forever. Abruptly, he turned and stalked out of the room, his guards following him. Colleen let out her breath. Jerry stood in the corner looking uncertain. When Colleen would have spoken, Flame shook her head and indicated the windowsills and along the door frame where Whitney's guards and been standing so quietly. Jerry went to look, and sure enough there were the usual bugs left behind.

"Do you still feel sick, Iris?" Colleen asked. "You have to stay hydrated when you're vomiting that much, that's why I'm putting an IV in you. I know you hate them. You can use the bathroom first if you want. And this is portable so you can move around with it. Once you're feeling better, I'll take it out. This is anti-nausea medicine. Hopefully, that will help as well. This is cold water as well as juice. Ice chips. I'll check on you every half hour. Dr. Whitney doesn't want you sick, he's trying to make you better. The medicine feels like it makes you worse, but it is supposed to kill the cancer."

Once she was back from the bathroom, after washing her face and brushing her teeth, Flame lay motionless in the bed, too exhausted to move while Colleen put in the IV. Jonquille slept in the vent, recouping her strength. She made the trip down to Flame's bed three times that night in the dark, her energy disrupting all recordings so she could work on the cancer eating away at Flame's body. After the first and second sessions she forced herself to climb back into the vent. Flame slept through all of the healing sessions.

The third healing session of the night, Jonquille knew she had to make it back to her room. She couldn't take the chance of sleeping in the vent even in the early morning hours. If it was reported to Whitney that she wasn't in her bed or she didn't make it to breakfast, he might suspect that she had been the one in the room with Flame. That she had killed Vern. When he found Flame's cancer reduced, he might suspect Jonquille of healing her.

Jonquille found herself back to the present, tears on her face. She rarely allowed herself to think about the other women in her past, those girls she had shared a nightmare childhood with. As she had grown and the electrical energy in her body had increased, the charging had grown worse and she had been forced to separate herself from the others in order to keep from drawing their energy to her. They would talk to her at night, but she couldn't be in the same room with them and it felt like isolation all the time. Whitney had clothes that helped, but he deliberately wouldn't let her wear them to be with the other girls unless she was training.

She wanted freedom. She wanted to be able to use her healing gift. Rubin was a doctor. He could help others. She was born to help others, but she couldn't do that. She could only live in the woods or in a small drab apartment and sneak into a laboratory at night and do her research to try to find a way to reverse the things Whitney had done to her.

She felt Rubin's presence before he actually reached her. He did something to her body. Usually, when she was close to other human beings, the energy fed the electrical charges in hers until she was so completely overwhelmed, she had to get away from everyone. Her core temperature would rise and she'd feel sick. Her skin would become prickly and tiny sparks would zap her all over. With Rubin, none of that happened. Well—unless she kissed him. Then it happened in a good way.

She caught up her sketch pad and bent over it, dashing at the tears on her face, hoping he wouldn't be able to catch the way she was blushing at the thought of kissing him, or the silly tears, or the fact that she was pretending. She glanced up through wet and spiky lashes. Did he have to be so utterly gorgeous?

He flashed her a grin and her heart immediately felt as though it skipped a beat. His smile faded and she hastily looked down at her blank sketch pad. He stepped closer and caught her chin between his finger and thumb, seemingly completely unaware of personal space. Tipping her head up, he studied her face.

His other hand came up, fingers moving with exquisite gentleness, and brushed at the tears, and then followed the tracks down her cheeks. "What made you cry, little lightning bug?"

A million thoughts crowded in. It wasn't his business. A sarcastic reply. A joke. Anything but the truth. Jonquille didn't say any of those things. "I heard a cry like a child in distress and for some reason it brought the past too close. I don't usually allow myself to go backward like that, but the memories just swept over me before I could shut that door."

Rubin brushed his hand very gently down the back of her hair and it felt too much like caring. When she was really little, the older girls had brushed her hair and treated her like a little doll, but then the buildup of energy had begun and they couldn't do that anymore. She'd watched them brush each other's hair and she'd been envious. She'd tried very hard not to be, but she couldn't help it. Having Rubin just use his palm and sweep his hand over the back of her scalp so gently tore at her heart. She didn't know what to do with that kind of gesture.

Jonquille knew she wasn't a woman who would ever have a home and family. This gentle, brilliant man whom Whitney had paired her with had the soul of a healer, the intellect of an Einstein and the fierceness of a warrior. He was everything a woman like Jonquille could possibly want or need yet could never have. She wanted to scream at the universe for such a betrayal.

"We all have those moments, Jonquille. I have them every single time I first arrive at the cabin. I remember each loss I suffered here and wish I had a do-over. I was a kid and doubt I would be able to change the outcome, but I always think I somehow would be wiser."

"Why do we do that to ourselves?"

"I don't know, sweetheart, but everyone does it."

He bent his head and her heart pounded. His lips were soft as he brushed kisses over her eyelids and along the tracks her tears had taken. "I love this time of the day. Sunset. Sunrise. Magical times. There's a reason those times are magical."

"You're supposed to be catching up on your sleep." Her brain was short-circuiting. That was all she could think to say because tenderness lit his dark eyes and sent her temperature soaring. There were sparks, and none of it had to do with electrical energy.

"I got plenty of sleep. Come on, but you have to stay quiet and we have to stay downwind."

She nodded and shoved her sketch pad into the pack on her back. Truthfully, she'd follow him anywhere. It was that scent he had on his skin. It was faint, but it was there. How had she missed it when she'd first stepped into the cabin? Every time she inhaled, she seemed to take him deeper into her lungs. That scent of red spruce, faint orangey citrus combined with leather and earth. He moved like he was part of the mountain, of the forest, of the land itself.

It was more than the scent on his skin. It was the way he could be so gentle when he touched her. He was alone with her, but he didn't push himself on her. Walking behind him where he couldn't see, she brought her fingertips up to her tingling lips. She couldn't help wondering about what it would be like kissing him again. She had no idea what she'd do if he kissed her. *Really* kissed her again.

She tried not to stare or think too hard about him because a part of her was afraid he could read her mind. The longer she was alone in close proximity with him, the more she seemed to be attracted to him. She'd dreamt about him all night. About the kiss. The moment she thought about the kiss, her blood pounded through her veins. Hot. Inflamed. Like her face. It was the most annoying thing ever. She didn't have these kinds of problems when she was by herself.

The first time she ever saw Rubin Campo, she remembered being so shocked at her reaction to him. She'd stared at him in awe when he walked out onto the podium to speak. The first few words he said, she didn't even hear him—and then when she did, his voice was like the whisper of fingertips brushing over her skin. She actually got goose bumps. It didn't make any sense. She was up in a balcony, completely alone, hidden in a corner, and she had been afraid she would light up like one of the fireflies dancing in the grass at sunset.

Jonquille followed Rubin a good distance from the cabin into much deeper forest until they came to a series of large trees, where he stopped and caught at her arm as he sank into a crouch. He indicated a very old oak that had toppled over several years earlier, the roots coming right out of the ground, leaving a large hole that curved back underneath the tree. Jonquille was silent, waiting for the wind and the sounds to tell her what Rubin wanted her to know.

Bobcat. A little female and her kits. They couldn't be more than a few days old, nursing. How many? She stretched her senses, wishing she could see them. Four? No, five. Definitely newborns. She turned her head slowly and looked at Rubin, smiling. If he'd given her a diamond, she wouldn't have liked it as well.

A female bobcat generally claimed a territory of about ten miles. In that territory she had her main den, usually a hole in the ground where she would have her babies, and then several auxiliary or shelter dens scattered throughout her territory. Those could be located near stumps or brush piles, anywhere in the less-traveled areas of her territory.

Like most of the predatory animals, the bobcats were hunted for their fur and driven out of their habitats when the areas were logged. Knowing a little female had established a den and had her kittens right there, a few miles from the cabin, was a testament to the fact that Rubin's and Diego's efforts at conservation and preserving their heritage were working. Having spent time in the mountains now, she recognized the beauty of their land and culture and wanted it saved as well.

They backed away slowly, careful not to make a sound. They didn't want the mother to feel threatened in any way. The last thing they wanted her to do was abandon her den and try to take her kittens to another, perhaps putting them in danger from a predator.

Once they were far enough away from the den, patrolling in a loose and wide circle around the cabin, Jonquille admitted to herself and him that she was happy to have actually seen the little cat.

"I was fairly certain the cry I heard was from a bobcat, but actually seeing her with my own eyes made me much less worried. I don't know what I was thinking—that a child was lost up here in the mountains? That would be silly, right?"

"No, of course not. It's happened. Just because we don't have close neighbors doesn't mean a child can't be lost. We have systematically bought up the neighboring properties when they've come up for sale in order to keep the land from being torn apart. That doesn't mean children weren't running loose playing or hunting at times. We certainly did. Also, more and more, we have backpackers who take the trail looking for places where few people go. Most are respectful of the land, but a few run wild. Some have children with them and don't watch them. It's good to check everything out, but always be on alert."

"It would be such a shame to lose all this to logging or mining," she said. "I've been going off trail to sketch some of the plants, and you've got some very rare species here, ones I'm certain have healing properties."

He nodded. "I'm sure you're right. My mother used to go out into the woods when the neighbors were ill and she'd find certain plants. She'd use the flowers or the roots. Sometimes she'd make tea or some other concoction. I remember my father laughing and saying she was making a witch's brew in her cauldron. That was sacrilegious. You were never supposed to make comments like that, but she laughed. When he was alive, she laughed all the time."

Jonquille glanced at him sharply. He sounded sad. She wished she could ask if he would allow her to draw him. She'd be embarrassed, but it would be worth it. She wanted to take a little bit of him with her when she had to go—and she had to go. She had a little time. There wasn't much, but some. She could take time and be with him before she went hunting, and she intended to hunt his enemies. Just because he showed up early didn't mean her plan wasn't solid. Now, after meeting him, she knew she was going to go through with it. Rubin Campo was too good of a man to let die. He would fight until his last breath, and she wasn't going to take any chances with his life.

"I didn't bring as many sketch pads as I should have," Jonquille admitted. "I only brought a few because I didn't think I'd be here that long and I don't like to carry extra weight."

He glanced at her as they walked a few feet in silence. Light was beginning to streak through the leaves of the canopy overhead, creating a theatrical effect. The early morning sun sent bizarre patterns spilling onto the forest floor. Rubin's eyes were so dark they looked like twin chips of black obsidian, weighing her truths against the lies she mixed in. That velvet gaze drifted over her face like the touch of fingers, bringing up the inevitable goose bumps.

Jonquille had no idea how he did that. He wasn't physically touching her, yet she felt as if he might be. It was just as well they weren't going to be partners, because if they had arguments, all he would have to do was look at her like that and she'd blurt out everything he'd want to know immediately.

"Jonquille." Even her name was a caress.

"I thought you said you didn't have relationships with women." She glared at him, narrowing her eyes belligerently. Maybe the only thing to do when she was alone with him was pick a fight. Push him away.

He stopped walking and turned, towering over her. She'd forgotten about their height difference. The uneven ground and his gentle demeanor had given her a false sense of security. Now he smoothly cut off her retreat. He looked down at her, his head tilted to one side, that dark gaze of his like a black velvet cloth moving over her skin in a slow perusal. He reached out and tucked a wild strand of her blond hair behind her ear. The pads of his fingertips shaping the tops of her ears sent tingles down her spine.

"I don't have relationships with women. You're my first one. Am I already making mistakes? What am I doing to upset you?" His gaze dropped to her mouth.

The moment he looked at her mouth, her mind went straight to the kiss. She couldn't help it. The sun was lighting up the forest floor. She was afraid if she kept looking at his mouth—and she couldn't pull her gaze away—she would be lighting up the entire forest because she was going to wrap her body around his and kiss him like there was no tomorrow. For her there wasn't one. So the hell with it.

Jonquille made the first move, stepping into him, close, going up onto her toes, wrapping her arms around his neck, one leg wrapping around his leg. She pulled his head down to hers. She didn't know what to expect. Rejection maybe. Anything but what she got. His lips were gentle, even tender, as they brushed across hers. There was no hesitation on his part. None. He tempted her further with little kisses along her lips.

Her stomach did a slow somersault, and she swore a million fireflies took wing all at once, sparking and dancing against her insides. His tongue teased the seam of her lips, and then his teeth bit down very gently on her lower lip. She opened to him and her entire world shifted. Tears burned behind her eyes. Her heart ached. This man. This one man. There truly was no one like him in the world. He treated her with such respect and gentleness. With tenderness. He gave her things no one in her life had ever given her.

Rubin swept her into another place, somewhere she hadn't known existed and hadn't ever dreamt of. She had lived her life with fire inside her, terrified it would get out. Those terrible electrical charges that could call down the lightning from the sky. Rubin was fire. He set the world around them on fire. He kissed her with absolute command. With confidence. Without fear. There was gentleness. Tenderness. Fiery heat. But never fear. He didn't leave room for that emotion.

Jonquille felt truly alive for the first time in her life. The lightning in her sizzled and crackled, singing in her veins. Rubin tasted feral, a wild predator, an untamed lover. She tasted his lust for her. His need of her. His absolute desire for her. He didn't try to hide those things from her. Heat sizzled between them. Electricity crackled. White-hot flames danced on the ground and spun in a blue circle of flames.

Rubin pulled back and rested his forehead against hers, working to get his breathing under control. "We really might set the forest on fire, Lightning Bug."

Jonquille laughed softly, her fists in his shirt, her heart hurting so much. He really was the best of the best. She was going to stay for a few days with him and just let herself be his partner. Just pretend she could keep him. Then she would know exactly why she was hunting and killing everyone who dared come after this man.

6

The wind blew through the canopy, throwing all sorts of patterns of light on the ground. On the forest floor, leaves were still, the trees so thick it was nearly impossible to penetrate. In most places in the mountains, Rubin knew it was no longer that way due to all the logging, but these lands had been mostly spared. What had been logged had been replanted, and the growth had been fairly fast.

He looked down at Jonquille's face. She was so beautiful to him and she looked so much a part of the woods, as if she belonged. He found himself smiling when he hadn't felt happiness in so long, he couldn't remember the feeling. His threaded his fingers through hers and turned away from temptation.

"Can you feel the storm coming?"

"Yes. There's always a kind of pull on my body."

Her voice was extremely soft. She had a way of turning her words. Not an accent really, but he liked the sound. He ran his thumb over the back of her hand. A little shiver ran through her body. She was very susceptible to him in the way he was to her, and he was grateful he wasn't alone in the intensity of his attraction.

"Mine too," he conceded. "Most likely in a different way. Part of the reason I came early was to conduct a few experiments. I knew we were expecting a series of intense thunderstorms. I would like to see a few patients. Luther Gunthrie lives down at the very bottom of the mountain. He's gotten up there in age and I'm always afraid I'll find he's passed sitting at his still. I like to check on him. He still considers me a twelve-year-old boy, but he lets me see to his ailments. Rose and Thomas Carter have a farm on the other side of Whiskey's Point, and they have several children. They were kids when Diego and I were young."

"I presume they're a little more modern than Luther Gunthrie."

Rubin glanced down at her. The early morning sun hit her face with a bright beam through the trees, lighting up the blue of her eyes. She looked a little mischievous. A little fey.

"Everyone is *much* more modern than Luther," he assured her. "Then there's the Sawyer family. I'm very fond of them."

"I can hear that in your voice," Jonquille said. "What is it about them?"

"It's important to see Patricia Sawyer. She married my brother-in-law Mathew, a couple of years after my sister Mary died. She raised Mary's son as her own. Patricia lost Mathew a few years ago to cancer. I tried to save him, but it was pancreatic cancer and it was too far advanced by the time I discovered it. Patricia's special. You'll see when you meet her."

Regret swept over him. They had come to the edge of a small clearing. Many of the animals came here to drink from the stream. He indicated the flatter rocks sticking out from where a larger tree had uprooted during a winter flash flood. Jonquille seated herself and he sank down beside her, tucking her in close to his body to provide warmth. She was dressed for the early morning hours, but they were exposed to the wind now and the gusts were biting cold.

"Rubin." Jonquille's voice was very gentle. A whisper of sound.

He looked down at her. Those vibrant blue eyes stole his breath. Her gaze drifted over his face as if he was really important to her. As if he mattered. Not the rare psychic surgeon. She didn't even know that about him. Not the healer. Not even the man who could direct energy from her. Just the man. She saw the man. Him. Rubin Campo. For the first time in his life, he felt like someone other than Diego saw inside of him and he counted for something.

She twisted his hand until his knuckles were on top, and she brought them to her mouth. Her lips were cool and soft. His hand enveloped hers. Swallowed it completely. Even as she kissed his knuckles, her blue eyes met his. There was a curious melting sensation in his chest, right over the region of his heart. He was a doctor and he knew it was impossible for a heart to actually melt, yet she managed to give him that illusion.

"You know, no matter how good of a healer you are, you can't save the world. I thought I could as well, but I learned it was impossible. You know that."

He nodded, expecting her to drop his hand back to her lap, but she didn't—she pressed their clasped hands under her chin, as if she held something valuable and precious to her close.

"I do, but sometimes it feels as if I'm continually saving strangers. I want to save them, but it isn't personal. It isn't the same as the ones I care so much about. I feel like I'm always losing them. I try to distance myself, but one by one they fall until I'm alone. I hold too tight to Diego. He's a good man. He deserves a life, and he could have it if he weren't so busy standing guard over me all the time."

"He knows he has a choice," she pointed out. "In any case, he probably feels exactly the same way. You're lucky you have each other."

Her voice had a way of working its way inside of him. He had to look away from the intensity of her blue eyes. If he didn't, he'd be kissing her again, and it took discipline and control to put the brakes on the last time. He'd all but run out of that.

"I try never to take him for granted," Rubin said. He slid his thumb over her knuckles. "I would try to always do the same with you, Jonquille. I know it bothers you to think that Whitney paired us and you don't want anything to do with that, but I've had the advantage of witnessing so many of his pairings really working out to be genuine love matches. I don't want to waste time fighting it. I'm not a dating kind of man. I'd rather accept what feels like a tremendous gift to me and go from there."

Her lashes fluttered down. Rubin wasn't certain if it was because her lashes were so long and thick but light colored, almost bluish silver they were so blond, that she appeared vulnerable when they veiled her eyes, but he instantly felt protective of her.

"I come at things as logically as I can. It just seems to me that we work, Jonquille. I can direct energy away from you so you can be in a room with others. You can use your healing skills when you feel the desire to do so. It isn't a perfect answer, but it buys us some time to find one. There is one, we just haven't found it yet."

Her gaze jumped back to his. "You can do that? Direct energy away from me?"

"I believe I can. I came up here to practice a little, directing lightning to specific targets. If I can direct that amount of energy, surely I can direct a much smaller amount. We can practice with Diego and then you can go with us to one of our regular patients and see how you do. If it doesn't work, you can wait outside."

She sent him a small smile, but there was hope in her eyes. "I might get pitchforked if I'm alone outside."

"That's only if they have an eligible daughter they want married off."

Jonquille groaned. "I hadn't even thought of that. An outsider comes up to the mountains and nabs the most eligible, hot-looking doctor around. I'm definitely not going to be popular." Her smile faded. "You were telling me about the Sawyer family. You said they were your favorite family and were telling me why."

"The Sawyers," he repeated. "They're really good people. Patricia has three sons, including my nephew, and a daughter. It's not easy to make a living up here. More than most, she's open to modern ways and education. She sent all of them to school and then to college. It wasn't easy, but she managed without them. That's the kind of woman she is. She would have been a pioneer."

"You admire strong women."

He smiled at her. "I do. I hope to introduce you to Wyatt's grandmother someday. She's a strong woman, and you would love her. I think you'd really like Patricia as well. Diego and I hired two of her sons to look after our property for us. Her youngest, Edward, went to school but really had a difficult time being away from the mountains and came back as soon as he could. One of his older brothers, Rory, had an accident in the mill where he was working as a supervisor, and he came home. He'd always been interested in keeping the trees healthy. He had studied the subject in college, minoring in it, but that was his real interest. Like Diego and me, he doesn't want to see West Virginia lose our part of the Appalachian Mountains."

"Where are Patricia's other two children now? The daughter and son?"

"Her daughter, Maggie, is in her last year of college. She's been studying in the field of artificial intelligence and robotic engineering. It just so happens that one of the leading experts in the field of AI has a research lab where I live in Louisiana and has been looking for someone really intelligent to work with her that would be open to traveling and giving lectures. I've asked her to keep an eye on Maggie. I'm hoping Maggie meets her requirements and she offers her a job. That way I can know she's safe."

"That is so like you."

"Nick, my nephew, joined the service. The Air Force. I keep an eye on him as well. He's doing very well. Patricia has some arthritis but nothing major yet that worries me. I'm watching her right shoulder. She broke her arm a couple of years ago. It was a fairly bad break, up high, in three places, and I didn't like the way it healed. She waited too long before she could get out of here to get help. The winter was bad and all of the kids were gone. Cells weren't working. It was pure luck that old man Gunthrie decided to check on her. It was a long trek for him in the snow in the middle of a blizzard. Who knows why he even decided to check on her."

"I can tell you really like him too."

"He's a strange man, Jonquille. I guess we're all a little strange. Luther is the kind of man who will give you the shirt off his back. Anything he has, unless you try to take it from him. Then he'll hunt you down and put you in the ground. He isn't a forgiving man either. He remembers everything. He doesn't own a car or a truck, and I can't recall that he ever did. There're miles, *miles* between his place and Patricia's, but he made that trek in a blizzard to check on her because he was worried. She has closer neighbors, but none of them thought to do it."

Rubin went silent when a family of raccoons, making tentative stops and starts, came out of the trees, going cautiously from rock to rock. Using the cover of grass, they made their way to the silver ribbon of water. Standing occasionally on their hind legs to peer around them for enemies, they dropped back down to eat and drink from the stream. The younger raccoons ignored the demands of their parents and rolled around together in several fights after chasing one another over the rocks and through the grass.

A pair of foxes came to the water's edge on the other side of the stream, eyed the raccoon family warily but drank and stayed for a short minute or two. Mice and lizards scurried underfoot. A few rabbits hurried to make their burrows before the sun was too high in the sky. The clouds continued to shift with the wind, blowing across the sky, by turns darkening it and then allowing the light to come shining through with stunning beauty.

They were silent as they watched the animals take turns in a truce, drinking together at the stream. Life could be like that. Little moments where the world held its breath and everyone got along, and then it would explode again and everyone would be enemies.

Rubin tightened his grasp on Jonquille's hand, pulling it to his chest. He had a very precarious hold on her, and all he could do was try to show her who he was as a person. Let her know he wasn't a soldier with Whitney. He wasn't any part of Whitney's bizarre world in spite of having started there. He was a soldier, yes. He was a GhostWalker, yes. He wanted a wife and a family. He wanted a partner. An equal. He wanted to give her time to get to know him and hopefully she would choose him.

He did have quite a lot he could offer her. He rubbed his chin on the back of her hand as he thought about it, his gaze fixed on a young buck walking cautiously to the stream to take his turn. The buck was clearly a juvenile, velvety buds for horns, his head bobbing as he took one guarded step after another. He would pause and swing his head around alertly. Freeze. Move forward a few more steps and then stop again. Finally, the little buck made it to the edge of the stream, where he dipped his muzzle in the water.

It was a calm scene. Jonquille remained just as still as he did. He kept all movements slow as he rubbed sensitive bristles on her soft skin. Drawing the energy from her shouldn't be difficult, not when he could direct it the way he could. He considered how to do it. The mechanics of it.

The juvenile buck raised its head abruptly, water streaming from its velvety muzzle. Instinctively, Rubin turned his body slightly to shield Jonquille's with his much larger one. "Slide back into deeper bush." He mouthed the command against her ear.

Jonquille slipped out from under his shoulder and off the rock noiselessly, her hand sliding inside her jacket to retrieve a weapon. Eyes on the deer, Rubin reached with all of his animal senses to scan the entire area for threats. A few minutes earlier the surrounding woods had been devoid of all enemies. He couldn't detect a human presence, but there was definitely the whisper of danger.

The presence of the bobcat had only been recent, just the last season. There had been no indication of any larger cats, but to Rubin the threat felt feline. Not the bobcat, although certainly a bobcat was capable of bringing down a deer. This felt much more ominous. Cougars were beautiful animals and ones he respected, but they were also pure killing machines. One didn't see them until it was too late.

He kept his gaze fixed on the nervous buck. The animal took a long time to settle before it went back to drinking water. The wind ruffled the leaves on the trees, and a silver beam scattered across the forest floor. On that breeze came a subtle scent of feral. It came and went as fast as the shifting of the clouds overhead, an ominous portent of what might be hidden in the bushes, waiting to strike at the unwary.

Rubin looked with the eyes of a bird into the bushes along the ground beside the trail leading to the water. It took a long time, long enough for the young buck to settle down and decide he was safe, before Rubin spotted the long body of the cat lying motionless beneath the sweeping branches of the red spruce fanning out on the ground right on the game trail leading to the water. The cat was completely covered by the maze of broken limbs and in the shadows, waiting for her unsuspecting prey. Clearly, she had stalked the young buck down to the clearing and was now awaiting his return.

Rubin felt the little shiver go through Jonquille's body as the deer turned from the stream and began his careful prancing back to the game trail to enter the cooler shadow of the trees, where he felt safer. Being in the open clearly made him nervous. He would stop and look around him, his head up alertly, looking in every direction. He never looked at the one spot he should have. He passed the cougar without so much as glancing her way.

The cat remained absolutely still. Rubin and Diego, as young children growing up on the mountain and providing for their family, had often sat high in the branches of the trees, observing wildlife and the way they hunted. Learning those same skills. The female cat was on the thinner side. Rubin guessed that, like the little bobcat, she had kittens stashed somewhere, and she needed food to sustain herself. The cycle of life for animals could be brutal, just as it was for soldiers.

The cougar burst from beneath her shelter of branches when the young buck was about seventeen feet down the trail from her. She sprinted fast, covering the ground, muscles bunching beneath her fur, driving with her back legs as she leapt into the air. She caught at the back haunches of the buck as he ran, digging her claws in tight on either side, using her weight against him, dragging him to an abrupt halt. Sinking her teeth into his spine, she pulled at him as he fought back, bucking and swinging around in a desperate attempt to get her off.

The cat used her sharp claws to move up his body toward his neck, using her weight and muscle in order to get him down. The buck swung his head in an attempt to use his horns, turning his body in circles, rearing up to try to dislodge her, but careful to keep his feet. Instinctively, he seemed to know she would have the advantage if he was on the ground.

The mountain lion held on, patient as always. She was a new mother and desperate in her own way. She had to provide for herself and her young. Her next move brought her to the buck's neck, where she sank her teeth deep and then flung her body to the side to drag his head around, in an effort to snap his neck. The buck tried to save himself, moving with her, but she was able to take him down.

He fought her ferociously, slashing at her with his hooves, kicking out with dangerous power, but she refused to back down, holding on to his neck, determined to suffocate him. The buck grew weaker, his attempts to fight feebler. As his thrashing and kicking grew less aggressive, her hold tightened on him until it was clear she had managed to secure her food for the next few days.

Rubin knew the controversy raged on about whether or not there were still cougars in the mountains, although sightings were reported all the time. Few people other than those living there believed it. He hadn't thought he would see one, and certainly not on his property. He turned to look at Jonquille and his heart clenched hard in his chest. Her gaze was riveted to the scene, eyes filled with liquid so they looked silvery and haunting. Tears tracked down her cheeks. It was the last thing he'd expected when she was clearly a warrior.

"Jonquille." He whispered her name and gathered her up without thinking, needing to hold her more than he needed to remain still and quiet for the wildlife around him.

Rubin pressed his back to the downed tree and put her in his lap, his arms around her. "What is it? Surely you're not upset because the cougar needed to eat. She has young to feed."

She rubbed her face against his jacket, trying to get rid of the tears. "I'm sorry. This is silly and I know it. I'm not like this. I'm really not."

He caught her hand when she went to brush away the tears. "Sweetheart, just tell me what's going on."

"I don't know why the memories are so close right now. That door opened and I can't seem to force it closed."

The little break in her voice tore at him. He found he was more susceptible to her emotions than he had first realized he would be. Her laughter. Her pain. When she was upset like this, it was very disturbing to him. When they were together, he wasn't going to be able to function properly if she was sad or angry with him.

"You don't want to hear these morbid stories."

"I do. I want to know everything about you, Jonquille." He did. The more he knew about her childhood, the more he understood her.

"One spring he brought us puppies. Whitney. We should have known better than to trust him, but he said it was to teach us responsibility. We could each choose one, and we were solely responsible for its care. We could have the puppy in our room, and it could even sleep in our bed with us if we wanted."

Rubin could hear the way she tried to distance herself, the notes

119

of horror in her voice, the strain when she told him, as if she couldn't quite believe what had happened. He had studied Whitney the way he did every enemy they went up against. He was a logical man and gathered as much information as possible without emotion in order to better learn. One could look at something from every angle that way. Whitney was a true megalomaniac. He was someone obsessed with his own power. He was both a narcissist and a psychopath. He had no conscience. Rubin would never be surprised by anything anyone told him Whitney did, unless it was betraying his country.

He ran his hand down the back of her head, feeling the thickness of all that soft blond hair before plunging his fingers deep to massage her scalp in an effort to soothe her. Retelling the childhood story after locking it away where she refused to even look at it was obviously reliving it again. He wanted to tell her she didn't need to tell him, he understood it was going to be bad, but she needed to share it with someone. He wanted to be her someone.

"All of us were so careful with our little charges. We were so happy that spring. We walked them and cuddled with them." She kept dashing at the tears. "We all loved them so much. We were required to keep up with our studies as well as our training, but we could take our dogs with us as long as they behaved. We trained them even at an early age using the crates provided. All of us worked so hard, and Whitney acted like he was proud of us for the jobs we were doing. We kept them for eighteen months."

She coughed and cleared her throat before looking up at him with pain-filled eyes. "He introduced a program to us he called survival of the fittest. At first the subject matter was all about nature and the food chain. We were kids, but we understood even though we were shown extremely graphic films. Then one evening instead of curfew, we were told to go to the arena that had been set up. We were to sit in the stands." She pressed a trembling hand to her mouth.

"Jonquille, sweetheart." He dropped his hand to the nape of her neck and tried to ease the tension out of her. She seemed so small and lost—very vulnerable—when before, in spite of her diminutive size, she was a little powerhouse. "You don't have to tell me."

"No, I do. Someone has to know besides us. There was no one to tell. He always got rid of our nurses after a few months. Even the guards, especially the nice ones. He only kept the ones that were very loyal to him, or that he could compromise in some way. We were little kids with no one to advocate for us and very confused as to what was wrong or right. Then there was Lily. She was treated differently than we were. We all loved her and thought she was one of us, but he didn't do to her the things he did to us."

Rubin felt very sorry for Lily Whitney. She had been officially adopted by Whitney, raised to believe she was his daughter. She didn't know about his experiments or that he had "bought" the girls from orphanages. She couldn't remember them at first. She didn't know about the experiments he did on the soldiers. When she found out, she was horrified. Eventually, with both sides not trusting her, she married Captain Ryland Miller, a GhostWalker from the first team. She had rescued Team One from the cages they were in. They were being stalked by a murderer and it was impossible for them to escape, locked up as they were.

"What you're saying is her puppy was safe, and the rest of you all had dogs at risk." He kept his voice quiet and soothing as he continued to massage her neck.

"Exactly. That night was one of sheer terror for all of us. We were instructed to leave our dogs in our rooms, which we did. The soldiers were sitting around the arena and they were all excited, and there were other soldiers there as well, men we'd never seen before. Whitney was standing at the bottom of the stairs with his guards, just to the right of where we were all seated, and there were guards heavily around us. He instructed them to bind our hands and feet so we couldn't move from where we were sitting."

He could feel her heart pounding when his palm curled around her nape, his fingers gently resting on her pulse. He tasted anger in his mouth. He rarely felt the emotion, but he knew what was coming.

"They brought in a big dog. It looked savage and it was snarling. Its eyes were red and horrifying, like something out of a movie. Across from it, they brought in Flame's dog. She was a sweet thing, and clearly, she didn't know what was expected. None of us did. The crowd roared when that horrible animal was let loose. It rushed straight at Flame's dog. She screamed and tried to break loose. All of us did. One by one we had to watch as our dogs were torn to pieces by various animals brought in to 'fight' them. Since our dogs weren't fighters, of course they lost. They weren't fit to live, according to Whitney. We were supposedly taught a valuable lesson. We hadn't taught them to survive."

She was sobbing and it was difficult to understand her. He held her tighter and let her cry, stroking her hair and murmuring soothing nonsense to her. What could anyone say to counteract the absolute cruelty of a man like Whitney?

"Some of the girls needed an anchor. They couldn't survive very well around violence without Flame or Lily or me. It wasn't well known that I was an anchor because I was so young. Lily was the one most of the girls relied on because Flame was so sick or put in solitary so often. But that night, Lily wasn't there. She didn't see what we saw. And her dog survived. What did that say about her? We didn't understand why she was treated so differently."

"He was already driving a wedge between you," he murmured,

nuzzling the top of her head. "I'm so sorry, Lightning Bug. Whitney deserves his own private spot in hell. There are no words for a man like him. None."

He placed his hand under her chin and tipped her face up because he was almost desperate to find a way to make things better for her, when he knew there was no way he could. This experience could never be erased from her mind. Still, he brushed kisses across her eyelids and down the tracks of her tears to the corner of her mouth. That beautiful mouth. It made no sense to him that anyone, even Whitney, could be that cruel to children. Life, yes, but a man, no.

He brushed his lips gently over hers, settling his hand at the bare nape of her neck. She responded tentatively at first. A hesitant movement of her lips, velvet soft, sliding along his, until his stomach did a strange somersault. He had never been into kissing that much, it always seemed far too intimate, but now, intimacy was extraordinary and necessary.

She opened her mouth under his, and he poured himself into her. That fire in her, contained in her body, an astonishing supply of sheer power, rose to meet the powerful energy in his. The two collided with the force of an erupting volcano, or a lightning bolt. Around them, just as earlier, he heard the sizzle and crackle of high voltage. He felt the static charge in the hairs on his body. Sparks played over his skin and flames rushed through his veins like currents of electricity.

Lights dazzled behind his eyes and he had to look, no matter the feeling of euphoria, or of being transported to somewhere else. His lightning bug had taken on her silvery glow. Her hair had gone wild, thick, standing out from her head as untamed as the storms overhead. She blinked as he lifted his head, calling attention to her eyelashes, those silvery-blue lashes. Her eyes had gone almost completely silver. Around her rib cage circled dazzling pulses of light, streaks of white-hot lasers that were so bright she really did resemble the famous fireflies that danced in the grass at sunset.

He let his breath out slowly. His palm shaped her face. "You're so beautiful, Jonquille. I can't imagine any other woman for me. Not ever. I can't see anyone else but you. Kissing another woman or touching them is out of the question."

The two of you had better not be off somewhere doing something you shouldn't, Diego intruded.

Such as? Rubin demanded. *I'm having a moment and you're interrupting.*

Such as impregnating her with my future niece or nephew. You don't yet know if she's on our side. We haven't completely vetted her.

I swear I'm going to shoot you, Diego.

That's going to be hard to do when I'm the one with the rifle.

I've got my rifle with me.

You don't. You left it here. Fat lot of good it's doing you when it's sitting in the dark where the potatoes are supposed to be. You went after her so fast you took everything but your rifle.

"You two are arguing again, aren't you?" Jonquille asked, amusement tinging her voice. "Is that the way it would be if we actually were in a romantic relationship? We'd be in the moment and your brother would interrupt and the two of you would start?"

Rubin was a little afraid it might really happen that way. *You are totally cramping my style. I thought you wanted to have a niece or nephew.*

"My brother is crazy."

"You both are a little crazy. Ask him if he's got breakfast ready."

Rubin was grateful for the respite from the assault on his body, and he suspected Jonquille was as well. Kissing his lightning bug was really like igniting an explosive. He set her carefully off his lap.

Do you have breakfast ready? We're starving after patrolling and keeping you safe while you slept.

My ass, you were patrolling.

"Did the cougar leave? We weren't exactly being quiet for a few minutes there."

"She's looking this way. She was eating, but now she's getting up and dragging her very large meal away from the game trail into the heavier bush," Jonquille reported.

That doesn't tell me if you have breakfast ready, Rubin pointed out.

He stood up, deliberately dropping his arm around Jonquille's shoulders. They watched as the cougar, across the clearing, the stream and some thirty or forty feet along the game trail, dragged the carcass of the buck into deeper brush. The fact that she hadn't done that earlier told him she probably hadn't eaten in several days.

Not yet. I didn't want it to get cold.

That was Diego. He might act tough, but in the end, he would think of that detail.

Can you make it back to the house in half an hour?

"He's going to make breakfast for us. Says he can have it ready in half an hour. We can make it back there cutting through the brush. If we take a trail, it will be longer." He gave her the option.

"I'm good with cutting through brush. I've got my good hiking boots and clothing on, so I'm prepared, and I'm really hungry. Kissing works up the appetite." There was laughter in her voice.

He liked to hear those notes of amusement after she'd been so upset. He knew he hadn't completely helped her close that door on her memories, but he'd definitely distanced her from them. Knowing she found the way he telepathically argued good-naturedly with his brother amusing made him even happier.

She's good with cutting through the brush so we can get there in half an hour.

"I told him we'd be there as soon as we could." He glanced up at the sky. "In a couple of hours, we're going to have a hell of a storm. I want to practice targeting the lightning. That might be fun."

She laughed softly. "I'm beginning to think there are quite a few things that I never considered could be fun that might be if done with you."

"Thanks, Lightning Bug," he replied gruffly. He thought it was a huge compliment and knew Jonquille didn't give those out, not that there was anyone for her to give them out to.

They hurried back to the cabin. Twice in the distance, thunder rolled ominously, but the storm was clearly a good distance away. Rubin could visibly see the pull on Jonquille's body and the way, even though the storm was so far away, the tension in her was so ingrained that she began to try to distance herself from him.

Rubin had a long reach, and he snagged her wrist easily and pulled her closer to him. "Sweetheart, the last thing you ever want to do when a storm comes is move away from me. You want to be close to me," he said. "I know that's a behavior that will have to be learned, but you should start now, when no one else is around."

She sent him a look from under those silvery lashes that told him she wasn't so certain. "Just because you think so doesn't mean you're right, Rubin. I'm not so willing to take chances with your life."

"We kissed and you didn't fry me."

A faint smile curved her lips and she looked away, shaking her head. "I don't know how you got so unlucky to have been paired with me, but that's probably the only reason you didn't get fried. That doesn't mean if a lightning bolt suddenly comes out of the sky and strikes somewhere in our vicinity, you aren't going to die."

"We're going to form a partnership, Jonquille." He poured confidence into his voice. "I've been working on ideas for a long time.

If you came to the conferences, you had to have heard some of them."

"Theories aren't the same as practical knowledge, Rubin, you know that. One mistake and you're dead. Just one. Lightning kills. Electrical charges kill. The amount of volts is beyond anything anyone really imagines. You talk about directing lightning. Do you know how fast it is?"

"Why, yes, I do, Miss Jonquille, now that you ask," Rubin said. "I happen to be well versed in my facts on lightning. Each bolt of lightning can contain as many as one billion volts of electricity." He flashed her a boyish grin. "The lead stroke from air to ground is much slower and can come in steps, a microsecond at a time. It's the return charge that's fast, traveling at speeds of 320,000,000 feet per second. We also know how hot you can get."

"Don't be cute. This isn't funny, Rubin. Were you really going to experiment?"

"That is exactly what I came up here to do, and I intend to do it. And it isn't my first time. Now that you're here with me, it will be fun. Don't get all grim and foreboding on me like Diego. He's all gloom and doom, sure we're both going to go up in smoke."

"You probably are." This time when she said it, she sounded a little more amused.

He sent her another quick smile. "We know you're hot as hell. How fast are you when you're not cheating?"

One silvery eyebrow shot up. "I don't cheat."

"Drawing energy from others and using it against them isn't cheating? If we're racing, you can't take my energy for yourself."

"I think you do that," she pointed out, giving him a little haughty chin lift.

He did do that, specifically with her. He could drain off quite a bit of that dazzling white-hot energy sizzling through her, but he wanted to see what she could do with it when she wasn't using it to call to the clouds.

Deliberately, he set a faster pace, breaking into a sprint through the brush, leaping over the first of a series of low bushes and choosing the ground with the least amount of foliage to run through. He was a big man, tall, with long legs and a long stride. She was short and her legs couldn't possibly cover the ground he could. He knew he was taking advantage, but she'd been so confident so many times and he wanted to see the skills she had.

A flash of light overhead distracted him for a moment and he nearly stumbled as he tilted his head to look up. She was so fast, gliding from tree branch to tree branch, her weight barely making the leaves shiver as she skillfully landed and took off for the next one. She outdistanced him fairly quickly, making her way to the cabin unerringly, as if she had been born in the mountains. Few others could have done that, found their way without a map or consulting a GPS, but she had some built-in chart in her head.

He arrived right behind her. She was waiting for him, standing right outside the mudroom, looking smug.

"If we were racing, I'd call that a win for the ladies," she announced.

"I'd have to agree." There was color in her normally pale cheeks, and her blue eyes were even brighter than normal. Rubin resisted pulling her into his arms, but he was blocking the door to the mudroom.

You two going to stand out there staring at each other like two lovebirds or come in here and eat while it's hot?

She's looking particularly beautiful, so standing out here and staring at her, deciding whether or not to kiss her, seems like a better idea than having you lecture me about taking precautions like leaving the cabin without my rifle.

Good grief, Rubin. Kiss her already and then come inside and eat before it gets cold.

Rubin sighed. "He's whining about the food being hot."

"Why aren't we going inside?"

He was blocking the door. "I'm debating whether or not kissing you again would get us in trouble."

Diego flung the door open. "Enough already. Pancakes taste like cardboard cold. If he has to talk about kissing, the moment's passed. I'll explain that to him later, Jonquille."

Rubin sighed and followed them inside, the sound of Jonquille's laughter lodging somewhere in the region of his heart.

7

The trail many hikers liked to take to the campground was one that had signs posted everywhere cautioning to check the weather forecast for storms. Diego, Rubin and Jonquille took a shortcut through the woods to get to the trail more frequented by hikers in order to reach the clearing near the top of the mountain. The place was perfect for the kinds of experiments Rubin hoped to conduct.

Rubin and Diego had traveled that route on their way to the cabin, posting warning signs and closing the area, hoping to keep any backcountry campers from hiking to the clearing for the spectacular views. They had the government credentials to close the area, but didn't want to use them unless it was strictly necessary. There was still a lot of distrust for the government among the locals in spite of a rise in education. The poverty level was still one of the worst, and neither man wanted the local people to quit trusting them as doctors when they returned to check on them year after year.

"I'm not certain what you want to do, Rubin," Jonquille said when they'd reached the large, mostly bald area rising over the top of one side of the mountain. Trees and brush were sparse. The grass was closely cropped as if it struggled to grow amid the rocks and dirt. "I did read all your published papers. And some that weren't published." She admitted that under her breath.

Rubin glanced at her sharply. "Any other papers I submitted were to the military or they were private."

She bit her lower lip and looked up at him for a full fifteen seconds. "I know," she finally admitted.

"You hacked into a military site?" he prompted.

"Not exactly. Well. Sort of. Your personal site." She mumbled the admission. "I'm sorry, I know that's bad. A terrible invasion of privacy."

Both men stared at her accusingly. Color stained her cheeks. She squirmed under their gazes. "Look, no one was going to help me. If I was going to be saved, I had to do it myself. The only way to do that was through research. I did as much on my own as I could. I pursued two different avenues, but both dead-ended. That's when I heard you give a talk. It was inspiring, and I was hopeful again. The only way I was going to learn anything was to find everything you wrote on the subject."

She sounded defiant and not in the least remorseful, but Rubin couldn't exactly blame her. He just didn't understand how she'd managed to hack his research site. He had two of the best computer experts checking his computer and ensuring his password couldn't be broken. He couldn't be hacked.

"How?" It was absolutely vital he know.

Both men stood in the open field, the gray clouds overhead, the silence occasionally broken by the sound of birds. She sighed. "You always used the same assistant to do your research at the military research laboratory when you traveled to Maryland to speak there."

"How do you know he went there? That's not *ever* common knowledge," Diego demanded.

"I'm a GhostWalker too, remember?" Jonquille pointed out. "I might be a flawed one, but I have excellent forged credentials to get onto military bases to work in laboratories. I research. That's how I was trying to figure out how to undo the enhancements Whitney had done to me. I knew I would have to live with some of them, but thought if I could find a way to ease them, I could be around people enough to use my healing gift and maybe even get my nursing degree or become a doctor. I'd have a chance at having a family."

Rubin heard the raw pain in her voice, but it still didn't tell him how she'd hacked his private account. He forced himself to keep looking at her when he really wanted to gather her up and hold her close to him—tell her he was proud of her skills. She'd slipped in and out of the research center often.

"Tell us how you did it," Diego snapped.

She shrugged. "I worked there at night." She stuck her chin out, her silvery-blue eyes flashing. "I'm considered quite brilliant."

Neither man said anything, although Rubin was beginning to think she rivaled even Trap's IQ, and he was the most intelligent man Rubin knew.

Jonquille sighed. "You have to be aware your researcher was adequate at best. He was sloppy and sometimes just plain lazy. He waited until the last minute, until you absolutely demanded what you needed, and then did the minimum. I didn't know why you put up with him as long as you did. I had a high security clearance and was working there as well."

Rubin didn't enlighten her that he was well aware of the man's lack of work ethic. If he hadn't been stretched so thin, he might have complained, but he couldn't be bothered. The work was definitely something off the normal path and the assistant had asked to be replaced several times.

"I made certain to sit next to him, and when his boss was there, every time he didn't know the answer to something you needed and he was complaining, I would just tell him without looking up from my work, which was totally unrelated. I made certain to sound as if I wasn't even paying any real attention. Eventually, his supervisor asked me how I knew the answers and I told him I just had one of those brains that remembered facts I was interested in and I studied storms and everything to do with them. Again, I made certain to sound very offhand. I kept returning my attention to my own research. Eventually, they just made me your new assistant. I'm Corporal D. Wynn."

Rubin exchanged a long look with Diego. He'd even remarked to his brother that the new woman was fast and efficient and provided him with facts. She'd cut his work in half. He'd actually begun corresponding with her over time. She'd made little notations in the margins a couple of times that put him thinking along a pathway he hadn't even considered, a pathway having to do with moving the actual strike from one section of an area to another.

"If you were caught . . ." Diego said.

"It would be no worse than the way I'm living now," Jonquille pointed out. "I don't have a life. I was trying to find a way to survive. I wasn't trying to steal national secrets. If anything, I was better at guarding them than Rubin's last assistant. Fortunately, he got moved out of there, although he was really good in other areas."

Rubin glanced at the sky. "As fascinating as this conversation is, we have to get busy. We're going to run out of time. Diego, you have to get to a lower elevation, but find a place where you can still record. Jonquille, are you certain you'll be safe?"

"You mean when I attract the charge? The lead stroke is going to come straight at me. It always does. Yes. I'll be fine." She pointed to the few straggly oak trees. "They're far taller than I am. The charge will bypass those and come straight for me. I can even be lying flat. What do you want to do?"

"I'm going to practice directing the bolt away. The lead is slower, but the ground-to-air is so much faster. I want to be able to hit it every time. If I can do that, you and I can eventually direct a strike away from a residence, a ball field, a place where there are people."

"I'm not going to be a weapon, Rubin," Jonquille stated quietly. "I know that's what Whitney hoped, probably if he could get us together, but I'm not killing masses of people for him."

"Nor would I expect you to. First, I'd like to see if we could actually do this together. Lightning causes over a billion dollars in damages to property as well as loss of lives. We might be able to find a way to stop that through our experiments. If you and I can redirect the strikes together, we can find a way to artificially redirect them."

Jonquille's blue eyes moved over his face, assessing him, trying to decide whether or not he was telling her the truth. He couldn't blame her, not after the few things she'd told him about her childhood. She'd been betrayed too many times. Why should she believe him?

She nodded slowly. "I suppose so, but I still don't see how you can do that without burning up, Rubin. Diego's going to be safe somewhere recording this, but you're going to be close. Too close."

"This isn't the first time I've attempted it," Rubin admitted. "I've had quite a bit of success. I don't want you here when the storm first moves in. Let me do a little work on my own, then we'll see how it works with you if you're up for it."

She looked around her. "If I'm up here, anywhere out in the open, no matter what you do, the lead stroke will find me."

"Then you'll have to go to lower ground with Diego and find somewhere you'll be safe."

Diego had turned away to start down the trail to find a refuge where he could still record but not be in the path of the lightning strikes. Using a camera so close to the actual storm could be dangerous. Jonquille didn't want to go with him. She wanted to stay with Rubin. She knew she could protect both of them by drawing the lightning away from Rubin. She thought he was crazy for attempting to direct the actual strikes when he had no decent protection.

"Diego, are you really all right with him doing this?"

"No, but you try talking him out of it," Diego groused. "He's stubborn as hell. You might want to remember that, Jonquille, when you're getting all melty over him. He has some really bad traits that outweigh the good ones."

"I don't know, Diego, those kisses kind of make up for a lot."

"He doesn't kiss me and I'm just fine with that. You coming?"

She didn't want to.

"Yes, she is," Rubin said. "Get moving."

She could feel the building energy in the air. The pull on her body was already showing in the form of white-hot light. The storm was moving toward them, the wind pushing it right where Rubin had predicted.

"He is bossy," she conceded. "The memory of those kisses is fading fast."

"I don't have time right now to remind you. Get under cover."

Rubin sprinted away from the two of them, across the bare, bald landscape, toward some spot that he seemed to have in mind.

"Move it," Diego snapped, proving he was just as bossy as his brother. He began to sprint in the opposite direction.

Jonquille followed him, but she wanted to be with Rubin. She wished she were in his mind the way Diego was. She had the capability, but she didn't have the pathway.

Diego and Jonquille had to travel quite a distance in order to get across a gorge to allow them to see the flat, bald top of the mountain where Rubin planned to conduct his experiment. Diego spotted a crevice Jonquille could fit her smaller body into to keep the lead stroke from finding her.

"Can you see Rubin?" There was no way to keep the anxiety out of her voice.

"Yeah, I've got him, he's lying flat just to the right of those boulders. See them? Left side up near the highest point."

Thunder rumbled. There was little to stop the wind or keep it from slamming into them. She couldn't imagine what it was doing to Rubin, exposed as he was. Overhead, the clouds were dark, black and purple. They lit up, lightning forking inside them as the charges bumped against one another repeatedly, causing enormous friction. The pull on her body was horrendous.

"You all right, Jonquille?" Diego asked. "You're glowing like a Christmas tree."

"Just keep your eyes on Rubin. I've done this a million times now."

"You really are worried about him. I'm sorry I thought about killing you so often. That would have been a tragedy."

She wasn't so certain, not when her core temperature was so hot now she felt like the ground around her was melting just from the contact with her body. This was never going to end for her. She'd done so much research. Rubin, as far as she knew, was the best mind in the field working on the possibilities, and yet he couldn't help. She'd been at her research for years. It didn't seem as if there was any hope for her. Maybe Diego's bullet would have been a kindness.

Static buildup was fast. The charge was coming. She couldn't help herself. She was folded into a little ball, crammed tight into the crevice, but she stuck her head out to look up at the sky just as the bolt of lightning slammed to earth. She saw the trajectory in her mind. Knew where it would hit. Out of nowhere a blast of energy every bit as strong hit it, diverting the path, knocking it off course so that the spear moved from its intended target to another. Sparks flew up in all directions.

"He did it. That son of a bitch actually did it." Elation poured out of Diego. "He said he could, and he hit the target dead-on."

"What target? There were no targets." Jonquille felt like a turtle, with her head stuck out of the crevice trying to peer at the bald mountaintop.

"Rubin mapped the entire mountaintop into various coordinates. He told me where each strike would be directed."

Another was coming. She felt the pull on her body. "Watch your eyes, Diego," she warned.

Thunder crashed directly overhead as the blinding flash of white-hot electrical energy burst down looking for the charge coming from the ground. Again, before it could reach its target, it was struck and knocked off course. Diego was muttering continually to himself. "This is insanity. No one can do this."

"Do you know how fast he has to be?" Jonquille demanded. She nearly crawled out of the crevice. "He hit it quicker that time. He knows it's coming the way I do. I want to go up there. I wish I could talk to him the way you do. I should have asked him if we could do that. It would have made things so much easier." She couldn't keep the excitement out of her voice.

"Hang on a moment and don't do anything dumb like move."

"There's another one coming," Jonquille warned again.

This one was very dangerous, directly over Rubin's position. He directed it with seeming ease this time. It was all Jonquille could do not to sprint back up the mountain toward him.

"I'm a strong telepath, Jonquille," Diego surprised her by saying. "I asked Rubin if he minded if I looped you in. He agreed, so I'll start you out. That way you can talk with either of us when you need to."

"That would be so perfect, thank you."

Rubin, she's all yours.

She is, Rubin agreed.

I'm coming up there. The minute I start moving, the lightning will start striking. The lead stroke will look for me.

Even down here? Diego asked. *We're quite a bit below Rubin's position.*

Yes. I'm fast though. After the next strike I'll start running. Rubin, do you think you can redirect when the lightning is targeting me?

Rubin was silent. She could tell he was thinking it over. *I know I could if you were up here. The idea is to practice for every situation though, so this is good for me. I don't want you hurt. It's building again. Stay put, Jonquille. Wait one more time.*

She wanted to get to him, but she waited, the pull terrible now, especially because it was doubly so, the need to get to Rubin almost as strong as the magnetic charging happening to her body.

Diego, your eyes. Both Rubin and Jonquille warned him at the exact same moment, and she realized Rubin had been warning his brother every strike. She thought it was significant that Rubin knew the strike was imminent the exact moment she did. The bolt slammed toward something Rubin must have laid out in the field to attract it, but this time, even faster, it was redirected much farther than the last one, hitting something she couldn't see and sending up enough sparks that it looked like the Fourth of July.

She didn't wait. She was up and running. She might be short, but she had been given enhancements as well, from Whitney, and she used them to her advantage, leaping huge distances, fully across the gorge, racing up the other side to get to the bald top.

Her body was lighting up. Glowing. Going hot. Her hair pulled straight out and up. Her eyes went fully silver. She was exactly what the lead stroke looked for when it came charging toward earth. She put her arms up. If the bolt struck her, as it did others so many times a year, she wouldn't be harmed in the way they were. She didn't have to huddle in fear. She would absorb the strike. She had no idea why, or how it was possible. Neither did Whitney. He only knew that she'd been born attracting energy and he'd enhanced that to the point that she had become a freak of nature, and there seemed to be no way of undoing what he'd done to her.

The cloud seemed to open and fire rained on the earth in the form of white-hot silvery jagged spears. She had known there were going to be multiple strikes, not just one. Rubin was going to have his hands full. She tended to attract more than one strike. She should have warned him. The bolts came so fast it was impossible to see them, so she hoped Diego was actually getting them on his recorder so they could slow it down later because Rubin managed to redirect every single one. The last came close enough that she felt the whisper of its burn before it was gone, whisked away by an astonishing force of energy every bit as strong and willful.

The storm was still moving, the wind pushing it toward the

valleys, where it was slowly dying down in strength. A few more streaks of lightning leapt at her sideways, and each time, Rubin pushed them away from her.

Shut it down, Rubin, you're getting too tired. You still have to go see Mama Patricia today, Diego said.

Jonquille realized it was true. Rubin was exhausted. She looked over at him, and he was lying in the blackened section where the first lightning strike had been directed. He lay motionless looking up at the clouds.

I'm sorry, Rubin, I can take a few hits. The storm's moving away. Just rest for a while. If the lightning keeps coming this way, it won't for long. You've practiced enough. She didn't dare go over to him, not when the top of the mountain was so bare. She'd lead a strike right to him.

Rubin didn't respond, but she sensed that he didn't like attention called to the fact that he was weak after using his particular talent. She wondered if that was because it was in front of her, but she didn't think so. Rubin wasn't that kind of man. It seemed as if he didn't like being weak in front of his brother either, as if he were letting both of them down.

Her hair went straight up again and she felt the charge of energy. This time the lightning bolt came from a distance. To her consternation, Rubin still shoved it away from her, again directing it toward a target he had placed in an area about forty yards away from her. It was a fairly small target, and the jagged stroke still hit it dead center.

Before Diego could reprimand him, she intervened. *You are such a show-off. Next time, we're going to build a huge tic-tac-toe game up here and we're playing.*

Her body had settled down, the sizzling, prickling sensations receding from her skin. She sank to the ground, knees drawn up, waiting for the storm clouds to move away completely. Rubin didn't get up, he just remained lying on his back, his hands locked behind his head. Diego came to them. He went to his brother first, digging through his backpack to get Rubin a bottle of water and a packet of something that looked like energy bars. Then he came to her. He gave her the same things before going around the open field collecting the targets Rubin had placed.

Some were lying flat on the ground. Some were standing a mere foot off the ground. One was about two feet high. All were made of different components. Diego collected each one using tongs and inserted them in what looked like hazardous material bags. He wrote on each one separately before putting the target into the bag. The one with the multiple strikes he took some time collecting. She wanted to see what he had written. Those strikes had mostly been directed to the flat targets on the ground.

Rubin took about half an hour to recover and then he was up as if nothing had happened. "That was impressive, Jonquille. You really are my lightning bug. You don't get to get snippy when I call you that."

She gave him a chin lift and narrowed her eyes at him, but she took his hand and let him pull her to her feet. "I never get snippy." That was a lie, but she considered it a small one.

Diego was back, and he gave a snort of derision, reaching down to snag his brother's pack. Rubin's hand got there first.

"You could carry my pack," Jonquille offered and tried batting her eyelashes at Diego.

He rolled his eyes. "You're going to have to work on that. Carry your own pack. If we're going to make Mama Patricia's, we've got to get a move on. I want to watch the sunset from her porch."

"You're not very nice," Jonquille said. "*At all*. If you ever get a girlfriend, I'm telling her to dump you fast."

"I kiss like sin. It makes up for a lot, or so you tell me." He kept walking.

"You'd better do a lot more than kiss like sin," she muttered under her breath.

"I have excellent hearing," Rubin reminded. "You can think about all the things I can do better than kissing like sin, but not him. In fact, don't think about him at all."

Jonquille burst out laughing. The two brothers really were a little crazy.

The Sawyers' home had a large porch that ran the length of the house. There were two rocking chairs, a stool, a long chest and a stump placed on the porch for company to sit on. Patricia Sawyer sat in one of the rocking chairs, but when Diego, Rubin and Jonquille approached, she stood, wrapping her hand around the post holding up the roof overhead. She smiled a welcome, but her gaze was on Jonquille, watching warily.

Rubin strode right up to her. "Mama Patricia," he greeted and kissed her cheek. "How have you been?"

Diego did the same. Neither man hesitated, although Patricia Sawyer blushed and looked as if she drew back just a little.

Rubin reached for Jonquille, pulling her right beneath his shoulder, very proprietorial. "This is Jonquille. My woman. Jonquille, Patricia Sawyer. The best of the best here on the mountain. She's always treated Diego and me like family."

Jonquille smiled shyly. "I'm so pleased to meet you. Rubin and Diego talk so much about you and your daughter and sons, I looked forward to meeting you."

Patricia raised her gaze from Jonquille to Rubin and then back. "You have a very pretty name, Jonquille. Rubin's mother was reputed to love Easter lilies, did you know that? I wonder what she would think of you."

"Since she's nearly better on a game trail than I am," Diego said, "I'd say she'd be all for Rubin taking her for his wife. She's also good at making a berry cobbler. *Great*, Mama Patricia," he corrected himself. "Almost, but not quite, rivals yours."

Patricia was really studying Jonquille now. "*Nearly* as good as you on a game trail is high praise, Diego. Why do I think you might be selling her a little short?"

"I'm a man, ma'am. I've got an ego," he said without repentance.

"Are you as good?" Patricia asked.

"No. I'm close. I don't have his experience, but I'm very close," Jonquille admitted. "And I have a little advantage in that I'm smaller and lightweight. I get into places easier than he can and go into branches he can't. Because I'm so light, I don't leave tracks so easily either."

"And the cobbler?"

"I haven't had the chance to eat yours, but I wouldn't mind trying it just for comparison," Jonquille said readily.

"I like her," Patricia said. "Have a seat. I'll get us something to drink."

"Are the boys home yet?" Rubin asked. "I was hoping to have a chance to speak with them." He followed her inside, used to her home, knowing he was welcome.

She glanced over her shoulder and then lowered her voice. "I would have thought it would be Diego bringing a woman home to us first, not you."

"She was . . . unexpected. She loves the same things I do. And she includes Diego in everything. She even finds the way we argue

143

amusing. She really is nearly as good in the woods as he is. Mostly, Mama Patricia, she doesn't make me want to scream when she starts talking. She's intelligent and she knows when to listen."

"Does she sound a little too good to be true?" Patricia asked as she gathered up tall glasses for her specialty apple cider drink she preferred to make.

He gave her a little smile. "If you mean, is she too good for me, undoubtedly she is. I haven't convinced her living in a swamp full time sounds like a dream come true, especially since I'm gone a good deal of the time."

"If she doesn't recognize how extraordinary you are, Rubin, she doesn't deserve you," Patricia said very quietly as she poured her special cider from a cold pitcher.

Rubin sighed and shoved a hand through his dark hair. "That's the problem right there, Mama Patricia. I'm so extraordinary. She recognizes it. Diego recognizes it. You do. My team does." He fought to keep the bitterness out of his voice and knew he hadn't succeeded when she put the pitcher down and turned to look at him with her all-seeing eyes.

Rubin shook his head and searched for a way to make her understand. She'd been in his life a long time and she knew he worked in a program in the military he couldn't talk very much about. She had eyes. She was intelligent. "Everyone is so careful to protect me they're willing to sacrifice their life for me. They don't see that I think they're just as extraordinary and just as necessary. I need the members of my team safe. I need Diego safe. I need Jonquille in my life and definitely safe. Like everyone else in my life, she's willing to protect me. That's not okay with me. She also thinks I'm this unbelievable man she can't possibly live up to. I'm so done with that way of thinking. If only they really knew what it was like to be me. To see my failures. They wouldn't be so quick to be ready to sacrifice their lives."

Patricia's soft features reflected her compassion. She was a mountain woman through and through, and tough as nails. She had gone through winters alone, providing for her children after she lost her husband. Through it all, she had retained her innate kindness, that empathy that drew so many to her. That trait was most likely the reason Luther Gunthrie had dared to put on his snowshoes and trek the dangerous miles of wilderness through a blizzard just to check up on her.

"Rubin, never think you're a failure in any way. The people who love you want to protect you, just as you want to protect them. I want the best for you and for my children. We look out for one another. If your Jonquille wants to protect you, it's because she does have feelings for you, and that's a good thing. You're intelligent and you can work with that." She turned back to her cider and the glasses. "I have every faith in your ability to win her over."

The confidence in her made him want to laugh in spite of the seriousness of the conversation. "Because I'm such a romantic man."

"You are, Rubin. You just aren't aware of it."

"You're mixing me up with Diego. He's the romantic one."

"Is he? Would you mind getting the cookie jar down, please? You know where it is. I have apple-walnut bars made. I know they're your favorite."

Rubin reached up into the cupboard Edward had made for his mother. Edward had a way with wood. During the heavy winter months, he would sand and shape each board into beautiful pieces for his mother's home. Although simple, her kitchen was a work of art. Rubin carefully laid the apple-walnut bars on a decorated hand-painted platter that had been in Patricia's family for generations.

"Why do you say it like that? Diego is good with women. I'm not."

Patricia sent him a quick amused look. "I think your Jonquille would say you do just fine." She put the glasses on a tray and he added the platter of cookies before picking it up.

"Where are the boys?"

"They went to Mire's Landing to get supplies for us. We're near out of everything." She led the way back through her house to the screen keeping out the multitude of insects. "They tend to go together. I prefer them to, with all the outsiders coming in to hike the trails. Edward and Rory both spend a good deal of time now patrolling to keep them off private land—yours as well as ours. The park ranger calls at least twice a month to ask them to volunteer to help find someone lost."

"There are clear signs on the trails and places for backpackers to camp." Rubin set the tray down on the little table Edward had built for his mother. The surface was smooth and the legs sturdy. Her son did good work.

"There are always that one or two that seem to go off trail and get lost," Patricia said. She smiled at Jonquille as she handed her a tall glass. "This is my special cider. I hope you like it, Jonquille."

"I'm sure I will. It looks very refreshing."

Patricia settled into her rocker. "Do your parents live in West Virginia?"

Jonquille shook her head. "I didn't ever know my parents. I grew up in an orphanage and then attended a military school where I received training as a medic. I do research mostly now in laboratories."

Rubin couldn't find fault in the least with Jonquille's matter-of-fact tone. She delivered the information as if she had many times. She didn't sound defensive or upset. She looked right at Patricia and gave her what appeared to be pertinent facts. When he went over what she'd said, in a way, she'd stuck very close to the exact truth.

"I don't even know what to say." Patricia seemed far more upset than Jonquille. "Not to grow up with parents. I'm so sorry, honey."

Jonquille smiled at her. "It seemed normal to me. I had the other girls and we formed a family unit. Later, when we pursued different types of training, as young as we were, we did lose touch, and that was hard, but fortunately, I love to travel and do quite a bit. I also spend a lot of time researching extremely interesting subjects. That keeps my mind occupied."

"Is that how you met Rubin?"

Jonquille nodded. "Yes. He needed a new research assistant and I had some knowledge in the field he was looking into. We were in two different states, but I sent him the things he needed and we started a few discussions." Jonquille lifted the glass of cider and took a slow sip. Her eyes went wide. "What did you put in this? It isn't just apple cider. I've tasted apple cider a lot of different ways and I can normally tell what's in a recipe . . ." She trailed off and took another sip, looking at Rubin over the rim of the glass. "This is amazing."

"Mama Patricia is a genius when it comes to her concoctions in the kitchen," Rubin stated.

Patricia blushed. "All of you say that. I think you just like to eat."

Diego had been quietly eating two of the apple-walnut bars and downing his first glass of cider. "You're right about the eating part, Mama Patricia." He helped himself to another glass of cider, tossing a grin to his brother when Patricia immediately put another cookie on his plate. "But you're definitely a genius in the kitchen."

Jonquille couldn't help herself. She had to try the apple-walnut bars before the two men finished them off completely. The view from the porch was beautiful. Like the Campo cabin, the Sawyer house had been built to the best scenic as well as defensible advantage. Sitting on the porch, they could see the wind playing over the grass while the family played music in the evening hours together or, like now, visited with guests as they drank cider and ate cookies.

There was no doubt in her mind, after two bites, that Patricia was a genius and would have been making quite a bit of money had she been out in the world somewhere with her astonishing recipes. "I think both the boys are a little on the crazy side, but I have to agree with them, the cider and these apple-walnut bars are amazing. If I was here too long, and ate like Diego, I'd have a weight problem." She glared at him. "I don't understand how you look like you do."

Diego's eyebrow shot up. "Extraordinary? All muscle? Not one ounce of fat? Is that what you're referring to? I'm glad you noticed."

Rubin groaned. "Don't get him started."

He sipped at the cider, but Jonquille noticed that while Diego was teasing, holding Patricia's attention, he was watching the older woman carefully, studying the way she moved. Paying close consideration to every detail of motion of her shoulder and arm. He didn't appear to be doing so—his legs were sprawled out in front of him, his eyes hooded. He looked casual, and she knew if she asked him, he could repeat what was being said verbatim, but he was really aware of everything about Patricia.

Jonquille realized Diego held Patricia's attention on purpose. The two men had obviously worked together smoothly many times with the individuals living in the very rural areas of the mountains. They visited and just talked with friends, laughing and getting reacquainted, talking about the things the people loved the most. Their hobbies. Their families.

Jonquille stayed quiet and listened as the two men steered the conversation toward the winter and how difficult it had been. Patricia was cheerful at first and then a few details slipped out. Things were easier now that the boys were home with her. Still, there were a couple of mornings that she had trouble getting her arm to cooperate. She must be getting up there in age. She laughed when she said it, but Jonquille noticed the worried note in her voice and knew both men couldn't fail to hear it as well.

Rubin's gentler questions would be interspersed with Diego's conversation with her. Jonquille was amazed at how much information the two men would draw out while simply visiting. They had incredible skill at knowing the exact topics to introduce, the little snippets of news about their own lives to share, a simple funny story that would draw Patricia into sharing one of her own and would lead to more data on her health in some way.

It came to light that she'd had the flu several times and hadn't really been eating much since. Rubin had picked up on the fact that while they had shared the apple-walnut bars, she hadn't. They'd always been her favorites, yet she hadn't touched them. Rubin paid attention to small details. That was one of his skills. He noticed. Both men did. They applied those skills not only to their tracking and hunting but also to working with patients who might not accept normal doctors.

Jonquille was so intrigued by the way the two brothers conducted the health visit, which really seemed more like a genuine call on a beloved neighbor, that she'd been at the Sawyer home for over an hour before she realized she didn't have a problem being around Patricia. The energy the woman was giving off, even when she was very animated, Rubin directed away from Jonquille. He did it so quietly, even as he had his attention centered on Patricia, that Jonquille hadn't noticed. More and more, his abilities astonished her. She had a fast learning curve and she remained as quiet as she could, unless Patricia or one of the men drew her into the conversation, so she could observe.

"Mama Patricia, now that Diego has eaten everything and the boys will get home and want to beat him to a bloody pulp, I'd like to ask a favor," Rubin said. His voice was extremely soft. Very gentle.

Jonquille recognized that small little push of persuasion in it. Nothing one could track, but it was there.

"Rubin, you do so much for us. You have only to ask."

"Jonquille is a natural healer, the way I am and my mother was. She is learning our old ways and the medicine plants. I've been working with her but only on people we trust. I would like her to see how modern medicine and the old ways can work together to aid someone, but we wouldn't want you to be uncomfortable." His gaze flicked to Jonquille.

She understood immediately. "Please know I won't be offended if you say no. I'm just learning and haven't gotten to Rubin's level at all yet."

"You have to learn somewhere," Patricia said briskly. "Rubin is family. If you're his woman, then you're going to be family as well. We best do this before the boys get home. Once they come, the noise will be deafening. Especially with Diego here."

Diego flashed a grin at them. "Sure, blame me. I can start dinner for us after I take a look around, Mama Patricia."

"I knew you were coming, Diego. I made your favorite. There's enough for everyone. The boys will fire up the grill and throw some fish and corn on it. They're real proud of their grillin' these days."

She got up, pushing off the wood arms of the rocker. This time Jonquille noticed one side was stronger than the other. Rubin picked up the tray and indicated to Jonquille to precede him into the house. She wanted to look around as she followed Patricia down a hall into a bedroom, but she'd caught on to the way Rubin and Diego worked. She was aware Diego was taking the opportunity to sweep the area around the cabin for signs of intruders. The brothers were rarely idle.

8

Jonquille forced her mind away from everything but what she was actually supposed to focus on. Rubin was giving her an unprecedented opportunity. Not only had she been close to becoming a doctor, but she had a healing gift and yearned to use it. That talent was often so strong that when she was at the laboratory and others were too near, there were times she could feel something not quite right with their bodies. The compulsion to do her best to heal them was terrifyingly intense at times, depending on the degree of the problem, yet she didn't dare, nor did she really know how to use that talent correctly. She'd never had the opportunity to develop it.

Jonquille observed Patricia as she walked. Her gait. The way she favored one side of her body just slightly. It was almost as if she protected her right side. In fact, twice she caught her right wrist with her left, as if just having the arm swinging free bothered her, yet she'd told Rubin it didn't hurt. No, she hadn't actually said that in so many words, she'd just acted stoic and laughed and said she was getting up there in age.

Rubin and Diego had gently steered the conversation without seeming to do so. They talked about family and the various times of year. The winter, how difficult it was, focusing first on her sons, asking her how they had fared. What they did. What it was like having them home. They asked about her absent children. Throughout the conversation they exchanged stories with her, getting her comfortable telling little details even about herself. What happened in the fall? The spring? The summer? They didn't ever act impatient, and had clearly come prepared to spend the rest of the day with her. Their secret, she realized, was that they were truly enjoying themselves. Jonquille wondered if that was what they did with every one of the patients in the mountains, or if Patricia was that special to them.

"Patricia is going to lie on the bed for us," Rubin said. "Jonquille, if you would just stand here beside me, I can show you what you're looking for."

Don't touch her physically. Don't ask her to remove her clothing. Do or say something to put her at ease.

For the first time in a long while, Jonquille was grateful for her smaller size. She knew she appeared nonthreatening as she moved close to Rubin, almost beneath his shoulder but still trying to give him room. She wasn't certain what to expect. How could he examine Patricia if he wasn't going to physically touch her? That didn't make sense. Excitement set in, but she forced it down, knowing the predator in him would hear her elevated heartbeat. The healer needed to be present, not the hunter.

"Mama Patricia, did you make this quilt?" She didn't have to make up the awe in her voice. The quilt covering the bed was handsewn. Stitch by tiny stitch. Each block was detailed, the pieces cut out of old material that had been used until it was faded and worn. She was certain those pieces had been material from her children's clothing when they were young, and others from her husband's clothing. This was a masterpiece. A remembrance quilt.

"Yes. Before the boys got me a sewing machine. I used the material from their baby clothes. I saved everything—well, at least the ones I didn't give to other families that needed clothing. Some pieces are from my husband's favorite shirts, ones I made for him, or mended over and over because he wouldn't part with them." She touched a square. "Our wedding clothes."

Rubin extended his hands, palms down, about four inches above Patricia's body. "Jonquille, you two can keep talking about the quilt. It's very interesting, but I want you to follow my hands with yours. The exact path."

Jonquille immediately followed his example, stretching her arms out to reach up beside Patricia's neck. She felt the pull there on her own body. Heat rose in her. Almost without thought, she could feel an alignment that was wrong.

"I love the design of this quilt, using the clothes from when your children were babies and other various ages as well as your husband's favorite shirts and your wedding clothes. How did you get that concept? Even the way each square depicts an individual story is so unique."

There's something wrong in her neck.

Good. Yes. Keep moving your hands down along her shoulder. This is the one she broke in so many places. Keep her distracted. She's in a lot of pain but refusing to acknowledge it to her sons or to me.

She's afraid it's something extremely serious like cancer. Jonquille was reluctant to keep moving her hands when she hadn't done anything to resolve the neck issue for Patricia, but she kept moving her palms slow and steady along the rounded shoulder.

"A lot of the quilters use their children's clothing for quilts, or their husband's if he's passed for a remembrance quilt. The designs are mine though. Each square I figured out ahead of time, cut it out and sewed it myself."

Her shoulder is a mess. No wonder she can barely move her arm, Rubin. Can you help her? There's so much scar tissue built up. Jonquille's body was warm, not from the energy Patricia was giving off—Rubin was directing that away from her—but from that well of healing inside of her. She felt it growing hotter, wanting to burst open, and that excited her. She'd never been this close to using it.

Yes, we'll both help her.

Rubin's voice felt like a caress in her mind.

"I've thought about using the sewing machine to reinforce the stitching so it will last longer, but none of the children want me to do it," Patricia continued. "They love the quilt the way it is."

"I have to admit," Jonquille said, "I agree with them. It's absolute perfection. The sewing machine might preserve it longer, but if my mother had made it, I'd repair any damage to it by sewing it by hand. I'd ask quilt experts how best to care for it."

Keep moving your hands down her arm. Don't make the mistake of stopping. With mountain people you rarely have a lot of time to assess. You want to know the worst immediately and then start working on healing as a whole, starting from worst to most minor.

Jonquille could see the wisdom in that. She followed Rubin's advice, although she did want to linger. Mapping out the damage was easier for him—he had far more experience. She was new at it. She knew anatomy, and that certainly helped, but the images in her mind weren't the same as seeing them on an X-ray or the results from imaging in a machine. It had taken a few stops and starts to get the images to visualize correctly in her brain.

Patricia beamed at Jonquille. "Quilting is something I've always been interested in. I'd hoped to pass the skill to my daughter, but she doesn't like sewing. She said when she has children, she will welcome all the clothes and blankets I want to make them, but she will not be making a single one. She doesn't have the patience."

"I'd love to learn," Jonquille said. "I sketch. I'm not a great artist, but I particularly love nature. Someday I hope to have my own garden with as many healing herbs and flowers as I can grow. My own natural pharmaceuticals. I always imagined living off the grid somewhere, growing my own food and living free. I'll have to add quilting to my list of things I want to learn."

The bones in her arm are twisting because the shoulder has locked up. The arm is trying to compensate. The neck is doing the same thing. When we get to her hip, you'll see that it's doing the same thing. Everything on that side of her body is working to keep her from falling or being off balance because she's in such pain. She can't lift that arm over her head. Or stretch it out in front of her. Not without excruciating pain. The entire body is trying to compensate.

"I've been working on quilts for all the children," Patricia confided. "If you're here for any length of time, you're welcome to come and work on squares and learn."

That's a huge concession, Jonquille. Huge.

"Mama Patricia, I can't thank you enough. No one has ever made me such a kind offer." Jonquille had to look away. Tears burned behind her eyes. She was getting too emotional around these people. They were too nice to her and she wasn't used to anyone treating her with respect or being kind.

Patricia's gaze jumped to Rubin. "She's a good girl, this one, Rubin. You were right. She is extraordinary." She squirmed a little on the bed. "Are you nearly finished?"

"Is it difficult to lie in that position?" Rubin asked.

Patricia hesitated.

"I am your doctor," Rubin reminded gently. "You have to tell your doctor the truth. Forget that I'm your adopted son too."

Jonquille had reached the end of Patricia's arm and hand and was moving as quickly as possible along the rib cage and down to the hip and leg, following Rubin's sure hands. He never hesitated and his arms were steady, not trembling, although he'd had them extended for a period of time. She needed to work harder on stamina. Rubin was putting her to shame.

"Yes, I'm uncomfortable lying in any position," Patricia admitted in a small voice. "Back, either side, even my belly now. I don't know why." There was worry in her voice. "Jane Rolly, you remember her, she got so she couldn't sleep much, her body hurt all the time. She got the cancer, Rubin, and she was dead in three months."

"You don't have cancer, Patricia," Rubin stated. "You're not going to die, so you can put that right out of your mind. You'll be cooking for those sons of yours, Diego and me, and now Jonquille, for many years to come. Probably old man Gunthrie as well. Has he been around?"

Jonquille knew the last question was asked partially to distract her so she could finish the examination. Rubin already had his palms so close to Patricia's neck Jonquille almost abandoned the last of her inspection of the leg and ankle, but she forced discipline and then hurriedly followed Rubin.

"Are you certain, Rubin?" Patricia whispered. "I was so certain."

"I'm certain. I'm going to work on you and show Jonquille how. You're going to feel warm, even hot, in some places. Once we work on this side, we will have to work on the other side. Then I'm going to insist on examining your back. You can't sleep because you're doing so much hard labor and lifting loads that are far too heavy. I've talked to you about that before."

Rubin's voice was very low, gentle even, but extremely firm. His tone carried authority that wasn't to be ignored, not by anyone. Jonquille found him fascinating. He didn't need to shout or look cold and unfeeling. He could deliver his orders in a gentle, caring way, infusing them with a command, but not a threat. He made those around him want to obey him. He didn't bully them into doing so. Her respect for him continued to grow.

The heat Rubin generated was far more than what Jonquille was summoning from the well inside of her, which didn't make sense since she drew energy and her temperature was always so hot. He was a miracle to her, moving with absolute confidence over every part of Patricia's neck and horribly scarred frozen shoulder.

Work with me, Jonquille.

Her heart skipped a beat. She might ruin everything. This was too big of a risk. Patricia was an incredible woman and she meant so much to him. If Jonquille made a mistake and hurt that fragile shoulder, making it worse . . . She shook her head.

Work with me. Feel the way the heat rises in you. Healing happens. You don't do it yourself. You already have knowledge of the body. The scar tissue has to go. The faster we get this done, the more on her body we can take care of. You were born to do this.

His absolute confidence in her was astounding. He didn't look at her. He looked at Patricia. He didn't order her. He simply acted as if he were stating facts. He believed in her. Jonquille allowed her palms to mimic Rubin's—settling over the scar tissue causing such problems, this time about three inches above the shoulder. She took a deep breath and concentrated on opening the well of healing deep inside her.

Heat rose fast, rushing up to spread out across her arms to her hands and fingers. She closed her eyes, visualizing that heat going straight to the scars on the shoulder, removing them, creating the clean lines again so Patricia wouldn't have pain or lack of movement.

Nice. Keep moving. Don't stop there. Look down the arm at her joints. Keep going.

He was moving around to the other side of the bed and Jonquille nearly panicked. *Where are you going? Rubin.*

You're doing just fine. Take each problem one step at a time but keep working steadily. Just as you assessed her, fix the problems. I hit the worst of them. I'll take care of this side and then we'll work on her back. After that we have to convince her sons to keep her from working so hard again. Maybe this time they'll listen.

For the first time she caught a little hint of anger toward the absent brothers who hadn't protected their mother more. She understood. Rubin's mother was buried in the graveyard behind his cabin. He couldn't save her no matter how many times he came back and helped other families. He'd cautioned Patricia and evidently her sons as well.

There was no change of expression on his face. Even in his mind, he appeared calm. Again, she liked that about him. Rubin wasn't a man given to losing his temper. He wouldn't fly into a rage. He could get angry if provoked, but he stayed in control.

The longer she worked, the more she grew in confidence. She didn't constantly check in her mind to make certain Rubin was right there overseeing her. The visualization came easier. She knew when she was on the right path and when something didn't feel right. Twice she caught the beginning of arthritis and was able to stop it. That was a victory for her. In Patricia's leg, one vein wasn't working quite as well as it should be. She went back and reassessed to see why the blood wasn't flowing properly.

Rubin glanced up and smiled at her. *Good work. I fixed the main problem. You fix the vein.*

She tried not to glow. She had never been praised in her life and it felt good to have someone acknowledge she did something right.

The vein took longer than she would have liked, mainly because she wasn't certain what she was doing. It had been a while since she'd studied every aspect of the human body, and she went slow until she felt confident she was on the right track again. By the time she was finished, Rubin had completed working on Patricia's entire right side.

"You'll have to turn over, Mama Patricia. I want to examine your back," Rubin said gently. There was the merest hesitation on her part. Rubin smoothed the pillowcase. "We want to finish before Edward and Rory get here. They'll be pulling in any minute, won't they? Jonquille, you might want to just observe and let me do this fast so we get it done. Patricia doesn't like the boys thinking she might be ill."

"Of course, no problem. I understand completely. Mama Patricia, it was so sweet of you to allow me to learn on you. Do you know very much about natural plants? I'm so interested in them and what they can do versus modern medicines."

Patricia turned over, presenting her back to Rubin, laying her head on her hands and looking at Jonquille when she positioned herself right where the older woman could see her. "I have an old handwritten book of plants, what they look like and what they are used for, to help when someone is sick or injured. Rubin's mother actually made it for Mary, and Mathew kept it. She was amazing at healing. She had the gift the way Rubin does. She would have loved talking to you about plants."

"I would love to see it, Mama Patricia. I've spent hours and hours in the woods sketching as many of the plants and roots as I could find that would be helpful. I added what I thought they could be used for. I'm embarrassed to have anyone look at it because I haven't checked to see if I'm right yet. I haven't looked them up, and who knows if there are any true experts left. I was going to experiment on myself if I couldn't find anyone to give me answers."

Rubin's gaze jumped to her face. *You won't be doing that.*

We can't lose the old ways. Just because no one is actually using the plants anymore, or they are being killed environmentally, doesn't mean they don't work.

We can have this discussion another time.

His voice was a gentle caress that slid like velvet against the walls of her mind and sent fingers of desire creeping down her spine. She supposed he was right. She felt too exposed and vulnerable right then, with Patricia looking up at her with her piercing eyes. She reached her hand out to Jonquille unexpectedly, making her wonder if the older woman had her own psychic gift. It was entirely possible.

"I think the book will help you a great deal. Rubin and Diego bought Edward and Rory a computer and printer and copier. The Internet hardly works most of the time, but when the satellite service is working, then they have a reason to argue about who gets to use it. My point being, I can have one of them copy the book. It's in Rubin's mother's handwriting. Beautifully penned and illustrated."

I had no idea. I would have wanted a copy of that book.

I will give it to you, of course, Jonquille said hastily.

She means for you to have it. I'll ask her if we can make two copies. I'll see if Diego wants his own. Perhaps three while we're at it. Thank you for even inquiring. I wouldn't have known.

How is her back?

Very messed up. She's lifting too much weight again. It's an ongoing battle I have with her. I don't know how to stop her.

"You're going to make me cry at your wonderful generosity, Mama Patricia. No one has ever been so kind to me. Growing up the way I did, everything was about duty. I suppose you know a lot about that, don't you? But you, at least, had the love of family to surround you and learn from."

"I did," Patricia said, squeezing her hand and reluctantly letting go. "Life could be hard here at times. We all had to work when it got tough, but we loved one another and that was felt. My husband was a good man. A really good man. Building this house was a big priority to him. He was so good with wood. You can see Edward takes after him."

She rubbed her palm lovingly along the carved bed frame. It wasn't intricate, but it was lovely. "My Matt was such a good man. He would come home at night after working all day and insist I sit and listen to the wind in the trees while he served dinner. I always made sure to have it ready or he would have insisted on cooking it. He said women aged too fast and died here. He was terrified whenever I got pregnant that I would die in childbirth."

My sister Mary died in childbirth. She was Matt's first wife. Their oldest son, Nick, is Mary's child. Patricia raised him like her own. Matt didn't like Patricia to get pregnant, but back then, there wasn't a lot about birth control here.

There was no bitterness in Rubin. He genuinely cared for Patricia and thought of her as family.

Jonquille nodded her head. "He sounds like an amazing man, Mama Patricia. You must miss him so much. I'm very certain he wouldn't be happy with all the heavy lifting you're doing though. I can see it's really hurting your body. Our spines have cushions called disks sitting between each of our vertebrae so they don't scrape against each other. That's all up and down your spinal cord, right? As we age, those cushions can start to dry out. If you put too much stress on your back, a disk can tear or break. The more weight you pick up, the more work you do, the more disks can rupture. That can cause your arms and legs to really hurt. Or they can feel numb or tingle."

Patricia's eyes went wide with shock. "Really? That happens to me all the time now, especially in my hands. It's from my back, you think?"

"Most likely. You *have* to take better care of yourself. You have two sons at home with you now. I know you're used to doing the work yourself, but you have to let them do it for you. One day, they'll find women of their own, right? Isn't that your hope for them? You want them to be men like your husband, looking out for their women the way he looked out for you. If you're always doing everything, they won't even notice the chores that are difficult."

"I hadn't thought of that," Patricia mused. "I do want them to be like their father. You're right, Jonquille. I'll have to do better about giving them the opportunity to do for me. I don't even ask them."

Rubin straightened slowly. Jonquille noted he looked a little pale. He stepped back from the bed and reached behind him to find the one chair Patricia had in the room. He sat down rather fast, almost as if his legs couldn't hold him up.

Jonquille smiled down at their patient. "I'm going to grab some water. You need to just rest for a couple of minutes. Would you like something cool to drink?"

"No, I'm fine," Patricia said. "I don't know why I'm always tired after Rubin does his natural healing on me, but sometimes, I feel like I can't move for a little while."

Jonquille glanced at Rubin for reassurance. He nodded at her.

"That's very normal," Jonquille comforted her. She hurried down the hall to the kitchen and filled a glass with water. It was definitely spring water. She brought it back to Rubin.

He took the glass with a faint smile. *Thanks. Always remember, using any gift, especially healing, takes energy out of you. You'll need to rest after. If you're in a combat situation and you're attempting to save someone, you have to reserve enough strength to get yourself and whoever you're working on to safety.*

She knew he was speaking from experience. She really admired him. She wondered how often he'd gone into combat and pulled soldiers out of dangerous situations to save their lives at the risk of his own. What did she do? Hide away from people in order to keep from attracting lightning to them. She couldn't even use her healing skills on them. This had been one of the few times she had been able to even try, and that was all because of Rubin. He'd drawn all energy away from her, giving her the opportunity.

Don't look so sad, Jonquille. We're going to have a good evening. You'll like her sons, and the food will be fantastic. We'll sort things out.

They would have a good evening. She knew they would. She lived life in the moment. She'd learned to do that. More than anything she would enjoy every second she had with Rubin. He was such a good man. Tonight, she would be grateful he was hers. They would settle into a routine at the cabin. Rubin would take first watch. Diego second and her last. When it was her turn, she would go hunting. She would find the threat to Rubin and hopefully eliminate them before they could find him. He was too good a man for anyone to harm. But she was taking this night to laugh and talk and pretend she was normal.

❧

Edward Sawyer was a good-looking mountain man with a dark beard, wide shoulders and a ready smile. He had an easy, relaxed way about him, although Jonquille wasn't the least bit fooled into thinking that meant he wasn't alert. His gaze constantly shifted to the terrain around the house, quartering each segment of land as he teased his mother while he competed with Diego for eating the most food.

Rory Sawyer was much more subdued, but very polite. He was quieter than his brother and no less watchful, also checking on their surroundings, and he would get up often and go through the back of the house to check on that side of the property. He made regular visits to the chicken coop to make certain the chickens were locked up so that any fox or skunk wasn't able to get to them. Twice, Rubin had gone with him. Jonquille was certain it was to talk about Patricia's need to take things easier.

The food was delicious, just as the Campo brothers had said it would be. Patricia could have made top dollar cooking for one of the restaurants springing up for tourists. Surprisingly, it was Diego and Edward who gathered the dishes and took them inside to wash before returning to the porch for evening conversation and drinks.

This time the cider had a little kick to it. Jonquille was startled by the slight, unexpected hint of fermented apple and pear. The cider was smooth and spicy, refreshing and delicious. It was also extremely dangerous in that one could easily drink several glasses of it without realizing it was actually an alcoholic beverage.

She smiled at Rubin. "I'm definitely not drinking more than one of these. Okay, maybe two."

Patricia laughed. "They sneak up on you."

"Not like Luther's alcohol. His is fiery smooth," Edward said. "Everyone wants his, but you know you're drinking it."

"I thought he made illegal moonshine. Isn't that really crude and will burn your stomach lining and all the rest of you as well?" Jonquille asked.

"He's been at it so long, he's perfected his moonshine into an art, just like Mama Patricia's cider," Rubin said. "No, his whiskey is the best."

"Can you work your natural healing on the brain, Rubin?" Edward asked, his voice teasing. "I think old man Gunthrie could use a little help upstairs, if you know what I mean."

Rory nodded. "Yeah, he's finally losing his marbles," he agreed. "Last winter he decided the government is watchin' him and wants to bust his still. You know how he gets over that still of his. Like they couldn't care less about it, but every couple of years, he's convinced they're comin' for him. He moves it from place to place."

"You don't know, Rory," Patricia said, her voice a mild reprimand. "They might be. His whiskey is very famous."

"In a hundred years, he's never been busted, Ma," Edward pointed out and burst out laughing. His brother joined him.

"Because he moves his still," she said. "See, he moves it for a reason."

"Right. Like he did last winter. You know how hard it is to move that thing at his age in winter, in the dead of night, leaving no tracks?" Edward demanded. "He's gone completely round the bend. He was suspicious of me when I told him I'd help him. He's known me since I was born and he asked me if I was a government spy on their payroll."

"Well, are you?" Jonquille asked.

There was another round of laughter, but Jonquille thought it was a perfectly good question. Rubin took her glass of cider and replaced it with a different one.

"Everyone has always thought he had the second sight," Patricia said. "There have been raids other places. I'm certain he's been investigated and he was never caught in them. They never found evidence of wrongdoing at his house. If he's making moonshine, why is it he's never caught?"

"He's making moonshine, Ma. Everyone knows it. We drink it. He brings it to the house. You've had it before. Don't pretend you haven't," Edward said. "That old man makes the best there is in these parts. He makes top dollar on it. Don't pretend you don't know that."

Patricia raised her eyebrow. "You know I knew his wife very well and visited her on many occasions. I never saw a still or evidence of one. As for Luther being crazy, he may be old, but he's just as sane as any of us."

"Ma, he doesn't have a car. He doesn't trust them," Edward said. "Calls them contraptions. He can shoot the wings off a fly, but he can't drive a car? He can move a still in the middle of the night on his own, but he can't talk to a backpacker? He can travel miles in a blizzard with snowshoes to check on you when the nearest neighbors can't, but he can't fit into the modern world at all? I could go on and on."

"Never forget he communes with the hornet people," Diego added with a little grin.

"Oh, not that," Patricia said.

Jonquille's eyebrow shot up. "What in the world?"

"There were so many stories and rumors about Luther," Patricia said. "Mostly to scare the teens. Lights in the middle of the night, ghosts, I don't know. The kids would dare one another to go to his property. Then they'd tell tall tales and scare each other more."

"He's a little out there, Ma," Edward repeated.

Rubin laughed. "He's wily, Edward. He likes to make everyone think he's crazy so they stay away from him. He's as sane as we are, although I'm not sure that's saying very much. The more active he stays, the better it is for his body, although moving that still of his around isn't the best thing for him. Last time I talked with him, he said he had a plan that would keep him from having to do it as he got older. I didn't point out that he was already well into his older years."

"I went to visit him," Rory said, "just to check on him, really, and that old man has been seeding wildflowers and transplanting ferns and other fast-spreading plants on the holler leading to his house. You can't even tell it's there anymore. I'm serious, Rubin. He's erased it on purpose. It's so overgrown now I don't see how he packs in his groceries."

"Mostly, he lives off the land now," Edward pointed out. "He has his own vegetable garden. He hunts and fishes. He does okay."

"I wish he interacted with others a bit more," Diego said. "The more he acts like a recluse, the more there's a chance he could die without anyone knowing."

"I keep an eye on him when I can," Rory admitted, glancing at his mother. "He came all this way in a blizzard to check on Ma when we were gone. I figure it isn't that hard to get down to his place once in a while to check on him. I bring him Ma's cider and some baked goods. That way he doesn't shoot me."

"Good plan," Edward said. "I should have thought of that. Maybe that's why he accused me of being a government spy. I didn't bring him any of Ma's cookies."

Patricia laughed. "I'm sure that's it. Luther does have a sweet tooth. Will you be seeing him this trip for certain, Rubin?"

"Yes," Rubin affirmed. "He doesn't like me to look after him, as he calls it, but he lets me, even though he still thinks I'm fourteen."

That got another laugh. Jonquille liked to listen to them talk. All of them spoke softly, blending in with the sounds of the night, the drone of the insects and calls of the night frogs. Occasionally there was the hoot of an owl or the song of one of the night birds. Something large splashed in the water, and Edward spotlighted a large, very well-fed doe. Her eyes shone at them, and when he put out the light, she was gone instantly.

Rubin's and Diego's accents seemed to get just a little more pronounced in the company of the Sawyer family as the night wore on, and for some reason, Jonquille found that extraordinarily sexy in Rubin. She was grateful she hadn't drunk any more of the cider because she was afraid she might have blurted that right out to him.

He was the one who ultimately ended the visit by standing and holding out his hand to her, pulling her to her feet and whispering to her to go inside and use the facilities quickly because they had to leave. She did so, and when she returned, he took her hand as if it were the most natural thing in the world and they walked together like that all the time.

Patricia kissed her cheek and told her to come back often. Edward and Rory pretended they were going to kiss her but backed off when Rubin threatened to shoot them. Diego moved to the other side of Jonquille so she had both brothers acting like they were looking out for her as they started up the trail toward their cabin. They were miles from home, and it had surprised Jonquille that they'd stayed so late.

They walked several miles along the trail before Diego suddenly veered into the woods. Rubin indicated for Jonquille to follow Diego. "There's a shortcut we take through here."

Diego was already slipping out of his "visiting" jacket and replacing it with his forest gear from his pack. Rubin was doing the same. He took Jonquille's nice jacket, folded it and pushed it into his pack. She pulled out her worn one and slipped into it. She was never without it in the woods.

"You okay in those hiking boots?" Rubin asked.

"Yes. I only have a couple of pairs of shoes. These work for almost every type of situation I run into." That wasn't altogether true. They weren't as cute as she would have liked, but when you wanted serious hiking boots, you sacrificed looks for performance. She really needed performance. Since she wasn't around people most of the time, it all worked out.

They shrugged into their packs and Diego took lead, setting a fast pace, cutting through the woods on a narrow game trail that he seemed very familiar with. He didn't slow no matter what obstacle was in his path. He leapt over small logs or large ones and clearly expected Jonquille to do the same. She did so effortlessly. In fact, her body welcomed the stretching after sitting for so long. She wasn't used to visiting with others and the activity felt good.

Rubin was behind her, at least she was pretty certain he was—she couldn't hear him breathing. She couldn't hear footfalls. Or twigs snapping. Or leaves brushing against his clothing. For that matter, Diego didn't make any noise. She was smaller than both men, so not snagging her clothing or hair or pack on brush as she moved through the denser woods should have been easier for her, but it didn't seem as if it mattered one way or the other.

She found she was enjoying herself. Her body felt like a machine, heart and lungs working perfectly, her eyes adjusting to the darkness, seeing everything. The nerve endings at the base of her hair follicles acted like radar, communicating where everything around her was so that she knew how close animals were to her. How close she was to trees or boulders, so she wouldn't trip or get too near a drop-off. Her hearing was more acute. Everything was just *more*.

They ran in formation for over an hour, covering the distance between the two homes until Diego slowed and then came to a stop. Immediately, Jonquille recognized where she was. They were on the Campo property and had been for some time. Diego had set a ground-eating pace, and with the shortcut they'd taken, even though it was all uphill, they'd made it in record time and were close to the cabin.

"I'll go ahead and hunt for signs just to make certain no one came to visit while we were out," Diego said. "You two can wait here."

Rubin shrugged out of his pack. "Or I can do it. You took lead."

Jonquille didn't like a little note in his voice. Just one single note. Or the look Diego shot Rubin over his shoulder. She'd recognized that first night when they'd arrived a difference of opinion between them, and it had to do with the way Diego looked after Rubin. Rubin didn't like it.

She felt protective toward Rubin as well. She understood Diego's need to watch over him. Rubin was a good man, and he looked after everyone around him. She could tell the two brothers were arguing again telepathically in that way they had. The energy between them flew back and forth. Rubin was more mild-mannered than Diego, but no less stubborn.

In the end, all three of them chose a direction and went out looking for signs. She could tell Diego wasn't happy, but neither was she. She took the area assigned to her and went over it very carefully. Nothing was out of place. There were no tracks. She didn't expect there to be. She had come well ahead of anyone looking for Rubin with the idea that she would be ready for them. She wanted a little time before she destroyed his enemies. She would leave in the early morning hours and go hunting them. Now that she'd met him and spent time with him, she knew she'd been right about him. He was a good man with a brilliant mind, and she wanted him alive in the world.

9

Rubin slid his weapons into the many loops of his mountain jacket and pulled on his gloves before stepping out of the cabin silently and into the night. He inhaled almost without thinking. It was so automatic to scan the world around him with every sense, every enhancement Whitney had given him. It was these times that he was grateful for the animal DNA giving him the ability to know every creature that was close. Every enemy approaching.

He wasn't going to allow his brother or Jonquille to slip away in the middle of the night to search for Whitney's team of soldiers. If Jonquille was there in his cabin, Rubin knew the soldiers weren't that far behind. Whitney had prepared for this moment. The man liked his little games. He couldn't have known about the terrorist cell or whoever the foreign team hunting Rubin was, but he would have waited for Jonquille to seek out Rubin so he could test his best soldiers against the pair.

Whitney would have given those soldiers his most advanced weapons and enhancements. They would have been psychics that had been rejected for one reason or another from the regular Ghost-Walker program but that Whitney had enticed with money to work for him. They rarely lasted long because he souped them up so much that their bodies couldn't take the overload. Rubin figured that sooner or later, just as Whitney had made improvements with his teams of GhostWalkers, he would with his own soldiers.

Rubin shouldered the small pack of supplies, water and provisions that he would need just for a day or two. He was traveling light, wanting to cover distance fast. He'd only have a four-hour start before his brother would be coming after him. Diego would be pissed, but then he'd be torn about whether to trust Jonquille enough to have her at their backs or to have to stay there to keep an eye on her—although by now, he most likely believed Jonquille wasn't their enemy.

He kept his movements in tune with the natural rhythm of the wilderness. Their property had been one of the wildest in the area, and nothing had changed in all the years since they'd been gone. When neighboring farms came up for sale, they paid top dollar for them in order to ensure their privacy. They didn't want the trees to be cut down as they had been in so many other parts of the country. Wildlife had a foothold in the extensive wilderness surrounding their cabin. Black bears, bobcats, coyotes, even a small wolf pack had come back, sustained by the ever-growing resources available to them.

Early on, when they'd first joined the military, they'd brought an expert on wolves with them to work with Edward Sawyer. He was interested in conservation. Every time Diego and Rubin talked to him about the surrounding wilderness and how they needed to protect the trees and wildlife, he actually listened. They hired him to manage their property for them. It turned out to be one of the best investments they'd ever made.

Edward then approached them about his older brother, Rory, who had had an accident at a mill and had returned home. He had spent hours talking with Edward, and had gone with him several times to the Campo property. He wanted to know if they would be interested in what he might be able to do for the forest itself. He had always had an interest in trees and plants. That next spring they brought up an arborist to talk specifically about the trees and flora and fauna in their area. Rory was hired to manage the woods.

More than anything else, hiring the two men helped the Sawyer family through harsh winters and provided them with a decent living. It also promoted goodwill. They weren't after the small wolf pack that had established a home there, although the wolves claimed a good hundred miles as their territory.

Rubin felt an affinity with the wolves. He had a bit of that DNA in him, enough that he could detect motion immediately and see easily in the dark. He had a highly developed sense of smell. The hairs on his neck and face had extra nerves that allowed him to process information around him, changes in the air current that might indicate activity close to him. He could determine the size of something he couldn't see, the speed it might be coming at him, even the shape of it. He could move fast, leap over objects, including downed tree trunks if necessary. He could move in absolute silence and go long distances at a steady run without getting winded.

The clouds had turned dark and ominous. In the distance, he could see a long row of dense, towering vertical clouds. *Cumulonimbus*. He was grateful Jonquille wasn't outside. The thunderclouds were a portent of a lightning storm. The storms could be quite severe in the mountains, and there were warnings on the trails for hikers to beware of lightning strikes.

The wind picked up, so the canopy overhead swayed above him. Once in cover of the thicker vegetation, he moved even faster. Whitney would know the location of the Campo property. His soldiers would avoid all contact with anyone living in the area. If an outsider was seen, even briefly, it would be noted and the news would go out immediately, carried on the local special channels. They didn't need telephones. They had age-old methods of leaving signs for one another outsiders weren't aware of. Most of the time outsiders didn't see them. A team of soldiers would be seen long before they would spot an old-timer or a young boy hunting rabbits or squirrels. The news would go out far and wide.

Whitney would be very aware that his team would be at a disadvantage. He wouldn't have them come in on any of the trails or roads backpackers might travel on. He would instruct them to avoid the little communities or farms at all costs. He would tell them not to touch any of the locals. Whitney knew Rubin and Diego's background. Two young boys who hunted down the men who had raped and killed their sister. They would never stand for anyone killing innocents. They would spend the rest of their lives hunting them. If they believed Whitney was responsible, they would turn their attention to hunting him. That was the last thing he wanted. He might want to pit his soldiers against them, but he wouldn't want an all-out war.

Which way would they come in? They wouldn't know Rubin had decided to come early. They would know Jonquille had. They might decide to try to acquire her and see if they could get him to try to take her away from them. Since he didn't know her, that wasn't the best of ideas. He doubted that they would want to do that. Most likely they weren't risking coming up the trails yet, so they wouldn't be on the mountain. Where would they be?

He picked up speed once he was a good distance from the cabin, choosing to follow the stream winding downhill. Both Jonquille and Diego were enhanced with animal DNA, which meant they had excellent hearing. They also had good instincts. Diego knew him. He'd been careful not to give any hints about his intentions, but that didn't mean Diego wouldn't guess what was on his mind.

He wasn't losing either of them. Not Diego or Jonquille. He'd watched over his younger brother for as long as he could remember. Diego, of course, thought he watched over Rubin. Now there was Jonquille. If Rubin had any doubts about her being the right one for him, those kisses had sealed her fate. He wasn't the kind of man who jumped in with both feet, all in, with women. He was careful. In fact, for the most part, he simply stayed away from them.

Rubin had been all about the catch-and-release program in the beginning, mainly because he wasn't a man who wanted one-night stands. He was looking for something permanent. The women that came around him seemed to be shallow. They all had agendas of some kind. He wasn't charming like Diego. He didn't have that ease of conversation, so the women usually came on to him. It didn't take long before his radar went off and he realized there was some hidden reason why he'd been singled out. Often, it was to get closer to Diego or one of the Fortunes brothers.

That reason should have bothered him or undermined his confidence in himself, but it hadn't. Rubin knew his own worth as a man, a soldier and a doctor. He also knew his bank account. He didn't come across as wealthy because he was quiet, dressed casually when he went out and talked with his slow mountain accent.

He'd acquired a great deal of money because he spent very little. There was no need to spend. He banked most everything he made and he was extremely good at investments.

Rubin slowed as he came to the fork the stream had forged. A waterfall spilling over rocks and tumbling over downed tree trunks divided the stream. Going south, the bed was wider and much faster moving, the downhill steeper. The water ran over a bed of rocks. Ferns and brush closely grew along the sides of the creek, interspersed with trees.

The bed to the east was thinner, a little sluggish, overgrown on the sides so that the ferns and foliage, at times, were hiding the sides of the stream. The amount of growth in many places made it difficult to see where the actual creek bed was. That wouldn't matter, but this was wild country and the stream could be very shallow or unexpectedly deep in places. The eastern slope appeared easier to travel because it wasn't as steep, but the terrain was far more treacherous once one got into it and off the trails. It was true wilderness. True mountains. Just what the predator in Rubin preferred. He took the eastern route.

He contemplated the war his mind continually struggled with—the reason he found a semblance of peace away from people. It was why he sought the solace of the swamp and the mountains. He was a healer. A psychic surgeon. He was compelled to heal others. It was so ingrained in him he couldn't stop himself. He was also a predator. He needed to hunt and to kill. That was ingrained in him as well. That was something he didn't share or talk about.

He knew he'd been born with the ability to push aside his feelings when he needed to. He wouldn't have been able to hunt his sister's killers otherwise. He had been the one to calmly get his rifle and tell his mother he was going after the men who had killed his sister—he'd be back when they were dead. He hadn't asked

Diego to come with him. He hadn't expected Diego to come, although it hadn't surprised him. Where he went, Diego went as well. They were like-minded. That was the dichotomy—killer and healer. Rubin accepted it, but it was hell to live with, his mind always at war.

Hunting the men who would kill his brother and Jonquille, the men who Whitney had been foolish enough to send after him, gave him a much-needed excuse to let the predator in him loose—the one he held so strictly in check.

A large animal moved off to his left and he hunkered down, crouching low, waiting for it to get a drink. Elk were returning slowly to the area but were rarely seen. He'd put miles between his cabin and where he was, but he was still surprised by the sight of the large animal dipping its head warily into the stream. The animal lifted his head twice and looked around as if sensing a possible hunter, but unable to find the hidden threat.

Rubin inhaled, once more letting his senses flare out to scan the night. There was no sound to alert him. Nothing that would tell him he was being hunted, but like the elk, he was suddenly uneasy. He eased into the deeper foliage and went perfectly still, fading completely into the dark of the shrubs. He was so quiet and stealthy, the elk never looked his way, as wary as the animal was.

Again, Rubin took stock of his surroundings, letting the wind talk to him, bring him information. An owl flew silently overhead. Shrews scurried under leaves and cones in an effort to stay hidden as they fed in the dense foliage, protected by the trees and brush. A family of raccoons chattered back and forth farther downstream, scolding a skunk that didn't care one way or the other, oblivious to whatever the elk seemed leery about.

It wasn't raining, but the wind was by turns gusting or still. The clouds were stacked overhead across the night sky, towers rising high. Occasionally Rubin could see flashes of light in the purple-and-black-laced edges, forked tongues like snakes lashing out at the restraining barriers holding the electrical energy in.

Several tree frogs serenaded back and forth, uninterrupted. Salamanders skittered through the leaves and debris on the forest floor near the stream bed. The night insects sang. Still, Rubin didn't move. Now the hairs on his body reacted, telling him something unseen was in motion. Something was coming toward him from his left and behind him. Low to the ground. It was in one of the tunnels foxes and other animals used to navigate quickly through heavy brush.

Rubin relaxed the fist that had been around the hilt of his knife at his waist. He stayed where he was, his hand still on the knife. That was no fox in that small tunnel. That was a small woman, a little lightning bug that could move fast and track just as well as Diego. If she was already coming after him, there was no doubt in his mind that his brother was as well. So where was Diego? Was he tracking Jonquille? Or him?

So much for any of them getting sleep. He thought about closing his eyes for a few minutes. It would take Jonquille another fifteen minutes at least before she made it to him, and that was if she didn't slow her pace, which she would if she didn't want to get caught. Diego was another matter altogether. Diego was a huge question mark. To reach him as fast as she had, Jonquille must have started after him almost as soon as he'd left. That meant Diego was already out of the cabin or she couldn't have gotten away safely.

If Diego had come after him first, he might not know Jonquille was tracking him as well. Rubin puzzled it all out in his mind. He liked puzzles. Diego was better in the woods than Rubin. There was no doubt about that. Rubin was good, but Diego was pure animal. He'd been good as a kid, but once Whitney had enhanced him, he'd gotten better. Not just better. Weirdly better.

Diego could track anything through any kind of terrain. He was quiet about it. Never talked about it. Few knew, even on the teams. They had elite trackers on their team, so Diego and Rubin didn't say much about either of their little-known gifts. It wasn't necessary and neither preferred the spotlight. They both were the type to fade into the background when at all possible. If they were needed, they came forward, but not until.

Another flash overhead, sizzling and bright, lighting the long series of clouds as if the bolts were igniting one another. The lighted forks were dazzling and then gone, leaving the woods even darker and more threatening.

Rubin didn't let his guard down because he had spotted Jonquille and knew Diego was close. The elk hadn't alerted to either of them. Something else was prowling around the stream very close to Rubin. He kept all his senses alert, hoping Jonquille was doing the same and not concentrating solely on him.

The small figure in the tunnel had ceased to move and was curled up in a little ball. His breath caught in his throat as he realized the activity overhead in the thunderclouds had to be a magnet for the electrical charges in her body. The overhead lightning was looking for just one lead stroke to carve a path to earth. She was doing her best to keep from responding. She wasn't out in the open, which was what had kept her from drawing the lightning to her.

Rubin studied the clouds. The weather was conducive to a thunderstorm, yes, but this one was much stronger than seemed warranted. The clouds rose higher, stringing in rows across the sky as if seeking a target . . . He turned that over in his mind. Was it possible that Whitney had developed a weapon to track Jonquille?

A way to call to the electrical activity in her? Why would he do that? She said the members of the others tracking him had strange weapons that she had never seen before. They were interested in lightning as weapons. They had attended the conferences he had attended. Was it possible they *did* know about Jonquille?

Something wasn't right about the clouds of lightning. She was secreted in the small animal tunnel, low to the ground, surrounded by tall trees and dense forest and brush. Those clouds continued to stretch for miles overhead, the lightning forks active, crackling and sizzling with hostile intent. The more he studied them, the more he was certain the lightning was an effort to draw Jonquille out. Eyes in the sky. Looking.

If he could make his way to her without giving away her position, that would stop any possible chance of an attack on her, or success of the threat to her. His presence alone would stop it. On the other hand, just moving might draw the hunter's attention. He had to know where the threat was coming from.

Jonquille didn't panic, and she had to know the clouds were a deliberate danger to her. Diego would be a ghost in the woods. Rubin studied the terrain. Where would the hunter most likely be? He thought Jonquille was alone. Why had he thought she might be near the stream? What had tipped him off to her presence?

The elk put one hoof in the stream and splashed through the water, his head up, eyes on a section of trees as he traveled without haste out of sight. The drone of the insects never stopped. An owl several hundred yards from him, in the direction Jonquille had come from, flew toward a tree, circled, talons out as if to land, and then veered off, wings beating hard to get lift again. It flew to a red spruce several yards away and settled in the branches there.

Rubin switched away from the vision he mostly used at night— that of a wolf. He was comfortable with that, but he switched his vision in order to see from an eagle's vision. The bird could see at night. He wanted to inspect that particular tree the owl had decided not to rest in. It had swerved off for a reason.

Crouched on a crooked limb, about thirty feet up, was a man. Dressed in camouflage gear, his face streaked with paint to reflect his surroundings, he nearly blended right into the tree itself. He wasn't armed with a rifle. Rather, he had a strange device in his hand and he was pointing it upward, not down toward the ground. Every now and then, he would look at something much smaller, nestled in his palm, that Rubin couldn't see.

Although it was clear the hunter was a patient man, he was also frustrated. He was pushing the clouds farther out, back toward the Campo cabin, as if whatever had made him think Jonquille was in the area he was rethinking. He consulted the device in his palm over and over.

Rubin watched the clouds move away from Jonquille. She wasn't entirely safe. She had to remain quite still until the electrical charges settled. They could be miles away and still find her, but she would know that. He didn't take his eyes off the hunter to look for Jonquille. He had to trust that she was every bit as trained as he believed she was.

The hunter in the trees remained still the entire time other than to glance between the two devices. There was no doubt in Rubin's mind that the man in the trees was forcing the thunderclouds to migrate across the sky toward the Campo cabin in search of Jonquille. Over the next few minutes, the towering clouds spread across the sky, the electrical storm lessening over the area so that the static charges dwindled significantly.

Rubin was concerned with the way the clouds were beginning to take shape overhead. From the original formation, the way the hunter was forcing them to move, they were taking on the appearance of an anvil. That could be very bad. Anvil clouds could produce lightning that could strike as much as ten miles away, where skies could appear blue and people would be completely unaware they were in danger.

The hunter abruptly leapt from the tree, into the nearest branches of the closest spruce, and then continued on to the next tree, his body taking on the appearance of a large flying squirrel. He moved so fast he blurred, his clothing blending into the needles and branches of the swaying limbs of the trees as he sprang in and out of them. It was difficult to track him, and would have been impossible had Rubin not been using his enhanced eyesight.

Rubin was up and after him, running full out, using every one of his many enhanced senses to keep track of the enemy as the man sprang from tree to tree. As he ran, Rubin, through the hairs on his body, felt the shift in the wind just enough to warn him that the clouds were moving back into place overhead. As their opponent ran, he was capable of thinking and acting. The foliage on the forest floor hadn't been that affected, but the canopy above them swayed.

Diego, he's going to attack with a lightning strike. Rubin crouched in place. *Keep your eyes on him at all times. Don't let him escape. I'll take care of the lightning.*

He worried about sending telepathic warnings to Jonquille. That involved using energy and it could enable that hunter to pinpoint her. Still. He knew she had strong protective instincts, just as he did. Just as Diego did. Their enemy had been after her, using the clouds he'd seeded to try to draw her out. *Don't answer me, Jonquille, and don't move. Let me take care of this.*

Lightning crackled, lighting up the bottoms of the clouds in forks, sizzling and building the negative charges, attracting the positive charges in the ground. Rubin couldn't imagine the pull on

Jonquille's body from the clouds and the ground both. He couldn't spare a glance in her direction. He couldn't look to see where the enemy was. The lightning strike would happen so fast even the human eye couldn't follow it, but his body's electrical perception and the hairs on his body would be able to act as a tracking system and trigger an interception. He needed to deflect the strike and keep it from hitting anywhere near his brother.

The buildup was shockingly fast. *Now.* He warned his brother. The light would be so bright after the dark of the night that it would hurt his eyesight. Diego would have to close his eyes against the flash and then open them to catch the movement of their enemy, who would take the opportunity to make a jump for another tree.

Rubin triggered his own electrical response, directing it precisely at the lead stroke that ran from cloud toward ground, so that it hit with deadly accuracy. Rubin was up and running, leaping over rotting tree trunks to cover as much ground as he could, heedless of the dense brush and the startled animals rushing before him. He heard Diego's rifle but didn't dare take his eyes from the clouds, where the charges were building faster and stronger.

He hunkered down as his body hairs rose. *Incoming. Eyes,* he warned his brother. Diego had gotten off a shot, but he hadn't hit their enemy, which was nearly unheard of. Their opponent was brutally fast.

Several jagged bolts of lightning struck like swords at a location not too distant from Rubin, where he suspected Diego was hunkering down. Rubin had been expecting the retaliation and he triggered his own response in anticipation, his electrical charges knocking the rods sideways, away from Diego. It wouldn't be long before the squirrel man would decide to take his next shot at him.

Immediately he was up and running again, toward the location the enemy had been in. Again, Diego's rifle sounded off. This time, there was a loud crack and a splintering sound as a branch gave way. Diego pulled the trigger again.

I didn't get a clean hit, but he's down.

He's fast. Rubin didn't slow down, although knowing his opponent was wounded didn't make him happy. He was a mountain man, a hunter. He knew to be cautious when tracking a wounded animal into the bush. *Wait for me. I've got your six.*

Rubin kept moving fast. He had pinpointed his brother's location by their telepathic communication. His brother was on the move but at a much slower, cautious pace. Coming behind him and off to his left, but keeping the same speed, he felt the static electricity that could only signal Jonquille moving through the brush as well. She was silent, not disturbing leaves or branches, not stepping on anything that would snap under her weight.

The ground was wet, so that meant one could step in unseen puddles. Sound carried at night, even ragged breathing, but the splash in a puddle would instantly give away position even in the thick brush to an experienced hunter. But Jonquille made no sound. Had it not been for the static charges on his body, he would never have known she was close to him.

He's in the tree branches, can't get a bead on him. I hit him. There's blood on the leaves.

Stay still, Jonquille. He's going to strike at Diego.

I can feel it. She sounded very calm. *I can steal his lead. I'm ground. Once I do, I can strike at him if you direct it.*

The charge was building fast. It was not only fast, but Rubin could tell their opponent meant to blast the entire area so he could get away. The hunter knew he was in trouble and had to get out under cover of the ferocious lightning storm.

Now, Rubin directed, orchestrating their own strike.

Jonquille was magnificent. Both Rubin and Diego could feel the staggering power of her enhancement as her electrical charges burst from her, rising up to meet the jolting forks descending like swords from the clouds. At the same time, Rubin took aim for the tree where the wounded hunter was lodged, and as Jonquille connected, so did he.

The powerful bolts rained down, exploding the tree the hunter was in, reducing it to splinters, as well as the trees closest to him.

He made it out of the tree before the bolt hit, Diego reported, already on the move. *That man is fast. He was a blur. Something warned him. He's on the ground running.*

Can you see him? Jonquille asked. She was moving as well, keeping pace with Rubin, but staying about ten feet to his left.

Diego kept going through brush, following a nearly nonexistent trail. Rain and ice fell from the clouds. Thunder rolled continuously.

Rubin answered for Diego. *Glimpses of him. Low to the ground, running in between the red spruce and oak trees just beyond the stream. He blends in, but he's so fast movement catches the eye.*

Got him. Am dropping ball lightning on him. It will run low to the ground. You should be able to direct it straight onto him. He might not see it coming or expect it.

Jonquille was right. Ball lightning was a rare atmospheric phenomenon few people had even heard of. Scientists weren't even certain how it was formed, although already the military in several countries were trying to find ways to utilize it as a weapon. Ball lightning rarely, if ever, occurred at high points where lightning strikes were inevitable. The phenomenon was much more likely to occur during a thunderstorm on flat ground. It would be the last thing their enemy would consider in the way of an attack on him.

Can you control it?

Inside a house or an enclosed area, a blast could be contained and stay relatively small in the way of damage for such an explosive event, but outside, the damage could be extreme.

I can't control anything. You will have to do your best.

Again, she was very honest, but Rubin felt her make every effort to control the charges building up in her. He felt the static rising in the hairs on his body. He knew Diego did as well. He was certain the enemy did, especially when the man suddenly dashed away from the stream, trying to put distance between his body and the shiny ribbon of water. He moved away from the taller trees, further adding to Rubin's belief that he was as tuned to electrical buildup as all three of his pursuers.

That would make sense in terms of Whitney pitting a team of supersoldiers against them. Sooner or later, he had to get a really good team of men who were enhanced with animal DNA to match theirs and psychic gifts that were on par with theirs. This opponent was the first one that Rubin had ever run across that Whitney— and he was assuming it was Whitney due to the man's capabilities— had sent after them that was truly a scary enemy. If an entire team was like this man, Rubin, Diego and Jonquille might really be in trouble if they went up against more than a few at a time.

Lightning forked in the bottom of the clouds, a jagged, hot, sizzling display, leaping from cloud to cloud overhead. Rubin noted where the enemy lay flat in the grass, using his toes and elbows to push forward, working his way toward an animal tunnel that would take him to thicker brush cover.

The ground ten feet away crackled with electrical energy, and he saw the white glow in the brush as Jonquille continued to run forward. Heat burst around him. Then she was still, lifting her arms wide, throwing them forward toward the meadow where their enemy had flattened, making himself small.

Thunder rolled, a deep booming drumbeat straight over their heads. All the while those lightning forks glowed and crackled ominously in the dark clouds above them. Bright spinning luminescent yellow spheres of various sizes surrounded by bluish-white halos dropped straight from the sky to rain on the meadow. Some seemed to detonate, while others traveled parallel to the ground. A few bounced low. All lasted longer than the brief flashes of lightning bolts, but at the most, ten to twelve seconds.

He's not moving. He's down, Diego reported.

Don't approach him, Rubin cautioned. *He's a wily opponent. I wouldn't be surprised if he's still alive and has some kind of killing bite or a way to shoot poison into one of us. Let's just wait until we see what he's going to do.*

Rubin came up beside his brother and crouched low, not taking his eyes off their prey. The squirrel man was lying facedown in the grass, unmoving. Rubin didn't take his gaze off the man. Both he and Diego could be utterly still for hours. He had no doubt that their enemy could as well, but he was wounded and he had been losing blood—a lot of it. He might not have the time to pretend.

Jonquille? She should have been right there beside him. There was a moment of hesitancy. His heart did a funny little hitch.

Be there in a minute.

His heart resumed beating normally, although she didn't *feel* normal. He couldn't take his gaze from their enemy long enough to look behind him to find her. *I need to know if you're doing all right, sweetheart.*

Diego spoke for the first time. *Jonquille, you have to tell us the truth. If using your gift tires you out, we need to know so we can take steps to protect you when we ask you to use it. We're a team and we work together. We'll do the same, let you know when we need you to take our backs.*

Like that's ever going to happen.

It happens all the time, Diego said. *We go into combat. We get shot. There are accidents.*

Rubin took over. *You seem to have a very big problem with the fact that you're the first-generation GhostWalker and we're the fourth. Team One, Ryland's team, is every bit as respected among the GhostWalkers as Team Four. We don't look at each other's psychic gifts and put one ahead of the other either. Or we shouldn't. Diego is a little arrogant because he thinks he's a hotshot tracker with mad skills, but now that you're with us, his status is in jeopardy.*

The man on the ground was definitely becoming much harder to see. The clouds had darkened. The electrical activity had died down, leaving behind very black clouds that were drifting away on the wind. The light from the moon came only in strange patterned tears like rips, streaks of thin stripes when the thick cloud formations parted just enough to allow a small beam to escape and slash across the ground. In a way, the streaks looked like a giant claw had ripped at the grass, tearing at it and leaving it blackened and torn in the wake of a massive cat taking its aggression out on the world.

Rubin thought in terms of a predatory animal. The man sprawled out on the ground didn't remind him of prey, not even now, when he should have been dead. He hadn't been struck by any of the lightning bolts or the plasma spheres—but he had been shot.

Can you tell if he is bleeding, Diego? Fresh blood. That would indicate he's alive.

He fell covering that side.

How convenient. More and more, Rubin was convinced their

quarry was not dead and that he was just as lethal now, if not more than he had been. *Don't approach him. I've got a bad feeling about him. Remember Whitney's last experiments? All of the women could inject lethal poisons. We don't know what this man is capable of. I don't believe he's dead. He may have been stunned for a few minutes, but he isn't dead.*

He isn't dead, Jonquille confirmed. She sounded a little stronger, but she wasn't closer to them. *I can feel him. He's very aware of us. Of me in particular.*

Rubin didn't like the sound of that. *What do you mean, of you in particular? Are you connected to him in some way? Did Whitney connect you? Pair you?* There was sharp demand in his mind. Even anger, when he wasn't an angry man.

Mellow out, Rubin. How could she possibly know the answer to that? Diego said. *I'd like to tell you he's sane most of the time, Jonquille, but since he's never been crazy over a woman before, I have nothing to go by. Judging by his behavior with you, I don't think there's much hope that he is.*

Jonquille's soft laughter sounded like music, a breath of fresh air, clearing out the dark stirrings of strange jealousy that had crept into Rubin's mind unbidden, striking such a discordant and unnatural note.

It doesn't feel like a pairing, Jonquille mused, after a moment. *But he's tuned specifically to me. That device he used was to draw me out. You weren't supposed to be here for another three or four weeks. If Whitney sent him to get me, why now? Why bring me in all of a sudden after all this time? That would mean the retrieval team is after me, not you.*

It was impossible not to catch the worry in her voice. Jonquille had thought of herself as being flawed, and because of that she was off of Whitney's radar. He shouldn't want her back. If Whitney had sent a team of very sophisticated supersoldiers after her, he meant business. He wouldn't risk his multimillion-dollar high-tech soldiers for the return of one flawed orphan experiment that had gone seriously wrong. She might be imperfect and a mess, but she was still lethal. Why risk his elite soldiers?

Rubin, none of this is making any sense. You and Diego should back off. This might be some elaborate trap. Diego? Can you sense anyone else near? Rubin? We've been concentrating on this man. Is it possible he's the bait? We're exposed out here just like he is.

Jonquille had a point. Not one thing about this squirrel man made sense. None of his actions did, unless he was deliberately holding their attention. They hadn't spotted him immediately. Rubin hadn't known he was there until the elk had been so nervous.

Diego, slide back into the thickest brush. Once you're under cover, no one can spot or track you. Take a look around and see if he's alone. Lightning Bug and I will be sitting ducks waiting for you to get back to us, so don't fall asleep on the job.

Diego didn't argue, although Rubin felt his reluctance. His brother slipped away, a silent wraith, moving quietly so he wouldn't disturb the insects or wildlife. Rubin didn't dare take his gaze from the man lying supposedly dead not thirty feet away.

Are you feeling any better, woman?

I thought it was Lightning Bug.

He let his laughter slip into her mind. *You can produce superb lightning. I was very impressed. I could use another pair of eyes on this character, although I'm beginning to think maybe we need to watch each other's backs.*

I'm watching your back, she assured. *I've got a bad feeling that man is faking it to keep us right where we are.*

I've got that same feeling. Rubin had the impression they were in real trouble. He just didn't know how or where it was coming from.

10

Rubin, Jonquille, I'm going to shoot that faker in his calf and the two of you slip back into the brush and get the hell out of there. I'll cover you. Meet me at the fork in the stream.

Diego didn't wait for either of them to protest. The bullet hit their quarry in the back of his right calf. He screamed, rolling for the nearest brush. Immediately, answering fire exploded from two different sites, a tree several yards away almost parallel to Rubin and one directly in front of him about thirty yards away. Both shooters directed their shots toward the highest part of a knoll several yards away, clearly trying to trace where Diego had shot from.

Rubin moved immediately, hoping Jonquille was doing the same. He knew Diego had changed positions the moment he fired that bullet. He would be already zeroing in on one of the two snipers in the trees. Sure enough, a single bullet was fired, and something heavy crashed through several branches before a body was hung up in the thick limbs.

Rubin made it into the thickest part of the underbrush, took a deep breath and turned to look around for Jonquille. There was no bright hair to mark her in the dark. There was no sound. He inhaled and took in the subtle fragrance of coral honeysuckle and daffodils. Very subtle, almost nonexistent, although he'd know her anywhere. She was very close to him.

You managed to hide your sparks.

I have to carry something with me at all times.

The night had gone silent again. Rubin was very familiar with Diego's hunting skills. There was a body hanging in the trees, possibly dead—possibly wounded on purpose, just as Diego had wounded their original prey. That meant the lone sniper would have to make a choice, and it was never a good one. Diego would have endless patience. That was the way Rubin had been taught when he was a child, and he'd passed that lesson on to his brother. The first to move was often the first to die. These men had come hunting them. They would never give quarter. Rubin had also taught Diego that.

You two are pretty ruthless, aren't you? Jonquille asked.

If the situation calls for it, Rubin replied. He chose a game trail and began moving through it, using elbows and toes to drive himself forward. *They came looking.*

He felt rather than heard Jonquille behind him. He was extremely aware of her presence now. She was very small and could move much faster than he could through the smaller game tunnels, but she never closed the gap between them.

A rabbit veered away from a downed tree trunk just across the stream from where Diego was hunting the last of the snipers before he went after the wounded squirrel man. Rubin instantly froze, his gaze on the rabbit. The rabbit stood on its hind legs and looked inquisitively at the tree trunk. Rubin did the same.

Diego, stay very still. You're being hunted. This is most likely a five-man team, maybe larger. We assumed they sent a small team after Jonquille, but there are more than the two snipers and the one with the device seeding the clouds. I'm putting eyes in the sky.

Diego didn't answer, but Rubin felt his acknowledgment.

Jonquille, stay curled up tight. They might try again to draw you out. I'm going hunting.

I'm capable of hunting. I'm not staying here safe while the two of you track these men, especially if you believe they were looking for me.

Do you recognize anything about them?

No.

She was adamant and Rubin believed her. He tuned his mind to the trees and the owls there. Diego was the expert, but Rubin could reach out and connect easily. He had done it often as a youth, hunting. He didn't want Diego's attention to be divided for even the slightest moment. This was life or death. This team—if Whitney had sent them—was superior to anything they'd ever come across. He wasn't so certain anymore that Whitney had sent them.

Rubin reached out until he found the owl he was looking for. Great horned owls were powerful, relentless and without fear. More than once, as children, the boys had enlisted the owls as hunting companions. The fierce raptors were ferocious when bringing down large prey, inflicting maximum damage in order to make certain of a quick kill with little or no resistance. The boys had learned a lot from the owls.

The owl was large, but with its coloration it had the ability to camouflage its body by positioning itself onto a tree limb, elongating its body to blend into the bark during the day. Few people would ever spot it. The boys often took to the trees to sleep in, molding their bodies to the tree limbs in an effort to hide from any enemies. Those lessons in stillness had been taught at an early age from their hunting companions.

The owl had been waiting in silence, perched on a limb, using her extraordinary senses to find a meal for the evening. Rubin turned her attention to finding his enemies. She would be his eyes and ears. It was always disorienting to first move from his vision into the vision of another creature, but he had done so often enough that the adjustment came quickly. The owl's night vision was one hundred times sharper than that of a human. He could see ten times clearer, and the owl had a 270-degree neck rotation, allowing him to see so much more.

Rubin studied the forest below him carefully, using the owl's vision and acute hearing. He saw squirrel man with his back to a small tree, one knee drawn up, the other outstretched at an awkward angle and bleeding. He was repairing a wound in his shoulder. He looked battered, but was definitely still alive. He'd found a good place to shelter, completely covered on all four sides. He was also very concerned about the wound in his calf. A field dressing was tight on it, but he fussed with it more than once.

Occasionally he would pause, head going up as if listening to someone speaking to him. He nodded once. Was someone speaking telepathically? The owl caught the whisper of a voice. No, it was a radio, but there was no sign of the receiver. If it was in his ear, it was deep.

The owl studied the body hanging from the tree, upside down, swinging macabrely. Definitely dead. That man wasn't faking. Rubin dismissed him and moved on. The third sniper was located in an old white oak, one of the rarer trees still left that hadn't been taken years earlier. Diego, undoubtedly, had already pinpointed his exact location.

Rubin continued to push to see the entire surrounding forest, the floor as well as the trees. He was patient. The great horned owl could be still for hours waiting for prey. The owl scanned carefully, sifting through the trees, each of the branches individually. It was an enormous task. An hour went by. A second one. He barely noticed the passing of time.

The wounded squirrel man on the ground drew the owl's attention twice when he shifted positions, trying to get comfortable at one point, and then whispered a complaint.

"I'm bleeding again. I think that bastard hand-loads his own bullets and he put something in them to make me bleed like this. Nothing is working to stop it."

There was silence for a long time. Then a slight buzzing sound that indicated someone was speaking. Rubin let the owl sort it out.

"You'd be dead by now if it was bleeding that much."

The owl's head snapped around, not toward the oak where the sniper lay in the crotch but behind the owl, farther away. Much farther. A mile? This man was in the trees as well. These men seemed at home in them. He might have eyes on Diego, but Rubin doubted it. Someone else closer. The one a mile out was the leader of the team, directing them, but the one hanging back, being so silent, he was their ace in the hole, just as Diego had been Rubin's.

Rubin was methodical. These men were comfortable in the trees. They could move fast in them, leaping from tree to tree like flying squirrels. Jonquille might eventually expect that, just as Rubin and Diego would. So their ace would most likely take to the ground. He would locate Diego by the direction of his bullets and creep up on him, using the cover of the dense underbrush.

Rubin directed the owl to sweep the forest floor in the area where Diego had gone to ground. If he was right, his brother would be pinned down by the sniper, unable to change positions while their assassin would be slowly stealing up on him. If Diego chose to defend himself against the one on the ground, the sniper would kill him. He was dead either way. Rubin had to find the assassin on the ground.

Movement caught the eye of the owl, and Rubin's heart stuttered for just one moment. The assassin was close, coming up on Diego from the south side. He knew he'd given Diego knowledge of him by the sudden stillness in his mind.

Don't move. Keep very still. Sending the owl. The leader is watching. Don't know if he's a sniper as well, but we have to assume that he is.

His heart accelerated overtime, something very unusual for him. Rubin always kept himself under control, but this was Diego in danger.

The great horned owl was a raptor, a ferocious hunter. This was her territory and she defended it without fear. She left the branch, lifting into the sky on her wings. She was a deadly killing machine, coming out of the darkness in complete silence and dropping low, talons outstretched toward her prey. The first slash was straight at her victim's eyes, tearing at the orbs with such strength she rolled the man over, removing one eye completely and leaving the other hanging out.

He screamed and threw his arms up in an effort to protect his face and continued rolling. She struck a second time, a terrible blow to the top of his head, leaving behind three four-inch gashes in his scalp. The owl was relentless, striking a third time, tearing with her talons down his arm as he rolled.

Rubin was up and running, leaping over fallen trees and shortened brush, calling to the owl, forcing her away from her prey.

Rifle shots reverberated through the night. One from the sniper covering Diego and one from Rubin's quarry, the team leader who clearly was taking a shot a mile out through trees, both aiming at the owl as she attacked the assassin.

It was too late, Rubin had already called her off and she had risen, circling back toward the sniper closest to Diego, her menacing yellow-orange eyes staring straight into his while her talons slashed at his chest and ripped the rifle from his hands. The sniper nearly fell from the tree and had to leap from one branch to the next in an effort to escape her.

Rubin called to the owl as he ran, using a series of hoots to get her to come to him, fearing the leader would shoot her. Sure enough, the sound of a rifle firing several shots told him the man was doing his best to hit his hunting companion. It only took a couple of minutes, but those two minutes were enough for someone enhanced, such as Rubin, to cover ground fast. He was nearly to the leader's tree.

Diego was up and running toward the wounded squirrel man on the ground, distracting the leader further. The leader was a little larger than the original squirrel man, but still able to move easily through branches and leap from tree to tree with blurring speed. He was small enough that he could land on the limbs of trees that might not hold bigger men like Diego and Rubin, so he could get higher in the canopy without fear of snapping off the more fragile branches.

Without hesitation, Rubin sent the horned owl straight at the leader, not wanting to risk allowing him to get a shot off at Diego. He hated risking the beautiful bird, but he couldn't let his brother get shot.

That wouldn't happen. I'm not that slow. Diego sounded aggravated with him.

Ignoring his brother, Rubin leapt for the lower branches of the tree and pulled himself up fast, using sheer brute strength while the owl began darting in and out of the branches.

An agonized scream heralded the arrival of Diego to the location of the original squirrel man. The leader squeezed off a couple of shots toward Diego and leapt for the next tree. He yelled as the owl tore a gash down his back before he was able to get into a protected shelter of branches where he could fend off the bird's repeated attacks.

Rubin was up the tree and into the next, climbing higher, keeping the pressure on the leader, not wanting to give him a chance to turn the rifle on Diego or the owl again. The great horned owl helped by continuously flapping its wings and darting in and out of the branches trying to get at the man with beak or talons.

Without warning, thunder rolled overhead, a continuous, ominous booming so loud the ground shook. Rubin, not a man given to cursing, knew, once again, the enemy had backup.

Jonquille. Are you safe?

I can handle a little lightning. They're trying to distract you both. They don't want Diego to get any information from the one on the ground. I don't know why, but we seem to be connected in some way. I killed the assassin the owl tore up. He was trying to get to Diego and the other one. He was mostly dead anyway. The persistence he showed told me the one Diego is questioning has important information.

Lightning crackled in the dark clouds directly over Diego's position. Rubin knew Jonquille was very close to his brother and the downed would-be assassin. He glanced down and saw a very small figure leap up from the darker brush. She looked like a tiny fairy, a true lightning bug, dancing like a firefly might at sunset across the tops of the grasses as she raced away from Diego and the man he interrogated. Her hair glowed, a wild display of platinum blond strands standing up like a halo around her head as she threw back the hood of her jacket to attract the lead stroke from the clouds.

Rubin's breath caught in his throat. Energy in the form of sparks circled her small waist, rib cage and outstretched arms and flashed around her legs as she ran, giving more and more the appearance of her dancing in the air. His heart sank as he felt the charging in the air increase.

Stop, Jonquille. You're playing right into their hands. They came for you. This is all about you. They've pulled you away from us. Go back toward Diego. Reverse directions. I can direct the strike away from him.

He knew it was too late. Lightning forked across the sky, cloud to cloud, and then the lead stroke found its path straight to her. He sent out the intercept to direct the bolt away from Diego, but it didn't matter. The target wasn't his brother. The target all along had been Jonquille. The team was desperate to acquire her. Casualties didn't matter, only getting Jonquille mattered.

The dart gun was silent, but he saw it hit her and she went down hard. Fast. One moment standing and the next dropping to the ground. Whatever they used was instantaneous. Rubin leapt from the branch he was on, although he doubted he would get there in time to stop the recovery team from taking Jonquille. He was too far away.

Kill him, Diego, and get to her. Kill as many as you can. At least we can handicap them as they're bringing her off the mountain, he ordered.

He ordered the owl to kill the prey in the tree at all costs. He knew the female raptor would never give up. It would be a battle of life or death between predator and prey. She would keep at him until she ripped every square inch of skin off him. Once on the ground, Rubin ran full out, using every enhanced bit of animal DNA he had to aid him.

He heard the bark of Diego's rifle twice and saw two men go down, but it seemed as if there were at least ten to fifteen men swarming around Jonquille. He counted eight lying prone in a semicircle around her, guns pointed toward Diego's location. These weren't rifles. They weren't semiautomatics. They looked as if they were new-age weapons built to take half the mountainside with them when fired.

Pull back, Diego. Get out of there fast.

The men began to fire simultaneously, making it impossible to see. Great clouds of smoke and debris rose into the air. Craters appeared in the mountain and trees exploded in every direction. They could do little but hunker down until it was over.

Rubin had the presence of mind to check on the owl. She'd managed to rip the rifle from the leader's hands, and once she'd done that, he'd tried to use a knife on her. That had been a mistake, getting him too close. The owl had killed him in much the same way she'd killed the assassin on the ground, going first for his eyes and then ripping at the soft parts of his body like the raptor she was.

The men retreated, two at a time, covering one another in pairs. Rubin raced to check on his brother. Diego had rolled through the brush just before the squirrel men had begun shooting and had found a wide crack just below the stream. He'd wedged himself in it and covered his face and ears while the guns had rained hell down on them.

"Who the hell are these people?" Rubin demanded, after giving his brother a quick inspection to make certain he wasn't injured other than a graze or two. "What did you get out of squirrel man?"

Diego rolled back out of the crevice, lying on his back for a moment, staring up at the smoky sky, breathing hard. "They aren't Whitney's men, and they aren't a terrorist cell either. They've been tracking her for some time." He sat up slowly, shaking his head several times, trying to clear his ears.

Rubin handed him water. They were going to have to move fast, but he needed Diego at full strength, and the concussion from the weapons had nearly knocked him out.

"She's been doing research in laboratories at night for a couple of years on how to reverse what Whitney did to her. She was careful, but apparently not careful enough." Diego got to his feet and slung his rifle in his scabbard. "Where are they taking her? We'll have to get there first."

"They have to have a plane to fly her out of here."

"With those kinds of weapons, they could make a landing strip," Diego said.

"True, but they won't. They can do what they did here, destroy everything and dig big craters in the ground, but they aren't going to be able to take off or land a plane. They have one somewhere. We have to figure out where and get there ahead of them," Rubin said.

"Whitney hired several different brilliant scientists to help him with his experiments," Diego said. "One was an American with way too much money, no morals and, unlike Whitney, no fanatical patriotism. He had ties to several of the men in the military and when he realized the GhostWalker program was successful, he wanted his own personal team. He also saw the potential to sell the abilities of his team for missions, especially when his main purpose for Whitney was developing weapons."

There was little doubt that members of Jonquille's recovery team would be waiting to ambush them when they came after her. There was no way for a group that size to cover their tracks, not when they were moving fast through heavy brush.

"They have a superior force," Diego reminded. "They may not

think they have to move fast. They may decide to send a few of their men after us. They don't care who we are. We're just in their way. They don't want to harm civilians or engage with them if it isn't necessary. They just want to take Jonquille and leave. They think we're civilians."

Rubin and Diego faded back into the trees. They didn't need to track the men holding Jonquille. They needed to figure out where they would take her. Rubin considered that carefully. These men wouldn't want to be seen. They were a large party. They liked to stay in trees. They seemed to be at home in the mountain environment, so much so that neither Rubin nor Diego had known they were anywhere near. The animals hadn't tipped them off.

They would need the least-traveled way possible but one where there might be a very clear meadow out of the woods at the very bottom of the trails. There was only one place that he knew of. Old man Gunthrie lived at the end of a holler, down a dirt road few ever traveled. It was at the very base of the mountain trail, but so far in and covered over that it was long forgotten. No cars or bicycles ever used it and hadn't for years. That suited Gunthrie just fine. Edward and Rory Sawyer had just mentioned that Gunthrie had even encouraged plants to cover the road further so that it had completely disappeared. According to them, there was no evidence of it off the main road.

Gunthrie had lost his wife six years earlier. They'd never had children. Neighbors moved away and he'd been forgotten. He didn't drive. He walked everywhere he went, even for supplies. A recluse, he had few manners, was gruff and surly to everyone, even those at the grocery store. He mainly trapped and fished for his food and had his own garden.

Rubin and Diego visited with him on their way when they were leaving the mountains, checking to make sure he was still alive.

They joked he would live forever. When they would talk with him, he would squat down in a crouch and give them his faint grin, remaining in that position for hours. He had no idea how old he was, but he was strangely ageless, with thick white hair that never seemed to thin. Rubin was suddenly very afraid for him.

Behind his shack, which was made up mostly of corrugated tin, and an outhouse stretched a long, inviting meadow. With a little work, one might be able to smooth it out, and if you had a good pilot, you could land a small plane in it.

"Gunthrie's place," Rubin guessed, a sense of dread filling him. The man might be old and strange, but he didn't deserve to be murdered at the hands of a bunch of strangers.

Diego nodded his head and the two began to set a fast, steady pace, not running, but a pace they could keep up for hours.

Tell me everything you learned from squirrel man, Rubin encouraged. Even as they moved fast through the forest, they maintained a ten-foot distance apart, barely disturbing the limbs or bushes as they hurried past.

This scientist, a man by the name of Oliver Chandler, who Whitney hired to develop weapons, began to study Whitney's advanced Ghost-Walker experiments. Chandler had access to Whitney's private notes because he would visit Whitney's laboratories to see the experiments on a regular basis. Whitney would discuss GhostWalkers with him and the failures of the female soldiers. In particular, he discussed Jonquille. She was a little girl at the time, but Whitney wanted to use lightning as a weapon. Oliver wanted his own GhostWalker team.

Rubin leapt over a particularly large downed tree trunk. Several rabbits ran in all directions, startled by his sudden presence. *Are you telling me this Chandler managed to make supersoldiers for himself better than Whitney?*

Whitney makes us for his country, Diego reminded. *He gives his best to his country. He continues experimenting with those he considers flawed. Oliver didn't necessarily recruit these men from a flawed genetic pool.*

Rubin let that process. Diego was right. Whitney might be insane, but he was a patriot. Everything he did, he did with the idea he was making his soldiers and his country safer. Like the girls he pulled from orphanages, the "flawed" soldiers were expendable, so Whitney performed all kinds of experiments on them. Apparently Oliver Chandler wanted superb GhostWalker soldiers for his own use.

Was Chandler just as capable as Whitney of performing the same surgeries? Enhancing psychic ability? Adding to the DNA sequencing? That's extremely precise surgery. Not everyone can do it. I wouldn't think that someone Whitney hired as a specialist in developing weapons would be a surgeon capable of what Whitney does.

He brought in a team from India, very advanced in this kind of thing. According to what squirrel man—and how did you start calling him that?—told me, that team was beyond excited with what little Chandler dangled in front of them to get them to come. They enhanced thirty-one soldiers. Seven died on the table. Twenty-four survived. Of those twenty-four, fifteen are in relatively good shape. Nine are . . . expendable. The soldiers don't consider one another expendable. Chandler considers them that way. The one I was interrogating was one of the expendable ones.

Relatively good shape? Rubin echoed. *They looked in good enough shape to me.*

They continued through the forest, rushing around trees and leaping over smaller bushes, ducking low-hanging branches but never slowing their pace. They had been running for at least two hours when a low hoot came off to Rubin's left. A great horned owl emerged out of the darkness close to his head, flying low and fast, shooting in and out of the trees.

Rubin and Diego both dropped to the forest floor and made their way to the heavier growth of trees a hundred feet in the middle of the grove they were passing through.

Company tracking us, Rubin announced. *Two of them. In the trees. Freaky little squirrel men. That's how I think of them. They jump from one tree to the next so fast, they remind me of flying squirrels.*

They are fast, Diego agreed. *Chandler blew up the plane that was taking that first team back home so they couldn't share what they knew about the GhostWalkers. But then he wasn't very happy with this team because they didn't want to run his private missions for him, the ones that would make him money. He wanted another team, one that was loyal to him. Chandler started noticing his team wasn't quite as up to par as he would have liked.*

Rubin hissed his displeasure with the unknown Chandler. He was even worse than Whitney. *Do these soldiers think they're committing to the actual GhostWalker program?*

I believe so, yes. They're pulled from every branch of the service and have to undergo and pass all testing. In any case, this first team is after Jonquille, and they are determined to acquire her at any cost. Five of those they consider expendables have some link to Jonquille. Each has something different. It was all genetic material that Whitney had slated for disposal but gave to Chandler to study in case it helped him in the development of his lightning weapons.

Again, Rubin took time to think that over. *That's how they track her. Get someone in her general vicinity and then seed the clouds to draw her out. What do they need her for? They've gone to a lot of trouble to get her.*

He went up a tree, using his hands only, careful not to leave any trace behind that he had stopped moving and was settled, waiting for the assassins coming up behind him. Very slowly, so that he didn't disturb any foliage or bark, he placed his pack in the tree and shifted positions again, knowing this particular oak would entice one of the squirrel men to use it as a springboard to the next one.

Rubin waited in silence. The wind ruffled the leaves of the trees. A light rain began to fall. The frogs increased their chorus to a joyful, loud cacophony of sounds. He could pick out the individual species, males calling to females, females enticing males. He heard the rustle of mice in the leaves on the forest floor. The skitter of lizards running over trees. Raccoons chattered at one another and skunks shuffled through the brush. Life moved in the forest.

He didn't move. Like the great horned owl that elongated its body and was frozen and still during the day, essentially becoming part of the tree it rested in unseen, Rubin was nearly invisible. The tree nearest his shivered, leaves shaking off droplets of water, and then something heavy landed nearly at his feet.

The man was lean and wiry, a compact combination of muscle and bone. He paused for a moment, taking a breath. Behind him, the tree came to unexpected life, Rubin materializing behind him, catching his head in a merciless lock. The squirrel man went crazy, knowing he was in a life-or-death struggle, throwing himself backward, trying to break the hold Rubin had on him. Rubin twisted, breaking the neck with his superior strength, lowering the body to the crotch of the tree, wedging it there so he could examine it.

One down, Diego. Radio is in the ear. Fingernails are longer than usual, and he's wearing special open-toed shoes that allow his toenails to work the way a squirrel's might. He's got venom sacs located along his ankle. Strange place for it, but that means a scratch with his toenails probably could kill, if this venom is lethal. We have to assume it is.

I noticed that the toenails and fingernails were extremely thick on the assassin I was interrogating, Diego said.

That's how they climb so well and cling to the branches when they land. The clothes they wear are aerodynamic as well. Each piece is streamlined, almost glued to their bodies, although very weatherproof. The vest looks more like you might expect with a wing suit, which when they leap gives them the appearance of a flying squirrel. They don't have wings or webbing, but they do have artificial help.

Why doesn't it get caught in the branches of the trees? Diego asked. *That would make them larger and bulkier.*

They have to train precisely to retract before they hit the branches, Rubin guessed. *They moved with such blurring speed. We can't underestimate them for a minute. Our advantage is going to be that they'll underestimate us.*

So far, I hadn't noticed that we have too many advantages, Diego said. *And we're on our home turf.*

Rubin had to agree with him there. The fact that they hadn't realized there was an entire team waiting to take Jonquille from them in their own forest, even with the great horned owl watching for them, was humbling. They were so sure of themselves in the woods, and that could have cost Jonquille dearly. Even if they lost her temporarily, they would get her back. He'd call in their team and find a way to track her. He was tenacious, if nothing else. She had to know he'd be coming for her.

Did you bring a tracker with you?

I always do, why? Diego asked.

Just in case, Rubin said. *I want to be ready for anything.*

We're going to get her back.

Yeah. I know. But Rubin wasn't so certain.

Have you located his partner? Diego asked.

No, but he has to be close. This one was no doubt lead. The second one is probably coming up behind him by a mile or so. The good news is, we know the number of men they have in their unit. They're losing them fast.

From his vantage point in the oak, Rubin looked at the surrounding trees. The oak was the largest and sturdiest of those growing in that particular region. The forest was particularly thick with spruce and oak. The section hadn't been logged in decades, and many of the original trees were still intact.

The two assassins were following Rubin and Diego to kill them. They didn't appear to know anything about either man. They hadn't expected them to be with Jonquille. They didn't expect either man to turn back on them and hunt them. The squirrel men were moving fast, clearly believing themselves superior to their adversaries. Would the second assassin take the line of least resistance and use the same tree as the first one? Rubin would have boxed Diego's ears for making a mistake like that, but it was possible these men had never been up against actual soldiers with the same skills and abilities as they had. One of their weaknesses might be that they were just a little bit lazy.

When you interrogated the squirrel man, what did he say he knew about Jonquille? Why did they want her?

He didn't have time to tell me. He died. That was the weird thing. He kept bleeding. That wound shouldn't have killed him, but it just wouldn't stop bleeding.

You didn't load your bullets with something to make him bleed out, did you? Rubin poured suspicion into his voice.

You're so funny, although that's not a bad idea.

It wasn't the wound, but something else. Could he have been using first-generation Zenith? By now, everyone knows not to use it. Whitney had to have warned all his colleagues that it does give any soldier in the field using it the necessary clotting to stop bleeding and the adrenaline to keep going, and then it does the exact opposite and kills them. That's common knowledge.

Diego's sigh was in his mind. *I saw no evidence of a Zenith patch, first or second generation. Whitney might not have warned Chandler because he wouldn't have known Chandler was creating his own personal army of elite soldiers. Whitney wouldn't have liked that, and he would have put a stop to it. I don't think he bled out because of Zenith. It was something else. Another reason.*

These men could be experiencing problems in the same way some of the other GhostWalkers do, Rubin guessed. *The squirrel man you interrogated said nine were expendable. Maybe that meant they weren't perfect. They had flaws like the orphans. Like Jonquille.*

The last thing he wanted was for Chandler to use Jonquille in more experiments. She'd been adamant that she wasn't going back to Whitney ever again. She'd rather be dead. No doubt she felt the same way if Chandler was going to experiment on her.

You said Jonquille was doing research in laboratories. What kind of research? Rubin asked. He wasn't going to get into a discussion with his brother on how to load his own bullets with some kind of chemical that might make a flesh wound bleed more, nor did he want to think about what kind of experiment they might perform on Jonquille instead of on one of their soldiers.

I would think it would have to be something to do with lightning. You're the lightning expert. They're developing weapons, right? That's Chandler's thing. She's the lightning bug, so to speak.

Rubin considered Jonquille *his* lightning bug, not the government's. Or Whitney's. Certainly not Oliver Chandler's. Or his team of elite soldiers. What did this team want with her, and what research was she doing? He shouldn't have treated her like an experiment. Diego was right, he didn't have any real social skills. He hadn't considered he might need them if he found the right woman. He'd never bothered. He didn't stay very long in anyone's company.

Did squirrel man mention which weapons they were developing?

Just about everything. The ball lightning—they have the use of that as a weapon. It isn't known. The project was stopped supposedly for a variety of reasons, but they found the answers they needed for a delivery system and shut down funding to all other research, leaving everyone else without a means to complete them. They can create ball lightning and shoot it at a target.

Rubin thought about that. He wasn't surprised by it. Several of the laboratories had been able to create ball lightning and shoot it at a target in the lab. He knew the military had the resources already sewn up in that area for weapons.

They also can do exactly what you did using Jonquille, although not quite as efficiently. Their ability to target using the real thing is not very effective because the split-second trajectory and timing even for a computer is not accurate.

Rubin believed that. Every experiment that he knew of had run into the same problem, other than the ones he'd personally conducted.

Why are you accurate when a computer isn't? Diego asked.

I'm accurate with Jonquille. Not with every lightning storm. I'm already tuned to her. I can feel the lightning just the way she can. Without her, I think I'd hit the same percentage as the computer, but with her, I'm going to be one hundred percent accurate every time.

A prickle of awareness went through his body, just as it did every time an enemy was close. *He's here. Coming closer. Not as fast as his partner.*

He hadn't heard the buzz of the radio in the partner's ear, so there was no contact between the two men. They definitely had confidence when they moved through the forest that they could track their prey. Like both Rubin and Diego, they used their enhancements—sight, smell, the senses of animals—to tell them what was happening in the forest around them.

Rubin and Diego gave off the scent of the woods. They blended in. They were accepted. The mountains were their domain and had been since they were born. Most of the creatures, like the raptors had at one time or another, hunted with them and benefited from it. They were conservators of the forest and its inhabitants. Both were careful of the fragile ecosystem, but they did their best to preserve their part of the Appalachian Mountains.

Once more, Rubin stayed very still, his body blending in with the thick tree trunk of the old oak. The assassin landed in a spruce about forty feet away, causing a brief little shiver of the branches. The tree went still and stayed that way for a good three minutes. Squirrel man didn't launch himself as expected into the next tree. He didn't seem to be in any hurry to catch up with his partner.

Rubin focused on him now that he knew where he was. Squir-rel man took a small envelope out of the tight vest he had zipped around him, slit it open with a long fingernail and emptied the contents into his mouth. He returned the envelope to the inside of the vest and zipped the vest again. Once zipped, the vest seemed to glue itself to him. The clothing was exceptional. Whitney was always working on camouflage clothing for the soldiers, wanting to ensure whatever they wore would allow them to fade completely into the background of whatever environment they were in. The clothes the squirrel men wore were very sophisticated.

The man turned to face the next large tree. There were several smaller ones in his way. Rubin wanted to see how he maneuvered through the branches of all the trees to get to the one he wanted. He realized the squirrel men didn't fly. It wasn't as if they could be in the air for long distances. They didn't have air packs. They literally were jumping from tree to tree.

He watched as the assassin took two steps on the branch and threw his body into the air, arms out and then in, out again, and then in, like a diver, moving with that amazing speed, just like one of the birds flying around the branches to get to the next tree. Rubin could see he'd already chosen his course. He knew where he was going, had mapped it out in his mind and had followed that path. He'd chosen the branch he was going to land on as well as the exact spot.

Again, the assassin took his time, settling on the limb, giving himself a little break before the next leap. Why? Rubin studied him carefully. As a doctor he was quick to see the elevation in breathing. The squirrel man's chest was heaving. He was taking deep, slow breaths to get his breathing back under control. The moment he did, he looked to the next tree—the large oak. This time the assassin didn't waste time. Again, he took the two steps and launched himself.

Rubin could have admired the speed and precision if it weren't for the need to move quickly to get to Gunthrie's place ahead of the team with Jonquille. Hopefully, the old-timer was alive. The old man had even survived his still blowing up once. Fortunately, he hadn't been around when it happened, but that just went to show you the luck the old man had. Rubin hoped his luck was still holding.

Squirrel man landed on the same branch the lead assassin had perched on. The moment his toenails dug into the branch, he must have smelled death, because he started to turn. Rubin was on him before that could happen. Once again, his tremendous strength and his own speed prevailed. He snapped the assassin's neck without giving him time to put up a fight.

This man seemed far less able to fight, too winded. Rubin didn't take the time to examine him, not even psychically, but he was certain if he did, he would find that this was one of the men considered "flawed" and expendable. He hoped Jonquille wasn't considered expendable. He had to get to her as fast as possible. He did take time to check the rifle the assassin was carrying. It was loaded with darts, not bullets.

11

Luther Gunthrie's home hadn't changed since he'd first found old used sheets of corrugated metal and carried them, one by one, over miles of trail, walking with each sheet over his head to bring it to the chosen spot where he'd decided to build his house. He was tenacious when he wanted something, and he loved the hidden piece of paradise he called his. He built the cabin with his own two hands. He built his outhouse next and then his outdoor shower.

He developed a spring that ran all year round to meet his water needs. There was plenty of fish. He could hunt or trap. He did have a bicycle for two once he married. His bride, Lotty, had been the love of his life. The two would pedal to the grocery store on the bike. You never saw one without the other. Luther always stayed close to his Lotty. They did everything together.

The trail leading to the rugged holler that went back to his home was so overgrown a person wouldn't recognize that it had ever been an actual path at one time. Gunthrie preferred it that way. Since his beloved Lotty had gone, he stayed more and more to himself and discouraged visitors, particularly the official kind that he believed came looking for his still.

One had to trek a long way from the main trail to find the entrance to the holler, and then it was another mile or so in before you came across his cabin. The building was nearly hidden among the trees and overgrown grasses and bush. One would never know that just another forty feet behind the building was the most magnificent clearing surrounded on all sides by woods. The meadow was gorgeous and Lotty had loved it. Luther had transplanted every kind of wildflower they found in the woods that she fell in love with, into the meadow, just for her.

She had a garden there that he had built a fence around to protect from the deer. He claimed he thought it silly, but she loved it, so she got it. Whatever Lotty wanted, she got, and in return, she spoiled Luther as best she could. She painstakingly patched every hole in his clothing and mended every sock. She bartered for skins so she could make him shoes and vests and jackets. She knitted blankets and crocheted lacy curtains.

Their little cabin was cozy and had little feminine touches meant to give Luther a sense of being cared for. There wasn't a time when he came home, even if he'd been gone for a while, that there wasn't a cooking pot on the fire. She massaged his feet for him, especially in the winter when he went out hunting, and warmed his hands the moment he came in. Lotty had been as devoted to Luther as he was to her.

Early on, when Rubin first came back home to visit, checking up on the couple, bringing them rabbits to put in the stewpot, Luther had yarn stretched between his hands while she knitted him a sweater. He glared at Rubin, daring him to say something, but Rubin took notice that a man should treat his woman good that way. Lotty always seemed happy. Rubin liked Gunthrie a lot, in spite of the man being a bit rascally at times.

Diego and Rubin stayed above the homestead, studying every inch of it, looking for signs of life. There weren't any high ridges to get over it, so they both had chosen one of the taller trees. Still, they needed a broader scope than what they were seeing. Both were tired. They'd been too long without sleep, but after running all night, they'd definitely gotten to the meadow before the soldiers who had taken Jonquille prisoner—if they had guessed the destination correctly.

Tired could equal mistakes, and getting Jonquille back was their first priority. That meant no mistakes could be made. The meadow looked as if it hadn't been touched. The flowers were in bloom. There were no holes or bare spots to indicate that anyone had been digging to try to smooth the meadow to prepare it for a plane to land.

Rubin's heart sank. Had he guessed wrong? He rubbed his jaw. The stubble there was beginning to get heavier. Each of those hairs was embedded in nerve endings, and those nerve endings helped to identify everything around him. He could find no evidence of the squirrel men. That didn't mean much. He hadn't been able to locate them when they had been secreted in the woods waiting to abduct Jonquille.

There's no sign of Gunthrie in his cabin, Diego said. *He's an early riser. He'd be up, moving around by now.*

Rubin was very aware of that. No matter his age, Gunthrie didn't believe in staying in bed. Even on days when he claimed his bones ached, he said it was better to get up and move around, which was right. Gunthrie chose to sleep on a woven mat on the floor. After Lotty passed away, Gunthrie burned their bed, the one he'd carved for her. He'd hauled the mattress all the way from

CHRISTINE FEEHAN

where the neighboring farm brought it on the back of their truck and left it by the entrance to the holler. He'd burned that mattress as well.

Others might not have understood, but Rubin did. That kind of gut-wrenching loss did things to you. Stayed with you and twisted you up inside. He knew why Gunthrie chose to live out his life alone in the backwoods, barely seeing anyone else. It hurt to lose the people you loved. It hurt to be afraid all the time that you were going to lose more.

Rubin was aware he held on to Diego too tightly, as he did Ezekiel, Mordichai, Malichai and now Jonquille. The squirrel men had made a mistake when they'd taken Jonquille. The healer in him, usually at the forefront, had been pushed far back and the predator was fully unleashed.

Do you think I was wrong? This was the only place they could possibly land a plane. It's possible they aren't going to fly her out. Another method of transport?

Diego continued to survey the peaceful scene below. *It's possible, Rubin. We made good time. We know the terrain and they don't. They were just as tired as we were. They have a large force and believe themselves invincible. They could have camped somewhere for the night and planned to bring her here sometime during the day. That means they'll send a crew here to get a landing strip ready. They wouldn't have bothered if they couldn't acquire her. They wouldn't want to raise suspicion.*

Diego was right. The ground crew had to be close by. Already here. They wouldn't use Gunthrie's shack. They'd camp out using high-tech gear. Where would they camp that any locals wouldn't ever spot them? And would they have spared Gunthrie until they actually needed to kill him? Probably not. He was a loose cannon. He would be too likely to spot them moving around in his part of the woods. At some point they would have to examine the meadow

218

to see how difficult it would be to quickly build a landing strip for a plane.

They're here, Diego, they're here somewhere. They came here and they made the decision to kill that old man.

We don't know that for certain. Diego was cautionary.

If there was one person on earth who knew Rubin, it was Diego. He knew that place inside of him that was deep and wide. Whitney had found it and just expanded it.

You know. Rubin breathed the truth into his brother's mind. The burn of rage was slow in coming and it wasn't red and volcanic. It was cold like ice, like a glacier. That cold. A flame that never died, that would hunt one to the ends of the earth if necessary, just keep going until it was done. That was Rubin's way. That was the way he felt now.

Just the thought of these men, these outsiders, cold-bloodedly coming to Luther Gunthrie's home and possibly killing him, took that last piece of civilization from him. He felt it go, just as he had felt it when he had found his sister's body so long ago in that cold stream. His mind shut down to everything but the task of hunting.

Diego instantly felt the difference in his mind. *We don't know if Luther's dead, Rubin.*

Doesn't much matter, Diego. They came here to kill him. An old man like that. They came here to take her. Wherever they plan to take her, it isn't somewhere good. They're here. I can feel them.

More, now that he was certain, now that he was fully in predator mode, he could smell them. They had set foot on Gunthrie land.

The ground crew won't be their elite soldiers, Rubin surmised. *They wouldn't expect any real opposition. Jonquille was their opposition. They expected a fight from her. They didn't know about us. They wouldn't waste manpower on locals, so the elite soldiers were reserved for acquiring her.*

The ground crew assigned to building a landing strip at the last minute will be ordinary soldiers with maybe one elite soldier leading them.

There were few meadows like the one Gunthrie had. It was long enough for a small plane to land and take off in. A good pilot could easily do it. If Jonquille had been alone, and she had been surprised as the soldiers had hoped, they would have taken their time bringing her down the mountain. The last thing these soldiers wanted was to draw attention to themselves. That meant they didn't want to tear up the meadow until they had to. Bulldozing the ground was definitely going to draw attention. The crew and equipment had to be close but hidden under camouflage, easy enough to do if one knew how.

Where are they, Rubin?

He thought about where the ground crew would be camping. They would be close enough to keep an eye on Gunthrie's property and the meadow. They would be out of sight, completely off the beaten path of any stray hikers or any of the locals.

Diego, put a bird in the air, one of the early morning songbirds. Have it search the entire area for Luther and then have it fly over the old mill by Huntington Falls. Let's see if anyone is camping there.

You still calling it that?

Rubin didn't reply. Yeah, he had always referred to the little series of waterfalls as Huntington Falls. No one else did because the falls were really nothing more than a series of large rocks with water pouring over them. Rubin had an imagination, and he would name everything so he could go back and tell his sisters his stories. Huntington Falls had become the home of many fairies who hid when the trolls came out.

When he and Diego would return to the mountains to check on patients, and Luther wasn't around, he would find himself telling Lotty the same silly stories he had told his sisters on the cold wintry nights that were so dreary and gloomy. She always acted delighted. Yeah, he would always call that place Huntington Falls and have fond memories of it.

Once, Lotty had gone with them and brought an armful of wild daffodils, and she'd thrown them into the whirling pool at the bottom of the falls, one by one, as he'd told her a story. She had made strawberry lemonade and cucumber and fish sandwiches for lunch for Diego and Rubin.

She never complained and always seemed happy, even though both men knew her life had to be somewhat lonely. When they came to check on her and visit, they always brought fresh meat, but also supplies and novelties such as jams and buttons and threads and things they knew Lotty would have trouble getting.

Once, she showed them a hand-croqueted lacy shawl their mother had sent to Lotty on her wedding day. Lotty treasured it. Rubin knew his mother would have needed that shawl herself, but she'd gifted it to Lotty. That was the way of the people they'd grown up with. No matter the dire circumstances, or the extreme poverty, they tried to help one another.

Huntington Falls was as sacred to Rubin as the Gunthrie property, another memory he associated with his sisters and Lotty. To have outsiders—killers—come in and desecrate it was disturbing to him on many levels.

Yeah. I'll always think of it as Huntington Falls. I took the twins there one time. Snuck them out of the house in the middle of the night. Thought we'd be back before sunup. Thought we'd make it back in time to get the chores done in the morning. You covered our asses, remember?

Diego had. He'd fed the few chickens the foxes hadn't gotten, collected eggs and done as many chores as possible before their mother had gotten up. Rubin and the twins had gotten in a whole hell of a lot of trouble. Rubin had taken it stoically, as he always did.

You always made up your mind to do something and you just did it.

That was the truth. It was a big part of his personality. If Rubin defied the rules, he always weighed the consequences ahead of time and decided whether it was worth it. Giving his sisters a little bit of magic in a grim world was worth a beating with a belt or the lack of dinner for a night or two. Usually, the girls or Diego snuck him food if that was the punishment. If they couldn't slip him food, he could go hungry. It was that simple.

You're still like that, Diego added.

Rubin couldn't argue with that assessment either. He was. Regardless of what those in authority said, he always acted on what he believed to be right or wrong. He had a strong sense of justice. He figured someday that was going to be the thing that got him in the end. He was in the service, and one couldn't flagrantly violate authority. Luckily, he was in the GhostWalker program, which allowed for some leeway, but he still had to answer to his unit.

He did try to do the right thing. He did follow his mother's advice. And Ezekiel's. They both pushed education. Rubin and Diego set up a scholarship fund for the families in their region to be educated. The money covered not only the tuition but books and lodging as well. The most difficult part was often getting the children comfortable with leaving the freedom of the mountains for what seemed the restrictions of city life.

Rubin loved the people, their connection to one another, their history and culture and their fierce independence. It could be said his history was one of tragedy, but when he was in the mountains long enough, he remembered why he came back every year. He remembered the moments of peace. Of happiness. There had been times of joy. Laughter. Not everything had been a struggle. The struggles had given him strength. The little moments had taught him the core values that made up who he was. Who Diego was. Those were the reasons he kept returning. Neighbors like Luther and Lotty Gunthrie. Mathew Sawyer. There were other families. He remembered them. Ones that had so little but were always willing to share what they had when it was needed.

Going to take a little time, Diego said.

Yeah. Get some sleep, Diego. Let the birds watch.

Rubin closed his eyes and let his body rest. That was another thing he'd learned at a very young age. Sleep when he could, especially when hunting human vermin. One often had to travel under the cover of darkness, and he learned he would have to exist on one or two hours of sleep. He could close his eyes and still be aware of danger. Like the great horned owl, he concealed himself in the trees and stayed very still, but he slept, waiting for Diego's songbird to return. He'd told Diego to let the birds watch for them, and they would, but both men would have their radars set to warn them just in case. They never left anything to chance.

Even resting, it was difficult to turn his brain off. At first his mind seemed quiet, but then he felt small pulses of energy, like tiny strikes of lightning hitting right around the edges, jabbing at him. Each poke felt like a tiny laser point that came and went fast. A fiery flick, no more. He kept his eyes closed and his breathing even. Waiting. Was it real? His mind jumped fast from one subject to the next.

The body was made up of all kinds of energy. That was one of the largest experiments that raged on teleportation. How did one actually teleport without destroying the body? Some scientists said it was impossible. He knew it wasn't, but no one knew how those that had that gift actually did it. Strides were being made in manipulating lightning. He was particularly interested in those studies. He'd contributed to them heavily.

A series of thunderstorms had been predicted in the coming weeks, another reason he'd come earlier than he'd originally planned. Thunderstorms brought lightning to the Appalachian trails, and he knew exactly where the most strikes generally occurred. He'd talked often with the major general and his team commander, Joe Spagnola, about how, inside laboratories, lightning was controlled with laser beams, but outside, they failed to work. He was certain he could figure out the reason. He was close to the answer. If he could, they could keep lightning from destroying personal property, crops, homes . . .

Those little strikes had faded. He didn't move. Didn't open his eyes. He thought about the weapon Oliver Chandler's elite team had used to abduct Jonquille. The weapon had seemed to utilize lightning. Not ball lightning. It was another kind of weapon shot from a very small handheld device that looked like a gun. It didn't look heavy. He hadn't had time to examine the craters or the way the trees had exploded, leaving nothing but splinters behind. Certainly, the weapon seemed to duplicate a lightning strike, sending an energy charge that reacted like a bolt, but it wasn't the same. It wasn't real lightning.

The other thing he needed to consider, Rubin decided, his mind becoming even more active, was the fact that the weapon used against them earlier was laser driven for certain, but mostly, rather than going for accuracy, they had tried to keep Diego and Rubin off them so they could get Jonquille away without a firefight. Hopefully, that meant they didn't want to chance harming her.

Those little pulses of energy returned, tiny strikes hitting around the edges of his mind, jabbing like laser points, that same fiery flick that he'd felt earlier. There was no mistake. The sensation was weak, but it was repeated, a series of quick beats. He took a breath and let it out but didn't react in any way. There was no feel of Jonquille. No pouring of her into his mind. The familiar, intimate energy that came with her entry was entirely missing.

What had Diego said? He had interrogated the squirrel man. Five of the assassins chasing her had been given a part of what Whitney had considered "garbage." He'd frozen Jonquille's DNA, and Oliver Chandler had used it. Was it possible one of the squirrel men was trying to trick him into revealing his location? Was it Jonquille? Was he losing his mind?

The sensation stopped again after approximately the same amount of time as the first sequence had run. Rubin played it back in his head over and over. Each beat. Slow fast. Each strike. If it was Jonquille, he needed to know she was alive and well and what she was trying to say to him. If she was reaching out this way, it meant someone could intercept. Could hear them even if they spoke telepathically—or at least know if she was speaking telepathically. If one was sensitive to energy, one could feel it. She was extremely sensitive. Anyone like her would know immediately if she was trying to communicate with him telepathically.

Diego. You awake?

I am now.

His brother made him want to smile. He always sounded like such a grump when he didn't get his sleep.

You're such a baby.

You woke me up to tell me that? I might remind you I do have my favorite rifle with me.

Rubin wanted to laugh even in the middle of the mess they were in. He loved his brother. *Fortunately for me, as bloodthirsty as you are, you'll have to wait until we've narrowed the odds down a bit. Even you need help.*

There was a little space of time, as if Diego were giving it some thought. Then a sigh in his mind. *Get to the point.*

This has happened twice now. Don't know if it's Jonquille, or someone else trying to draw me out. I think it's her. Listen to the beats and tell me what you think she's trying to say.

Rubin replayed the little lightning strikes for his brother. The first sequence, and then the second. Diego replayed them several times in his mind.

Definitely identical and man-made. You didn't make those up.

That was a little bit of a relief. Rubin had been concerned he was so worried about Jonquille that he might have been seeking any sign of her while he was allowing his mind to drift in his sleep. Making up things just to convince himself he hadn't deserted her.

It has a rhythm to it, Rubin. One that's repeated and has to mean something. A code of some kind? When you corresponded, did you two have shorthand you typed in?

Rubin didn't answer right away. He hadn't thought of Jonquille as his research assistant. She was his lightning bug. She was brilliant. A healer. A mountain woman. Tough as nails, yet soft inside. He should have known. His researcher had been brilliant. She could keep up with him on anything he asked for.

Give me a minute, the songbird is back, Diego said. *I need to get the information.* He was silent for several minutes. *Six men camping at Huntington Falls,* Diego reported.

Relief swept through Rubin. He'd been right. He knew they were there. He didn't like that they were close to Gunthrie's home, but he knew where they were bringing Jonquille.

They'll need more than six men to make that meadow into a landing strip fast. *There have to be more. And someone has to be watching Gunthrie's place as well as the main road. Did the bird spot anyone?*

Diego sighed. *You used to have patience. I was getting to that. It looks like heavy machinery and trucks concealed under netting and branches about three miles in along the holler going into Gunthrie's home. Close, but not quite there.*

Rubin wasn't a man given to cursing. There was no way Luther would fail to feel the vibration of heavy trucks coming toward his home even if he didn't hear it—and no one said his hearing had gone.

Four men with the machinery. They looked to be heavily armed, Rubin.

That still didn't account for roving guards or Luther. This was a large force for one small woman. They really wanted Jonquille. They weren't taking any chances with losing her. With the force of elite soldiers surrounding her and those here waiting, the puzzle was growing. It couldn't just be about her ability to attract lightning, could it? That didn't make sense. The abduction had been planned carefully and carried out fast and efficiently. If Rubin and Diego hadn't come early to the mountains, no one would have known that Jonquille existed. She would simply have disappeared, and no one would ever have been the wiser.

Sentries? he prompted.

One is close to Luther's house, roving. He's moving clockwise. The other is moving counterclockwise in a larger circle to the outside of the shack, taking in the meadow, but also keeping an eye on the shack.

What did that mean? Could Luther be alive? Why would they worry about the house? They weren't entering it. He took a breath. He had to know.

Luther?

No sign of the old coot. Songbird went over the ridge where he last had his still. Wasn't there.

Rubin closed his eyes for a brief moment. That didn't mean Luther was dead. He was cunning. This was his turf. He would have had advance warning—maybe. Rubin wanted to think so. He reluctantly opened his eyes and took another slow scan of the area, studying Luther's shack, the outhouse, the outside shower and then the surrounding woods and brush.

His heart stilled when he saw the birds beginning to circle. A lazy glide in the sky to the south of him. It was only three, but three meant more were coming.

You notice a few vultures circling a couple of miles from here? Along that ridge where the old still used to be?

Could be Luther caught a couple of rabbits in his traps, Diego said hopefully.

If Luther had caught rabbits in a trap, he would have pulled them out of the trap, even with danger circling him. He didn't waste meat. He'd cache it somewhere, just like one of the larger animals would.

Rubin gathered up his gear. He wasn't wasting time. If Luther was injured, he would need help fast, especially if he was being hunted. The team leader wouldn't send his unit after an old man. At most he'd send two soldiers. He wouldn't know that old man would be hard to kill. Rubin was going to make certain that if Luther was still alive, he would remain that way. If he wasn't, someone was going to pay for his death.

Send the songbirds to track Jonquille and the squirrel men. I want advance warning so we know where they are at all times. Have sentries posted at Huntington Falls to keep us informed, and more with the trucks.

Give me a minute, Diego said. *Getting a flock that big to do what I want isn't easy. You'll need backup, Rubin.*

Like hell, he would. *Catch up later.*

Rubin scanned the area one last time and then jumped from the tree, landing in a crouch on the ground, his legs absorbing the shock. He stayed still, listening for sounds, letting the wind carry information to him. Just because he was making an educated guess that the elite soldiers weren't going to waste manpower on a ground crew for grunt work didn't mean he was right. Even if he was right, more than likely the leader of the ground crew was one of the elite. Those soldiers were every bit as good in the woods as Diego. At least some of them were.

He began to pick his way through the heavier brush to find a trail that led up toward the ridge, one that wouldn't give movement away. This was mostly flatland. The uphill was sparse with few trees, and those were scrub pine, sugar pine and one or two straggly spruce trees rising above the thick brush. Animal tunnels abounded. Rabbits and foxes clearly made their way through the brambles of wild berries and thorns. Some of the branches were dried and could easily snap, alerting both wildlife and any sentry. If Luther was being hunted, his killers would hear.

In some places Rubin went to his belly and crawled through the tunnels, in others he stayed low using the uneven terrain to hide his forward movement. He was good at blending in, blurring his image when he needed to and using every advantage that he had. He covered the distance quickly, eating up the first mile fast, the second half mile just as quickly and then slowing significantly, circling around to come at what appeared to be something large the birds were interested in.

The vultures were still high, wings spread wide, a lazy, slow perusal, but their eyes were on a prize below them. They hadn't settled on the ground, or in a nearby bush—they were still checking out their intended meal. That made Rubin wary, and maybe hopeful that if that was a body—Luther's body—he was still alive.

He trilled softly, a short series of low singing notes like an early morning songbird. He waited for a few minutes, hunkered down in the dirt. There was no answer. He was going to have to move closer.

Even another three feet higher, the grass would barely cover his head if he was lying flat. There were more boulders than brush until one hit the actual ridge. The wide expanse of ground cover looked like a giant layer of rocks wedged into the sparse grasses before once again turning into brush and timber. It was as if there were a band around that section of earth. The uphill was slight, not at all like the trails leading to his cabin, where the elevation was much steeper.

Rubin went into his "gecko" mode. He flattened his body as much as possible and allowed his skin coloring to change to match the background of the rocks and grass. His clothing reflected the terrain around him, blending perfectly. He stretched his senses, looking for eyes in the sky, on the rocks, on the ground, anywhere at all. He inhaled and used the hairs on his body to try to find his enemy. If there was one close, they were excellent at blending in and staying downwind.

Using his toes and fingers, he began to drag himself over the ground to a better spot where he could visually see a larger area, including the one the vultures were interested in. He didn't hurry. There was always that one small whisper in the mind that urged one to do so when a friend might be in trouble, but getting killed wouldn't help. He inched his way to the position he knew would be safe and backed into cover before lifting his head until only his eyes showed.

The wind touched his face and brought with it the scent of death. For a moment, his heart reacted with a lurch. There was a body. He could see part of it, one side, arm, leg and rib cage. Definitely male in combat gear. He let himself breathe a sigh of relief. That wasn't Luther. If this man was dead, Luther had to have killed him. So where was Luther? He had no doubt that Luther had more than one dead body buried deep on his property. Why not this one? No time? Was Luther hurt? Why hadn't he answered when Rubin had sent out a bird call?

That Luther? There was tightness in Diego's voice.

No. One of the soldiers. I put out a call for Luther, but he didn't answer. This one isn't buried, and you know Luther would have buried him deep if he could have.

Without warning the little lightning strikes were back, pulses of energy beating at the edges of his mind. Fiery flicks, faint jabs, that same precise sequence, over and over and then gone again. Rubin knew it was Jonquille. It wasn't one of the others trying to trip him up. It was definitely her and she was trying to convey something to him.

Did you get that, Diego? That's Jonquille. She's afraid they'll catch her communicating with us.

Yeah, I'm getting that. She's letting us know to keep it light and very short. No more than that precise time or under. Not words. So, code of some sort.

Rubin took a deep breath, let it out. He was merged with Diego. The two of them held a strong bond. They always had. He was a fairly capable telepath and Diego was immensely strong. He'd been known to build bridges for the entire team, even members who weren't strong telepaths.

We have to follow her trail now, while it's fresh, or we'll lose it, Rubin said.

You're lying out in the open, Rubin. If I . . . Diego broke off.

Rubin wasn't about to argue with him. He was going to at least let Jonquille know they heard her and they would be waiting to take her back. More, they'd figure out that she was sending a code, and once they had a key, they would be able to talk to her. Diego didn't want to stretch his mind that far when he was trying to cover his brother. Rubin got it, but Jonquille mattered too much to him.

She needed reassurance that she wasn't going to be left to another madman to be experimented on. He'd made a commitment to her. He meant that commitment. He wasn't a man who went back on his word. He knew she would have walked through the fires of hell to come after him. He wouldn't do less for her.

They kept a strong merge and followed that faint trace to Jonquille's mind. It wasn't a way to find her location on the mountain; rather, the pathway would direct them to reach straight into only *her* mind. She hadn't wanted to take a chance that one of the other squirrel men implanted with some strand of her DNA might overhear them communicate with her. His woman was so brilliant.

I think we're as close as we're going to get without giving ourselves away, Rubin. Do whatever you're planning to do.

Rubin replayed the sequence in his mind. Very, very softly, he repeated the first half of the strikes as gently as possible, sending them directly into Jonquille's mind, letting her know he heard her. They were there, and they would be waiting for her. He paused after the first half and counted out the rest of the beats deliberately, then repeated the first half a second time. He wanted her to know it was on purpose. He might not have decoded the message yet, but he understood it came from her and he was there.

There was silence for what seemed an eternity. He didn't realize he was holding his breath. He needed to know she was alive. That she was unhurt. That those men hadn't touched her. Violated her. She'd been so confident in her ability to protect herself and yet they'd brought her down with a dart, knocking her out and taking her right out from under him and Diego in spite of their enhanced abilities.

There were so many of the elite soldiers. Of the ground crew. What could they possibly want with Jonquille? He was supposed to be so smart and yet he wasn't even close to that answer. He wanted to call out to her that he was right there, that he wasn't leaving her alone. She had to feel so alone, just as she'd been for so many years. In isolation. Abandoned.

The fiery flicks touched the outer edges of his mind gently, and this time there was a hint of a feminine touch. Just the barest hint. Relief swept through him. Triumph. He took a terrible chance and pressed his fingers to the corners of his eyes tight to relieve the pressure that had built up. Communication was possible in ways the squirrel men might never suspect.

Abruptly, Diego pulled back, breaking the bridge. *You're lying out there totally exposed, Rubin. If the enemy has eyes on that slope, you just moved.*

Yeah. I get that. She's alive. Rubin didn't care that Diego was royally angry with him—and his brother was. As a rule—as in never—Rubin didn't make mistakes when he was out in the field surrounded by enemies. He hadn't realized just how much he needed to have affirmation that Jonquille was on the other end of those little lightning strikes in his mind.

I get that too, but you dying isn't going to get her back.

Rubin had to get his head in the game, and that meant pushing his woman out. *You're right. We have to find Luther before they do and then take this crew out before the others get here.*

He could just be lying low until they leave. There're so many of them, he may have decided to just wait it out safely. Again, there was a hopeful note in Diego's mind.

Rubin considered that for less than a second. *You know the old man better than that. He would never let an army take over his property. This is his home and he would defend it from the devil with his last breath.*

Rubin began a slow retreat back down the slope, employing the same method he'd used coming up it. Inch by slow inch. If the enemy had eyes on the slope, if they'd spotted the vultures, he didn't want them spotting him.

You're right. Where the hell is he?

He didn't bury the dead body completely, Diego, and he would have, especially knowing there's a larger force out there. He'd want them to wonder what happened to their sentry. He's got to be wounded.

He didn't want to think about the old man being hurt, but there was no other explanation. Luther Gunthrie had survived too long not to know how to fight a larger force. He would become a ghost and use a bow and arrow, employ silent weapons, stealth, never letting the enemy see him. When possible, he'd make the kills disappear completely so his enemies would never find the bodies. He would create a nightmare for his enemies. Leave no tracks. No trace. They would never imagine an old man could do the damage Luther could do.

I think he's wounded, Diego. Where would he go if he's hurt? We need to get to him fast. They will have sent someone to look for a sentry that hasn't checked in. We have to find him before they do.

Rubin wanted to find him alive.

12

Diego joined Rubin for a brief conference at the very bottom of the slope in the dip that Luther had hollowed out at one time to put in a wine barrel to use as a culvert.

"The songbirds couldn't find a trace of that old man anywhere," Diego said.

Rubin frowned and ran his fingers through his hair in agitation. He rarely showed emotion by physical tells, but losing Luther to the ground crew was intolerable. They knew Gunthrie. They knew the area. Surely, they could find him.

"You're certain the birds didn't give a hint the crew had a prisoner."

"Absolutely certain," Diego reiterated. "He's not there."

"And he's not in his house. The sentries are looking for him." Rubin mused, "Where are you, Luther?" He frowned and looked at his brother. "Where's his still? It isn't up on the ridge. It's not in any of the other places he had it before. Where did he put it?"

They looked at each other for a long time. Diego trilled several notes and several of his birds took to the air, flying in various directions over Luther's property. Both Rubin and Diego connected with them, seeing for themselves what the birds were seeing. Men were moving on the ground below, clearly searching for someone. They were trying to be stealthy as they hunted in pairs through the woods and around the meadow. Two were making the rounds near Luther's house, traveling in circles, trying to find tracks.

"That's a good question," Diego mused aloud, even as he paid attention to what the birds could see.

Rubin didn't talk. Looking through the eyes of flying birds was disorienting and he didn't want to miss a detail. As it was, he was nearly distracted by the pair of soldiers in camouflage clothing working their way around a spot toward the back of the particularly flat area in the woods Rubin had been in often. It was close to the Gunthrie house, right out back, just inside the tree line.

"Have the birds go back to just there, Diego," Rubin directed quietly, sending him the exact visual.

Diego didn't question him. The flock of birds changed direction, coming together, circling and flying over the house and woods, dropping lower and then circling higher to settle in the tree branches.

"What is it?" Diego asked. "Other than the soldiers?"

"The ground. It's not right. Look at the ground."

His brother went silent, taking his time. Like Rubin, he was familiar with the area. They'd been there numerous times over the years, visiting first Luther and Lotty, and then Luther, to check on his health whether he liked it or not. When they did, he liked to walk around his property, and they always obliged, walking with him, keeping him company, knowing he was proud of his place.

"Not enough ground cover. Should be a little more overgrown than that," Diego said.

"Yeah. He tore that up for some reason." Rubin blinked rapidly to get his vision back to normal and then waited until his brother did the same before looking at him. "Are you thinking what I am?"

"That he put that still underground?"

"What else? Where is it? He would never get rid of it. You know he wouldn't." Rubin was certain of that.

"He's got to be seventy or eighty. How could he possibly build an underground room for a still?" Diego demanded.

"Because he's a genius," Rubin said. "Everyone always underestimates him. Just because he doesn't want to drive a car doesn't mean he doesn't have the ability. I'll bet if those soldiers go to start up their equipment, none of it will work. Luther Gunthrie is intelligent and quite capable of building an underground maze if he chose."

Diego's head snapped up. "Rubin. He could have discovered a cave."

"Or a cave system," Rubin said. "We talked about it that one time at Huntington Falls. We were on that picnic with Lotty. She said something about Luther being so excited over someplace he liked to go. He'd taken her there, but she didn't like him going because it seemed like a lot of mud and he had to crawl in places. Or pull himself through on his belly. That just terrified her, so she asked him not to go back there. She was afraid it would cave in on him. As far as she knew he never did again. She used the words 'cave in on him.' She used that as one of the examples of what a man might do for his wife when she was really afraid of something."

Diego nodded. "Is that what you call it? A picnic? You were assessing her condition, as I recall, and had me chatting about everything and getting her to throw rocks into the water." He fished around in his jacket until he came up with a packet. Tearing it open, he emptied part of the rations into his mouth and then zipped the packet closed and returned it to the pocket. "But, yeah, now that you say that, Lotty did mention he'd found some muddy place that was dangerous he liked to go. Luther never spoke of it. At least not to me. If he'd mentioned it to the Sawyers, they would have said something."

"Luther's closemouthed about anything on his property. He doesn't like outsiders coming onto his land. Spelunkers like to explore caves. If they got wind there was even a small system, someone would try to find it. You know Luther. He'd shoot a trespasser if they didn't get off his land when he told them to," Rubin said. "If this muddy place he found was a cave system, he wouldn't say a word."

"He would have several ways to get to this underground hiding place, especially if he keeps his still there. He would keep supplies there. Weapons. Emergency equipment," Diego speculated.

Rubin nodded. "He has an entrance in that section of land that he recently replanted. But he's got one in his house. Lotty's been dead for six years, Diego. He's had time to prepare. He knew he would be getting old. He deliberately became a recluse and discouraged people from visiting, including Edward. Edward told us how Luther acted like he believed he was a government spy. Luther Gunthrie on his worst day would know Edward Sawyer isn't a government spy. He didn't want Edward to see what he was up to."

Rubin was already considering the best way to get into Luther's cabin without being seen by the sentries who were patrolling. He wasn't worried about the two men hunting for Luther in the woods— they were already moving on, quartering another area, doing a thorough, systematic search.

Rubin sent the songbirds into the air, specifically looking for snipers, or any of the ground crew who might be sitting up high in the branches of a tree with high-powered lenses looking for signs of Luther—or even them. It was possible, even probable, the elite soldiers had warned them that Rubin and Diego might be on their way. How they could guess this would be their destination, he didn't know, but he wasn't going to rule it out.

Once the birds were in the air, he accessed their vision, studying the trees and tops of the highest boulders that might be used. He even sent one bird to check the ridge just to be safe. Once he was certain no one was watching, he called the birds back, waited until they settled once more on the branches of the trees around Luther's home and then gave them the command to warn him if the sentries became interested in Diego or him.

We'll time the two sentries and slide inside the cabin between their rounds. He signaled to Diego to move forward while he covered his brother.

Diego kept low to the ground, but he was fast, running through the brush to a spectacular flowering shrub that was a good ten feet high and fifteen feet wide. It had low, sweeping branches, riddled with leaves and clusters of brilliant flaming-red flowers. The flame azalea was part of the rhododendron family, and when the brothers had first seen it, the shrub and been small.

Luther had planted that shrub for Lotty so she could wake up every morning and look out her window and see the flowers growing heavy on the branches. She always called it one of her greatest joys. He still carefully maintained it, snipping the dead flowers off so new ones could grow. His care could be seen in the health and size of the plant.

Diego utilized the sweeping branches, sliding under them and changing his coloring to reflect the plant. Immediately, he slid his weapon into his hand, the familiar stock feeling a part of him. His sense of smell was uninterrupted, as the five-inch funnel-shaped clusters of flaming flowers gave off no fragrance. There was little wind to give him much in the way of information. Still, he took his time inspecting the ground around the Gunthrie cabin.

Someone had tried to erase the tracks around the house, but they weren't up to Luther's expertise or his. He could see crushed grass in places and a bruised leaf here and there. He checked the roof and the sides of the building. Luther kept the branches of the trees cut back so there was no chance of one falling on his home. He'd always said he liked the sound of the rain falling on the metal. More than likely, he liked it because Lotty had liked it.

Another few minutes and the sentry should pass, Diego informed Rubin.

Let him go for now. We'll get him later.

Rubin worried him. His brother was the gentlest man he knew, but there was this side to him few ever saw. He could become a merciless hunter when the occasion called for it. He would strike without warning and leave bodies without ever looking back. When he did, Diego could never detect a stirring of remorse or afterthought. The Rubin he knew wasn't that man. He was unfailingly kind and giving. He was the man who would put himself in dangerous situations over and over to save others. But when this predator slipped loose, he was as cold as ice and no enemy was safe. Diego often wondered if Whitney knew what he was enhancing when he had gotten ahold of the two of them.

Diego laid his hand on the ground and felt the strange stillness. As a rule, the leaves and grasses would be teeming with life, insects and lizards would be rushing around carrying on with their normal routines. A heavy footfall, the crush of boots coming down on brush, snapping twigs, quieting the drone of bugs for just a moment was another warning the sentry was close. Diego didn't move, blending with the flame azalea, that declaration of love Luther Gunthrie had planted for his wife. The low-hanging branches wept over him, caging him in, a heavy curtain of leaves and clusters of flowers that meant nothing to this soldier who would kill Lotty's husband.

We'll find him, Rubin assured, reading his need for action.

Diego had wanted to spring out of the azalea shrub and cut the soldier's throat. He wasn't nearly as gentle as Rubin. He had more of a temper until Rubin actually got angry.

Just the idea that they're hunting that old man like this, so many of them, Rubin, makes me want to rip their heads off.

We'll get them. Rubin was calm. Steady.

Diego remembered how it was when they were boys. It didn't matter what happened. How bad it was. What they had to do. Rubin did it. He faced it with that same calmness and he did it. He hunted, with absolute determination, the animals who had killed their sister. Diego had known he would never stop until he had gotten all four of them. He knew then, like he knew now, that these men who may have killed Luther Gunthrie were already dead. They didn't know it, but Rubin was going to find them and he was going to make certain they didn't go after any other old men who were just minding their own business in their homes.

Yeah, we will, Diego agreed.

There was silence while they both waited for the sentry to make his rounds. The guard might not be a woodsman, but he was thorough. He checked the cabin and all around it. He opened the door and peered in. He did try to be careful of brushing up against the plants near the house and cursed under his breath when he backed into the bottlebrush in full bloom, knocking a multitude of the bright spikes to the ground. He stood there a moment, looking down at the damage, and then shook his head and crouched low to sweep them up with his hand.

It took effort to collect all the spikes lying among the dirt and leaves. The soldier turned his head several times toward the flaming azalea and looked directly at Diego. Diego never moved. He barely breathed, releasing air one slow breath at a time. He wasn't particularly worried. Rubin had this man in his sights, but more, he could kill him before the soldier could react. He was prepared. Diego was also confident in his ability to camouflage himself. Eventually, the sentry was satisfied with his job of cleaning up his mistake, and he glanced at his watch and hurried off.

It's clear, Rubin reported. *Head inside. I'll be right behind you.*

Diego didn't like that Rubin was guarding him. That never sat well with him. It wasn't just the fact that Rubin was his only living relative and he was determined not to lose him. Rubin was extraordinary in that he was a gifted healer, but being a psychic surgeon was beyond measure. Rubin might not like having a talent that defined him, but Diego knew he was needed in the world, particularly in the world of GhostWalkers. Rubin didn't want to hear it, but it was true. All of the GhostWalkers knew they needed him, and they took extra precautions with him. Rubin detested that.

Rubin was suddenly crouching beside Luther's door, sliding it open just enough to gain entrance. Diego slithered out from under the azalea shrub, careful not to disturb the clusters of flowers. He looked with disdain at the job the soldier had made of cleaning up the ground. He'd brushed it with it fingers and strewn a few leaves over the area. It didn't look in the least bit natural. Luther would have known immediately that someone had been snooping around.

Rubin shook his head. *Get a move on, Diego. The other sentry will be here in a few minutes. We have to find Luther's entrance to the underground system. It's not like he has many places for us to hide in his shack.*

Rubin waited for Diego to go in first, covering his brother all the way. He knew it annoyed Diego, but that was too bad. He was already upset at possibly losing Luther—at Jonquille being in the hands of the squirrel men. He wasn't going to take chances with his brother. He was well aware Diego thought to protect him. He was damn sick of everyone thinking he needed that protection. He was the last one to need protection. It was just that no one saw into him.

Rubin hadn't been inside Luther's home since Lotty had passed away. When they met with the old man, he always talked to them outside, and they respected that distancing. He didn't know what he expected from Gunthrie, but the almost obsessively neat interior was a surprise. Even a shock. The fact that Luther had burned the marriage bed and had told Rubin he slept on a mat on the floor had conjured up images in Rubin's mind that were very far from the truth. The home remained much like it had looked when Lotty was alive. The only thing missing was the bed.

There was no mess at all. The woodstove Lotty had loved so much to cook on, even when she had a much more modern stove, looked well cared for. Everything was in its place. The blankets she'd knitted or quilted were lovingly displayed on walls or folded at the end of the mat where Luther slept. The entire interior was a shrine to Lotty.

Rubin's chest hurt at the thought of losing the old man. "We've got to find his door, Diego." He glanced at his watch. "We're running out of time."

The cabin was small, essentially everything in one room. They each took a side and carefully inspected the floor to see if they could find where Luther had installed a trap door. Rubin moved his mat several times, thinking it had to be there, but how would his mat be moved back in the exact spot again? There were no signs of an entrance to an underground cavern.

"We're going to have to get out of here," Rubin warned. "Luther, you cunning old coot. Where would you put the entrance?" It had to be in his shack. He would want to be able to disappear fast. If not his mat, what else could hide a trapdoor?

There was the woodstove. The one chair. The little modern stove and sink. His gaze went back to the sink. Like his sink in the cabin, it had been modernized long after the cabin was built. They used the dark beneath it for storage. He crouched down and examined the interior. A wooden crate holding a few potatoes sat beneath the sink. He lifted it, and as he did, he felt his fingers catch under the crate. He lifted it higher. There was definitely a manmade mechanism attached to the crate, although it looked like it belonged there.

Rubin studied it for a moment. Luther acted as if he refused to come into the modern world and everyone bought into that, but Rubin wasn't necessarily convinced. His whiskey was too good. Too smooth. His still was always maintained and kept in working order. He managed it himself. He always had the ingredients he needed. His product was in high demand. He sold to exclusive stores. For a man not able to understand the modern world, he was living in it quite nicely. Rubin passed his hand over the small mechanism.

For a moment it seemed to flash at him. There was no way to type anything into it. If it required a password, it had to be audio. "Lotty4ever," he murmured. Nothing happened. He stared at it for another few minutes, more convinced than ever that he was right.

Luther loved Lotty with everything in him. What would he use? His world revolved around her.

"Diego, what did Luther always call Lotty? After she passed? It wasn't his angel. But something like that."

"His way to heaven. No, his wings to heaven," Diego said. "I always thought it was so sweet. He would say Lotty was his wings to heaven."

Rubin repeated that very clearly. "Lotty, my wings to heaven." That was the phrase Luther used for her. Rubin remembered it was one of the few times Luther had stopped talking and seemed choked up. Rubin had continued to examine him and pretended not to notice, knowing Luther would have simply walked away and disappeared had Rubin said anything to him.

The moment he finished saying the password, a small portion of the floor beneath the sink retracted, leaving a hole. It wasn't a big hole. He had wide shoulders, as did Diego. He studied it, wondering if either of them would fit.

"You're up, Diego, you go first. Looks like there's a rickety old ladder. Hope you don't break it. You ate a lot last night."

Diego didn't bother to argue with him about who was going first—both were too conscious of the second sentry making his rounds. Diego stripped off his gear and jacket, handed them to Rubin and then stepped through the hole. It was definitely a tight fit and required a little engineering of shoulders and body to slide through. It wasn't easy at all. Rubin watched his brother carefully and then handed him his rifle, gear and coat before stripping his own gear and passing it to Diego.

He slid the crate of potatoes as close to the hole as possible in the hopes it would slide in place and relock once they were inside. He followed Diego into that narrow opening. His boot found the rung on the ladder easily, but it took a lot of patient maneuvering to get his shoulders through the limited space. He was aware of minutes ticking by as he did so.

His head dropped below the hole when he heard the sentry at the door. Very slowly, he slid his hand to the knife concealed between his shoulder blades. It would be a very difficult kill. The last sentry hadn't entered the house. He'd only taken a cursory look inside. They'd most likely looked in a hundred times. There was no bathroom, no reason to enter. Neither brother had disturbed anything other than the crate, and it was beneath the sink in the dark.

The sentry would have to actually enter, walk to the sink, crouch down and inspect underneath to find it. Rubin practiced, over and over in his mind, raising one arm and slitting the man's throat. There was no way he could get his head and shoulders through that opening in time to make the kill. He'd have to do it blind, using instinct alone, the stubble embedded in his jaw guiding him, telling him exactly where his enemy was, how close, his shape and where to make his strike.

He waited in silence, the dark surrounding him, as he heard a grunt and then shuffling. The door to the shack closed and then there was silence again. Still, he waited. There was the faint smell of sweat. Heavy breathing. Measured treads coming closer. The water at the sink went on and then the soldier muttered something to himself. Water drops splashed on the floor. Rubin couldn't see them, but he heard them. The sentry didn't like the humidity. Abruptly, the man turned off the water and hastily left the shack.

Rubin shook his head. The sentry hadn't been one of the elite soldiers. Rubin whispered the password a second time, and just as the floor had opened, it closed. He heard the crate slide into position.

That old man is a genius, Diego. He knows technology whether he'll ever admit it or not. He built that little unit. He ordered the parts and he put it together.

They say not to judge a book by its cover and I guess they were right. Luther deliberately made himself an old stereotype, Diego agreed, climbing the rest of the way down the ladder.

There wasn't a great distance to go before they were in the shaft itself. They had to bend down to walk through the man-made tunnel Luther had painstakingly dug to connect with the cave system he had discovered. He'd shored it up with metal, rebar and cement. The tunnel was long and dark, twisting and turning, going uphill and then down, taking them toward the woods and toward the Huntington Falls area.

How long do you think it took him to dig this from his house? Diego asked.

He obviously spent years on it, Rubin said. Luther was tenacious. His respect for the man just continued to grow. This had taken careful planning. The cement had to be brought in. The dirt had to be carried out and concealed. *This is a feat beyond measure for one man.*

It's possible he caught trespassers and made them help him and then killed them, Diego said dryly.

Rubin laughed. *If he could have, he would have made everyone believe that about him. He does so love his reputation.*

The heat in the tunnel was giving way to cold air. Abruptly, they came to a wide-open cavern with layers of rock, beautifully and unexpectedly colored. It was the last thing either of them thought they'd see. It was as if it came out of nowhere. They both just stopped and stared in disbelief.

Rubin guessed they were near Huntington Falls, but very far underground, so their voices wouldn't carry. Still, he spoke in a low tone. "Luther's known this cave system has been here probably since he first bought this property, and he never told anyone but Lotty."

"If he had, it would have been overrun. Look at it, Rubin. It's beautiful."

A stalactite hung from the ceiling like a chandelier, its color nearly a pure white with a bizarre red band running around it. The band was wider at the top, tapering as it came toward the bottom. He'd never seen anything like it. The red was more rust than an actual red, but it was really amazing. There were other stalactites on the ceiling of the cave, but none as large or as striking as the one with the red band.

The stalagmites rising from the cave floor looked like beautiful columns of pale blue, purple and rusty red. The stalagmite rising just beneath the stalactite hanging from the ceiling was close to reaching it to form one complete pillar.

They picked their way carefully around the limestone, trying not to touch anything, not wanting to disturb the fragile balance inside the cave. The sound of water dripping was continuous. The rocks gave way completely until there was only water on the floor of the cave, like a shallow stream. The rock wall appeared orangey, with rust along the edges of the water. The water was dark in places, but Rubin could see that the floor was solid rock.

There was nowhere to walk other than in the water. Rubin took lead, stepping into the water. The water was barely moving. Water trickled from the walls of the cave on either side of them, from up above and in various locations. As they went forward, the minerals mixing with the calcite had to have changed slightly, because so did the various formations and colors surrounding them.

Rubin felt he was walking on an alien planet—one that was ever changing. The walls were thick with the growth of what looked like tubes in various shades of yellow. Huge tubes that formed columns of what looked like shawls to him, rising from the floor. They were pencil thin or huge and round and fat.

Then there were the blue stalactites, ranging from pale to almost royal blue, hanging from the ceiling. They were large and thick, vying for space, so much so they practically looked like a wall dropping down on one side, adding to the extreme beauty of the cave.

He was so busy looking at the sights around him, he almost missed the narrow corridor that veered off from the main direction of the water bed. He stopped and indicated the darkened tunnel. It didn't look quite so beautiful or inviting. Rubin stayed very still, right where he was in the center of the rocky water bed, studying the tight, shadowy passage that was really no more than a wide crack between two giant slips of rock.

He's in there, Diego. If he's wounded, he's dangerous. If he's dead, I'm not sure I want to know.

If he was dead, we'd smell him. Diego was pragmatic about it.

Rubin shot him a look that bounced right off his brother. They had no idea how far back that tunnel went, and it was very narrow. That meant they would have to go one at a time and Luther would have the advantage. If he was trigger-happy, they'd be dead.

Rubin sent out the call of an early morning songbird. It was one of Lotty's favorite birds. Luther would know the brothers would remember that bit of information. He took a step toward the opening between the towering rocks. Diego got there first, smoothly cutting in front of him.

What the hell do you think you're doing?

I'm more sensitive than you in situations like this. Just stay quiet for a few minutes and let me feel for him.

Diego rarely pointed out the difference in their abilities when it came to tracking or hunting in the mountains or woods. He was always humble about his skills, but Rubin was well aware his brother had extraordinary talents. He stepped back without another protest. His objection hadn't been ego, it had been worry for Diego's safety.

Diego moved silently even coming out of the water into the mud and then onto the slippery rock. Rubin found himself admiring his brother as he moved over the rock and began to insert his larger body sideways into that crack. He did so without making a single sound, not even his clothing seeming to whisper against the rock. He didn't shift a grain of dirt. Rubin wasn't certain if he prevented debris from being disturbed with his mind or if his body was just that careful. Whatever it was, Diego was a master at moving nearly unseen and unheard through most environments.

I can feel someone ahead, Rubin. Pain crashing through them. Smell fresh blood.

Rubin let out his breath slowly. It had to be Luther. He was alive, then. *He'll be doubly dangerous,* he couldn't help but warn his brother. Luther would be like a wounded animal.

Diego sent out Lotty's favorite morning birdcall again. She had had a real fondness for the indigo bunting, with his brilliant blue feathers and his love for his lady, with her much more subdued coloring. His notes were so perfect it was as if the bird were singing to its mate. There was a long silence. Diego waited patiently and then sent the male's call a second time, singing his song perfectly. Indigo buntings learned songs from the other males around them and could sing up to one hundred songs an hour. This time, an indigo bunting answered from somewhere deeper inside the cavern.

"Diego and Rubin coming in, Luther," Rubin called, not wanting to leave anything to chance.

"Come on in, then, and don't make such a ruckus." Luther's voice sounded thin and shaky.

Diego moved forward, going around one more bend. A faint light spilled out, this one artificial, revealing the smears of blood on the rock leading to the larger, hollowed-out chamber where Luther half lay, his back to the wall, bloody leg stretched out in front of him.

Rubin and Diego dropped their gear as they approached him, both coming up on either side to take a look at the wound. He'd been shot, and the bullet had done a lot of damage. He'd lost a lot of blood.

I told you he isn't really human, Diego said. *This should have killed him.*

"You got yourself in a fine mess, Luther. Saw the body you left up on the ridge. You normally bury those. Why'd you leave it?"

"I was keeping him in reserve in case I needed to live off of him whilst they were livin' down in the house," Luther said.

Rubin turned his head and gave the old man the once-over. He raised his eyebrow at Diego. He went back to his gear and pulled out the field kit he always carried. It wasn't the best, but it was all he had. It would have to do.

Diego scowled at him. *He's been on his own far too long.*

Rubin tried to be practical. "There are bad diseases you can get from cannibalism, Luther. One called kuru can eat away at your brain. Bad way to go." He tried to be simplistic but make it as bad as he could think to make it.

Luther snorted. "Was just joshin' with you, kid. You lost your sense of humor. Would have just buried him like all the rest, but with this leg the way it was, didn't think I could get back to the house and in the cave before they got me."

It made Rubin wonder how many other bodies were buried somewhere around the Gunthrie property. It wasn't as if Rubin and Diego could say much, although they hadn't buried the ones they'd killed. Luther had been wiser and kinder than they had been.

"Wait a minute," Diego said. "You were shot up on the ridge like this? And you made it all the way down to your house? There were no tracks, Luther."

Luther had already cut the material away from the wound and tried to clean it. He'd attempted to build a fire and clearly was going to cauterize it in an effort to stop the bleeding. Rubin ignored the two men and began to work as fast as he could on the older man. He handed him water. He was clearly dehydrated. Running his palms just above his leg, he found he could see the damage done to the muscles and bone. The artery wasn't hit, but the veins were a mess.

"You think you're the only one any good in the woods, boy?" Luther challenged.

Diego thought about it. "Well." He rubbed the bristles on his chin, distracting the older man as Rubin examined the wound. "Yeah. There aren't very many as good as me. Rubin's pretty good. I thought you were getting up there in age and maybe had lost a few of your abilities."

Luther visibly objected. "I can still run rings around you. Don't let age fool you."

"I can see where I may have gone wrong there," Diego said. "And this cave system, Luther. It's unbelievable. Really, amazing and beautiful."

Luther's body shuddered with pain. Diego glanced anxiously at Rubin. To find him and then lose him at this late date would be terrible. Neither brother wanted that. Rubin was very aware of Diego counting on him. He was always aware of the GhostWalkers counting on him when those they loved were so close to death—and Luther was close to death. They both could smell it there in the cavern.

He pushed all thoughts away but the well of healing fire in his body. He didn't have his surgical instruments, or IVs to save Luther, but he had his gifts. "Do you know your blood type?"

"Yeah. I served," Luther told him abruptly. "What are you doing here?"

"The men that came to your place want to land a plane in your meadow. Other soldiers took my woman, and they're bringing her down the mountain to fly her out of here. We got here first," Rubin said. "I need to know your blood type."

"You let candy-ass babies take your woman, Rubin?" Luther demanded, pouring outrage into his voice, but he closed his eyes. "Was going to go join my Lotty, but guess you're going to need me." He murmured his blood type and then seemed to drift into a sleep.

"Rubin?" Diego asked. He was already rolling up his sleeve. He reached into Rubin's field kit and began hastily preparing for a blood transfusion.

"I don't know. Don't interrupt me."

Rubin couldn't think about anything but taking the repairs one step at a time. The inside of Luther's leg was mangled. He hadn't done it any favors by dragging himself through the fields over rocks and then the cave through the water. Rubin had no idea what kind of bacteria had gotten into the wound. Infections happened fast and killed easily. He shoved that out of his head so he could concentrate.

Just using his healing abilities on Luther wasn't going to be enough to save him. Rubin could see that immediately. He had no choice if he was going to save the old man. Being a psychic surgeon wasn't quite as cool as everyone thought it was. There was an exchange taking place. It was an extremely dangerous practice. One couldn't cure cancer. No matter how much he might be tempted to save someone on the battlefield, he knew he might be exchanging his life for theirs or losing both their lives. It was always a balance.

When he desperately wanted to save an individual or a loved one, it was difficult if not impossible to make the decision to walk away. He knew he should walk away now, but Luther belonged to his past. He was a connection bridging the time between his youth, the family he couldn't save and the present. And there was Lotty. They all adored Lotty. She tied them together even with her beloved songbirds and her azaleas. Jonquille was his future. She was his Lotty, and she would want this as much as he did.

He opened the well of healing energy and began to do the surgery through his mind, moving the shattered pieces of Luther's bone, muscle and veins back into place and meticulously mending each one. He had no idea of time passing. He never did. It could have been hours or days. When he came back to himself, he could only slump against the side of the cavern wall, right alongside Luther, unable to move.

Rubin's arms felt like lead weights. His throat was parched. His heartbeat was off, as if it had taken on Luther's uneven beat. He was aware of Diego holding a water bottle to his lips and he forced himself to drink, but he couldn't lift his hand to take the bottle from his brother.

"Even out your pulse, Rubin," Diego advised.

Rubin shook his head, trying to convey that he was unable to.

"You can. Take a slow, deep breath. You need oxygen. Give yourself air."

Rubin's lungs were burning. His body felt like it was slowly shutting down. Too little oxygen. Diego was right. His heart wasn't pumping efficiently. His leg was on fire. There was an odd, persistent jabbing in his head that refused to go away, or he would have just drifted off.

"Rubin. You need to take a deep breath," Diego persisted. "Right now. Do it now."

His brother really was a pain sometimes. He just wanted to sleep. Close his eyes and go to sleep. He was wounded. His leg—couldn't he see that and maybe, just this once, give him a break? But no, Diego was gripping him by the shoulder, shaking him hard.

"Take a breath. Now. Right now."

Rubin tried to tell him he would, but no sound emerged, so he just did it to shut him up. He drew in a deep lungful of air. It burned at first, as if his lungs had forgotten how to breathe in and out. He frowned and concentrated on the mechanics of breathing. Finally, his lungs caught on as if remembering a long-ago performance and they began to work automatically. The air circulated through his system.

You happy? His voice wouldn't work, but he managed to get the words out—he thought—to his brother telepathically. Maybe he hadn't or he'd slurred them. Who knew? He just wanted sleep.

13

Luther glanced over his shoulder at Rubin and Diego as he led the way through the labyrinth below the ground. It might not be the largest cave system, but it was big enough, with so many twists and turns that the brothers were more than impressed with it. "Shouldn't even be alive, let alone up and walking, yet here I am. You boys are a bit on the scary side."

"You're the one that has more lives than a cat," Diego pointed out.

"No way could I live through that one. Which one of you did the mumbo jumbo?" He threw another suspicious look over his shoulder.

"Diego gave you his blood," Rubin volunteered. "Figured you were both ornery, so if you got any more bad-tempered no one would notice."

"I guess I oughta thank you for the blood, kid," Luther said.

The old man limped as he walked, but other than that, he

showed no additional signs that he'd had such a severe injury that he should be dead. His color was good and he ate his portion of the rations Rubin and Diego shared with him. It was Rubin who looked pale. If one looked closely, he walked with a limp as well. He was directly behind Luther, with Diego bringing up the rear. He hadn't objected when Diego had silently picked up Rubin's heaviest pack and shouldered it along with his own, something Rubin would ordinarily never allow.

They were going into combat, and Rubin knew he had to recover. That meant resting. He'd slept, and that had helped, but they didn't want to take any chances that the elite soldiers would get to the Gunthrie property before they took out the ground crew and could keep the plane from landing. They meant to take back Jonquille before the soldiers could take her wherever they were planning on doing their experiments on her. He wasn't willing to risk waiting any longer.

Luther kept walking, but when Diego remained silent, he shot another look over his shoulder, his gaze assessing Rubin this time. "You did the mumbo jumbo, then, Rubin," he said. "Suspected for some time you had the gift. 'Course, what you got is more powerful than any I've ever witnessed. Shouldn't have wasted it on an old man like me when you got to have your strength to take back your woman."

Rubin didn't respond. He kept walking. Luther was fishing. He knew their mother had had the healing gift, but he also was astute. He'd been watching them closely each time they came back to the mountains. Knowing how intelligent Luther really was, Rubin was wondering just how much Diego and he had inadvertently given away.

"We'll get Jonquille back," Diego said, confidence in his voice.

"Did you take out their equipment?" If he had, that would be one less thing to do.

"'Course I did. You think cuz I'm old I lost my brains?"

"I'll ponder on that for a piece before I answer," Diego responded.

Rubin wasn't so certain he wanted to be between the two of them. *Diego, I've been thinking quite a bit about that sequence of strikes Jonquille hit me with. After we used the indigo bunting, I remembered a conversation we had about songs. It was all about various songs we knew about that had lightning in the lyrics. Some were modern, some not. We knew most of the same ones, but she mentioned one I hadn't heard of. It was by a group out of Liverpool, I believe. In any case, she repeated the lyrics to me and then sang a phrase. She repeated it several times. When she did, she tapped the rhythm on her thigh. I watched her fingers moving, and it was fascinating how she did it.*

Diego processed in his mind, watching the images Rubin replayed.

The little strikes with Jonquille's fingers on her thigh as she tapped were not as if she were playing an instrument but as if she were the lightning striking a specific target on the ground. The rhythm to the song was mellow, almost sweet, not at all hard-hitting like a bolt of lightning would be. When I matched those taps on her thigh to the ones of the sequence, they seem to fit.

Rubin waited for his brother's assessment. If he was right, they could use the sequence to write short messages to Jonquille. Clearly, she didn't feel any communication longer than that specific sequence was safe, even using code. Someone had to be able to monitor her telepathically.

I think you're right, Rubin. I think that's exactly what she's using, Diego agreed.

Why are you baiting Luther?

So he doesn't notice that you look like crap. Not that it's working. Diego sounded rueful. *And he likes it.*

"We're coming up on the tunnel leading to the spring where those soldiers are camping. The entrance to the caves is much closer to their campsite than I'd like." Luther had dropped his voice to a whisper. "The opening there is a natural one. That's how I first discovered the caves." He stopped altogether and turned to face them. "Their campsite is almost below the entrance by about twenty yards. It's a slope with rocks and grass. They only went to the top to try to get better views, but they didn't do much in the way of exploring, not that they would have seen the entrance, at least I don't think they would have."

"I'll go out first," Diego said. "Can you give me a good layout of their camp?"

Luther nodded. "I spent some time studying it before I decided to take them on. Might have left them alone, but they decided to hunt me. On my own land too."

"Probably heard about your reputation," Diego said. "Didn't want you coming after them."

"You said they were there to tear up my meadow? The minute they started that, I would have declared war," Luther said decisively. Never once did he forget to whisper. "I like your woman's name, Rubin. Easter lily. Or daffodil. Your ma would have liked her name."

Rubin nodded. "She would have liked her. She's a good woman. Lotty would have approved of her too."

"When you first go out of the cave, you have to be careful. The camp is right below. They aren't great in the woods, but they are watchful. They're nervous. I noticed that right away. They have one good man, the boss. You're going to have to take him out as fast as possible. He's not only the brains, but he's got eyes and ears."

"The ones coming with Jonquille are like him. Maybe even better," Rubin supplied. "They're fast in the trees. Like flying squirrels. Never saw anything like it, Luther."

Luther was silent for a long moment and then he sighed. "I served my country in several wars. Men go to their graves carrying secrets they swore to keep, and I'm no different, but I don't think you're going to be too surprised when I tell you that experiments began years ago, far before you were ever born, to make men different. Better. Stronger. At least that was the hope."

What is he saying, Rubin? Diego asked, shock in his mind.

Rubin considered all the times Luther had managed feats of strength and endurance others far younger could never have done. All the times he survived when he shouldn't have. Why had he served his country in multiple wars? How had he managed to move his still on his own at his age? To dig out the tunnel to the caves?

How come it had been so easy for Luther to accept Diego's blood and so difficult for Rubin to put the pieces of his body back together again? Rubin had spent a long time trying to put together muscle and bone that should have matched up easily but instead, had been weirdly different. Working on Luther had really taken a toll on him—the kind of cost to him that happened when he made an exchange not only with a gravely ill patient but with an enhanced GhostWalker.

He should have recognized that Luther was different. Everything about him was slightly different, from his blood cells to his muscle mass and the density of his bones. Looking back over the years, from the time he was a child to the times he had returned, there had always been whispers about the goings-on in the woods surrounding Gunthrie's property.

There were always stories. Rumors. Old tales of sightings of ghosts, and some even said Gunthrie's woods were home to the "Hornet Man," only because several teens trying to sneak up on Luther's still had reported seeing red eyes and flying creatures landing in the meadow from time to time. The giant bodies were shaped like hornets, and they swore old man Gunthrie went out to the meadow and petted one of them, ducking his head to avoid getting it bitten off. There were weird lights that flashed. Strobes? Helicopters coming in at night? So many years earlier, late at night, when boys were scared and possibly drinking, they might make that mistake. Others were dared to go, and the stories grew. Luther would feed those rumors.

"You saying that, Luther," Rubin said carefully, "I think that's exactly what the soldiers who took Jonquille are. They're just too fast. They aren't flying from tree to tree, they leap, but it's so fast, they're a blur when they move. Even getting a shot at them, they're already gone. Their clothes blend into their surroundings. They have weapons that can tear up the ground and literally explode trees apart. They have instruments that can move a storm overhead and then feed that storm so they can blast the area with lightning."

"Why do they want your woman?" Luther persisted. "Tell me about her again."

Rubin frowned. "I don't know why they want her. She doesn't know. She was working at a research facility, studying lightning. That's how we met. I can only surmise it has something to do with that. At first, we thought they were after me. I occasionally give talks on various theories I have at conferences. We were together, all three of us, and had no idea they had more than a five-man team hunting us. That's how good they are in the woods."

"Diego was with you?" Luther was all business now, no longer even trying to put up any kind of a front. He was deadly serious.

"Yes. We had eyes in the sky. You know we've hunted with birds. They didn't spot the others either. Not until we realized Diego was targeted. Then it was no longer our hunt, we had to scramble to stay alive. At the last moment we comprehended the real target was Jonquille, but we couldn't get to her and she couldn't get back to us. They put a dart into her and dropped her like a stone. There were so many of them, although Diego killed a couple before they used that blasting weapon on him."

"How did he get away?" Luther asked. "If they have this great weapon and they're that fast, how did Diego get away?"

"There was a buildup of energy, almost like before a lightning strike." Rubin was honest.

"I always look around me for escape routes," Diego added. "When I knew I might be in trouble, I dove for the nearest crevice and hoped it was deep enough to save me. I got lucky."

"They control the clouds and try to use lightning," Luther mused. "She worked researching weather, lightning in particular. Could she have stumbled onto something that would have been useful to them to help them weaponize lightning? That's been talked about for years."

"She would have told me," Rubin said. "I don't think she has any knowledge of making weapons."

"What else can she do? I presume she's quite intelligent or you never would have taken a second look at her. A man like you wants a woman with a brain, someone he can discuss things with. She has talents, Rubin. What are they?"

He's as sharp as a tack. What happened to the stereotypical old recluse coot with the still, which, by the way, I never even caught a glimpse of? Diego said.

"She has a gift for healing although she isn't trained. She went through medical school to become a doctor, but was never able to finish. She wasn't given the chance. She has problems if she's around others too long."

Luther regarded both men in silence. He shook his head. "None of this is adding up. They would have been better off grabbing one of you. She has to have something they need."

"We were unexpected. We came a month early. I don't think they know who we are," Diego offered.

"I don't think I'm violating any big government secret when I ask if you two can still communicate like you did when you were kids. I could tell back then, you'd look at each other and suddenly one of you would do something right quick. You had a way with animals too. If you can reach out to the woman . . ."

Is he fishing? Diego asked.

Who knows? He's helping us. And he's a government secret same as we are.

"We've always been able to talk to each other. We just always had that, like twins or something," Rubin was casual about it. "Diego is stronger than I am with it. He can reach much farther. But, no, we can't contact Jonquille that way. I think those squirrel men—that's what we call them, because they remind me of flying squirrels—can feel telepathic energy."

We do need to contact her. Find out how far out they are, Diego warned.

I've been thinking how to send a short message to see if she understands. I want her to know we're here waiting for her. I just don't want to chance tipping them off.

"We'll find a way to get a message to her, Luther," Rubin said. "I'm thinking on it. A code of some sort, to let her know we're waiting for her."

Luther nodded. "One thing before we start this little war. I want a promise from you boys. Your word of honor. I know you'll keep it." Luther looked each of them in the eyes. "If I don't make it, you text Jacob at the mortuary immediately. Right then. The moment you know I'm dead. You just text *LGDEAD*. That's it. Make absolutely certain he gets my body. He'll cremate me immediately before they can come for me. I gave Lotty my word I would lie with her in the hereafter. Ashes to ashes. Dust to dust. I have never broken my word to her. Never. I served my country with honor. I gave them my entire life. They'll come for my body, but that's the one thing I won't give them. That belongs to Lotty. I trust you boys will make sure I keep my word to my angel. She's my wings. Jacob will bring me to her and bury me with her."

"You think they'll come for your body?" Diego asked.

"I *know* they will, and they won't waste any time." Luther was absolute. "So, if you agree, you have to text Jacob the moment I go down, even if the bullets are still flying. Just add an X—*LGDEADX*—for 'battle ongoing' and he'll know. He'll come."

"You have my word," Rubin said. "Absolutely, Luther. If I could, I'd take you to Jacob."

"You have my word as well," Diego said. "No one is going to take you from Lotty."

"Appreciate it, boys. I'll draw out their camp right here for you. And show you a little extra firepower I've got stashed in the way of explosives. We're not exactly naked here."

"Nice." Diego approved. "I do like explosives. Show me what you've got."

"Tell me you brought a couple of those little transmitters Mordichai put together for Wyatt's girls so they don't get lost," Rubin said.

Diego patted his pocket. "Why?"

"I want to get into position when we know they're here, first thing, and get two of those in her, just in case. That way, if something goes wrong, we can track her."

"Rubin." Diego injected caution into his voice. He glanced at Luther.

Luther held up his hands. "Don't mind me, boys. I don't hear nothin'. Got to uncover my stash of weapons anyway." He began to make his way back down the tunnel.

"Her body will just render them useless. You know that. She already told us it happened when a tracking system was tried before."

"Apparently you weren't listening when Mordichai explained to everyone how these worked," Rubin answered. "No one wanted Whitney to accidentally pick up on a signal and be able to track the girls. This doesn't look like a regular signal. You have to know what you're looking for." He sighed. "Just get it in her. I'll warn her you're going to shoot her and not to treat it as anything other than a bug bite."

"You're the boss, but we'll get her back, Rubin," Diego assured. "Let's go see what Luther has in his stash."

Rubin shouldn't have been surprised that Luther's weapons were up to date. Just the fact that Luther was worried that someone was going to come immediately for his body, even in the middle of a fight, should have tipped him off that Luther was being monitored. He had to have fought in the Vietnam War. If he'd been in more than one war, did that mean he'd run missions in Iraq and Afghanistan? His age alone should have prevented that from happening, but if Luther was considered a weapon, just as the Ghost-Walkers were, would the military use him? Most likely.

Luther painstakingly drew out every detail of the camp the soldiers had set up at Huntington Falls. He added in those guarding the machinery and their routes and times and the roving sentries.

"This is the one you have to get to, Rubin," he pointed out, using the tip of his knife to show an unseen leader who often went from one of the boulders near the falls to the trees in the woods. "He's running the show. He's most likely one of your squirrel men. The others are very alert when he's around and they defer fast to him."

"Have you seen him move?" Diego asked.

Luther shook his head. "No, but I was surprised when I had him in my sight on the boulder at the falls and I turned my head to look at another soldier. The next time I spotted him he was in the trees. I knew then he was something different. I pulled back to study the rest of the soldiers just in case they were like he was."

That explained why Luther hadn't engaged with them immediately. He had sabotaged their equipment without their knowledge. Until they went to use it, they wouldn't know.

"You'll have to find the leader's location first. If he sees you and you don't see him, you're as good as dead," Luther reiterated.

"I'm going out first," Diego said. "I'll put eyes in the sky before I go." He didn't look at Rubin, knowing his brother would object.

"Diego."

"I'm better than you out there. You're still not one hundred percent. Try to reach Jonquille while I'm sending the birds." Diego refused to look at him, but began to make his way to the front of the very narrow tunnel.

The entrance leading outside by Huntington Falls was natural. This was how Luther had first discovered the cave system. The tunnel sloped gently uphill, and all three of them had to stoop as the roof overhead was low. Rubin's and Diego's shoulders scraped on the walls of either side. There was a rock blocking most of the entryway, with grasses growing over and around it.

The vegetation was thick in the area and particularly right

where the rocks were. Grasses grew from every crack, creating a seemingly impenetrable wall. If anyone did look at what appeared to be a small hole, they might think it was an animal's den. Luther had encouraged the brush to grow and added the appearance of small animals living in the area. Nothing big enough to hunt, but if anyone was curious, it would explain the cozy little nest in the dark space. Very few would explore beyond that. Rubin couldn't help but marvel at the man's ingenuity.

He watched as Diego sent his birds into the air to find the leader of the soldiers as well as to find the location of as many of the other soldiers as possible. Diego had switched from the early morning songbirds to hawks. He sent the sharp-eyed raptors into the air from several locations.

While they waited for the information, Rubin composed a short sequence of notes to Jonquille to let her know he was aware of the code. He wanted her to know they were close. Waiting. She wasn't alone.

He had to be careful. If any of the others shared the pathway because they shared her genetic makeup and he touched them, they couldn't realize someone was communicating with Jonquille. She'd been very cautious. He had to be equally cautious. He followed the psychic footprints leading to her, sending little flicks and strikes very gently and softly, a melody of lightning using one of the actual refrains from the song she loved. He waited, knowing he was right but still worried that his woman was out there with a number of men and perhaps helpless.

A few flicks answered him. The relief was tremendous. He had already composed the next line. *You right.* He chose actual lyrics so he could use the notes, flicking them with ease. When he needed to, he would compose a detailed message, using the sequence, but for now, he'd find out if she was being treated humanely.

She let a few moments go by while his heart thudded in reaction to the wait. *Yes. Delaying them.*

She was giving them time to set up to find a way to retrieve her. He took his time trying to figure out the best thing to ask next. *Gunthrie's?* They had talked at length about Luther Gunthrie at the Sawyers'. Would the squirrel men risk talking in front of her? Or, like those she feared would be able to hear them speaking telepathically to her, could she hear them?

The little flicks came after what seemed forever. Time seemed to be rushing past. He had no idea how close the elite soldiers were, but if they didn't take out the ground crew, they would be overwhelmed with sheer numbers. It would be impossible to get Jonquille back. *Heard kill old man twice coming from someone there. The leader here objected. The one there said it was done.*

For some reason hearing that, even though he already knew it, sent a spark of anger through Rubin all over again. These soldiers had no idea Luther was anything but a gentle old man protecting his home and his still. The orders were very clear to hunt him down and kill him. That was why there was so much activity. They wanted him found and out of the way. And the team leader here had lied to the one in the field. Luther wasn't dead. The ground crew was still hunting him. Why did that man want him killed?

Arrival?

Just before dark.

She answered that immediately and then fell silent. He had the feeling she wouldn't respond again. It made sense that the soldiers would bring in a plane just before dark. They would want to ensure it would be when few travelers would be on the road. The plane would be small and would fly only Jonquille and a couple of the elite soldiers out with her. The others would go by road. They wouldn't want to be seen. Once the plane was in the air, they would wait for nightfall and they would leave, taking their equipment with them. Luther would be dead, but what was the death of one old man? If they buried him deep, they would expect that no one would look too hard for him.

Squirrel man is in the tree above the falls. He's sitting up there with a pair of binoculars, directing his crew. He's talking to someone though. Do you want me to figure out what he's saying? I can read lips.

Yes.

Diego was silent a moment. *Some kind of double cross going on here, Rubin. This man is saying the major doesn't suspect anything. They'll get the package on the plane and once it's in the air, they'll kill all the soldiers. His men will surround them and kill them. They won't be expecting it, so they won't have a chance to fight back.*

He was silent again, watching the leader as he listened to whomever was on the other end of the phone. *He's talking to someone higher up. Said the major trusts him implicitly. Now that that pilot has been taken prisoner, replaced with their pilot, she'll be going to this person's laboratory. A lot of laughter. The person on the phone will get information from pilot. Has chemicals and his men can practice techniques on extracting information. It should be fun for them. This bozo says not to worry, he will handle everything here and won't let anything happen to the package.*

Rubin rubbed his temple, shaking his head. That was all they needed. A conspiracy. A double cross. *Take him out when you have the shot.*

I've got a clear shot to him right now. Rubin, once I do, we'll have to move fast, pick a spot and get out of here. There are two left in camp. We don't want them to get to their radios before we get to them.

Rubin marked his targets. He could hit them on the run. *You take the leader, I'll take the other two.* "Luther, back us up, but stay out of the way. When we hunt, we don't usually worry about anyone but the two of us."

"You don't worry about me. Do what you have to do."

Rubin took the man at his word. He'd survived this long, and he'd had a good run knowing his own strengths. *Let's do this, Diego.*

Diego, staying in the shadow of the tunnel so as not to chance alerting the squirrel man with movement, slid his rifle forward. He took better care of his rifle than any other piece of equipment he had. That rifle was a part of him. He knew every little quirk she had. Squirrel man came into his vision, barking orders to his men, anger on his face. Diego squeezed the trigger.

Rubin took his targets instantly, first one then the second one as he slid from the tunnel onto the ground and came up behind the brush he'd chosen, his guns in hand already firing a second time just to be certain. The sound of the bullets was so close they sounded as if they were on top of one another even though he'd fired two shots from inside the tunnel and two out.

Rubin's targets were down and the squirrel man was crumpling, falling from the tree in a macabre, slow-motion fall that had him bouncing from branch to branch.

You certain he's dead, Diego? Rubin remembered how difficult the squirrel men seemed to be to kill.

He's dead, Diego confirmed.

Red-shouldered hawk flying over two soldiers just to the south of us, Diego said. *They alerted to the sound of gunfire and are heading this way. One is talking into his radio.*

Diego shared the exact images with Rubin so he could see where the two soldiers were and how fast they were coming toward them. The two brothers took off together, sprinting through the brush, rushing to intercept, staying low as they ran, keeping a space of about twenty feet.

The hawk above them let out a distinctive *kee-ahh* cry. The sound was one used for alarm or a claim on his territory. In this case, the bird warned Diego the soldiers were closing in on the two brothers fast. Diego dropped to one knee. Rubin did the same. This time, both men used the bow, wanting silence. They hadn't had room in the tunnel, but here, in the woods, they did. Not only did Luther have bows and arrows, crossbows and arrows, he had explosives as well that could be fired using them.

They heard the two soldiers before they saw them. Heavy breathing. The snapping of twigs. A branch creaking as one of them shoved it out of the way. A muffled curse.

"Do you think that old man got him?"

"No way in hell. Something's wrong with the radio is all. That old man is up there dead. That's what the vultures are after."

Diego and Rubin released arrows at the same time. They'd grown up hunting with arrows long before bullets. Bullets were a luxury. The arrows flew straight and true, going straight through the throats of both men. The second arrow took them through the heart.

Two over by Luther's shack. They're looking at the equipment. Met up with one of the sentries. The other sentry is on his way around. Must have called him, Diego reported.

They were bound to check the equipment.

One's trying to start up one of the heavy-duty backhoes. It's not co-operating. They don't look too happy. In fact, the sentry is backing away from the guard. He looks nervous.

Diego and Rubin were already on the move, using the same sprinting pace they'd used before, running through the woods in a low almost crouch, a good twenty feet apart so they'd be difficult to spot. They knew the easiest and fastest routes from Huntington Falls to the Gunthrie cabin and which ones had the most cover. They stayed under branches, avoided hitting brush that might give them away to anyone watching for them.

As they neared the edge of the woods where Gunthrie had built his home, they swung around it to intersect with the long holler leading to his residence. The equipment the soldiers planned to use to build a runway was lined up in a row just around a bend from the Gunthrie home.

One man was peering inside the first machine, a frown on his face. "Just about every wire is cut. *Every* wire. What wasn't cut was smashed or bent. I don't know how that old man could have done this much damage by himself, Bert. You have to take a look at this."

The soldier in charge, Bert, stalked over just as the second sentry arrived. Bert peered inside the machine. "What the hell? Is every one of them like this one?"

The others opened the machines up to examine them. Bert looked inside with obvious disgust. "How could he do this without making a racket? You're telling me you didn't hear him?" He straightened and turned toward the other three soldiers, all grouped together.

Diego and Rubin shot them with arrows, the first two hitting Bert and his partner in the throat, the second two the sentries. They each shot two more, hitting their targets in the heart before they had fallen to the ground.

A red-tailed hawk to the west is in a spruce looking down on two soldiers moving through the woods heading up toward the ridge. They finally spotted the vultures. About time. There's quite a few now. Must be going to take a look at the body.

Still have two more somewhere. Going onto the ridge is risky without knowing where those two are, Rubin cautioned. *Have to get eyes on them.*

Diego was silent, reaching for the various hawks he had in the sky. *Two are walking the meadow. Pacing it off. Presumably to map out the runway.*

We take them first, Rubin decided.

They're in plain sight. The ones on the ridge can see them. If we kill the ones in the meadow, the ones on the ridge are going to know they're being hunted.

Either way, one of the pair was going to be tipped off. If they took the ones on the ridge, those in the meadow would no doubt know. Luther might get them. And was that the problem? Was he protecting the old man? Luther had done enough for his country. Given enough. Put his life on the line over and over.

Diego smirked at him. *That protective streak in you is growing, bro. I don't say that like it's a good thing. Luther wouldn't appreciate it. You're taking his fun. I can't imagine what it's going to be like when you have children. You're going to make those kids crazy.*

Diego was right—the logical thing to do was go up the ridge and remove that threat. They could always find the last two soldiers. They knew the woods and Huntington Falls far better than the two men who would be looking for their team members to back them up. Even if they radioed to the squirrel men holding Jonquille, the elite soldiers would have no choice but to continue with their plan to bring her to the meadow. They didn't yet know the equipment was useless. Hopefully, Luther killed the two in the meadow before they relayed that information or the fact that the ground crew was dead.

Rubin sighed. *Fine. We'll head for the ridge. But if anything happens to that old man, I'm holding you responsible.*

He's a vampire, Rubin. He lives underground and sleeps in a coffin. That's his secret. The military found a way to make him into a vampire. He lives on blood.

Rubin wouldn't have been altogether surprised if that turned out to be the truth.

That's why he stayed in the tunnel when we came out of it. He's got a trapdoor in the meadow though. You wait and see. He'll pull those two poor soldiers through and feed off them for the next twenty years. That's why his buddy Jacob has to cremate his body so fast.

And I thought I was the storyteller. Have that hawk keep a close watch on the pair. Let's move fast.

The two again began to make their way to the ridge, this time through Gunthrie's woods and brush, heading in the direction of the mountain itself. The slope was gentle at first, deceptive in its climb. Rubin thought about Luther taking his still up to the ridge where he actually had it for a while. Why? He'd moved the still around his property to various spots, fueling the rumors of a paranoid man certain the feds were after him for his illegal making of moonshine. That whiskey was considered some of the best in the state and was sought after by some of the best stores. Luther made a fortune off of it. How? Rubin had never thought too much about it. He should have.

They stayed low in the cover of the brush until there was no more brush and then both dropped to the ground, blending into the rocky surface. Grasses and the occasional straggly wildflower grew on the slope leading up to the ridge, but quite a lot of the mountain was made up of rock. This particular side had sparse vegetation and was dark in color, with various-size rocks jutting out.

They used their abilities to pull themselves up with sheer strength, climbing faster than they would ordinarily, but trusting Luther to take care of the two soldiers mapping out the meadow. The two in the meadow seemed very occupied with their job. They needed to get their runway right, and it was clear from the images the hawk had shared with Diego that they had hastily made runways before.

The equipment used was small for a reason. It didn't look military. The backhoes would blend in with farming equipment in the area. Anyone seeing the backhoes being transported on the trailers wouldn't think twice about them.

Rubin sent up a silent prayer to the universe that Luther was as good as he thought he was. He would have to time his taking of the soldiers for the moment Rubin and Diego killed the two on the ridge. If they spotted the ones being killed in the meadow, they would be on full alert. As it was, they were nervous with communication being down between everyone. It was the fact that those in the meadow were carrying on with their job as if nothing was wrong that kept the two soldiers searching the ridge for Luther. Rubin could hear them now, he was that close.

"I hate these damn radios, Parker. They never work. And they're a bitch to put in the ear and then take out."

Rubin noted that Parker wore combat boots and dark cargo pants. He looked seriously capable, with multiple weapons hanging from his belt and his gun rock steady in his hands.

"You know who the package is, Kurt, and why they want her? This is a lot of work for one tiny chick. Everyone's a little afraid of her," Parker answered.

Rubin had been about to rise up behind Kurt, but he froze, waiting for him to give an answer. Diego didn't move either, lying full out behind Parker. Either man could be seen. They blended into the terrain and were very still, controlling their breathing and heartbeats, but they could be stepped on, or a good soldier might spot them.

"Why would you think I know?" Kurt asked, his tone suddenly

wary. He glanced up at the sky. "Those vultures are getting lower and lower. Some are already on the ground just up there. I'm hoping it's the old man, but Daryl didn't come back. We couldn't get him on the radio."

"You just complained the radios were shit, Kurt, and they are," Parker said. "You do know why they want this woman. It's not a big deal if you tell me. Who am I going to tell?"

"No one, because I don't know shit. If I did know anything and it got out that I told someone, those soldiers would cut me into little pieces and hang me from a tree. They're not anyone you want to mess with."

Parker shrugged and patted his weapon lovingly. "A bullet kills anyone, Kurt, even them. They try to mess with me, they're dead, same as anyone else."

"Yeah, well, you don't know these men. I see them every day and what they can do. Let's go see what the vultures are feasting on."

He isn't going to talk. He's too afraid of the squirrel men, Rubin conveyed to Diego.

My take too, Diego agreed.

Kurt took a step. It was the last step of his life. Rubin rose up behind him and slammed a knife into the base of his skull. Diego did the same to Parker. Neither man saw death coming, nor did they smell it. Very carefully, bodies held upright in front of them, Rubin and Diego looked toward the meadow. Luther was dragging the first body off the meadow. The second lay on the ground with an arrow sticking out of his chest.

Diego grinned at Rubin as he lowered Parker to the ground. "That old man. He's got the skills. I might be right about the vampire thing. He might live forever. He hasn't lost his touch."

Rubin was respectful of the body of the soldier as well. Kurt was just doing his job. Too bad it was on the wrong side. "Luther definitely hasn't lost his touch. We're going to need a cleanup crew before this is over. I'm not into burying all these bodies myself."

"You're getting lazy," Diego said and sat down abruptly, wiping his face with both hands.

Rubin gave him a quick look. He had no real idea what toll it took on his brother to use his psychic gifts. "That I am. Getting a little up there in age." He sat down beside his brother and took in the view. "I love this valley. I always have."

Diego just nodded. They sat together in silence for just a little while, letting the peace of their birthplace seep into their hearts.

14

Jonquille did her best to observe as much as she could about the men who had kidnapped her. The results were daunting. These were elite soldiers. They weren't anything like the ones she'd seen Whitney create from the flawed men who'd agreed to genetic and psychic enhancements once they'd failed their tests. Those men desperately wanted to be faster and stronger than others for money. They believed they were superior already and being enhanced was just another step. Those men eventually went insane.

These elite soldiers were the exact opposite. She kept her eyes half-closed, watching the efficiency as they broke camp. They worked together as a unit, almost as one person. They were courteous to her when they spoke to her. They provided blankets to cover her when they rested and it was cold. When she had to go into the bushes, two guards went with her, but they turned their backs after receiving her word that she wouldn't try to escape.

Jonquille thought long and hard about that. Why believe her?

She had even considered escaping from them, but she'd always kept her word. It was a matter of pride with her. She detested that Whitney lied so much and used the girls' emotions and their caring for one another against them. She had vowed never to be like him. Did that count when your freedom was at stake?

The leader of the elite soldiers came over to sit in front of her. He always had a relaxed air about him. He didn't bark orders at his men, rather they acted as if they had a great comradery. In some ways it made her lonelier than ever. She didn't have that. Well, she was feeling as if she had a chance of it with Rubin and Diego.

The men treated her with a kind of respect she'd never gotten from Whitney's soldiers or guards. There were one or two who had sympathized, but they were quickly removed. These men acted as if she was their equal, not a lab project to be feared, or one to sneer at. Still, she wasn't going to be lulled into thinking they were good when they'd kidnapped her, just because they treated her as a human being.

"My name is Sean O'Connell. I'm a major in the United States Air Force. I know the circumstances don't look good, but we need your help. Finding you and getting a chance to talk to you seemed very slim. We thought once you were back with us at our home, you would see the dire situation we're in and you'd agree to help us out."

It was the last thing Jonquille had expected him to say. She sat up slowly, careful to keep her distance, very cognizant of the rifles pointed at her from the trees. The moment she got into an upright position, her head felt like it was going to shatter into a million pieces. Her stomach lurched, protesting the last vestiges of the drug in her system. She refused to allow any discomfort to show on her face.

The major didn't appear afraid of her, but he still wasn't taking chances. She pushed back her thick, wild hair as it settled around her chin. She had it short to keep it from going crazy when the storms came in, but it was still practically untamable. Rubin seemed to like it that way. She wished he was there now.

She lowered her lashes as if thinking about what Sean was saying, but really, she was judging how close his hands were to her. He was wearing gloves. The only actual bare skin she had access to was his face. The snipers could get a shot off before she killed him.

"How exactly can I help you? I'm sure Whitney has told you I'm his greatest failure. That's the reason he left me alone."

"Whitney has no idea what you're capable of. We do. We are not affiliated with him."

"Yet you're obviously enhanced both genetically and psychically." She wasn't going to beat around the bush. "As far as I know, only Whitney is experimenting on human beings, and he's doing that covertly. So, where did you come from?"

Sean sighed. "We would like to break camp soon and get to our destination. You could come with us willingly, or we will have to drug you again and carry you."

"I'm not about to trade one prison for another. You tell me what's going on before I make that decision. Otherwise you'll have to drug me, and when I'm awake, all bets are off."

Little fiery taps beat in her head. She dug her fingers into her thigh to keep from following the beat. She knew that the last time, one of the guards had suddenly watched her fingers and she had to force herself to stop midmessage. It was an obsessive-compulsive habit she'd developed in isolation, counting out rhythms on her thighs. Now it helped her cope, but if any of the others felt that light tapping in their mind, they might associate it with the tapping on her thigh and know she was receiving or sending messages.

Rubin wanted her to slap her body loudly when she was bitten by a bug. Or at least make a big deal about it in some way. They were going to shoot a transmitter into her bloodstream, one that wouldn't transmit in the normal way. It would be undetected and the energy in her body wouldn't devour it. She was already at capacity with these men and she could tell they put off very little energy, the way Rubin and Diego did. They would suddenly have flares of violent energy that swarmed to her, and then just as suddenly they would dissipate, sometimes before they reached her.

"Who were the men helping?" Sean asked.

She blinked. "Does it matter?"

"They were . . . unexpected. Let's just say no one thought we would have casualties."

"Because you underestimated what someone on their own turf can do. They know the country and they're good in the woods. The best." She let her admiration show. It was genuine and he would recognize that.

"Again, who are they?"

"If I gave you that information, you'd have two of your soldiers round up someone they love and hold a gun to their head so they'll leave you alone. You aren't innocent, Sean. I overhead that some old man was killed just because you wanted to use his property. And then there's kidnapping."

"I'm sorry you had to hear that. Yes, some hard decisions are necessary for the protection of my men. I have to put them first. Just as we made the decision to acquire you. It was put to a vote, but ultimately, I had to agree and plan the mission. You are very good in the woods yourself."

Again, Jonquille felt his respect for her. She pushed down the part where he had to make hard decisions. She didn't want to think too much about what that meant to the people he decided to kill. "Where are you taking me if not to Whitney's? More experiments?"

He looked genuinely shocked. "Is that what you think? No. Absolutely not. We need your help. You won't be hurt. I give you my word as an officer in the Air Force."

She tapped very gently, using the lightning sequence to give Rubin Sean's name and rank in the Air Force. He appeared to think he was acting on active duty.

"Are you under orders?"

Sean looked around at the others and then slowly shook his head. "No, we took our leave at the same time and only have a short window to get this done."

"If you would tell me, I might be able to determine whether or not I can help."

"We know you can," Sean said, his voice filled with conviction. "It's a matter of whether you will agree to or not."

"Why make it a huge mystery?" she challenged.

"Because we sound like we're nutty if we talk about it. It's easier to show you. I'm telling you we don't want you hurt in any way. We aren't going to use you for experiments. We aren't going to turn you over to Whitney whether you help or not. He isn't a part of this."

"And the person who enhanced you?"

Sean rubbed his chest as if it ached. "Dr. Oliver Chandler was hired by Whitney to think up futuristic weapons. Believe me, he's very good at it. Whitney and he were talking about harnessing lightning, and Whitney showed Chandler some of the experiments the doc had tried using you. Chandler was intrigued and began to obsess over developing a lightning weapon. At the same time, he noticed the soldiers Whitney surrounded himself with."

"Those are as much his failed experiments as the little girls he claims are failures," Jonquille said. "Why would your boss be so enamored with those soldiers?"

"Whitney didn't stop there. He showed Chandler the experiments he had done with you girls. Then the soldiers failing psych tests, that was to show him the importance of getting the best to complete the experiments. And then he had a few descriptions of a team he called the GhostWalkers.

"Chandler went back to his lab and he began to obsess over wanting his own elite soldiers. We'd been with him awhile, guarding him. He's a brilliant man. His work goes to the Department of Defense to protect our soldiers."

"*All* of it? Does everything go there, or does he sell some of his ideas and fancy weapons to foreign countries, Sean?" Jonquille asked softly.

Sean shook his head. "I don't know that answer anymore. I can tell you that I would have bet my last dollar that he was a patriot and would never do something like that a couple of years ago, but lately . . . Suddenly, people aren't human beings to him. Not even us, and we've been with him almost from the start."

Jonquille could hear the truth in his voice. Whatever agenda he had for her, this was clearly the truth and he felt very real sorrow, mixed with anger, when he told her. She knew and understood feelings of betrayal. She took a careful look around from under her lashes, keeping her head straight, seemingly looking at Sean. The others were watching her closely, trying to interpret how she was taking the information Sean was giving her.

"He wanted his own supersoldiers," she prompted.

Sean nodded. "Exactly, but not flawed the way Whitney's are. He wanted them superior to anything on the planet, like the GhostWalkers. He wanted better than the GhostWalkers. He began doing research into who was doing work on genetics. What kinds of work and how advanced they were. He found a team he thought was willing to do what he wanted and brought them to the States to his lab. They did the first round of operations and then flew home thinking they had all the information in their briefcases. The plane blew up and all the information was mysteriously lost."

"Of course it was," Jonquille said in disgust.

"We weren't all perfect. That made him crazy. He wanted perfection. And he wanted psychically enhanced soldiers as well. He went for a second round of soldiers, and I'm not certain he was any happier. Now he's even more obsessed."

"I can't possibly help with either one."

Sean sat there for a long time just looking at her. "No, but you've been doing research into psychic healing. Abel, one of my men, used the computer after you. It was locked, of course, and password protected, but he found some way to duplicate or mirror what you were doing. We thought you were a spy, actually. Imagine our surprise when you turned out to be anything but."

Jonquille turned to look at Abel, their computer genius. He looked a little guilty, but gave her a salute. A mosquito bit her neck and she smacked it with the palm of her hand loud enough for the others to react. She gave them a little girlie smile. "I always get a reaction to bug bites. Not a big one, but enough to drive me crazy with itching.

"Yes, I was researching healing as a natural form. Here, in the Appalachian Mountains, there are still some people who are suspicious of medical practices and outsiders. I have a small gift for healing. I know people don't believe in that, so go ahead and sneer if you want, but I was hoping to learn more about how to use it."

She kept her voice low and even to cover the lie. She felt bad lying to him—almost. She had no way of helping these people. And they'd *kidnapped* her.

Sean shook his head. "I read every single article you read. We went over and over the links you followed. We could almost feel your frustration when you ran into dead ends. You were looking for something besides the ability for natural healing."

The little lightning flicks hit her again. She rubbed her temples. Rubin was seriously upset now that he knew who had kidnapped her. He wanted her to tell Sean who he was going to be dealing with.

She tapped out a big fat *no*. Rubin's protection was in the fact that Sean was unaware of who Rubin was.

Rubin came right back at her. If she didn't drop the bomb, he would do so himself—by contacting her telepathically so those listening in would hear.

Jonquille closed her eyes for a moment, feeling as if she were being forced to give Rubin up.

"Jonquille?" Sean persisted. "You were looking for something besides the ability for natural healing."

Jonquille took her time before responding, breathing deeply in and out. She made certain she kept her facial expression exactly the same. She wasn't about to give this man any intelligence on what she had been looking for. It was a pipe dream anyway. Maybe she should just come clean and tell him that. As far as she knew, no one could do what she had hoped—remove the psychic enhancements Whitney had put on them.

"I wasn't nearly as clever in the laboratory as I thought I was," she finally said. "All those months of research on lightning and healing. I thought I was very clever sneaking in under a different name."

"You were, actually," Sean agreed. "We caught you in a random security screening that we do on and off. We never tell anyone ahead of time, we just conduct them. Your prints matched, everything did. In fact, your profile was so impeccable I nearly passed it over, but then I looked at you again. Really looked at you. Those eyes. That hair. You're very small. You look almost fragile. There's no hiding you even in baggy clothes. I'd seen you in films countless times. Chandler had watched them over and over. I knew you were the same Jonquille from Whitney's lab. You were either spying for him or for someone else."

"I can see how you'd come to that conclusion," Jonquille agreed noncommittally. "I'd never spy for Whitney. He could pull my fingernails out one by one. As for another country, that just would never happen. If I did get one thing out of being with that bastard, it was to love my country. So, no, I wasn't spying. Just doing research and helping out someone who needed an assistant."

"You say you were researching to learn natural healing to help those here in the mountains who refuse traditional medical aid because they don't like outsiders," Sean continued. "You aren't from the Appalachian Mountains, so wouldn't you be considered an outsider?"

Jonquille drew up her legs, promptly swatted another mosquito and then gave the men a faint apologetic smile. "I can take a bullet better than a bug bite. I *detest* them. There's something about that silly bug chowing down on me."

It was rather ironic playing such a girlie girl when she practically lived in the woods half the time—and Rubin called her Lightning Bug.

"Yes, to answer your questions, I would be considered an outsider and wouldn't get in the front door, but fortunately, I have friends here and they introduced me. So far, I've been accepted and I count myself very lucky. The people I've met have been lovely."

"You're a research assistant for Colonel Rubin Campo. There isn't much known about him other than that he is out in the field with his unit bringing back wounded. A colonel, no less. They say he actually goes to the hot spots and doesn't have the others go, but then most of those in his unit are officers now, aren't they? In fact, they get regular promotions quite often."

There it was. Her opening. Her heart accelerated and she had to force it back under control. She refused to be the rabbit. She stayed mute, rubbing at her neck as though it itched. *Fishing, Sean. You can do better.* She didn't blink.

"It would be friendly if you would answer the question."

"How could I possibly know if his unit gets promotions? I don't ask him that. Most of his work is classified, so even if I wanted to tell you about it, I couldn't."

"Do you know the colonel outside of work?"

Whoa. Sean didn't back off from the hard questions. She smiled up at him angelically, knowing she was about to drop a bomb on him. "Well, actually, yes. I know him quite well. In fact, I was here to visit with him. And Diego, his brother. They're very, very close, in case you're unaware of Diego. He's good in the forest. *Extremely* good."

There was a silence, so much so that the wind seemed to pause, as if holding its breath right along with them all. Very slowly, the men looked at one another and then to Sean.

"I need you to clarify this for me, Jonquille. Are you saying that you were with Rubin and Diego Campo in the forest when we acquired you?"

"Yes." She answered without hesitation. "That's exactly what I'm saying."

"Why were you with the Campo brothers?" Sean persisted through clenched teeth.

"Rubin is my fiancé," Jonquille said. "He's been working with me on healing as well. He's very good at it. He has a natural gift for it." She gave them her sweetest smile and rubbed her thigh over the supposed mosquito bite.

She sent a message to Rubin, hoping he wouldn't be upset with her, using little fiery flicks of the sequence and keeping it short. As she sent the message, she watched the others under the veil of her eyelashes, trying to figure out if any of them felt those jabbing spears of hot lightning on the outer edges of the brain. *Blew yr cover. Told them U healer if that's what they want. Not happy.*

She really hated that she had blown it for Rubin and Diego. Part of their advantage was that this group had no idea who they were dealing with. They still didn't know for certain the brothers were GhostWalkers, but they had to be guessing. Sean was intelligent. She didn't understand why Rubin was so insistent, but she knew the news had really shaken Sean.

Rubin let some time go by so there was no way to associate the tiny jabs with communication. She noticed that two of the soldiers rubbed their temples. It could have been coincidence, but she'd noticed them before when messages had come in from Rubin. One was called Hudson, the other Andrew.

"We attacked a colonel in the Air Force, his brother who happens to be a lieutenant colonel, and kidnapped the fiancée of the colonel." Abel rubbed the corners of his eyes. "We're going to be court-martialed. The keys to our cells are going to be thrown away."

"We knew going into this that it could go wrong," Sean reminded the others. "We all agreed it was our only chance. We voted on it. The only thing we can do is go forward and try to talk to the colonel and hope he has some understanding of our situation." He turned his attention back to Jonquille, his gaze moving over her in a dark, moody way she wasn't certain she liked.

"Does he have a radio on him?"

She frowned. "Why would he have a radio? He wasn't lurking around in the woods playing soldier. He's a doctor. He came to check on patients. He does every year, twice a year. There are people, families, that won't seek out normal medical attention. Rubin and Diego were born here. They're accepted and can go into those homes and provide care for those that would otherwise never have it."

"If the colonel came up here to play doctor, why was he loaded for bear?"

"They always go armed. I've never seen either of them without weapons. I don't go into the woods without weapons. And Diego doesn't ever go anywhere without his rifle." The moment the words were out she wanted to clap her hand over her mouth and shove them back inside. It was too late. Far too late.

"Diego," one of the men whispered, his voice filled with fear. "Sean. That's not just anyone she's talking about." He suddenly glared at Jonquille as if she had deliberately set them up. "Tell us who he is." He shouted the command at her.

"Hudson, calm down. It isn't her fault we're in this mess. What are you worried about?"

"This Diego she's talking about. The colonel's brother. He's known, Sean. He can shoot the wings off a fly. They say he's a GhostWalker. That he can disappear and then suddenly he's right in your face and knifes you, slices you from the belly up. Then before you even drop to the ground, he disappears again."

"That's what they say about him, do they?" Sean asked, gritting his teeth. He scowled at Jonquille. "Is Diego Campo a Ghost-Walker?"

"If Diego Campo was a GhostWalker, wouldn't that be considered classified information? Technically, all of you are GhostWalkers, and so am I. By definition, it's someone genetically and psychically enhanced. I believe we all fall into that category."

The little flicks were back, rapid but short. Diego had found them. He was lying up on the hillside, Sean in his sights. Give the word, he'd pull the trigger.

No, no, no. She was adamant and fast reacting just in case.

Both Hudson and Andrew rubbed their temples and then the back of their necks. Jonquille winced. She didn't like that she'd answered so quickly, compounding the problem. She was too close to the two men to use telepathy, not when they would feel what she was doing.

He's going 2 shoot U.

Her heart accelerated. She remembered his earlier messages to her. She was to treat the shot like a bug bite. That meant she would feel whatever he was shooting at her. She couldn't believe Diego was right there, out in the forest, so close. She wanted Rubin, which was stupid. Rubin didn't need to be anywhere near the elite soldiers. Luck eventually ran out, and Diego and Rubin were outnumbered by quite a few.

Where are U. She couldn't help herself, she had to ask.

On the heels of that burst of fiery flicks, she was shot with a high-powered rifle. The sound was muffled, barely discernible. The sting as the object entered into her body was terrible. She slapped her hand over the entry point and scowled. It burned like hell. A drop of blood told her the tiny object had entered a vein. Or the artery in her neck.

Sorry, I know that hurts, Lightning Bug. It was the longest and sweetest message Rubin had sent her so far. *I'm with Luther. All soldiers here departed.*

She didn't know how to feel about that. Rubin and Diego had

killed the *entire* ground crew and now there was no way for the plane to land. She didn't mind that the plane couldn't land. She did think it was nearly impossible for them to kill so many when it was only the two of them. She was relieved that Luther was still alive.

"We need to get moving, Jonquille. Are you willing to cooperate with us?" Sean demanded. "Walk on your own without trying to escape?"

Jonquille nodded slowly. She needed to stretch her legs and back. Her insides hurt from the drug in her system. Everything hurt. She didn't want more of the drug in her system. She was careful to keep all movements slow so no one thought she was a danger to Sean, but she did put her legs out in front of her.

"I can walk. I just need to stretch. Every muscle feels sore."

Her neck throbbed. She was almost afraid to take her palm away. She rubbed and then massaged the back of her neck so no one was suspicious. Even turning her mind inward, trying to find whatever device Diego had put into her body, seemed difficult, as if her brain was still a little sluggish from the drug. The only things she could "see" when looking inward were occasional flashes of light in her bloodstream, like butterflies dancing. Now she was really getting fanciful.

"I'm sorry, Jonquille." Sean sounded as if he meant it. "People react to the drug in various ways. We knew we had to put you out fast. According to the file we have on you, you can be rather dangerous. We didn't want you to feel as if you had to defend yourself and put you or any of us in a situation where someone could get hurt. We had no way of knowing that you were meeting anyone up here. You're always alone."

That was the truth. And she hadn't really planned on meeting Rubin and Diego. She was going to lead these people and the others she thought might be following her away from the Appalachian Mountains, and she would kill as many of them as possible before they killed her.

She was over experiments. Completely, utterly over them. Heat shimmered around her. The air crackled. Tiny hairs on the back of her neck stood up. She felt energy, white hot, swirling like her life's blood flowing through her veins. That feeling of power was familiar to her. Around her, dimly, she heard shouts. Men scrambled. She saw them, although her vision was different, not at all her usual eyesight. This was like a veil of silver over everything.

Her captors were running, looking over their shoulders back at her, and she could make out the fear on their faces. They were fast too, little blurs as they ran. Still, they gave off energy now, where before it was so low it was difficult to even pick up on. Now the energy surged fiery and fierce, great dark streams of it rushing to her, as if she were a magnet, collecting from all of the men, feeding the bright white-hot storm inside her.

"Jonquille." Sean's voice was calm. "What's wrong? Tell me what upset you."

She turned her blurred, silvery-blue vision on him. He was the last man standing. He was alone, one hand up as if to placate her. In spite of his calm exterior she could see the lines of strain around his eyes and mouth.

"Experiments." She could barely get the word out. "Get away from me." She needed open ground to make everyone safe. "Not running." She wouldn't break her word. She indicated to him that she was going toward the one clearing so she could get out in the open.

Out of the corner of her eye, she saw him turn toward Hudson and Andrew. Yeah, she'd been right about the two men. They were the ones that could read her. Maybe it wasn't so easy when her mind was consumed with chaos, with the need to explode with the buildup of blazing energy. Anyone coming near her would be killed. It was that simple. She was trying to save lives, not run away.

Her legs were so rubbery, not at all steady and sure as they'd always been. She could barely trust them. Without thinking she reached out to him. *Rubin.* It was a cry for help.

The moment she did, she felt the two men go on alert. "She's trying to contact him. Rubin Campo." Hudson ratted on her immediately.

"She sounds very distressed," Andrew said. "Very. I've never heard her like that. She's always in control. Let her talk to him. We can't stop what's happening. She's trying to protect us. We can't help her walk, and she's definitely struggling to do that. That damn drug is the problem, Sean. It's affected her muscles."

Jonquille forced her mind to concentrate on just getting one foot in front of the other. She couldn't think about the buildup of electricity and how the white-hot energy was zipping in circles around her midsection in a fiery display like the Fourth of July. She had to get away from the trees. From humans. She couldn't start a forest fire or kill these men. She didn't know if they were good men or bad ones yet.

Right here, Lightning Bug. Rubin's voice soothed her. *You've got this.*

Just his voice allowed her to take a real breath, drawing air into her burning, raw lungs. *Having trouble walking. Drug messed me up. Is there a way for me to combat it? Don't want to hurt anyone. So close to drawing the lightning.*

She kept walking, but she was like a blind drunk, stumbling, going to her knees, struggling to stand and then managing one or two steps before going down again. Her stomach lurched and her head felt like it might shatter with each step. All the while that energy built the power in her body so that the two sides, power and utter weakness, clashed and fought for supremacy.

You have a reservoir of healing in you, Jonquille. You saw how it worked. Pass your palm over your legs. Keep your palm about an inch from your skin. Visualize what's wrong and repair it as you go. That will get you up faster than anything. Once you release the energy, you can heal the rest of you.

Rubin. She whispered his name again, as if holding on to him. She felt that if she let him go, she would lose him.

You can do this, my little lightning bug. I'll come for you, no matter where they take you, I'll come for you. We all will. Every single Ghost-Walker. That's a promise. So, whoever is listening, you might want to tell your boss I'll be coming for him. For all of you.

Of course Rubin would issue a challenge to the squirrel men. There was a quietness in him. He was like the mountains. Calm. Peaceful. But rile him, and he would bring the wrath of centuries down on you. He was every predator rolled into one. He would hunt them, and he had their scent.

She was already on the ground, shaking with the effort to contain the energy swirling around her. Very slowly, with care, she passed her palm over her left leg. Her muscles were like Jell-O. It felt odd to fix her own body, to bring up that heat inside her and pour it over her damaged muscles, shape them, firm them and make them strong again. She did the same with her right leg and then was on her feet and running.

Rubin. Her hero. Her man. Maybe even her fiancé for real. She wanted to believe there was a way for her to have a home and a family. She hadn't believed it until she'd gone to the Sawyers' with him. She'd actually been there all evening and not once had she had a problem. In time, with Rubin, maybe she could learn to control the energy that rushed to her.

She sprinted to the clearing. The clouds overhead swirled in an ominous display of power. Colors of purple, gray and black were stacked from bottom to top and they lit up over and over as lightning zigzagged in forks through the cloud, looking for a way out. The lead stroke was going to break free and come to ground, seeking a target. In a few more minutes the wind would have driven the clouds away from them, but it was too late. The energy in her body was too strong and too attractive to the lead stroke. It would come straight to her.

She made it to the clearing just as the charge around her built to an astonishing level and she knew the strike was coming. Lifting her arms, she released the energy, allowing it to meet the lead stroke, so that the two charges detonated into a blast of jagged lightning that lit the skies and sent thunder rolling, shaking the ground. She'd forgotten what it felt like to have that tremendous release after holding in so much energy. All the anger. All the fury. Even fear and sorrow. All emotion had energy, and those things found her when she was with others, weighing her down until she had to do this, stand in the clearing, arms outstretched, welcoming the lightning.

Jonquille let the lightning play over her for several strikes, washing away the drug in her system completely so she could think clearly again. She sent the lightning to meet the storm, great jagged spears that pierced the black and purple clouds so that they opened up and poured a cleansing rain down on her. The rain was warm, each drop on her skin a welcome purging.

Finally, the wind shifted the clouds away from her and she sank down into the grass, exhausted as she always was after a meeting with lightning. She lay with her hands behind her head, a makeshift pillow, waiting for the men to approach her, hoping they weren't so afraid by that little display that they chose to drug her again.

"Are you all right, Jonquille?" Sean asked.

He was first, of course. She should have known. The man had courage. She had a lot of respect for him, and that scared her just a little. She didn't want to like him. "Yes, just tired. Weak. It will pass. Give me a few minutes and I can walk." Her voice was scratchy, another by-product of using her strange talent.

"Are you thirsty?"

Naturally, Sean would notice. He was that good of a guy. She *really* didn't want to see him in that light. "Yes. Water would be good."

He disappeared and came back right away with a canteen filled with water. "Spring water," he told her as if she might suspect the drug was in the water.

She wouldn't have cared. Her throat hurt. Propping herself up on one elbow, she allowed the cool water to run down her throat a little bit at a time, easing the terrible burn. It felt wonderful. She managed a smile. "Thanks, Sean. I really needed this."

"Watching that light show was pretty incredible."

"Whitney wasn't so appreciative. Did you read that part in my file? I was one of his greatest failures."

Sean nodded gravely. "Yes. I saw the word stamped over and over in big red letters on many of the hundreds of experiments he tried with you."

"He was always stamp happy. I had this persistent nightmare that he would tattoo 'FAILURE' in bright red letters across my forehead."

Sean laughed. "I can imagine. Whitney always did seem uptight. Chandler is a kiss-ass and he plays the part very well. Whitney eats it up."

"Don't trust him," Jonquille warned. "He can spot a kiss-ass a mile away. He might not know that Chandler is creating elite soldiers for himself. I believe he'd shut that project down, but he wouldn't fully trust him."

"So far, he's given Chandler everything he's asked for."

Sean sounded so tired that Jonquille sat all the way up and studied his face, trying to look at him not as her kidnapper but as another human being. There were lines of strain around his face, lines etched deep. Kidnapping her had really been out of desperation.

"Maybe you should tell me what's really going on, Sean. If you don't get Rubin on your side, you know you don't have a chance in hell of coming out of this alive. Any of you. I think you already know that."

He stood there for a long time and then paced away from her. "Can you reach him again? Ask him to talk before he tries to kill any of us?"

"Yes. Whether or not he'll agree is something I can't guarantee."

Sean nodded. "I understand why you both would feel that way."

"It's Luther."

"Who's Luther?"

A little spurt of anger flashed through her and no doubt he could see it in her eyes. Heat crackled around her. "The man who owns the property your ground crew decided they could use to land a plane on. The man they decided they would kill."

"Whoa." He put his hand up. "Wait a minute. That place looked deserted. We didn't think anyone even lived there. Suddenly I'm told we have a dead sentry and blood on the ground. Then the old man vanishes like he's a ghost. The man is waging war on us and we've never laid eyes on him. I told them to take him prisoner, not to hurt him, but Terry told me he was dead already. I'm really sorry about that. We didn't come here with the intention of harming any civilian."

"You had taken over his home," she pointed out. "Wouldn't you defend your home?"

Sean was silent. "I get your point. I'm not able to raise any of my crew, Jonquille. Not a single one of them. Do you know if they're alive?"

Jonquille didn't want to tell him. She could already see sorrow in his eyes. Her silence told him. He shook his head and then stared down at the ground, the rain falling softly on his head, running down his face like tears.

"You can go if you want to. This was never going to work anyway. It was madness. We were so desperate we didn't think our plan through. We sure didn't count on Rubin or Diego Campo interfering. Just go, Jonquille, before I change my mind, or one of them does." He jerked his thumb at the other men still sitting a distance away. Sean sounded tired.

"You still haven't explained to me what's going on. If you did, it might make all the difference in the world. Why don't you let me set up a meeting between you and Rubin? Just tell him what's going on. If he can help, he will. If he can't, you just walk away." It was the best she could offer him. She wasn't certain Rubin was in a helpful mood—or if Diego and Rubin at this point would let any of them walk away—but she would try.

15

Rubin didn't like that Jonquille was sitting right out in the open where one of the squirrel men could kill her if something went wrong. These men were elite soldiers. GhostWalkers in their own right. They might have different skills, but they were seriously good in the woods and they could handle themselves in a firefight.

Diego was secreted somewhere with his rifle. He would never take that aim off Sean the entire duration of the meeting. Luther was backup, but that was two against an army of GhostWalkers. Rubin had no idea how he'd allowed Jonquille to talk him into this. Still, it was done, and he refused to show anything but absolute confidence.

"You might just skip to the part that tells me what's going on," Rubin said, his tone mild. That was his way. Low. Calm. His eyes on Sean's face. Unblinking like the predator he was. He was judge and jury. Maybe executioner. "I don't want to hear bullshit, Major. I want to hear absolute truth."

Rubin, he really is sorry about this entire mess.

This was not the way to handle it. If there was a reason, he got a lot of men killed for nothing, and I killed them.

"Oliver Chandler was not only envious of Whitney's army of soldiers, but he decided to create his own army. He decided what he wanted in them, and like Whitney, he canvassed the ranks of various branches of the service for men who scored high on the tests who would be willing to serve in what we thought was the GhostWalker program. All of us signed up for that program. There were rumors about it and we were willing to take our service another step further. Our psych evals were good, as well as our physicals, and we all had clean records."

Sean pushed an unsteady hand through his hair. "He was so pleased with his army. There were problems with some of us, but he was willing to overlook them, at least at first. Then he started talking about some of us being expendable. Those he considered flawed were used for high-risk assignments. He had 'special' assignments he needed done personally. Those missions had nothing to do with our country and everything to do with lining his pockets. We knew he was developing weapons for Whitney to turn over to the United States, but he held back on some. He held auctions for those weapons."

Rubin was suddenly alert. *You getting all this, Diego?*

Yeah, letting Luther know as well.

I despise traitors, Luther chipped in.

"The men came to me and told me what was going on, even though they weren't supposed to talk to anyone about their 'covert missions.' Chandler not only was auctioning off weapons but he was renting his soldiers to the highest bidders for operations that had nothing to do with the United States. Drug trafficking. Planting bombs. Guarding crime lords. You name it. Chandler considered these men expendable because they weren't perfect. He held the rest of us back to defend him. We were his personal army."

There was bitterness in Sean's voice. He shook his head. "No soldier in my unit is expendable. We're in this together. We all took the same oath to serve our country. Chandler is selling our country out. When I tried to go up the chain of command, I was shut down."

Rubin understood a little better the one-sided conversation they briefly overheard between the one soldier leading the ground crew and the unidentified person he was talking to.

"Just before we hunted the ground crew, we heard a very brief conversation between the soldier that was enhanced and giving orders and someone on the phone. Apparently the pilot you had flying the plane was taken prisoner and their pilot had comman- deered the plane. I don't know who 'they' are, but now it sounds as if that could be Chandler. If you're acting outside of him, he is aware of it."

"Are you certain it was Barry? He's one of us. I was worried so I didn't tell everyone the plan. I knew we had a leak somewhere, but I never suspected Barry. I thought it was . . . another man." He trailed off, shaking his head. "Man, I feel bad. I was pretty abrupt with him. Now he's dead. He died trying to get us all help. And they have our pilot? The Swamp Man?"

"Apparently they want to get information out of him."

"They will never get him to talk. He's the last person to ever talk," Sean said. He closed his eyes and shook his head. "Barry. I can't believe he'd betray us. Sell Swamp down the river to Chandler. This doesn't make sense."

"The plan was to get Jonquille on the plane and then to surround all of you and kill you. They planned on taking her to Chandler. Where were you taking her?"

Rubin kept his voice even. Gentle. He never took his gaze from the major's face. He could detect lies fairly easily. So far, Sean seemed to be telling the truth. He had no real reason to be lying to Rubin, other than that he knew Diego had a rifle pointed at him, and Diego wasn't a man who missed.

"I have a place in Louisiana Chandler doesn't know about. The property is in the middle of nowhere. Wasn't developed. I only told my best friends about it. We went in and fixed it up. We built a barracks of sorts and a small cabin. A friend helped with electricity, plumbing, that sort of thing. She'd be safe there. Chandler wouldn't find her, and we've stocked enough firepower to defend the place. Each time any of us went, we brought more firepower, including the new weapons."

Rubin thought it was a strange coincidence that Major Sean O'Connell of the Air Force would end up in the state of Louisiana, where the members of Rubin's GhostWalker team resided. They had women and children to protect. Sometimes Whitney set up elaborate plans to get to those children. He wanted them. Others wanted them dead.

"Where in Louisiana?"

Sean hesitated for the first time. "It's the only place I can take my men where we can go and live out our lives. We're not going to last very long, but at least we won't be used to betray our country."

Rubin. He's so sad. I can feel the weight on him. He can't fake that. What does he mean, they aren't going to last very long? Ask him.

Jonquille sounded close to tears. Somehow she'd formed an attachment to Sean. Rubin didn't like it. Not because he was jealous but because he worried that they might have to kill this man and she would hesitate, or always hold it against him.

It might be better if you slip away, Jonquille, head for woods, where the trees are thickest. We could use another person watching. And yes, I'll ask him what he means. You'll be looped in to the conversation.

Jonquille gave him such a stubborn look, her chin going up, her silvery-blue eyes flashing such little silver sparks at him, that it was all he could do not to lean over, frame her face with both hands and kiss her. It was the silliest impulse in the middle of a crisis situation and showed him why taking his woman into battle wasn't a great idea. She was distracting. Instead of kissing her, he cupped the side of her face and ran his thumb over her soft skin just once.

I was so worried about you, Jonquille. I think we're going to have to get married immediately so you stay very close to me. No more running off on your own. You took ten years off my life. He dropped his hand, still looking into her unusual eyes. He found them beautiful no matter if they were blue or silver or a mixture of both.

She burst out laughing, the low, soft notes skittering over his skin like caresses. *I was kidnapped. I didn't run off, you goof.*

She touched his face every bit as gently as he had hers. He felt love in her touch. When had that happened? When had that emotion slipped in for both of them? Caring. Affection. Real love. He knew it was real for him. He had hoped it was the same for her. That touch told him it was.

Rubin turned back to the major, who was looking at the two of them with the realization that they were speaking telepathically to each other. Sean couldn't be surprised. He'd known she could. She had set up the meeting between them that way.

"I understand you want to protect your men. I'm willing to bet that it's no surprise to you that I'm a member of a GhostWalker team."

"No, sir, it is not," Sean answered honestly. "I was unaware that you were here or that you were associated in any way with Jonquille."

"Are you aware of where my GhostWalker team resides?"

Sean looked uncomfortable. He sighed. "Chandler made it a

point, once he learned about the GhostWalkers, to find them. He is very obsessed with them. So the answer is yes, I know where your home is."

"Whitney told Oliver Chandler about the GhostWalkers?" Rubin asked.

"Whitney had soldiers around him all the time. He showed Chandler his experiments, especially Jonquille, as she was one he claimed was a failure when it came to using her as a weapon for lightning. Chandler's job is to develop weapons, and Whitney really wanted to harness lightning. That led to talks about the GhostWalkers and how Whitney used his failures to develop perfection in his soldiers, specifically the GhostWalkers. Eventually, he showed training films of what all of you could do."

Rubin sighed. Of course Whitney would. He would want to show off his genius to another scientist. It wouldn't occur to him that a man interested in developing weapons for his country might not be a great patriot. He might want to sell out his country. He might want his own soldiers to be used for his own ruthless purposes.

"So, Chandler was able to get his hands on how Whitney enhanced soldiers." Rubin made it a statement, but he was skeptical. Whitney wouldn't share that information, and he wouldn't leave it lying around.

Sean frowned. "I don't know exactly how he managed to find out the process. I wasn't around at that time. I had been sent to Chandler's property to guard him and the laboratory because he developed weapons for the United States, so I did know a little more than some of the others. I was recruited thinking I was applying for the actual GhostWalker program. I met all the requirements and was given an invitation to apply."

That very well could be true. That was how many of them had been recruited.

"You still haven't told me where in Louisiana your home is. You know where mine is, but you are refusing to give me the location of yours. I have to tell you up front, that makes me very uncomfortable. We have women and children to protect. Whitney periodically makes a try for those children. If this is one of his elaborate schemes to get them, and you're a part of that . . ." Rubin allowed the threat to just trail off.

He waited a heartbeat or two. "You have your men to protect. I have women and children to protect. It seems we may be at an impasse. If that's the case, we'll call it a day, you walk away, I take Jonquille with me and we disappear. I will say if you or any of your men come after us, you won't get a second chance. My team and the members of the other teams will be after you, and they don't miss."

Rubin. Jonquille was clearly heartsick. Her mind dripped with tears, but nothing showed on her face.

Rubin wanted to take her hand, but hands were weapons. He didn't tie up one of his weapons, not even to comfort her.

I know, Lightning Bug. I like him too. I wish we could help, but he has to be more forthcoming.

"Sean, you have to trust someone," Jonquille said. Like Rubin, she kept her voice very low. Soft. She looked him straight in the eyes. "You obviously were taking me to this place for a reason. You thought I could help you. Eventually, you would have had to tell me what I was there for. Tell Rubin what he wants to know. I guarantee you, the GhostWalkers will find out very fast where you are anyway. You're one of them. You don't work for Whitney. You don't work for Chandler. You're enhanced. That makes you a

GhostWalker. They have loyalty to one another. They're not going to betray your trust if you're worthy of it."

Sean glanced up toward the woods and then out over the ridge, the lines in his face more pronounced than ever. Rubin felt sorry for him. This man carried a tremendous burden. Sean turned his attention back to Rubin, studying him for a long time.

"I own an island in the swamp. It's about forty minutes by boat from where you are. I know we have a mutual friend, Donny. He owns an island close to mine. He's the one who helped me with electricity and plumbing."

If Rubin were a swearing man, he would have said a few choice words. Donny certainly could have warned them what was going on just forty minutes away from the fortress they were building to protect the children. But Donny played everything close to his chest. He was a Vietnam vet and loyal as hell to his friends. A nightmare to his enemies. If you asked him to keep something confidential, he wouldn't talk if his life depended on it.

"How is it Chandler doesn't know about this island of yours?"

"I'd never been there. It was land my maternal grandmother inherited. It was in her name. I inherited it from her. The title goes way back in our family on my mother's side. To be honest, I'd forgotten about it until I needed somewhere for my men to go. I only told three of my men about it and contacted Donny to help me set it up for the others to stay there."

Rubin nodded. Luther was looped into the conversation through Diego. He was then texting to Colonel Joe Spagnola, the commander of Rubin's unit. They were leaving nothing to chance. If something went wrong and Rubin and Diego were killed, his team would find Sean and the others and take them out. Or, if Sean and his men did have another agenda and were after the children, Rubin's team could be prepared. While he was conversing with Sean, facts could be checked.

"What is the name of your maternal grandmother?" Rubin asked.

"Arelia Catoire," he said without hesitation. "She never lived on that land. They had a nice house with a courtyard in New Orleans. I remember visiting her quite often when I was a kid. We didn't go into the swamp."

"Why did you kidnap my woman?"

Jonquille reacted, sitting up straighter, shocked that Rubin would put the question to Sean in such an abrupt manner when he'd been almost gentle about everything else.

Sean looked like he'd been slapped. He shook his head for the first time, his gaze sliding away. "That was wrong. I'm sorry, Jonquille. I think I let desperation take over and I lost my mind. I convinced myself that because I knew we weren't going to harm you, that it would be okay. It wasn't. None of this was okay. That old man, my men Rubin and Diego killed, all the ground crew, even Barry. Their deaths are on me."

"Luther is alive and well. Barry and the ground crew planned to kill you. The pilot being taken prisoner, and the ones we killed, that's a different story," Rubin said. He couldn't absolve him of those deaths.

Sean shook his head. "Barry? I just can't wrap my head around the traitor being Barry. My men were using nonlethal bullets when they shot at you and your brother, sir, although you had no way of knowing that. When they blasted you with the lightning weapon, it was to give us a chance to get away with Jonquille, and they were careful to aim in front of both of you."

"Why did you go to such lengths to acquire Jonquille?" Rubin forced himself to repeat the question in a gentler fashion. He still went back and forth between feeling sorry for the major and wanting to rip his head off.

Sean gave Rubin a little half smile. "You asked me if Chandler had gotten Whitney's formula for creating perfect GhostWalkers. Evidently, he did not. He must have thought he was genius enough to fill in the blanks. He brought in teams from other countries who were experts, and they eagerly performed their miracle surgeries. Some of the men died. I guess Chandler thought that was an acceptable loss. Some had obvious 'flaws.' Those he deemed expendable. The rest of us, he called his elite team. He'd repeat that all the time, thinking we'd believe it."

Rubin studied his face. There was anger there, but not in Sean's voice. His eyes were alive with buried rage.

"He just dismissed those men as if their sacrifices meant nothing. He was willing to send them out to run missions for him. He put them in dicey situations, positions normal men wouldn't survive, just to line his pockets, but he sneered at them behind their backs. He kept telling the rest of us how much better we were. He wanted us to feel superior to our brothers. That was . . . maddening to me. To the rest of us. Well, maybe not Barry. He must have believed the crap Chandler was handing out to him."

"You thought Jonquille could help these men Chandler deemed expendable?"

"I hoped she could help all of us. All of us are flawed. Chandler just doesn't know it. At least he didn't seem aware of it. Maybe Barry told him. He brought in a second team to try again because he wanted more soldiers. We weren't as cooperative as he liked. He didn't like the questions we were asking him about the covert operations he was sending us on. When the second plane went down with an explosion, we knew he had rigged both planes."

"You were unaware he had killed the first surgical team?"

"No, he seemed to be such good friends with them. At the time the plane went down, I was still recovering from surgery. In the beginning, we all liked him. He's charming. Personable. It wasn't until some time after I was enhanced that I realized he was an ass-kisser to get his way and his charm wasn't genuine. He wasn't interested in other people, only in furthering his own agenda."

Rubin continued to look steadily at Sean. "How did you think Jonquille could help you?"

"She was researching psychic healing. We know we don't have much time. Maybe Chandler has this new, improved crew, but if he does, he figured it out in record time. I thought he just wanted to add to his army—you know, look like a bigger man and have more soldiers to rent out to terrorists. If that's the case, those soldiers are going to find themselves in the same boat we are. They're already dying, they just don't know it yet."

"You went to a medic? Chandler must have one there for you."

"He had no idea what to do with us."

Quite frankly, Rubin wasn't so certain what to do with them either. An entire unit of GhostWalkers in medical trouble. He couldn't examine them there. He had only Diego, Jonquille and Luther to back him up. If he tried healing someone and he grew weak, they would be in a world of hurt. He needed to know just how bad the issue was if it was true.

"Do all of you have the same problem?"

"All of us have similar issues, although some have extreme medical side effects and psychic hiccups." Sean gave Jonquille a faint smile. "That's what we call them. Hiccups."

"You mean like my lightning? Misdirecting it?"

"Yeah. Just a little hiccup."

Her laughter did that same thing to Rubin, the notes feeling like a physical touch to him. He took a deep breath. Healer or predator. Always at war.

Don't do it. That was Diego. Reading his mind. His need.

I need to know. We need to know. If he's telling the truth, we have to help them. We have no choice. They're GhostWalkers. We have to get them comfortable, safe, triage them so we know who is in the worst shape and start there. We don't leave them behind.

He was serious about that. They were fellow soldiers if it came to that. He wasn't going to lose them if they were in need.

I can do it. I can examine him, Jonquille offered.

Rubin turned his head to look at her. Her eyes met his. There was silver ringing the blue. Her otherworldly eyes. Those long lashes sweeping down and then back up, giving him that slow assault on his stomach. That mouth of hers. Lips pressing together and then her semiconfident nod. She wasn't certain, but she was willing to try.

You can talk me through it, Rubin.

Great. Then both of you are concentrating on the major, and anyone can pull something unexpected. Just stay out of the way of my shot. I mean it. You try to step into my shot, I'll move and take him out. I'm not playing games here. I can't protect you from everyone, and you're making it as difficult as you possibly can.

His brother was definitely against the idea. Rubin understood. They were out in the open with a dozen rifles aimed at them. There had to be a better way to do this. Diego would take the shot if one of them stepped into his line of fire, and when examining a patient, a healer easily lost themselves in what they were doing and forgot about their surroundings.

Not now, Jonquille.

"It's possible I can help you. Or Jonquille can. Perhaps both of us. There is an entire unit of GhostWalkers ready to help if you are what you claim. I can't take you to my home, but I'm willing to accompany you to your island and check you and the others out."

The hell you will. Diego's rage spread through the woods straight to them. The black emotions unsettled the birds in the trees so that the hawks rose into the air and screeched repeatedly, as if defending their territory. *You are not going anywhere with these people without protection, Rubin. We have to know everything about them and we don't know anything. How do we know he's telling the truth? Get away from him. Back off now. You can wait for our unit.*

Diego was really angry. He was throwing off so much powerful energy, it was coming across the little ravine straight to Jonquille, drawn like a magnet. Along the way, the dark emotion filled every crack, every nook, stuck to every blade of grass. Every man hiding with their weapon trained on the group was shaken by the force of that rage.

"What's wrong?" Sean asked immediately.

"My brother didn't like my suggestion. He believes everyone is out to kill me. Probably because I'm a pain in the ass," Rubin said easily, giving Sean a faint smile.

You are a pain in the ass. Rubin, you never think about security.

He thought about security all the time. Just not for himself. He thought about it for Diego. Now he'd be thinking about it for Jonquille.

"Tell your men to stand down, Major. We're going to let that plane land, if he's able, in the meadow, and see what the pilot has to say. Then you're going to your island and I give you my word as an officer in the United States Air Force that my unit will come to you and bring your men aid if we can in any way help you."

"We're running out of time. We have two men that are pretty sick. Chandler abandoned seven men that he determined were defective from the last batch he had enhanced. He thinks they were executed and buried. We took them to the island. They aren't in the best of shape. I've got a couple of my men pretty sick."

Rubin didn't react, but Jonquille did. Her hand went to her stomach, pressing deep. "This Chandler, the man you're assigned to guard, just ruthlessly ordered seven soldiers executed? How is he going to explain their deaths?"

"The way they make all soldiers disappear. They were on an operation and ambushed. Or their vehicle went over a mine. Their plane went down. There are so many ways now to explain the deaths of multiple soldiers." Sean sounded bitter again.

Rubin, maybe I should go with him now. I'm not great at healing, but I might be able to give them time until you can get there. Couldn't some of your team meet me there?

He could hear the plea in her voice. Feel the compassion in her, that healer rising to drown out every other part of her. She ignored the way her hair was still reacting to Diego's dark energy swirling aggressively through the valley, and Sean's men's reactive emotions feeding into that same stream. Her body was lit up like a white-hot candle. She was used to her core temperature rising and the sparks running in a wild dance of beautiful fireworks around her rib cage. He leaned closer to her, their thighs touching, allowing his energy to slowly drain the excess from her. Just a small bit at a time, so Sean and his team wouldn't notice.

You will not be going with them. You will be going with me. I told you, Lightning Bug, you took ten years off my life. No more scaring me like that. Stick close for a while until I get over it. Rubin looked at her face. That beloved little pixie face. She wasn't a woman who liked being told what to do. *Please.* She smiled at him unexpectedly, turning his heart over.

Would the two of you have a moment some other time when I'm not holding a rifle on a potential enemy? Can't you take anything seriously?

Jonquille, I thought you'd have some sense. One of you has to. Don't look at him like that.

Like what? She sounded dreamy, and Rubin knew she deliberately sounded that way on purpose to tease Diego.

Like you worship him or something. You look goofy. Pull it together. We're not out of the woods yet, even if Sean is one of the good guys.

"Sir, I believe the plane is about to make another call. He'll be looking for clearance to land. I'd like to talk him into trying to land in the meadow in spite of the fact that there's no landing strip. See if he'll do it," Sean said.

I was looking at him like he's hot as hell, Diego. There is a difference.

If you're supposed to have Sean in your sights, how come you're looking at Jonquille? Rubin asked.

She's prettier than he is. And much more interesting. And she was glowing. I'm tired of looking at him, Rubin. Call this off and send him home.

I did already.

I know, that's why I'm looking at Jonquille.

Rubin sighed. "Will he be able to land in the meadow? It's full of holes and bumpy at present. The grass and rocks alone will make it difficult."

"If he's any kind of pilot, he should be able to set it down. Whether he wants to or not is another story."

"Major, once more, I'm giving you an order to have your men stand down. We're finished here. We need to get into position to allow the plane to land. He needs to see Jonquille as a prisoner. I want to see a clear signal to your men to lower their weapons."

Sean winced, but he lifted his hand in the air and signed to his men in every direction to lower their weapons.

Rubin waited for confirmation that Sean's men were obedient to the command before he rose, stretching as he did so, taking his time, presenting a target, putting his body in front of Jonquille's as a shield. He was very careful to leave his brother a good line on the major. Jonquille started to stand.

Wait. I'll let you know when I think it's safe enough to get up.

You're making yourself a target. She wasn't in the least happy with him.

She didn't sound angry like his brother, or feel angry, but she was upset and for some unaccountable reason, his heart clenched and then ached. He didn't like that she was upset. He'd never cared much when others were distressed when he knew he was doing the right thing. He figured they'd have to get over it eventually. His woman was concerned for his safety, the same as his brother.

Get used to it, Jonquille. Rubin's an ass. He's one of the most talented men on the planet, but he's a total ass. Think twice about looking at him with adoring eyes. He's going to make your life hell, Diego weighed in.

Sean stood up as well, and one by one his men came out from behind the trees they were secreted in. Only when Diego signaled it appeared all were accounted for did Rubin extend his hand to Jonquille.

Are you telling us you wouldn't protect your lady, Diego?

Get out of there. Tell Sean to get his men out of the open. I've got this gut thing going on. Don't much like it. Thought it was Sean and his men. Now I'm not so sure. Might be that plane coming in. There was no more joking in Diego's voice. He was all business.

"Sean, get your men back under cover. Might be nothing, but when Diego says he's got a gut feeling something's not right, we act on it. Nine times out of ten, he's dead-on."

Rubin tightened his fingers around Jonquille's hand. He had no intention of being separated from her again. "Let's get to the meadow and see if the pilot will bring that plane in. It's up to you to talk him into it, Sean. He's going to be leery. Chandler's spy, Barry, hasn't been talking to him for a while now."

"Yeah, I got that." Sean was still bitter over the traitor in his unit.

The three of them jogged from out in the open to the relative cover of the woods. Rubin and Sean blended immediately. Jonquille stood out like a sore thumb. She began to pull a gray, black and olive green hoodie from her pocket. It was folded into a very small square, almost the size of a handkerchief, but when she opened it, it fell nearly to her knees. The minute she put it on, it adhered to her body, pressing any clothing she had on under it tight so it was like another layer of skin. She instantly blended as well.

Sean spoke into his radio and it took only a couple of minutes after the three of them making it to the edge of the meadow for two of Sean's men to join them. Sean immediately contacted the plane.

There was a short silence and the pilot answered, his tone wary, obviously expecting Barry to be contacting him.

Sean didn't reply immediately, then he snapped out a command. "This is Major Sean O'Connell. Identify yourself."

The pilot replied reluctantly, admitting who he was, and he wasn't Sean's pilot. "Lieutenant Owen Abbey."

"Swamp Man was supposed to be flying that plane. What happened to him?"

"I explained this to Barry . . ."

"He's dead. The entire ground crew is dead. They were attacked, and all machines needed to effectively build a decent landing strip were destroyed. I needed Swamp Man, he can land in anything. You didn't tell me where he is." Sean's implication was that this pilot couldn't land the plane.

"He was sick and I offered to collect the package for him. He gave me the instructions."

"We have the package, but the landing will be rough."

"Give me a minute."

Sean glanced back at Rubin. "I'll bet any amount of money he's consulting with Chandler, asking him what to do."

They waited in the shadows of the tree. Diego was up in the branches of the trees above their heads. If the plane circled around and looked as if it was in any way threatening, he would shoot it down. He was very good at that. He had backup this time. Several of Sean's men were scattered among the trees with the same idea. They didn't like that Chandler had one of their "brothers" in his hands, possibly torturing him to find out their intentions.

"I'll set her down," the pilot eventually agreed. "Will need two soldiers to accompany package to destination."

Sean waited to see if the pilot gave him preferences. Rubin thought it was an intelligent move on his part. If the pilot did specifically name someone, that meant there were more traitors among Sean's men. The plane was in sight now. Circling the meadow.

"You have anyone in mind?"

"Your best. I don't want trouble on the flight back."

The relief on Sean's face showed instantly. He took a breath and let it out. The men in his unit were close, the way Rubin's were. They were GhostWalkers, men set apart with nowhere to go, so they had to rely heavily on one another. To have someone turn traitor was abhorrent to them.

They were silent watching as the pilot circled the meadow low, looking for the best way to land the small plane. It was a large meadow and the grass was short. Most of the large debris had already been removed by the ground crew. The pilot circled once more and then came in low, clearly determined to set down.

"I don't want him to see Jonquille until the last minute after he lands," Rubin said. "We'll take him prisoner and turn him over to our commander. We know he's taking a cut of the profits. Once we take a look at all of you and hopefully get you on your feet and in good working order, Chandler can be dealt with. Any of the new soldiers can decide whether they're working for the United States or for profit. The government will have to deal with that."

He hoped what he said was true. Too often it wasn't. If a Ghost-Walker went rogue, only another GhostWalker had a good chance of tracking him and taking him out. Fortunately, that wasn't something that happened often.

Diego joined them as the plane made its way to the meadow. Rubin had to hand it to the pilot. He knew his stuff. He circled twice, coming in low, studying the terrain before he made his commitment to the actual landing. When he did make the commitment, there was no hesitation. He was a good pilot. The plane was controlled, steady, came in low, against the wind to help slow it, where the grass was short and the dirt was smoothest.

As far as Rubin could see, they could have already built a landing strip for the pilot. He set the plane down, turned it in a long circle and pointed it back in the direction he'd come, setting up to take off.

"He's got skills," Rubin acknowledged to Sean.

"Yeah, he does. Swamp Man taught him and then that son of a bitch betrayed him." Sean was very clear about that. "You were the one to tell me he was well aware Chandler had taken Swamp prisoner and was most likely torturing him to find out why they wanted this 'package' where they were taking her. The lieutenant didn't seem to mind."

That much was the truth again. Rubin sighed. Sometimes the psychological testing done for the GhostWalker program failed to weed out the ones that shouldn't be enhanced. If they had no empathy for others, being jacked up so much could turn them into beings who believed they were so superior to others they would torture and kill without a qualm. They had no morals. No code. They didn't belong in a program like the GhostWalkers.

Sean, with Abel and Hudson on either side of him, walked toward the plane. Diego, with Rubin and Andrew, stayed in the shadows to cover them. The other squirrel men went up into the trees as a precaution. Sean walked with confidence, acting as if he didn't think anything was wrong. Jonquille was seated in sight, at the edge of the meadow with two men on either side of her. She had only to roll into the woods and lie flat to disappear. Diego and Rubin were right there, close to her. Luther was somewhere close. Hidden.

The door to the plane opened and the pilot stepped out smiling, giving Sean a brief salute. He started forward and then suddenly veered to the side and dove under the plane.

"Down!" Diego yelled. He fired shot after shot, moving forward at an angle, dropping the first two men coming out of the plane.

The squirrel men fired, trying to keep a spray of bullets all over the plane to give Sean, Hudson and Abel time to move back to cover. The three men ran in a crouch toward the nearest brush as a third man burst from the plane spraying bullets everywhere. Diego shot at the third man as the pilot lifted his gun, aiming squarely at Diego.

Rubin came out of nowhere, throwing his body in front of his brother, his gun spouting death even as he took the bullet meant for Diego.

Jonquille saw the exact trajectory, knew where it went and heard herself screaming in her mind. *Diego, get him, take him to the cave.*

Luther. We need you now. Fast. We'll lose him. Take him now. Go. Go. Nearest entrance, Luther. Fast. Life or death.

She was already up and running, meeting them as she ran to thrust her hands into the wound, a shirt from somewhere in her hands to put pressure as they went to the nearest entrance directed by Luther. Heartbeat thundering in her ears, she matched her steps to Diego's and wouldn't let her mind think about anything but Rubin living.

16

Diego dragged his brother into the woods toward the entrance to the cave, Jonquille running beside him, her mind completely consumed with Rubin's internal body. She hadn't hesitated to place her hands over the damage to him to see where the bullet's path had torn through him and the destruction it had caused. The moment they were in the shelter of the cave, Diego had Rubin down and his shirt open. He tried to stem the tide of blood pouring out, but it was useless.

"Get the med kit. Get a line into him," Jonquille snapped. "His veins are going to collapse. I can only hold his artery so long."

Luther was already rushing back with the medical supplies, dropping to his knees beside Rubin and finding a vein quickly.

"I'm compatible with him," Jonquille said.

"We need you to save him," Diego said. "You save him."

She didn't look at Diego. She didn't dare take her vision from the inside of Rubin's body. Never in her life had she performed the kind of surgery she was attempting. Never. She'd studied it, but that was with instruments, not with her mind. Not with healing energy, with white-hot energy that could kill as easily as it could heal. If she made one mistake, she could kill him as surely as the bullet. If she did nothing he would die. The map she needed was there in his mind, which meant it was in hers. He'd laid it out for her because . . . well . . . he was Rubin and he was extraordinary.

"Give him my blood," she said, almost growling. "You don't, we lose him."

She was already envisioning the repair, moving on to his heart, going over the arterial bleeding and how she had to reroute everything to get to the mess that used to be a major artery. Then there was nothing but the work in front of her. She blocked out her surroundings and became only energy, using her mind to move Rubin's insides as delicately as possible, as if she were a surgeon and he were on her table.

A light shone on him everywhere her palms lay over his skin, and heat blasted through her core, welling up like a volcano to feed the instruments she needed to wield to save him. It was long, tedious, meticulous, exhausting work. She didn't know how many times she swayed and almost collapsed, only to have Diego wipe her face with a cool cloth, lift a bottle of water to her mouth and whisper to her that Rubin was still breathing.

She knew Rubin was still breathing. Just. She kept track of that. Kept track of his blood supply. He'd lost so much. She couldn't afford to give him what he needed.

We had already called in our team—they're on their way, Diego said. *They have our blood on hand. Another ten minutes out.*

She hadn't known Diego was monitoring her, and then, for one moment, she realized she was on her knees beside Rubin's body and Diego was behind her, his hands supporting her. She was able to continue, repairing the artery and then moving to the heart, where the bullet had damaged one small portion of that as well. She had rerouted the blood flow earlier so she was able to evaluate the damage and see what needed to be done. Again, it was a matter of taking her time and making certain she didn't make one mistake no matter how tired she was. Finally, when she had triple-checked her work over and over, she took a deep breath and allowed the blood to flow through the artery she'd repaired to his heart and the damaged chamber. She watched for leakage. For any sign of weakness. When she could find none, she slowly pulled her vision out of Rubin.

Her eyes nearly refused to work. There were others surrounding her, men she didn't know, and it made her uncomfortable. She was too weak to move, collapsing back into Diego.

I've got you, he whispered. *These are GhostWalkers. They've come to take us home. You'll be safe with us.*

"Do you know what she is?" the man beside Diego asked, his voice very quiet, keeping the question between the two of them, but she heard.

Jonquille was too tired to turn her head and really look at him. Everyone knew what she was. She was a lightning rod. Rubin called her his lightning bug, but he said it affectionately.

"She's a psychic surgeon, Diego. I couldn't have done what she did, and I'm a trained healer. I'm good at what I do, but I'm not capable of that level of expertise. I watched her closely and she performed surgery just as precisely as Rubin does, but with her mind. Did you know?" The man whispered the question.

"Yeah, Joe, Rubin said it was a possibility because he is and she's his woman. His other half. He knew she was his right away. He's completely bonded to her. Gone on her. I'm telling you that because we have to keep her safe. You know Rubin. He's seriously one-track minded when you get him riled. She's family to me, so I feel the same way about her."

There was a little warning note in Diego's voice. Jonquille didn't want to sort out what it all meant. She just wanted to sleep. She leaned back, let her lashes droop all the way and was out.

~

Jonquille heard someone crying. Sobbing. It was a great distance away, but the woman was really in distress. She needed to get up and help her. She tried to move, but her body wouldn't cooperate. Her arms and legs felt like leaden weights. Her head, when she tried to roll over, felt like it might shatter, and every organ in her chest felt as if it had shifted in her body. There was no way to pry her eyelids open. It was too much trouble, but that persistent crying was heartbreaking and she couldn't stand not to help.

"There, there, sweet girl," a voice said. "You're safe here. Everything's fine. Everyone's fine. There's no need to cry like that, you'll make yourself sick."

Someone patted her arm. The voice sounded gentle and older, had a very pronounced Cajun accent. A cool cloth wiped her face.

"You're among friends. Diego and Rubin are here."

More face wiping. The cool cloth felt good. Too good to be just water. There was some kind of natural healing compound blended together being stroked over her skin. It felt just as soothing as that voice.

"I'm Grace Fontenot. Everyone calls me Nonny. You're here at my home and very welcome too. I understand you saved Rubin's life. Thank you for that. We all thank you for that. Shh, honey, you're all right, just exhausted."

Her mouth and throat were so dry. Why did it feel as if her insides were torn apart? She tried to lift her arm again, but she had no strength. She tried to ask what was wrong with her, but no sound came out of her mouth, and that was terrifying. Her heart accelerated, pumping far too fast, but she couldn't control the fear coursing through her. Something was terribly wrong with her, but she couldn't figure out what it was. If Rubin was alive, where was he? Why couldn't she move?

"Jonquille."

That was another voice. A man's voice, and one she was very familiar with. Diego. He sounded stern. Commanding. Of course he would want to take charge when she was unable to even glare at him.

"You can't do the kind of healing you did on Rubin without repercussions to your own body. You have to rest and let yourself heal. He's in the other room doing much better than you are. In fact, he's been up walking around and has been in to see you twice this morning. He's not happy with any of us that we let you heal him. Like we had a choice. I told him you took charge, but he's gotten all growly on us and no one can live with him."

Nonny had been wiping her face and neck with the cooling cloth, but she stopped abruptly. "Diego, Rubin is never growly. I have never heard that man be anything but a true gentleman." The gentle strokes continued.

"Now, Nonny, my brother would never growl in front of you. You have to admit that," Diego said in his most pacifying voice.

Jonquille wanted to smile, and she definitely wanted to open her eyes and see Nonny, the woman who could cause Diego to back-track immediately and sound like he might weep if she didn't for-give him. She loved the way the two brothers were together, and the easy way Diego could sound so charming. She wished she knew how much time had passed. She was worried about Rubin, but she was also worried about Sean and his men.

She tried to reach out to Diego. *Sean?* The moment she did, her head exploded with pain and she cried out. Now she knew why that woman was crying. She knew for certain the woman was her. She was the big baby, sobbing away, because her head threatened to shatter into a million pieces. Her brain was fragmented and it hurt just to think, let alone try to reach out to Diego telepathically.

"Don't, Jonquille," he cautioned sharply.

At the same time, Rubin barked an order from the doorway. "Stop that right now, Jonquille. What are you thinking? Do you want to fry your brain completely? You could have burned out your talent, for all we know. I can't even examine you yet."

She didn't hear him move across the room, nor did she feel his energy, but he was suddenly sinking down onto the bed beside her, taking her hand, gripping it tightly.

"You do sound like a bear, Rubin," Nonny chastised, but she sounded gentle. "Don't growl at her. She's emotional and very frightened. You need to reassure her, not upset her."

"I know, Nonny. I'm sorry, Lightning Bug. You scared me again. I don't seem to do well with you scaring me. Maybe we'll have to put you in a little room for the next few months where I know you're safe, just to let me breathe." He brought her hand to his mouth so he could press kisses to the center of her palm. "Thank you for saving my life. What you did was impressive, to say the least, but it could have killed you." There was warning in his voice.

Jonquille reached for her voice. She might not be able to pry open her eyelids to see his beloved face, although she was determined that she would. Her hand trembled in his with the effort to rub one finger along his, that was how weak she was. "There is no living without you, apparently."

Her voice was more of a whisper, a thin wispy sound barely moving from her mouth to his ear, but he heard. She knew he did because he tightened his hand around hers and suddenly leaned down to her face.

"I'm in love with you, Jonquille. I know you think that's impossible because we haven't really been together, but I am. We've shared minds, so I can see who you are. It was impossible not to, and hopefully you could do the same with me."

It had never occurred to her that a man like Rubin would ever truly be in love with her. He might be paired with her because Whitney had set it up that way, but to actually love her for herself, that seemed unlikely. Rubin wasn't a man to lie. It wasn't in him. She had to open her eyes. As if Nonny could read her mind, that soothing cloth passed gently over her eyelids with a cool liquid and her lashes fluttered.

She forced her eyes open. Just a little. Not a lot. She wasn't asking for the moon, she just needed to see his face. That face. She loved his face. She needed to see him desperately. To know he was alive and well. She would forever relive that moment when that bullet had torn into his chest and she'd seen the destructive path it had taken. For her, it had been slow motion.

She had envisioned it in her mind. She was already running, calling to Diego. To Luther. Ignoring everyone else on the field. There was only Rubin. Her Rubin. She had to save him. She knew what that bullet was doing inside his chest, and she was determined that he wasn't going to die. The one thing about her few understood was that she could be determined, or stubborn if you preferred. She didn't stop if she set herself on a path, and her path had been to save this man.

She got her eyelids to cooperate just enough. He was there, filling her blurry vision. She didn't know if there were tears in her eyes or if her vision was messed up from using her talent, but it didn't matter. She would have given her life to save his.

He leaned close again, kissing the knuckles of her hand, looking into her eyes with his dark, dark ones. His hair was thick and a little unruly at the moment. She would have brushed it back from where it tumbled on his forehead, but she couldn't find the energy to lift her hand, so she just took in his chiseled features. Rubin was a handsome man. At least she thought he was. His jaw was firm, with a perpetual shadow on it. She liked that too.

"Glad you woke up, Jonquille. You had me worried."

His voice was soft. Intimate. Just for her. She could see he really had been worried. Her stomach did a crazy little somersault. "Sean?" She mouthed the name more than said it aloud. She was worried.

"Joe went to assess his men. A few of our team went with him for safety. We've got eyes on them. It's been two days. We'll go when you're on your feet. Wyatt's going tomorrow. Joe sent for him. Apparently there are two men in bad shape and they need help right away. Wyatt is an excellent doctor. They'll try medically first. We'll help them, Lightning Bug, no worries, if those two can't. You just need to rest and heal. In another day, I'll be able to help you heal faster. Nonny is a healer and she's been working on you. Zeke looked you over for me. He's an excellent doctor."

She hadn't meant to pull back slightly, but she had. She wasn't used to anyone getting near her. Nonny, she was all right with. She liked Nonny with her soothing touch. She appeared to be an older woman, small, almost fragile-looking until you looked into her sharp, faded blue eyes. She had silver hair she wrapped into a bun on top of her head. Her movements were calming and very graceful.

"Zeke?"

"Ezekiel saved our lives when we were kids," Rubin said. "He took us in. Diego and me. We would have died on those streets. We understood the mountain, but not the city. He taught us how to live on the streets and the value of education. He's family, sweetheart."

She wasn't so certain they would have died. They might have been criminals, but they wouldn't have died. They were survivors. She was certain Ezekiel had to be a survivor as well. If he valued education, he had led Rubin and Diego to where they were now. She decided she might like the man.

"Zeke is a doctor as well. All of us in this unit are now. Some specialize. We fly into hotspots and drag our soldiers out of nasty places. You know the drill. It's what we do."

He rubbed his chin back and forth over her knuckles. She found the feeling of his day-old growth mesmerizing.

If she didn't move her head at all, not even one tiny bit, the excruciating pain could be held at bay. Otherwise, she was certain her head would shatter. The insides of her chest felt like they were floating around with nothing to anchor them, smashing into one another if she moved so much as an inch. She decided animation while she talked wasn't worth it. She knew how to be still when she needed to be, and she forced herself to remain still.

"Zeke's going with Wyatt in the morning. I'm going to work on you and then we'll go when you're ready. Once we get Sean's men in shape, we're going to visit Chandler. None of us like the idea that the pilot has been in his hands this long. We can only hope he's okay."

She had forgotten about the other pilot. Her brain wasn't thinking clearly. "Luther?"

"Not a scratch. That man is like a cat, but with a million lives. How did you know about his caves? Diego said you told him to take me to the caves."

"It was in your mind. All of it. The surgery, all of it. I followed what was in your mind. I wouldn't have been able to do that on my own." She wouldn't have. Rubin had envisioned the cave, then his chest and more precisely the surgery. He had continued to do so as long as he was conscious. That had been a lot longer than she thought he could possibly be. The pain alone should have knocked him out, but he'd mapped out the entire surgical procedure for her.

"I remember that now. Barely, in the back of my mind. You said you don't forget things you see. I counted on that. I stayed awake as long as I could. You really don't forget anything."

"I thought, at first, I was following the things I learned in med school, but the surgery was too advanced and all done with my mind, not my hands. Using my mind versus my hands was difficult. The impulse to use hands was so strong. Of course I had no instruments. I felt like I was torturing you. It was intense. The heat was intense. Keeping that controlled so I was repairing your insides and not burning you to a crisp was a fine balance that terrified me." That confession came out in a little rush.

She was very pleased that her voice was stronger. Rubin pressed another cloth to her lips. This one had clean, pure water. He wanted her to open her mouth so he could give her ice chips. She realized she had an IV in her arm and they were giving her fluids to keep her from being dehydrated. They knew it was impossible for her to sit up and drink anything.

"You were amazing. I was proud of you." He leaned down and brushed strands of hair from her face with his fingertips.

The gesture was so gentle she wanted to cry.

"You were looking up surgeries online, was that to visualize them?"

Jonquille just barely managed to stop herself from shaking her head. "I kept putting words like 'psychic surgeon' into the search engine with the hopes that someone before me had thought up a way to reverse psychic enhancements."

Rubin was silent for a few moments, his expression thoughtful.

She liked that so much about him. He always took time to actually listen to her and think over what she was saying as if it mattered to him.

"You were actually looking up psychic surgeons online in hopes of finding out how to repair psychic damage, not physical damage?" There was speculation in his voice. "I've always thought in terms of physical damage. I'm a doctor and a surgeon. I fly into hot spots where our soldiers are torn up. I've never thought in any other terms."

"I've had to think about failed experiments, Rubin. There was Dahlia in a mental institution because she couldn't control fire. What if we could find a way to at least lessen those reactions? There has to be a way. He enhanced us. The DNA part, we can't change that. Even somewhat, I agree, the psychic enhancement we want, but not to the degree that those of us who are suffering and can't live in society can't be fixed."

Rubin sat for a long time just looking at her. He framed her face with both hands. "I don't know how I got so lucky, Jonquille. This actually never occurred to me. Not once, and I've been living with Pepper, who can't be touched by anyone but her husband, Wyatt. It's absolute hell for her. There are others as well we could help—maybe. We'd have to look at the side effects as well. The bond between pairs is extremely strong. We don't want to weaken that in any way. That could be a part of the psychic weave, and messing with that could cause damage to a bonded couple. We don't want to be responsible for that."

He didn't want to lose her. She heard that in his voice. She understood. She didn't want to lose him either, but he didn't understand what it was like to be her. At the moment, she was secluded in a bedroom, down a long hall, away from anyone else in the house. She heard the sound of children and the low murmur of other voices. She knew there were others in the house. Every single person had energy. All of them had emotions. Those emotions had energy. That energy would feed into her until she would light up like a Christmas tree and be dangerous. She couldn't be around people. Rubin didn't know what that was like. As much as he wanted to have empathy, he didn't really understand.

Those dark eyes bored into hers. Looked right into her as if looking into her soul. She'd forgotten that they were so connected, that because she'd used psychic healing, that had connected them even more. He was there in her mind and very aware of what she was thinking.

"If I could give you the freedom of being around people but it would break our bond, would you trade being with me for that kind of absolute freedom?"

He didn't take his gaze from hers, nor did he leave her mind. She felt him inside her. Waiting. Her heart accelerated. Would she? Was that even a fair question? She'd spent a good portion of her life researching a way to help herself and others like her.

"Would you give me that freedom if it meant giving me up, Rubin?" she asked.

"If that was what you wanted and I was capable. It would hurt like hell, Jonquille, but you deserve to be happy. If that is what it takes to make you happy, I'll give that to you." He answered without hesitation.

Her heart lurched. That was the kind of man he was. Purposeful. No-nonsense. Looking her straight in the eye. Refusing to pull out of her mind so she could see what was in his heart. He would give that to her. It might break his heart, but he would do it for her. How could a woman not fall hard for him? Her lashes fluttered. She tried not to move when she wanted to fling herself into his arms.

"You make me want to kiss you, Rubin, and if I move, my head will fall off. Literally. Fall off. Diego will like that, so I'm not moving. I don't want him playing some weird Diego game with my head."

"I don't know why you think I'd do that, although you'd look pretty cute being used as a bowling ball. All sparkles flying down the lane. Maybe lighting up when you hit the pins."

"See? I told you. Don't let your brother near my head," Jonquille cautioned.

"I'm going to take some of the pain away, sweetheart," Rubin said. "Lie still and forget about my brother. If he gets out of line, Nonny's here. She'll make him behave."

"I had no idea Diego ever misbehaved," Nonny said. "He's always been such a quiet boy. He just eats, cleans the kitchen for me and goes off into the swamp."

"Quiet?" Rubin glanced over his shoulder at his brother. "Nonny, Diego never stops talking. He wants his way in all things."

Nonny looked taken aback. "Is that true?"

Diego shrugged with a casual roll of his wide shoulders. "That may be the truth, but it's only because Rubin doesn't pay any attention to his security, Nonny. I have to watch over him. If he'd been doing what he was supposed to do, he wouldn't have gotten shot."

"I did notice everyone was extremely upset, Rubin," Nonny said.

"They'd be extremely upset if Diego had been shot, don't you think?" Rubin asked.

"Of course."

"He was about to get shot. He was covering some soldiers, helping them to get out of the line of fire, and someone turned a weapon in his direction."

Nonny regarded Rubin and Diego soberly. "My boys. Always gettin' shot at. I don' suppose there will come a time when you're safe and can just be home with your loved ones. I'm proud of you takin' care of one another. And your woman for takin' care of you, Rubin. She's one that will stand with you through anythin' life is going to throw at you."

"I think you're right, Nonny." Rubin kissed Jonquille's knuckles again. "I plan on keeping her. Marrying her the minute I can."

Nonny nodded. "Nice to know you have the sense the good God gave you. Diego, I'm not gettin' any younger."

Diego stiffened. *"Grandmère?"*

"I want to see you settled before I go. No more of this runnin' around like you do. I see you flirtin' with all the ladies, but nothin' comin' of it. You need to find the right one here fairly soon."

Both men looked up quickly. "What does that mean, Nonny?" Rubin demanded. "You aren't feeling ill, are you?"

"No, no. I'm fit as a fiddle. Just want this boy to get a move on. Want to see more grandbabies."

"You don't think Wyatt and Trap have provided enough? Good grief. Any more and we'll be overrun with children," Diego said. "Little vipers running around sinking their teeth into our ankles."

"Pardon me?" Nonny asked with great dignity.

Diego paled beneath his olive skin. "You know how children go through that teething phase and want to bite your ankle. That's what I was referring to." He slid off the bed. "I think it best if I leave you now, Jonquille. You're in good hands. I'm starving and the smell of food is getting to me. If I don't eat soon, Mordichai and Malichai are going to eat everything before I get into the kitchen."

"I think you're slinking off," Rubin observed. "A cowardly retreat."

Jonquille loved listening to the brothers and the way they gave each other a bad time. Usually, they did so telepathically, but she knew they were bantering back and forth with each other aloud for Nonny's sake.

"Retreat or not, at least I'm going to get decent food that I didn't cook myself," Diego declared. He bent his head and brushed a kiss over Jonquille's cheek. "You get better fast. I think with Nonny and Rubin looking after you, you'll be up giving us trouble in no time."

She gave him a faint smile. Aside from Rubin, Diego was her favorite person in the entire world. Rubin gave her a little grin. *You don't know too many others very well.*

That was true too. But still. Diego really was like a brother. Her heart had ached for family, now it felt as if she had that.

"There is plenty tonight, shrimp, chicken and andouille jambalaya. It's on the stove, Diego. Fresh-baked bread. Greens. Plenty of food. The girls made cobblers for dessert. I think you'll be happy tonight."

"Cobbler?" Diego perked up.

Jonquille started to laugh, but the movement hurt her head. She couldn't even grab her skull to keep it from shattering while she laughed.

I've got you, Lightning Bug.

Almost immediately, she felt Rubin in her mind. There were ragged breaks, little tears, that he seemed to be carefully gluing, making them seamless. He did one at a time. Not many. Just a few.

I can't do them all or I won't be any good later on. I have to rest in between. That's important to remember, Jonquille. Whenever you have the chance, take it.

Rubin continued to hold her hand, but she could visibly see the difference in him. His skin was pale and there were lines of strain around his mouth.

"Nonny, when was the last time Wyatt gave you a checkup?" Rubin asked the question casually, as if it were of no importance.

The older woman laughed, the sound contagious. "You aren't

foolin' an old woman, Rubin. It was a while ago. I'm pretty certain I'd know if somethin' was wrong, but if it makes you feel better, you can do your mumbo jumbo and look inside me just to check."

Jonquille felt the skitter of alarm that went down Rubin's neck. This woman was extremely important to him, and he was suddenly very worried about her, but Jonquille wasn't sure why. She raised one eyebrow to ask.

She would never suggest that I give her the once-over unless she's concerned about something.

"It won't take long, Nonny, and it would make me feel better. I appreciate it," Rubin said immediately, as if afraid she might change her mind. He got up and went around to the other side of the bed.

Jonquille had seen him scan Patricia Sawyer using his palms, and he did the same with Nonny. He held his palms about an inch from her body as he moved them over her. Every now and then, he lingered in one spot longer than Jonquille thought he should and she found herself holding her breath. The light seemed to grow brighter and the warmth grew hotter. Nonny never complained or moved. She didn't say he was taking too long or try to get away from what Jonquille was certain was extremely hot heat at times.

Those hands moved slowly all up and down the older woman's body from her toes to her brain, not missing a single part, much like a scan would do. Rubin was thorough. It was Nonny. Jonquille strengthened her connection with Rubin so she could see what was going on. He was finding little problems. Arthritis. He eased that. A minor knee problem. That was fixable. He made it as good as new. A small adjustment in her back. Nonny appeared to have the body of a much younger woman. Jonquille wondered if the healers worked on her all the time or if it was genetics and her diet and the work she did.

Jonquille felt Rubin's sudden stillness again. He'd found something he didn't like. He was very cautious now, going through the arteries and veins surrounding her heart and neck. He inspected each one. Jonquille could see the damage in two of them, the buildup that had significantly narrowed the artery, that sudden buildup of plaque that threatened to close off the much-needed blood supply.

Rubin worked with extreme care. Nonny was older and her arteries were a little thinner than normal, although in remarkable condition. She was the epitome of a woman in good health at her age. Jonquille found it a bit shocking that Nonny could have a buildup of plaque when she ate right and did manual physical labor even at her age. She kept a large vegetable garden as well as an extensive herb garden.

Once Rubin had taken care of the arteries, he moved on to the heart, checking to make certain there were no repercussions to it. From there he examined her lungs thoroughly. Jonquille could tell he was expecting to find something there. When he found nothing, he moved on to her brain, clearly looking for evidence of small brain strokes. When he found none, he once again checked her legs to be certain he hadn't missed anything. Only when he was positive she was going to be fine did he pull back.

He staggered and sank down onto the bed, reaching back to find the mattress as if that could hold him up. Jonquille inched her hand toward his. Their fingers touched, and he moved his hand enough to envelop hers.

"Just sit there for a minute, Nonny," Rubin instructed. "We'll talk when I'm up to it."

Nonny remained quiet. She'd known something was wrong. She'd had the symptoms of a blockage and she hadn't complained.

Women like Nonny rarely did, but she'd known all along. Her son was a doctor. She was surrounded by doctors, and she should have spoken up right away. She could have had a stroke at any time.

Eventually, it was Nonny who moved first, rinsing out the soothing cloth she'd been using on Jonquille. She put the bowl aside. "I know you have to talk to Wyatt and Gator about this, Rubin. Is it somethin' bad? I suspected. Is it the cancer?" She looked as if she braced herself for the worst news. "From my pipe? I do so love my pipe at the end of the day. I try not to smoke it every night."

Rubin reached his other hand out to her. Nonny's hand trembled as she took his. "You can tell me, boy. I don' fall apart, you know. I was scared to face it for a while. Upstairs, at night, in my room, but once you got home, I knew I had to say somethin'."

Jonquille wasn't certain Nonny *had* said anything. Rubin had been listening and interpreting what she'd been saying or he would have missed it. Jonquille wouldn't have thought to examine the woman from the little she'd said. In fact, she'd reassured them all that she was just fine. Diego had taken her at her word. Only Rubin had been alarmed. She respected Rubin all the more for his ability to understand women like Patricia and Nonny. She wanted to be able to do the same. Was it experience? Or just natural ability? She had the feeling it was a little of both.

Rubin sat up a little straighter. Jonquille sensed that he was still weak, but Nonny needed to hear his assessment. She'd lived with her fears much longer than she wanted to admit. She was a healer, and one very sensitive. She'd likely noticed the symptoms coming on earlier than most people would have. Shortness of breath. She worked hard. She wouldn't have said anything, but she gathered her own herbs and mixed her own medicines for the people in the swamp who came to her when they were ill. She gave cooking lessons to the women there in the household and cooked nightly for the men. She would have noticed having difficulty breathing or extreme fatigue.

"You don't have cancer, Nonny," Rubin said decisively.

Nonny looked shocked. She had braced herself to receive the news. She was so surprised she nearly slumped down on the bed. Instead, she got up and turned away from them, clearly working to get her emotions under control.

"It was bad. I could tell, Rubin, from the work you had to do." Her voice trembled.

"It was troubling, in that had you mentioned the problem earlier it would have been easier to take care of. Nonny, you can't neglect your health this way." Rubin waited until the older woman sat down in the chair and faced them, gripping the arms tightly with her fingers.

"I know, Rubin. I didn't want to trouble anyone when you all have so much work. I took healing herbs and thought that would work. When it didn't, I thought I had the cancer and nothing would do for it. I'm not young anymore, and sooner or later, it's bound to get me."

"Not everyone gets cancer, Nonny," Rubin pointed out. "Two of your arteries were clogged. That put you in danger of having a stroke or heart attack. Either could have killed you or left you in a vegetative state. Ordinarily, you would have to go into the hospital or have one of the others operate here for that. I took care of it, but I would prefer that you don't discuss that with anyone but Wyatt and Gator. Naturally, that's up to you."

Jonquille thought that was another thing about Rubin that was so brilliant—the way he gave choices. He didn't tell Nonny she couldn't tell everyone about the doctor who had saved her life. His preference was that she didn't talk about him, but it was her choice.

Nonny was very private, and Jonquille doubted that she'd ever give up Rubin's secret to anyone but her grandsons.

"Thank you for taking care of me, Rubin. I don't think anyone else has to know. Is this because I smoke my pipe?"

"Smoking may have contributed, but I checked your lungs and your brain and both are perfectly fine. No signs of small strokes or the beginnings of COPD, most likely because the tobacco is your own blend, without all the harmful additives, and you only smoke one bowl at night. I'm not going to tell you to stop at this late date. It's something you enjoy. Wyatt and Gator might have a different opinion, but that's between the three of you."

Jonquille was with Rubin on that. If Nonny were having lung issues and having to use oxygen, or her blood pressure was up, anything that might have indicated her smoking that pipe at night was a major health problem, Jonquille would have advised against it. At eighty, Nonny still worked hard. Taking away her one vice wasn't going to do much good or harm either way.

"I'll leave you two alone for a while," Nonny said, pushing herself up. "You do need to eat, Rubin. Would you like me to bring you dinner?"

"That would be wonderful, thank you, Nonny," Rubin said.

Jonquille knew he wasn't hungry, but Nonny needed to repay him in some way, and he had to allow it. Food was her way of showing her affection.

When the older woman had left the room, Jonquille found herself looking into those dark eyes again. Immediately, her heart reacted, clenching hard in her chest. "What?" There was no looking away.

"I told you I would do my best to heal you, Jonquille, even if it meant losing you. You didn't say if you'd leave me."

She studied his face. Those lines carved so deep. She wanted to lift her hand and smooth the lines with her fingers, but she was still too weak. She knew if she chose wrong, she would mourn her loss every single day. Men like Rubin didn't come along often.

"I would never give you up, Rubin. Not for any price. If I have to live apart from the rest of the world and have just the two of us, it would be worth it to me. Still, I think we owe it to everyone to see if it's possible to help them tone Whitney's enhancements down just a little."

She knew she'd given Rubin the right answer. Brightness came into his dark brown eyes slowly, but it kept building until there was sheer joy lighting his handsome features.

17

"Rubin, this house is beautiful. Is it really yours?" Jonquille walked through the empty rooms with the vaulted ceilings. It was all cypress. All wood, the planks fit tightly into one another, just as the Fontenot home had been built. The wood had been carefully treated to make certain it would last. This was a home built with care and kept with love.

Rubin had appreciated the craftsmanship the moment he'd walked into it. There wasn't a single space that hadn't been designed without thought. He knew excellent work when he saw it. The house sat just back from the river with weeping trees close, but not so close that they might fall on the structure. He could see enemies coming at him. He had several escape routes for him and his family should he need them. He could get to the Fontenot property or to Trap's fortress, both places of relative safety. The swamp surrounded his property, and he had the waterway as well.

"How many bedrooms?"

He liked that she asked that question. She wasn't thinking about visitors. She had to be open to the possibility of children. "Three, although the attic runs the entire length of the house and can be converted to a third story. The builder had started on that project when his wife died unexpectedly."

Jonquille spun around, right there in the middle of the dining room. It had the same high ceilings as the entire house, and one wall was dedicated to a long built-in gas fireplace. When it was turned on, small flames danced along that wall, adding to the warmth of the room but also giving the old-growth cypress throughout the room and ceiling a beautiful glow.

"That's so sad. It reminds me of Luther. I feel so bad for him losing his wife."

Rubin nodded. For the first time in his life he knew what it would be like to lose someone like Lotty. He was watching Jonquille closely. She'd only taken one day to rest after she'd woken, with Nonny and Rubin both attending her. She was on her feet and determined to see everything, declaring she felt absolutely fine, but he had examined her that morning and she was still bruised internally.

"Luther loves Lotty to this day. Everything he does, he does with Lotty in mind."

"Diego was a little obsessed with finding his still. Does Luther actually have one?"

"Oh, he has one, all right. And he makes the best whiskey around, which he does sell to the highest bidders. Luther is no fool. He knows what his product is worth. He also knows there are some people who want to steal from him."

"Do you know where that still is?"

He shook his head. Her hair drew him like a magnet. He wanted to touch all that silk. He had since she came out of the shower early in the morning, toweling the mop of blond strands dry while she chattered happily about going to see the house he'd bought. He'd suggested it early in the morning and prepared a picnic in the hopes she'd go with him. Deliberately dangling the house in front of her was low, but he wanted to show her what he had to offer.

Naturally they'd been delayed by several hours, and he thought they'd never be alone. Then the weather had turned on them, the rain deciding to fall in little stops and starts. Already the sun was determined to set, but Rubin was equally determined to have one night alone with Jonquille. So far, she hadn't objected and asked to go back to the Fontenot house.

"Luther must have planned all along to conceal the still in the caves. He's had plenty of time to do it over the years and find a place he could vent while he works on his whiskey," Rubin explained, filling her in on the older man they'd all come to be fond of.

"Don't you think it's extraordinary that these experiments have been taking place since the beginning of the Vietnam War, Rubin? Most likely before?"

"I heard rumors from the time I was a little boy about him. All the pieces of the puzzles involving Luther fit now that I can put them together. He must have really had fun feeding the gossip. Even giving Edward Sawyer a bad time about being a spy for the government. Of course all that did was get me worried about him."

"I think it worried Edward's brother, Rory, as well," Jonquille pointed out.

Rubin liked that she'd picked up on that detail. "You're right. Rory was concerned for Luther. The old man had trudged through a blizzard to check on his mother. He wasn't going to turn his back on him if he'd grown senile or had turned just plain ornery. The Sawyers are good people."

"I think a lot of your friends are good people, Rubin."

"The ones in my unit certainly are. I'm glad you like the house, Lightning Bug. I was hoping you'd like it enough to want to live here with me." He kept pushing her for the commitment. Needing her to mean it.

Those silvery-blue eyes turned fully on him. So unusual. Rare. Unsettling and as beautiful as the storms she seemed to dance in.

"If I point out to you that I've said yes to you several times, Rubin, a preacher won't suddenly leap out and marry us, will he?" Laughter lit the blue in those eyes of hers.

"Had I thought of that, it would happen," he conceded.

"I would love to live in this house. It's such a find. In my wildest dreams, I never thought I'd have you, and then a home like this one." She walked over to the wall and put her hand on the wood. "How sad that the builder gave this up."

"He had two brothers. They both had property on either side of him. One was single, and he built his home with the help of both brothers. The oldest brother was married and had a young daughter. The oldest brother and his wife were robbed and murdered on the way home from a night out in the French Quarter. The police found the two men who killed them, but they got off on a technicality. They walked out of the courthouse laughing."

"Rubin, that's horrible. Really horrible. This poor family seems as if they live under a curse." Her hand went to her throat, and for one moment white-hot sparks of light danced around her midsection like fireworks, betraying her emotions. "If I could, I would track those murderers down and deliver a little real justice to them."

He found himself laughing. "It's a good thing Diego isn't around to hear you say that. He'd never let either one of us hear the end of it. As it happens, someone did just that. It seems they found both men, several weeks later, dead. They liked to visit Bourbon Street in New Orleans, and apparently they were the victims of robbery and murder themselves. Many people thought it was a fitting end for them. The detectives have never found who killed them."

"That really was a fitting way for them to die." Jonquille frowned. "Were there other robberies? Like a series of them?"

"That's the strange thing. No other robberies. Just those two. And not one single tiny bit of evidence. No camera on the street or business recorded anything. There wasn't so much as a hair on the bodies or ground. No tread of a boot. No witness. Absolutely nothing. That just doesn't happen, Jonquille. There's always some little thing, even if the evidence doesn't lead anywhere, but there was nothing."

"How were they killed?"

"According to the police, they were executed military style. A knife to the base of the skull. They each died looking at the other one being executed."

"The knife? Or knives?"

"Taken from the crime scene."

"You think the brothers killed them, don't you?" Jonquille guessed.

"If they killed Diego, I'd hunt them to the ends of the earth," Rubin said. "They'd die knowing I killed them. And no one else would ever know I did it. So yes, that's my guess. All three brothers served their country, but that doesn't mean they were the ones that killed those men. They put the three properties up for sale, took their niece and moved away from here about a year after those men were killed. Said it was too hard on her with all the memories."

Jonquille lifted her chin. "If someone killed Diego, I'd help you."

He believed her. He held out his hand. "Let's go see the rest of the house."

"Did you buy the other two properties?" She took his hand.

Rubin had to smile. She knew him better than he'd thought she did. He wasn't going to take chances that anyone was going to move close to him—or Diego. He also wasn't going to let anyone ruin the craft the original builders had put into the homes. In his opinion, too many people modernized everything without first looking to see how to preserve the culture, history and beauty of what was already there.

"Diego bought one of the properties, and we went in together on the second one. We're close to Trap and the Fontenots." He brought her hand up to his mouth and nibbled on her knuckles.

"I didn't meet Trap."

"That was deliberate." He gave her a faint grin. "Cayenne and he just had triplets, and they're getting used to taking care of their babies. Trap also can be a bit of a difficult personality if you don't know him, but he's loyal, brilliant and you can't ask for a better brother in arms. Trap has Asperger syndrome and he can't always read everyone's expressions."

"I'll be fine with your friends, Rubin," Jonquille assured. "You have to remember, I haven't been around people at all in years. I worked in the laboratories at night when no one was around. I went to the conferences, but sat up in the balconies where no one was. I'm a loner. I understand the principle."

"I don't want you to be a loner forever, Jonquille. You'll have me, and you're comfortable with Diego."

"He's low energy until he's really angry." She sent Rubin a small smile. "Neither one of you put off much energy. You don't seem to have tempers, but then when you do get angry you go all out, super high octane. It's crazy."

"Ezekiel says we store it up."

"Has he ever really seen you angry?"

He was leading her very carefully to the master bedroom. There was little furniture in the house. The kitchen had a table and chairs and cooking items. The master bedroom had a bed and two chairs and the master bath had towels and washcloths with toothbrushes and little else. He'd brought food, and both of them always carried a pack with their personal items in them. He really thought the most essential thing in the entire house was the bed, and quite frankly, he could do without that if necessary. He had Jonquille alone. That was the *most* necessary of all.

Rubin stopped just outside the bedroom door and swung around to face her. He was suddenly aware of the difference in their sizes. Jonquille was always so confident in herself. He certainly thought of her as his equal. It never occurred to him she might be nervous because of his temper or his size or any of his abilities.

"Did I upset you with my temper? You need to tell me if I did, Jonquille. It's important for us to always have truth between us."

Her eyes widened. One hand went to his chest. "No, I'm not in the least upset because you have a bit of a temper. I'm all about lightning, Rubin. Diego and I were kidding around about what happens if I get upset, but maybe not so much. Under the right circumstances, it isn't a good idea to be around me. I might just slam a few lightning bolts into your favorite car or the house accidentally."

He couldn't help himself. He burst out laughing. "Woman, you're going to make my life fun. Especially living in close proximity to Trap. His woman can wrap people up in spiderwebs. Mine can toss around lightning. This is going to be a really fun neighborhood."

"Nonny might object to our strange ways."

Jonquille might point that out, but she was laughing with him and that was all that mattered. He loved the sound of her laughter, the way it seemed to wash over and into him. Little sparks of light surrounded her, or maybe that was just the way he saw her.

He had his hand on the master bedroom doorknob, but he didn't want to blindside her. "This is our bedroom, Jonquille. A bank of windows face the river so when you open your eyes, that will be the first thing you see."

The laughter faded from her eyes. She shook her head and stepped very close to him, her blue eyes very blue, ringed with that brilliant silver, meeting his.

Jonquille looked up at Rubin, her eyes searching his dark ones for a long time. Her stomach seemed as if every butterfly in the world had taken up residency and then taken flight. To her, Rubin was the epitome of what a man should be. Not just his features, the ones she loved so much. She knew every line in his face by heart. The way his laugh lines around his eyes crinkled before he smiled. It was the actual man, the soul of him, she loved. His gentleness. The way he was inside.

She had avoided others most of her life, and it had become a kind of self-preservation as well as a way to keep others safe. It was a way of life for her—until Rubin. Just looking into his eyes she was lost. There was no thought of saving herself. Looking into that scorching intensity, seeing desire smoldering, burning so blatantly for her, made it impossible to resist him.

Jonquille touched his face almost reverently. "Rubin." She whispered his name. Stroked a caress along his cheekbone as the rain fell in a kind of musical symphony outside. Not a wild storm, like the one in her heart, but a sensual, dreamy accompaniment.

She was very aware of his hand on the doorknob and what that meant. They were alone in the house together. She had come with him every step of the way, wanting this journey. Hoping for it.

"The first thing I want to see when I wake up in the morning is your face."

"You're sure, Jonquille?"

He was giving her a chance to back out. That was so like Rubin. Always the gentleman when she could see, but beneath that sweet exterior, he could be a ruthless predator. The combination could be both exhilarating and terrifying. She supposed others would find her opposing traits the same way.

"I'm absolutely certain of every step I take with you, Rubin." She was. If he really wanted her—and it was more than obvious his interest went far beyond Whitney's pairing of them—then she wanted to be with him with all of her heart. He was a good man. For her—the best.

Rubin took his time, bending his head slowly toward hers, giving her every opportunity to pull away. Her stomach dropped. Did somersaults. Those butterflies had a field day. Then his mouth was on hers and sparks flew. It was the Fourth of July. Fireflies danced and zipped around them. Lightning streaked through her bloodstream like white-hot fire, and thunder roared in her ears. She slid her arms around his neck and let him lift her, carry her like some bride across the threshold into their bedroom.

Jonquille was featherlight in Rubin's arms. He always forgot how tiny she was because she carried herself with so much confidence. He kissed her over and over, fire raging in his body, but it had been ever since he'd first laid eyes on her—since he'd heard her laughter. That low voice that turned him inside out. He took her straight to the bed and sat her right on the edge, reluctantly lifting his head so he could kneel down and remove her boots and then his own.

She kept her gaze on his for the longest time, remaining silent, and then, finally, she looked around the room, and then at the windows framing the view of the river. Rain was falling in earnest now, peppering the water with drops. Rubin had always liked the peace of the rain when it came, and the wild of the storms when they grew into turbulence. Right now, his mind was on the fierceness of the storm building in his own body, and in hers. He could already see the little white-hot dots of energy sparking like fireflies, lighting his woman up just for him. He stood and drew her to the center of their bed. He liked that. Their bed.

Rubin framed Jonquille's face with both hands, looking into those unique eyes. So different. So strange. "So mine," he murmured, astonished that she had given herself to him. That her choice was really him. The silver ringed the blue, and he let himself fall into that circle of fiery heat. His little lightning bug. A force to be reckoned with. A delicate pixie dancing in the grass, lighting up the sunset, flashing fire, a warrior when needed. She was all of that.

Jonquille reached up to touch his face. She did that a lot and the feel of her fingertips on his skin was a paintbrush stroke of pure sensuality, taking his breath. She didn't have a clue how truly sexy he found her. He leaned down, taking his time, looking into her eyes, watching those long, silvery-blue lashes flutter and close as he took possession of her generous, perfect mouth. He loved her mouth. Her soft lips. The way they curved into her heart-stopping smile. The way they melted under his.

She stilled, like a little wild thing in the woods she spent so much time in. He transferred one hand to her thick hair at the back of her skull, anchoring himself in all that silvery silk, holding it so she wouldn't escape. Her lips trembled under his while he slid his tongue along that soft seam, coaxing compliance. She opened her mouth to him and he took possession without hesitation.

At once, pure lightning charged through his bloodstream—

through hers. Bright streaks of supercharged electricity, crackling and snapping, sparks everywhere, raining down on his skin, inside him, through his veins and arteries, straight to his groin. He caught fire, the rush volcanic, spreading with lightning strikes everywhere. He pulled her closer. Held her tighter. Kissed her over and over until neither one of them could breathe. His belly tightened at the same time his heart nearly shattered. For a man of science who should think with his head and not his body, she was destroying him rather rapidly with just her kisses.

He had imagined a lot of things when he found his woman, but not this. Not this kind of powerful passion or overwhelming emotion. The kind of emotion that could destroy a man if he lost her. He understood so many things now. The way Trap was with Cayenne. Luther with his Lotty. Just kissing Jonquille gave him entrance into a world he'd never imagined existed. He'd always thought he'd find his pairing and he'd love her, but he hadn't expected this—passion. Streaks of bright, hot love so strong he knew he'd give his life for her, that he'd live a half existence if he lost her.

In his arms, next to his enormous strength, her little body felt fragile and feminine. Slight. Delicate like a fairy from another realm, and yet she had a core of steel, was a warrior every bit as strong and enduring as he was. He lifted his head and kissed his way down her chin, that stubborn little chin he'd come to love.

Outside the rain came down in a soft melody, the drops falling into the river and up onto the bank, hitting the trees and the roof of the house. Each note was different depending on where the droplets fell, orchestrating a song for them. He reached down and caught at the hem of her T-shirt and tugged. She lifted her arms without any hesitancy, and his breath caught as he pulled the top free. He'd seen her body before that first night in the cabin, but this time she was giving herself to him and it felt very different.

"You're so beautiful, Jonquille." He kissed his way from her chin to her throat—from her throat to the swell of her breasts.

She reached behind her to unhook her bra, giving him access to the soft weight, tumbling into his waiting hands. His heart accelerated. She was just giving herself to him, the way she did with her kisses. All in. No hesitation. He inhaled the scent of her skin. That fragrance of coral honeysuckle and daffodils.

Shockingly, need was clawing at him, a monster raging at his belly and groin, something that had never happened to him. He'd never considered that it could happen. Love for her kept his touch gentle and him ignoring his own needs. He kissed his way over and around her breasts, avoiding her nipples. He ran his exploring tongue along her ribs and then nibbled his way back up to the undersides of her breasts.

Her legs moved restlessly as he pinned her hips under his. Just having her there on his bed was a miracle, the raining drumming on the roof, matching the pounding of the blood rushing hotly through his veins. His body had never been so thick or so full. He took the time to strip his clothes away, the feel of the fabric against his skin too heavy of an encumbrance. He tugged her jeans from her hips as well, drawing them down and tossing them to the floor so there was nothing left between them.

Skin to skin. He had wanted her like this. All that soft skin. He nuzzled her left nipple, heard her gasp and then drew that stiff little peak into the hot cavern of his mouth and suckled strongly. She let out a soft little cry and arched into him. He tugged gently and rolled her right nipple while her hips jerked and her entire body shuddered under his as his tongue teased her. He used his every expertise to bring her the greatest pleasure, his tongue a rasp of velvet, lapping, teasing, and then suddenly a little rougher and more demanding before switching to her other breast to ensure the same treatment.

Nipping gently with his teeth as he pulled back, eyes on hers, he watched desire flare hot and bright through her with satisfaction. He couldn't help the way he ran his hand possessively from her throat to the tiny silvery curls covering her mound. Her legs shifted restlessly under him again.

"In my wildest dreams, Lightning Bug, I never thought I'd feel this way about a woman. I can't even put into words how I feel about you."

The scent of her was driving him insane. The way every inch of her was soft beyond measure. Pleasure coursed through his body, as hot as the lightning strikes that seemed to flash bright white and scorching through his bloodstream straight to his cock. His mouth was back at her breasts, while his hand slid along her inner thigh, urging her legs apart for him.

Very gently he bit down on her nipple while he stroked caresses along her thigh upward, toward all the smoldering heat, until he brushed at her silvery curls with his knuckles. She gasped. The silver circling the blue of her eyes thickened even more and her breath caught in her throat. *Rubin.* Even telepathically, her voice was breathless.

Watching her reaction, feeling and seeing her heightened desire, just fueled the fire building in him. His heart beat wildly in reaction as his palm inevitably covered the moist heat between her legs. Her body flushed, the color creeping up her belly, breasts, into her neck and face until she was a beautiful rose color. Her breath caught on a moan, a soft sound that made his cock jerk with his own desperate need.

I don't think I can breathe.

He found himself smiling as he kissed his way along her rib cage, exploring her soft skin. Lower still. She had a darling little belly button. He took his time there, while he settled his wide shoulders between her thighs, spreading her legs wide for him.

You can breathe, Lightning Bug. Her hands were in his hair. Fingers twisting in his scalp. He liked that. He slipped his finger into her slick heat and her lashes fluttered. Lips parted in a startled soft cry and her hips bucked.

Jonquille stared up at Rubin's face, the lines carved deep with a harsh sensuality. His eyes were dark and hooded, his desire stark, raw and intense. He dipped his head and lapped at her belly button, fingers tugging at her right nipple. One finger slid into her sex, making her gasp. Lightning was fierce, white hot and jagged, sizzling through her bloodstream, striking at her core. Thunder crashed and roared in her ears while the tension coiled tighter and tighter in her body with an unrelenting, merciless pressure.

Rubin stroked his tongue down her belly in a series of caresses that took her breath and had her squirming, her breath coming in hot, ragged pants. "Honestly, Lightning Bug, I've wondered if the flavor of you would match the scent of your skin and the taste of your kisses."

His voice, always unfailingly low and soft, was rougher, rumbling over her body like a roll of thunder. Dark hunger was etched deep into the lines of his face, was there in the raw desire so intense in his hooded eyes. She could barely breathe with wanting him. With the anticipation of his every touch. Of every stroke of his tongue. He looked, not for the first time, like a hungry predator, about to devour her. A little thrill of nerves shot down her spine, but she was desperate for him to continue.

As always, Rubin took his time, kissing his way around her belly button to her mound and the tiny silvery curls there. Her hips jerked as he very slowly and deliberately spread her thighs apart, opening her to him.

"So beautiful, Lightning," he whispered.

The rain intensified, falling harder, hitting the leaves of the trees, the roof, and the river, producing various sounds to go with her soft moans as he shifted his body, his wide shoulders between her thighs. She could see his face, those planes and angles she'd fallen so in love with. She knew them by memory. She'd drawn them. She had them in her mind. Mapped them with the pads of her fingers. Outside, the wind had picked up and blew through the trees, making them sway, casting shadows throughout the room through the wide windows. Casting shadows over Rubin.

Her breath caught in her lungs as she watched the way his eyes went from dark brown, almost black, to those of an animal on the hunt at night. He had the frightening yellow glow of the wolf staring at her hungrily. He seemed to almost disappear for a moment in those shifting shadows, but his grip on her legs didn't waver. She blinked, her heart pounding, and once more his features were fully there again, a harsh mask of pure sensuality. Those wolf's eyes were focused utterly and completely on her, so intense it was shocking.

He dipped his head slowly, that wealth of dark hair spilling around his forehead. It should have made him look feminine, just like his long lashes, but there was nothing feminine about him. He had too strong of a jaw, too intensely masculine.

Rubin's tongue did a slow foray up the inside of her right thigh, stopping just beside her pulsing clit. She wasn't certain she was going to survive. She wouldn't have been able to stay still if he weren't holding her legs. The anticipation was shocking. He did the same on the left side. Her entire body jerked. She felt his warm breath. Every nerve ending in her body was acutely aware of him, sizzled with fire, with electrical currents, running from her deepest core to her breasts, to her brain. Throughout her bloodstream. She'd never been so aware of herself as female and so aware of a man as utterly male.

His tongue suddenly, without warning, swiped through her hot, needy folds. A streak of lightning stunned her, racing straight up her body in a shimmering bolt of white-hot fire to flash behind her eyes, nearly blinding her with alarming, unexpected and quite shocking pleasure. His hands gripped her thighs. She'd forgotten his enormous strength and he was wielding it, yet even with his strength, his thumb moved back and forth against her skin in a caress meant to soothe her.

You have that taste I crave, Lightning. Coral honeysuckle and wild daffodils. All Jonquille. My beautiful woman.

His tongue lapped at her. Two leisurely strokes and then he began to lap as if he was a wolf in the wild, greedily devouring the cream spilling from her.

Just like that the air in her lungs was gone, leaving her gasping. Her mind stopped all coherent thought. There was only room for feeling. Her body needed. Desperately needed. It wasn't simply a want, a desire, it was a need growing beyond anything she'd ever experienced. Electricity surged through her bloodstream, threatening to burn so hot she was afraid she would burn both of them from the inside out. Waves of sensation poured over her. Into her. Swamped her until she cried out, trying to anchor herself by clutching at his shoulders and then his hair.

That only seemed to drive him on. He used his tongue to penetrate her, stabbing deep and then pulling back, going shallow, thrusting rough and then gentle. Every muscle in her body tightened in response. Every nerve ending caught fire. The lightning strikes increased in her bloodstream, driving straight to her deepest core, one after another, until she was breathless. Raw. Fear ripped through her, as tension gathered in her center, coiling tighter and tighter.

Rubin? She dug her nails into his shoulders.

I've got you. I'll always have you. Relax, Lightning Bug. Trust me.

She did trust him. She made the effort to let pleasure take her, to turn her body over to him, but his mouth was aggressive, his tongue driving into her, then flattening to flick her sensitive button. She heard herself cry out, a cross between a sob and a moan. A desperate cry of need, and then his mouth was over her clit, suckling. Hot, bright light burst behind her eyes as the pleasure surged over her, radiating outward and upward in waves.

Rubin knelt up between her thighs, looking at that beauty laid out in his bed. His woman, one he loved. One he felt passion for. One he thought he'd never have. He cupped her small bottom in his hands and dragged her all the way to him, keeping her legs on either side of his body. She was small and delicate looking, but Jonquille was anything but fragile. Still, she was afraid, and he didn't want to lose her now.

His cock was merciless, so thick and hard he feared he would lose control if he waited too much longer. With the base of his throbbing, painful shaft in one tight fist, he lodged the broad, weeping crown in her slick, hot entrance. Just that contact took his breath. She was scorching. Her body fighting to draw him deep. It was difficult to think with his blood roaring like thunder in his ears. He had to find a way to stay in control when he was skating the very edge, a shock when he was always in control.

"Look at me, Jonquille. Eyes on mine." He had to see her. Make certain she was all right. He wasn't hurting her. She was so small. "You tell me if we have to stop." It would kill him, but he would.

He waited until those silvery-blue eyes jumped to his and then, holding her gaze captive, he slowly began to invade her scorching-hot sheath. He knew she would be hot, she was lightning, but this . . . An inferno of silken muscles clamped around his cock like the tightest fist, taking his breath. The friction of that steady invasion was threatening to cause him to lose what little control he had left. Nothing had ever felt this good. Nothing.

"Do you have any idea how you're making me feel? What you're doing to me?" He dropped one hand to her thigh to rub soothing caresses, trying to steady her. Even to his own ears he sounded a little hoarse. He didn't know who needed soothing—Jonquille or him. He had to clench his teeth and breathe to keep from letting his body take control and plunge deep and hard the way it so desperately needed to. The fire. The heat. The scorching-hot silken fist surrounding him. It was all a perfect sensation. He shared that feeling with her.

"You gave me this, my little Lightning Bug. You did this for me. You're always giving to me when I'm trying to give to you."

He wanted to distract her by showing her what she was doing to him. She was tight and the sensation was amazing, beyond comprehension for him, but it was uncomfortable for her. Burning. Stretching. He felt her discomfort just as she felt his near euphoria.

He continued to move slowly, boring inch by inch of his thick shaft into her, watching her blue eyes and those rings of silver deepen. She panted, little ragged gasps that had her breasts jolting and swaying, adding to the pleasure coursing through him. He couldn't help but love the sight of her body stretched around his. He was right there. She needed to stop him now or he was going to take her all the way.

"You ready for this?"

Her gaze clung to his, those large eyes a little dazed but dark blue with desire. Her skin was flushed, nipples hard little pebbles. "More. All of you."

Rubin didn't wait. He drew his hips back, was rewarded with a gasp and a shake of her head. He plunged deep, driving through her thin barrier and burying his body fully in hers. Her core temperature seemed to grow even hotter. White-hot friction sizzled through his body. Sent electrical currents raging. Their combined thunderstorm threatened to burn out of control.

He tried to stay gentle, but Jonquille caught the rhythm and made her own demands, moving into him, crying out with a sobbing breath for more. He plunged deep, dragging his heavy cock over her sensitive bundle of nerves over and over. Her velvet-soft muscles squeezed and stroked his cock mercilessly with what felt like a thousand tongues of scalding heat, giving him such exquisite pleasure he wasn't certain he would survive.

Jonquille moaned his name. Chanted it. Her nails dug into his shoulder. Slid down his back. Her hips rose to meet his eagerly. Rubin pulled her body even closer to him, sliding her legs easily over his arms, giving him a different angle. He never took his gaze from hers. Or his mind from hers. He wanted to know if there was one single sign of discomfort.

Her sheath was hot—scorching hot—and growing hotter with every fiery plunge he took. He set up a hard, fast, very deep rhythm. She felt like a sweet tunnel of pure silken lightning, that white-hot fist gripping him in a fierce, possessive clasp. He just continued to burn hotter and hotter. Or she did. Or they did. His balls tightened. Power coiled hot and bright.

"Keep looking at me, Jonquille. Let go with me." She was close as well. He felt her.

Jonquille didn't—couldn't—look away. Everything Rubin did to her sent pleasure spiraling through every nerve ending. It was as if he was so connected to her that he could tune to the electrical charges in her body and set them on fire. Her mind was nothing but sheer chaos. Rubin's cock pistoned into her over and over, and each time sent lightning zigzagging through her body from core to breasts and back. The electrical storm between them was so fierce and connective that even without the lead strokes coming from the clouds, little sparks like fireflies danced around her outer skin and leapt from his body to hers.

The streaks of fiery light didn't deter Rubin at all. His features were a mask of pure sensuality, his eyes intense, focused, primal, almost feral. He moved fast and hard in her, his relentless, burning cock threatening to destroy her. Flames sizzled inside her with every thrust, streaked through her, around her, around them. The crackling bolts burned through her body, taking her higher and higher, that pressure deep inside coiling tighter and tighter until she was afraid she would lose her mind.

The fireball inside her roared and thundered, spun and ricocheted off the walls of her body, but she couldn't breathe or think. The tension kept building. She'd always been hot. Too hot. Afraid she would burn from the inside out. Now it was really true. All around her she would see the evidence of the lightning bugs spilling out of her body, too hot to be contained. Zipping through the air all around her.

Rubin continued to surge into her, and she never wanted him to stop because she was desperate. She needed. But she didn't know what. But this time, the fire was too hot. The lightning too close, with nowhere to let it go. The electrical charges were going to destroy her—destroy him. She couldn't let that happen, but she didn't know how to stop it.

My lightning bug. Just step off the cliff with me and fly.

Rubin's hands tightened on her. There was love in his eyes. Tenderness. Right there for her to see. It had been there all along. Looking into his eyes, she let the strength of the sensations rushing through her body take her over. Fear receded enough to allow her to feel the intensity of the roaring fire as all pleasure. His shaft swelled even more, pressing tightly against her channel. In reaction, her silken muscles clamped down on his cock hard, like a vise, even while he pumped in and out of her, causing the friction to be wilder. Hotter.

She felt the contractions, the ripples of pleasure spreading through her entire body. This was a storm at its best, an electrical outpouring of heat and fiery fury rushing through her in a torrent of flames. Her body locked down almost viciously on his, grasping greedily, squeezing and milking his thick, long cock with her scalding-hot muscles, forcing him with her.

Her blood had never been this hot, pumping through her body in a complete firestorm while thunder crashed in her ears. Flames, white hot and sparking like fireflies, burned over her skin and behind her eyes. The lightning storm in her body seemed endless, the waves crashing through her strong and fierce, a beautiful fury rocking her. She heard her own cry. Heard his hoarse shout. Her bones seemed to melt until she became pure energy, just a white-hot streak twined with Rubin, melded together, wearing the same skin, sharing the same mind where she floated in nothing but pleasure.

Around the room little fireflies seemed to dance and then slowly settled while her heart pounded like crazy and she tried desperately to find a way to breathe. Rubin very gently lowered her legs to the bed.

I have to know you're all right. We got a little out of control, Jonquille.

She had to smile because he used telepathy instead of trying to talk. He wasn't getting any more air than she was. *I'm just fine. Perfect. You are perfect.*

He was. Everything about him was perfect.

But I'm not moving. If you think we're going to jump up and head back to the Fontenots', you're going by yourself. I can't move.

Rubin laughed. She loved his laugh. She knew that not too many people got his laughter, but he gave that to her. He sounded younger. He looked younger. He turned away from her and went to the master bath. She heard water running and wished she had energy enough to move so she could clean up, but that wasn't happening. Not yet.

Rubin returned with a hot washcloth and towel. Of course he would. He was Rubin. He was already clean, and he gently cleaned her. She didn't know why she wasn't embarrassed, but she wasn't. He was thorough too. Just as he had been when he asked her all sorts of personal questions about sex and birth control. He was frank and uninhibited about his sexual practices. It wasn't like she could have sexual practices when she might accidentally electrocute someone, but she was careful enough to stay on birth control.

She was a woman alone. If Whitney ever did reacquire her, she didn't want him to get the chance to use her in his breeding program. In spite of the fact that she was lethal herself, she could be overpowered by sheer numbers, and if she was raped, she didn't want to have to go to a clinic and then decide what to do. Jonquille was extremely practical and thought about things in advance and tried to prepare for every possibility.

Rubin lifted her into his arms, cradling her close as he lay down in the center of the bed on his back, pulling her over his body so that she sprawled over the top of him like a blanket.

Jonquille laughed, nuzzling his neck. "Do you expect me to fall asleep like this?"

His hand crept slowly, almost seductively, from her bottom, up the curve of her spine to the nape of her neck. "Yes. But don't count on much sleep, Lightning Bug. Not tonight. I've got other plans."

A shiver of excitement went through her. Anticipation. That particular tone of his was mesmerizing. Compelling. She turned her head and kissed his shoulder. "Plans?"

That hand made the same slow assault on her senses, returning to her bottom, this time lingering on her left cheek. Rubbing. Little lazy circles. Massaging. More circles. There was a comfortable intimacy Rubin established between them, yet it was charged with such sensuality even now, and as sated and limp as she was, she was acutely aware of his body beneath hers and every touch of his strong fingers on her.

"I waited a lifetime for you, Jonquille. Once I found you, I felt like I had to wait even longer. I'm not wasting any time making sure you know who your man is."

She had no doubts who her man was, but she didn't mind in the least if he wanted to show her, or reaffirm as many times as possible.

18

Jonquille felt safe with Rubin and Diego. Both men gave off such a low level of energy she had no problem being around them. Being with several men from their unit in close proximity, even out in the open, was quite frankly terrifying. The men were quiet, and weirdly, so were the two boats, as they made their way through the swamp toward the location of the island Sean had inherited from his maternal grandmother.

Jonquille found herself sandwiched between Diego and Rubin. In the boat with them was Ezekiel, clearly the man they deferred to. Mordichai and Malichai were both on board. Malichai had a prosthetic leg, which didn't seem to slow him down. Malichai was married to a woman named Amaryllis who had opted to stay home and help protect the children with the other women staying back with Nonny. Jonquille could tell the brothers were close and included Diego and Rubin in their family. Ezekiel's wife, Bellisia, was very small, much the same build as Jonquille, with blue eyes and blond hair. Rubin had informed Jonquille that there were few better—or deadlier—in the water than Bellisia.

Gino Mazza was silent and scary and put out no energy at all unless one counted a black, forbidding kind of darkness like the heralding of death. She knew he was married. She'd met his wife several times in the kitchen with Nonny. Zara loved to cook, and she spent time with Nonny and the other women. She limped when she walked, which wasn't that often because she was supposed to stay off her feet. Zara seemed the epitome of light, the opposite of Gino.

Several times, Rubin had wandered over to Zara when she was sitting on the counter with Gino's arm around her waist while Nonny was explaining a recipe. Jonquille had watched his gaze flick to Gino and then Gino nod almost imperceptibly. The exchange was so small, no one else even noticed. Jonquille was aware of everything Rubin did, and she'd been drawn to Zara from the moment she'd been introduced to her. Rubin had forbidden her to attempt to heal anyone after she'd nearly burned herself out healing him, so she'd kept a distance, but the pull was tremendous. Something was very wrong with Zara's feet.

While Nonny gave her cooking lesson to a roomful of women—and Gino—Rubin just happened to position himself very close to Zara. His palms moved over the tops of her bare feet, approximately an inch from her skin. Zara must have felt the sudden heat, because she looked startled and nearly jerked her feet away, but Gino leaned into her and she didn't move. Her man brushed a kiss along her temple and whispered something in her ear. She nodded and kept her attention on Nonny.

The boat took a particularly hard swat on the water, nearly

throwing her into Rubin. He put his arm around her to steady her. She should have been ready for the pitch and sway of the boat on the water, but she'd been too busy thinking back on that midmorning before Rubin had taken her on a "picnic" and to see the house he'd bought.

Diego frowned at her. *You doing okay?*

For some reason, Diego's concern made her feel a part of a larger family, not just Rubin's but his family. She smiled at him to reassure him. *Was just thinking about how hot your brother is instead of keeping my mind on business.* She made certain to include Rubin just as Diego automatically had.

Diego's frown turned into a dark scowl. *That's ridiculous. There's nothing hot about him. You keep that up and he's going to be an arrogant ass if it's not already too late.*

You want to share with the rest of us? Ezekiel asked, proving he could read the waves of energy even though they were small.

Diego shrugged, and to Jonquille's mortification he repeated the conversation for the others. *This is not the first time she's told him this kind of crap.*

Rubin drew her deeper beneath his shoulder—he had broad shoulders. Jonquille lifted her chin at Diego as the others in the boat laughed. She drew on the electrical currents in her body, feeling them moving through her in little rushes, culminating in the fingers of one hand. Spreading her fingers wide, she held on to Rubin with her other hand just to be absolutely certain of control and touched Diego's thigh with her fingertips, zapping him.

He jumped nearly off the seat. She returned her hand to Rubin, looking as innocent as possible. *I only tell the truth, Diego. I don't understand how you can't see how utterly gorgeous he is. Although he doesn't follow his own advice. He told me I wasn't to heal anyone and then he does it after he got shot and shouldn't have been doing any such thing, especially when we're going to this island to attempt to help these men. So he can be . . . um . . . difficult.*

What do you mean, he healed someone? All humor faded from Diego's mind and he pinned his brother with dark, angry eyes. *You know this is too soon for both of you. Jonquille shouldn't be going to this island and neither should you. I let you talk me into it, but we agreed you'd be careful. Who the hell did you decide was important enough to risk your life healing, Rubin?*

There was dead silence. Ezekiel was suddenly looking at Rubin as well. His eyes were a strange amber color, and when he turned that piercing gaze on you, it was as if he could see inside of you. Jonquille could see he wasn't happy and he was waiting for an explanation. Rubin sighed and shook his head. She felt that well of stubbornness in him and knew he wasn't going to answer.

Jonquille felt terrible that she'd said anything. She'd been teasing Diego. She hadn't thought he would get angry at Rubin—that anyone would. She rubbed her chin on his ribs. *I'm sorry, Rubin. I had no idea Diego, or anyone else, would react that way.*

"I asked him to take a look at Zara's feet," Gino said. "It isn't on Rubin. All this time, all of us have been working on her, but she can barely walk, and not a single day goes by that she isn't in pain. Not an hour. She never complains. Never. But I see it in her. I can feel it. It breaks my heart. Nonny's beside herself. Wyatt and I have discussed trying to operate. Joe's worked on her multiple times. She isn't getting better, Zeke. Diego, I didn't know there was a risk with him looking."

They'll be the same about anything you do, Lightning. They get overprotective. I'm fine. You're in my head. You can tell I am. If my brother cared to, he could look as well. He doesn't like the fact that we're going to this island. He wanted to go and check it out ahead of us.

She noticed he hadn't just included Diego when he said "overprotective." He'd used the pronoun "they." She glanced around the boat. None of them looked that happy, although after Gino's explanation, they were a little more accepting.

Was there a risk to your life, Rubin? Ezekiel asked, straight to the point.

No, examining a patient is simply checking to see what's beneath the skin, much like a scan. There's no threat to me whatsoever. She barely noticed.

Rubin was telling the strict truth. There wasn't a risk when one scanned a patient. All the healer was doing was conducting an examination to see what was wrong. The healing was much more difficult. What had taken place with Patricia Sawyer and Nonny was difficult and tiring, but the "surgeries" Rubin had performed on Luther and she had on Rubin were something completely unheard-of. Something none of them talked about or wanted others to know about. That kind of surgery was life-threatening.

Did you just examine her or did you attempt to heal her injury? Ezekiel pursued.

Jonquille knew Rubin and Diego had told Joe and Ezekiel about her ability. They had asked her first. They'd explained what her talent was and how it differed from being a healer. How rare it was and how she could never allow Whitney to know about that particular psychic capability. There were only a handful of people, as far as they knew, who could perform surgery with their minds. She was one of them.

Jonquille denied she had the ability. Rubin had mapped out what she needed to do. She'd followed his instructions to the letter. It had taken some persuasion to convince her that she had the same gift as Rubin and he would help her develop it. She wanted that, was excited about it, but knew the cost to him was great, so at the same time was apprehensive. Now, seeing the way the others went so still, even though they all, including Gino, were extremely concerned for Zara, they were more uneasy over risking Rubin.

She knew a healer would have a difficult time examining a patient and then not following through to try to help them. She'd been in the room with Zara, and her need had called to Jonquille. It was only her promise to Rubin that had kept her from at least trying to help her. The answer to Ezekiel's question was of course he had tried. Rubin couldn't do anything else but try to heal Zara. She had the feeling every single person aboard the boat knew that about him—and they would eventually know that about her. She realized what Rubin had to have felt all the time living in a glaring spotlight with others making his decisions for him as if he were one of the triplets at Nonny's.

I spent a very small amount of time working on the tendons. They've been severely damaged. I knew I had to come here, so I told Gino I would try again when I could really take my time, Rubin admitted. *Zara has an interesting problem. The man who attacked her knew anatomy, and he knew what he was doing. He did the most damage to her tendons that he could possibly do without actually severing them.*

Jonquille heard the interest in his voice. He wasn't going to drop it. He would find a way to help Zara no matter what. He might not get her to a point where she was running like the wind, but he didn't want her in pain. She couldn't help but smile up at him. That was her Rubin. No matter how many others might frown on him, he would go his own way.

You didn't exactly answer my original question, Ezekiel persisted. *Did you put your life in danger?*

For God's sake, Zeke, do I look two to you? No, my life wasn't in danger. I did a favor for my brother. I looked at his wife, who has been in pain for weeks. I've wanted to help out, but no one asked me, so I kept a distance. I was grateful he asked me. It doesn't feel all that good constantly being kept out of the family circle.

There was a long silence. Rubin's tone was low, not at all accusatory or self-pitying, but just his words alone told the others he'd been hurt.

It's meant for your protection, not to push you out, Ezekiel said eventually.

Rubin didn't reply, but Jonquille was firmly entrenched in his mind when she realized he'd already detached from the others. He looked out over the water, his dark sunglasses shielding his eyes and his expression as unreadable as ever. He appeared remote. Distant. Just as she'd first seen him in the cabin when he'd confronted her. This was the man who went off by himself so often. She felt the affection the others had for him. Their respect. Their need to keep him alive at any cost, even when he didn't want them watching over him. This was how they made him feel. Alone in the middle of a crowd. In the middle of his family. Pushed out. Held at a distance.

She glanced at Diego. He was looking at her. It was just as difficult to read the expression on his face as it was Rubin's. He had also pushed his sunglasses over his eyes. She felt his regret, but she also felt a subtle flow of power drifting from him. It was so subtle that had she not been close to him, she would never have caught it. It was a steady stream that spread out and encompassed everyone in the boat.

She took a quick look around. All these men and women had psychic abilities. They were all enhanced, and each one of them had alarm systems built in. They'd been around Diego far longer than she had. Rubin didn't appear to notice either, and he was closer to Diego than anyone. What exactly was Diego doing? That steady stream ensured that everyone continued to need to protect Rubin, and somehow, now, she was included in that.

What are you doing? she demanded. *Stop it, Diego. If your brother ever finds out what you're doing, he will kill you. I might kill you.*

Diego couldn't quite conceal the shock flaring in his mind. At once, Rubin's dark gaze flicked from his brother to Jonquille and then back to his brother again. That was dangerous. Rubin had capabilities of replaying images and memories just as she did.

What's the plan when we reach the island? she asked Ezekiel, mostly to distract Rubin.

The plan is to protect all of you working on the men there. Once you get that done, we're going to pay Chandler a visit and get the pilot back, hopefully in one piece. Ezekiel's voice was grim.

There was a note in his tone that suddenly warned her. She tightened her fingers in Rubin's. *The other soldiers he enhanced? The newer ones he's surrounded himself with? They might fight you.*

Those men are soldiers in the service of the United States, not Chandler. They are only on loan to Chandler. He enhanced them without the consent of the government and for his own private use, even if they did agree to it. They are accepting private pay over the pay of their government. If they are running operations for Chandler outside their government orders, they will answer for that.

Jonquille leaned closer to Rubin. Again, that note in Ezekiel's voice told her that GhostWalkers answered very differently for their crimes than other soldiers. Being on her own had been difficult, but she made up her own rules. She didn't have to worry that if she made a misstep she would be hunted by grim-faced men who were elite trackers. She glanced at Gino Mazza. He was definitely someone she didn't want coming after her, any more than she would want Rubin or Diego tracking her. They would never stop. Never.

Her heart accelerated in spite of her effort to keep it under control. These men were predators and every one of them heard. Rubin shifted just slightly to angle his body protectively to cover hers. To her shock, Diego did the same, so it was nearly impossible for anyone to see her sandwiched between the two much larger men.

Lightning Bug? Rubin's voice was gentle. His thumb moved back and forth in a caress over her hand. *What is it?*

Jonquille? Diego was looking out over the water as if something was hunting them.

Your people have a lot of rules, and if you don't follow them, I think the price could be death. That's what Ezekiel is saying.

Rubin pulled Jonquille tighter into his body, her front to his side, clamping her close with one arm while he looked a little despairingly at his brother. *She said "your people," Diego. She's pulling away from me.*

She's not pulling away from you. She's in a crowd, something she's never been in, and it's scary. There are rules. It is different. Give her a break, Rubin. Nothing's going to take her from us. Nothing. Not even her fear. She's tough. She looks like a little wimp . . .

Are you two arguing again? Jonquille broke in.

He was calling you a little wimp, Rubin said in a pious tone.

Don't you zap me again. Diego glared at her. *I didn't call you a little wimp, I said you* looked *like a little wimp. There's a difference.*

I do not look like a little wimp. She sounded indignant. Her eyes went mostly silver, and for a moment little sparkling lights zinged around her rib cage. *You take that back, Diego. I'm not little either. If you're going to call someone little, Bellisia is little.*

Diego coughed. Cleared his throat. Rubin met his eyes and tried not to laugh. It was extremely difficult. Jonquille tilted her chin up and narrowed her eyes at him. *What?*

Rubin couldn't resist. He'd never be able to resist the combination of that stubborn little chin and those gorgeous eyes. He brought his mouth down on hers. He meant to just brush his lips gently over hers, but it didn't seem to happen that way. The moment his mouth was on hers, sparks erupted. Lightning sizzled, streaked down his throat, roared through his veins and thundered in his groin. His mind turned to complete chaos.

The toe of a boot smacked him hard in the shin, and he jerked his head up to glare at his brother, who just looked smug.

Woman, you are dangerous. Rubin brushed another kiss on top of her head.

I hate to break this to you, pixie, Diego said, sounding as smug as he looked, *but you're the exact same height as Bellisia.*

The boat began to slow as they came up on their destination. Rubin thought it was a good thing as Jonquille drew herself up, her body almost glowing—never a good sign with her. Even her hair glowed and stood out a little from her head. Rubin knew Diego was deliberately teasing her, keeping her from thinking about the things Ezekiel had said about what might happen to GhostWalkers who decided to go against their code of honor. That, and Diego had accepted her as a sister. As his family. He treated her with affection. He meant what he'd said about not losing her for any reason.

Two men waited on the dock. *Thirty yards. Tall cypress straight ahead. Sniper,* Rubin reported, all business.

Rooftop on taller of the three buildings, sniper, Diego added.

We've got eyes on them, Ezekiel assured.

The second boat was nowhere in sight. The team leader, Joe Spagnola, Wyatt Fontenot, Draden Freeman and his wife, Shylah, as well as Trap Dawkins and his wife, Cayenne, had all completely disappeared. Rubin knew they had already made their way around to the other side of the island, shrouding their boat in mist, muting the sound so it would be impossible to detect them as they invaded. Already they would be moving through the woods to protect their fellow GhostWalkers.

Ezekiel and Mordichai exited the boat first, and the two men greeting them saluted instantly, going ramrod stiff when they were introduced. Zeke was no one to mess around with, and it showed when he wanted it to. He was making them aware of his rank in order to take any attention off Rubin, which Rubin detested. Still, he sat quietly, waiting for his turn to get off, watching Malichai manage to step from the boat to the pier with an easy, practiced grace. Rubin knew what that cost him. He knew how hard Malichai worked to make that transition happen.

Diego stood, his body blocking both Jonquille's and Rubin's from the line of the sniper in the cypress tree as well as forcing the one on the roof to switch to a different angle if he was trying for either of them. Rubin cursed under his breath, something he rarely did. Jonquille's hand moved in his.

You have to let him have this, Rubin. Gift it to him. He needs it.

Her voice blew through the fierce anger building in his mind like a breath of fresh air. He pressed her hand to his chest over his heart. *I need him to be safe.*

You have to look at him. Really look at him without seeing yourself. He's barely holding on. You're seeing what you want to see in him, not what he actually is. You see charming and easygoing. You see that he's fine. Look at him, Rubin, with your eyes and mind open. Don't be afraid to—I'm right here with you.

Rubin almost pulled away from Jonquille. He didn't like what she'd said and wanted to deny every word. Her voice was very matter-of-fact, very calm. Her hand was steady in his, just the way her mind remained. Taking a breath, he forced himself to really go over what she asked of him. Had he been afraid to really look deeply at his brother? Was she right about that? He had never been afraid to confront anything in his life. He'd met every problem without flinching. But his brother . . . Diego . . .

What had Jonquille asked of him? *You have to let him have this, Rubin. Gift it to him. He needs it.* She had seen a terrible need in his brother that he had refused to see. She had seen something in his brother he had known all along but had been so terrified of that he had deliberately turned away from it, finding every excuse not to examine it too closely.

Rubin knew Jonquille was right. Diego needed to protect him. Now he had to protect Jonquille as well. He needed her almost as much as Rubin did.

"Let's go," Diego said. "I'll lead to the pier and then step aside. Gino will help you out of the boat on that side, Jonquille. Rubin on this side. Let them. Don't give them any guff about your abilities."

"I don't suppose Bellisia needed . . ." She broke off and looked around. Bellisia was nowhere to be seen. She wasn't in the boat, and she wasn't on the pier.

She's in the water. She'll guard the boat. Nothing will get by her in the water, Rubin advised.

"Stay close to me," Rubin said aloud. "If they test the draw of your electromagnetic energy, I can pull it away from you."

"I planned to do that anyway," Jonquille said. "Diego? You'll be right behind us?"

"Yes. I don't like any of us out in the open like this, although Shylah has the one on the roof in her sights and can take him out if he blinks wrong. Cayenne is hovering above the squirrel man in the tree and he doesn't even notice the spiderwebs, not to mention Joe has him lined up in his scope as well. Draden and Trap have combed the area for guards and found and sent the location to our men. I'm going with you into the barracks to watch your backs as you try to heal the worst of them."

"I thought Joe and Wyatt would be helping us," Jonquille said.

Rubin kept his hand on Jonquille's elbow, pretending to steady her as they walked along the boat to the very side of it where Gino waited. "They'll come in if you indicate they're needed, and Mordichai and Gino will take their places," he explained. "Remember, they've been here earlier, while we were convalescing."

Ha! Is that what you call it? Diego sneered.

Jonquille started to turn, but Gino had a firm grasp on one arm while Rubin had the other. She was nearly lifted off the boat. Rubin stepped in close behind Jonquille, crowding her little body, her back to his front, Gino solidly in front of her while Diego stepped off the boat and casually filed in after Rubin. They followed the two men, who led them all to the barracks where Sean and his men waited for them.

Just as they got to the barracks and the guard at the door opened it and stepped aside for them, Mordichai moved up in front of Ezekiel and stepped inside while the others waited. He stood still, his gaze moving through the extremely neat, spacious room with the bunks, inspecting the area carefully. He took his time, scanning the ceiling, the walls, the beds and every possible space for potential threats before he stepped aside and allowed the others into the barracks.

Rubin inhaled the smell of death. He glanced at Jonquille. She was frowning. She smelled it too. He pushed right past his guards without thinking, not paying any attention to what Sean was saying in greeting, and walked straight to the bed where a young soldier lay looking up at the bunk above him. He turned his head slightly toward Rubin and gave him a faint smile. His breathing was erratic. Wheezing.

"Little." Gasp. "Too." Gurgle. "Late, Doc."

"You think so?" Rubin didn't ask permission, he simply yanked back the thin cover and put his hands over the bare chest, an inch from the man's skin. "Jonquille. Get on the other side." He snapped the order without thinking.

This man was in a bad way. Really bad. Wyatt had told him to be prepared to lose one or two. Rubin wasn't going to lose this one, not if he could help it. Jonquille moved into position on the other side of the bunk and did the same, lowering her palms over his chest.

"His name is Leon," Sean said, coming up behind them. "A good man. A good soldier."

Rubin ignored him. "Do you see that, Jonquille?" *Those idiots act like they know what they're doing and they don't. They mess with the human body and then walk away saying it's all for science.*

How do we fix this? Can we fix this?

The heart was struggling because everything going to it was a mess. Leon's insides were a mixture of animal and human parts, most not fitting together properly. Rubin had no idea how he had managed to live this long. He glanced around the room and saw the others were all watching closely. The others had taken care of him. This was one Joe and Wyatt had said was impossible to save medically.

"Tell us what you need to help him," Sean said. "Anything."

"Zeke, have the men set up for an operation immediately. I'll need Bellisia. Call her back for me. I need a line into him now, Malichai," Rubin ordered. He looked at Sean. "The other one you said was in bad shape. Where is he?"

Sean indicated across the room toward another lower bunk. "His name is Milo. We've been giving him oxygen, but . . ." He trailed off.

Rubin removed the thin sheet without preamble, opened the shirt covering the man's chest. He was dotted in sweat, just as Leon was, only more so. Had Sean not been providing oxygen, Rubin doubted if he would have survived another hour. Milo was well aware of it too. He looked at Rubin in despair, shaking his head slightly and lifting his hand barely off the mattress to flutter his fingers toward Leon, indicating for Rubin to help his friend.

Rubin found the same problems inside the man as were in the first patient—a mixture of animal and human parts that just didn't fit. "I need you to clear your men out of here, Sean. The men who are capable of hearing telepathically anything Jonquille hears, I need identified. Don't screw around. We don't have time for that. I'll be giving her instructions to try to save one of these men and I can't have interference. Identify them now, before they leave this room."

"Andrew and Hudson are both capable of hearing what Jonquille hears," Sean said.

"Malichai, I need lines in this patient as well. He's going to need oxygen and blood. We have to put him out. I don't want his veins collapsing. Same with Leon. I'll need them side by side, but with enough room for me or Jonquille to get around both patients. I need water for both of us to drink. Two good chairs. If possible, darken the windows in here. If not, keep everyone away. Zeke, I'll need Joe and Wyatt. Get them here fast. Sean, I need a couple of volunteers willing to donate body parts if necessary, but they have to be the closest to these two in DNA that you are aware of."

"That would be Christian and Simon," Sean identified without hesitation.

"If they agree, bring them here along with Hudson and Andrew." Rubin was snapping orders, aware time was slipping away.

His team was setting up fast as they always did in the field. They were good at it, sterilizing the operating tables, getting lines into veins, transferring patients onto the tables. They had two more makeshift cots waiting for the donors who would be put out as well. Bellisia hurried in, a towel wrapped around her, clothes in hand, looking for a bathroom in which to change. Her blood type was RH-null, a very rare type that was compatible with all types, making her blood very sought after. It meant she was born without any antigens in her blood.

Sean hurried away to find his volunteers and the two men the GhostWalkers had to make absolutely certain they couldn't hear one single word said between Rubin and Jonquille. Surgery would be done in this room on the two patients, but it wouldn't be done with scalpels. It would be done with minds. No one could have that information outside their own unit.

Of the two patients, Milo was really laboring to breathe. Both struggled, but Milo couldn't seem to pull oxygen into his lungs and from his lungs into his bloodstream. Rubin again positioned himself over the man, his palms a scant inch from his chest, Jonquille on the other side, mimicking his action. Her gaze flicked to him.

Rubin gave a slight shake of his head. "We still have company," he reminded.

Hudson and Andrew were sitting in chairs, frowns on their faces, no doubt wondering what they were doing while doctors appeared to be setting up a makeshift operating room. Malichai approached, asked their names, leaned over them and gave each one a shot. Within moments they slumped over.

"Out. I'll keep checking them, Rubin. You've got a go here," he reported.

"Our donors are heading to sleep slowly," Ezekiel said. "They're both strong and very cooperative. Bellisia despises giving blood, it really hurts her, but she's ready whenever you need her to transfuse."

Rubin nodded, his concentration on Milo, assessing the damage to the man's insides, what parts were usable and then how they could best connect them and make them work long-term. He blocked everything out but the task ahead of him.

This is impossible.

No, it is simply one thing at a time. Surgery, just as if you were in an operating room. We have to keep him breathing. He's struggling. So that first. Then his blood pumping. Once we deal with those two things, we can fix each problem. He kept his voice calm and certain, infusing her with confidence.

Jonquille followed his lead, dealing with the lung issues first, making certain their patient could get oxygen to his lungs, into his bloodstream, heart and brain. They would have to reroute the blood away from the heart to deal with the heart issues, but one thing at a time.

Once we stabilize Milo, we'll do the same for Leon and then you'll have to operate on one while I take the other.

Jonquille's head snapped up. She shook her head. "No. Absolutely not. This is complete reconstructive surgery of the entire inside of his body, Rubin. I'm not capable of that. In an operating room I wouldn't be capable. No." She started to back away, complete panic on her face. "I would kill him."

"Jonquille. I don't believe you noticed, but our patients are dying. They don't have anyone else. If Zeke could operate, he would. If Wyatt could, he would have done so already. We are their only chance. We don't have time for discussion. I know you can do it. You just follow what I'm doing." Rubin was very calm. "Look at him. You're all he's got. Take a breath. We'll do this one step at a time. Joe will be with you for anything you need. He's experienced and fast. Wyatt's right here as well. Look to me if you get into trouble."

Deliberately, as if he had complete confidence she would step back to their patient's side, he indicated Milo. *He isn't able to get the oxygen to his lungs properly because the parts aren't fitting together. It's like they took pieces of pipes and connected all the wrong tubing. Check Leon and see if he's the same way. I want a good look at Milo's lungs. You do the same with Leon.*

Starting with assessing the damage would give Jonquille confidence. She could see the inside of both men's bodies easily. She had a strong healing ability, and that transferred into a need to help, no matter how afraid she was.

Rubin didn't take his mental image off the inside of Milo's chest. Over time, he had learned to treat surgery exactly as if he were in an operating room. He had to deal with all the same body parts. It was a matter of moving everything with his mind, rather than his hands. The problem was, Milo's body parts weren't exactly all human, and they really were like a mismatched puzzle.

The inside of the body appeared as if a child had thrown pieces together, connecting the organs with too-small veins and arteries— even the chambers of the heart were mismatched, as if the creator had taken leftover parts and shoved them together. Blood leaked everywhere. It was a wonder the man had lasted this long. It was a testament to his strength of will and the care his fellow Ghost-Walkers gave him.

Leon appears to be a mirror image of Milo as far as I can see, Rubin. Jonquille filled his mind with an image of Leon's upper chest. If they put the two bodies on top of each other, they would pretty much have the same problems, other than a few of Leon's veins and arteries allowed for better blood flow.

Let's get it done, Rubin said. They had to reroute the blood so they could fix the veins and arteries, give both men ones that would actually work. It was a time-consuming and dangerous surgery. Extremely meticulous. Sorting out what amounted to what carried the life's stream of blood and oxygen supply throughout the human body and making certain it was the correct size and shape for every major organ was a nightmare.

We have to go very slow and take our time. You have to take breaks, Jonquille, when you need them. Self-care is just as important as patient care in this instance, or we won't survive.

He remained steady and calm, moving through Milo's body with complete care and confidence so that Jonquille could follow his every action doing the same for Leon. She had to learn control of her ability along with the actual surgical skills. He took great pride in her for following the map he laid out for her, but also for listening to Joe's quiet instructions when it came to pulling back her heat as she sealed connections with white-hot energy. Joe was very experienced in psychic healing. He might not be a psychic surgeon, but he was extremely good at healing most wounds or illnesses. Rubin knew his experience would help to steady Jonquille.

This type of surgery wasn't the same as trauma surgery. There wasn't an exchange so much as an actual surgery. It was just time-consuming because one had to use the mind to move everything inside the body. It was extremely difficult and took an amazing amount of energy, draining the body and mind until one felt as if they couldn't move or even think.

Time passed and Jonquille staggered. Joe caught her and lowered her into the chair they'd provided, quickly pushing water at her and wiping her face. Rubin sank into the chair behind him. They needed to continue. They had to take a break after hours of work, but they were both exhausted.

"We need some way to get energy fast, Diego," Rubin said. "If Jonquille could absorb it, she could feed it to me. We've got several more hours of work to do."

"That's what you need, Rubin?" Ezekiel asked.

Rubin sighed. "A lot of it. She's like a magnet. She can absorb it, but everyone here is so low-level . . ."

"I can give her whatever she needs," he said. "The others need to go to the other side of the room for a few minutes though, just leave us." He waved them away.

Joe, their team leader, stood looking at Ezekiel for a moment, shook his head and then followed the others across the room.

Ezekiel crouched down beside Jonquille's chair. Bellisia took her hand. "You really can absorb energy, Jonquille?" Ezekiel asked quietly.

She nodded but kept her eyes closed.

"It's going to be dark and powerful."

She gave him a faint smile. "Best kind."

Around them the air crackled, began to heat. Power amassed in Ezekiel and poured off him in waves. They could see sparks snapping all around Jonquille, as the dark energy streamed straight to her and was swallowed up immediately until her body was glowing. Humming. Static electricity made her hair stand out. Little dots of light snapped and crackled, leaping from Jonquille to Rubin.

Ezekiel sank all the way to the floor and pulled Bellisia onto his lap. "That's the first time anyone's ever taken energy like that. It's never happened before. I didn't think it could happen."

"There was no way for anyone to see what happened," Bellisia answered. "It was gone too fast. I think your secret's safe." She looked to the couple. "Right? His secret is safe?"

"It goes without saying, Bellisia," Rubin said quietly. "Thanks, Zeke," he added. "Jonquille? We've got to get back to work."

It took several more hours of complicated surgery, and blood from Bellisia, before Rubin and Jonquille were able to turn the rest of the process over to Joe and Wyatt so they could once again collapse. This time, neither one bothered to try to open their eyes, even for the boat ride home.

19

"Colonel Joseph Spagnola to see Oliver Chandler. I will also need to see Major Sidney Kingsley immediately. Have him meet me now and walk with me to Chandler's office." Joe spoke with complete authority. On either side of him were Ezekiel and Gino, both in full uniform. Flanking them, in rows, came Draden, Mordichai and Wyatt, and then Trap, Malichai, Diego and Rubin, also in full uniform. All officers. All were armed and all were grim-faced.

The guard at the gate blanched. "Yes, sir. I'll call the major now. I didn't know you were coming. You're not on the list."

"Get the major here now," Joe said crisply. He continued to walk briskly, not even slowing down.

"Yes, sir. Yes, sir."

Heads turned as the GhostWalkers continued up the broad cobblestone walkway leading to Oliver Chandler's sprawling building. The layout had been studied and committed to memory. They had not only the satellite images, the plans Major General Tennessee Milton had provided, but also the meticulously drawn blueprints Sean and his men had given them as well.

This time, their unit had not come alone to this piece of property Oliver Chandler owned and thought he protected with his government-paid employees. He was so certain he could get away with anything. He had created his own army without permission, going beyond his contracts, using his protections and believing himself above the law, believing he would never have to answer to anyone. Oliver Chandler had more money than he knew what to do with. He liked his position as a respected and high-level security defense contractor. Most likely, having a couple of colonels and a full unit of GhostWalkers coming to investigate the disappearance of a team that had gone AWOL would make him very happy, although Chandler and his guards would have no way of knowing the officers coming to see him were GhostWalkers.

Two men approached them, angling across the grass to cut off their direct trajectory to the building. Joe halted his forward progress when the major and his companion, a tall, well-built, athletic-looking man, were directly in front of them. Joe waited, looking the two men up and down in that way he had. Rubin wanted to smile. The major's companion came to attention immediately, saluting. The major was much slower, but eventually—and sullenly—followed suit. Only then did Joe deign to speak.

"I'm Colonel Joseph Spagnola, Major Kingsley." Deliberately, Joe used the major's name to show he knew exactly who he was. "I want you to call your men out onto the field now. Immediately. All of them."

Kingsley looked over the group of men in their uniforms, managing to look insolent. "I'm afraid I can't do that . . . sir." The major flashed a barely there smile. "Had you called ahead, we could have accommodated you, but today is a bad day. Mr. Chandler is testing weapons today, and we don't allow any outsiders on the premises while the tests are being conducted. I'm sure you can understand."

The man standing beside him gasped and swung his head toward Kingsley, frowning. When the major glared at him, he looked at the ground. Rubin knew that was Jarod Barnard, recruited from the elite Marine Raider Regiment. He was a good soldier with an excellent record.

Joe raised an eyebrow. "I gave you a direct order, Major Kingsley. I didn't ask for an excuse." His voice was low, but there was a whip of command in it—one that said, *I'm a commanding officer and you had better remember that.*

The smile vanished instantly from the major's face. His shoulders straightened as he stiffened, annoyance crossing his features. It was clear that few ever questioned him, probably since he'd been enhanced. The fingers of his right hand curled into a fist. "Yes, sir. Right away, sir."

Joe looked bored and turned away from him, dismissing him, knowing that would aggravate him more than anything else. This was a man who had suddenly discovered he had a small kingdom and ruled it with an iron fist. They needed to see just how far gone he really was, and they needed to know very quickly. These men were sworn to uphold their duty to their country. They served in various branches of the services, but they were all men who had served with distinction, and they upheld their code of honor with pride.

Rubin felt bad for Kingsley. They had no idea what kind of DNA had been put into him. He was in the Air Force and his record was spotless. He wouldn't have been chosen for this assignment had it not been. He never would have passed the requirements for the GhostWalker program if he'd had any kind of psychological problems. Whatever had been done to him had caused the damage. The enhancement had pushed his natural aggression and testosterone levels off the charts, ripping away his basic kindness and humanity. Fortunately, his training kicked in and he obeyed his commanding officer, albeit reluctantly.

They still didn't have the full list of men who had applied for the GhostWalker program under Oliver Chandler. They had lists of men who had been assigned to guard him over the last four years, but it was impossible to tell which ones he'd given the tests to and then chosen for the operations. Two of their best hackers had tried to get into Chandler's computer and failed. His work had to be taken off the computer and stored until it could be looked at, but right now, it was imperative to see what shape these soldiers were in. And they had to find the missing pilot from the first group of soldiers—the squirrel men—Chandler had had enhanced.

The fate of these men was in Joe's hands. Rubin didn't envy him those life-or-death decisions. There were no trials for GhostWalkers. They signed on knowing that. If they ever went rogue, they would be hunted by other GhostWalkers and they would be destroyed. There was no real choice. All of them understood that when they signed the papers and agreed to be psychically enhanced. Technically, none of them had agreed to physical enhancements, but once it was done, there was no way to undo it. They all had to live with it. Rubin feared for Major Kingsley. He looked by turns confused, belligerent, resigned and grateful they were there.

Men began appearing, hurrying out of buildings to the lawn in various states of disarray. Three were being helped and they were obviously in bad shape. Rubin's every instinct was to go to them. The healer in him was so strong he actually took a step toward them, but Diego and Ezekiel blocked his forward progress with their bodies.

Wait, Rubin. Let's just assess what's going on here first before any-thing else, Ezekiel cautioned. *My understanding was that this group of GhostWalkers was in much better shape than the others, but it doesn't look like that's the case. There are fewer of them and they look sick. Either they aren't all here, in which case we have weapons pointed at us, or Sean was very wrong. This isn't a good scenario.*

The men lined up. Rubin counted no more than twelve men who looked fit, three very ill and three others that were iffy. Ezekiel was right. It wasn't a good scenario. Why would Sean think these men were the "perfect" ones as opposed to the squirrel men? They didn't seem all that perfect to him. In fact, given that Major Kingsley had obvious problems, and he was certain Barry, the man who had betrayed Sean's team, did as well, there was an underlying sickness Rubin needed to find and address in these men.

Joe walked slowly up and down the line of soldiers. When he came to one of the men swaying with illness but doing his best to stand, the colonel stopped in front of him for several long mo-ments. Rubin knew he was assessing his condition.

"Sit in the grass, soldier."

"Sir, I am fine, sir."

"That was an order, soldier," Joe said and moved on to the next man.

His insides are messed up, not like we saw with the squirrel men. This man has all human organs and parts, but he isn't put together prop-erly. He's leaking blood internally. I don't know who did these opera-tions, but they didn't know what the hell they were doing.

Joe was always calm. Always steady. The hint of anger, that lash to his voice that rumbled through their minds, was a warning. Joe's powers unleashed could be devastating.

When he had all three of the obviously invalid men sitting in the grass and had moved to the second row, Ezekiel reached out to their allies. *Ryland, you see anyone with eyes on us? I can't feel them, but clearly this isn't enough men. The major seemed too cocky to me, as if he could turn away officers without any repercussions.*

We've searched the entire complex, and other than the few guards on the perimeters, and those are babies, certainly not GhostWalkers, there are no others. Kaden, Ian, Kyle, Tucker and Jonas have been all around the buildings and rooftops. So far, nothing. They aren't even protecting that laboratory as they should.

Rubin thought that over. The major was relying too heavily on his enhancements. He was feeling the newness of his souped-up body. His acute hearing and sharp eyesight. He believed himself superior, and with his fellow soldiers failing to live up to the new standards, that only increased his own belief that he was even greater.

A man wearing a charcoal suit and sunglasses emerged from the main building on the left. He walked purposefully but with measured steps, taking his time to reach them. When he did, he ignored the officers, instead going straight to the major.

"Sidney, would you please explain to me what is going on here?"

Chandler had a mild French accent, one Rubin was very aware was more affected than real. He had deliberately turned his back on Joe, a sign of disrespect, in order to show Kingsley he didn't have to fear repercussions by not following orders.

"The colonel wanted to inspect the men, sir."

"The colonel has no right to inspect the men, Major. This is private property, not a military base." Chandler turned, removed his glasses and looked Joe up and down dismissively. "These men are my private security force, and this is private property. You have no right to be here, and I want you to leave immediately."

"These men are soldiers of the United States government, in service to that government, Mr. Chandler," Joe responded mildly.

"You are very much mistaken if you think they are your private security force. They are under my command."

Chandler had a difficult time keeping his expression pleasant. "You don't really understand . . ." He trailed off expectantly.

"Colonel Spagnola," Joe supplied.

"Well then, Colonel Spagnola. I do important work here for the United States government. Top security clearance only. I have to have a security team I trust surrounding me. I've worked with these men and know them. They're on loan to me. I don't, however, know you. So, if you don't mind . . ."

"You have several very sick soldiers here, Mr. Chandler."

"If you and your men don't leave, Colonel, I'll have you escorted off the property."

"That is an impossibility, as I outrank your security force and they are under my orders, Mr. Chandler. I am under orders. That is what the military is all about. We follow orders."

"Then if I call someone with higher rank than you and he orders you to leave this property, you will have no choice but to do so," Chandler said smugly. He pulled out his cell phone.

Be ready, Ryland. He's calling now, Ezekiel advised.

At long last. Rubin knew they had been chasing an elusive tie to a White House enemy for some time, but could never find out who it was. If Chandler actually called someone there, they would have a name. Somewhere to start.

"Good afternoon, Tracy, Chandler here. Put me through to Barron. I have a situation here I'd like him to take care of for me."

They were all silent. Rubin observed the men. Most looked tired. Those on the ground, a little hopeless, where before, when Joe had been inspecting them, there had been a ray of light. Now, most of them looked as if they were already defeated. Kingsley went back and forth, one moment appearing triumphant, the next upset, especially when he looked at his men. Rubin had never seen men more desperate for help than these soldiers—or more stoic. They had resigned themselves to dying a slow death.

"Have a bit of a problem, Barron, need you to tell this colonel to leave my property. He seems to think he can throw his weight around. Wants to inspect my men." Chandler listened for a moment and then laughed. "Sure thing. Next time I'm there, we'll have lunch. Thanks for this." He extended his arm, phone in hand. "Barron Scotsdale, aide to the vice president, would like a word with you."

Joe took the phone. "Mr. Scotsdale. Colonel Spagnola. Yes, sir, I understand completely. Yes, sir, I understand, but the only one that can rescind my orders is Major General Tennessee Milton. He sent me here with specific orders and until he rescinds those orders, I am obligated to carry them out. You can call him and have him call me. In the meantime, I will continue to follow them." More listening. "Yes, sir. I know who you are. I will expect to hear from Major General immediately."

Instead of placing the phone in Chandler's outstretched hand, Joe hit the end call button and pocketed the phone. "Gino and Mordichai, please place Mr. Chandler under arrest for his numerous treasonous crimes against the United States of America." Joe's voice turned crisp, all military commander.

"What?" Chandler backpedaled. Tried to put himself behind the major. "Kingsley, do something. It's your job to protect me from these people."

"Major Kingsley is a soldier serving his country, Chandler," Joe said calmly. "He does not serve a man who would willingly sell out his country."

Gino and Mordichai closed in on Chandler and grasped him by either arm. They had him in shackles, his arms behind his back.

"This is not necessary. I demand to talk to my lawyer. You have no proof whatsoever."

Joe ignored him. "I believe it is safe enough to bring your wife in to access Mr. Chandler's computers, Major Mazza. If you would escort her?"

"It's impossible to access my computers without a password, and that's not going to happen," Chandler snapped.

"There is a pilot being held prisoner here. He was a member of the other security team sent here that Chandler had enhanced," Joe continued as if Chandler wasn't speaking.

Most of the men looked at one another, clearly puzzled. They weren't aware of the pilot's presence on the property. Rubin and Ezekiel continued to look at Major Kingsley and Jarod Barnard. They had exchanged an uneasy look.

"Major Kingsley, why was this pilot brought here?" Joe asked.

"Sir, he has knowledge needed to help my men recover from their present illness, which he steadfastly has refused to give up." Kingsley barked the information to the open field, refusing to meet the colonel's eyes.

"You are certain he has this information?"

"Yes, sir."

"Was Chandler the one who told you this?"

"No, sir. We discovered the other soldiers had been investigating a woman who worked in a research laboratory."

"How did you discover that?"

The major hesitated, looked down at the ground and shook his head. "One of the soldiers in the other unit told Mr. Chandler, sir."

"He betrayed his unit?" Joe pushed.

Kingsley looked even more uncomfortable. "Things were done to him. To us . . ."

"Shut up," Chandler snapped. "That's classified information."

"I'm a GhostWalker, Major Kingsley," Joe said. "You have no need to worry that anything you say to me will be used against you. I need the information as fast as possible to help your unit. The other unit sent us here to aid yours and recover their pilot."

There was a hushed silence, as if the wind itself stood still at the announcement. Rubin was always surprised that one GhostWalker didn't recognize another. They all watched as Zara Hightower Mazza was escorted into the main building by her husband, Gino. It was easy enough to recognize Zara. Her face was plastered everywhere. She was a leading expert in the field of artificial intelligence. She was also an enhanced GhostWalker. One of her greatest gifts was her ability to talk to machines. They liked to talk back to her and give her all their information when she asked for it.

It just so happened that the satellite that Oliver Chandler relied on was one purchased from Samurai Telecommunications. No one had the software in audio or video like they did. The developers had installed it themselves and taught Chandler how to use the program. He worked with them directly, never knowing that Azami Yoshiie was married to Sam Johnson, a GhostWalker and member of Team One. There was always a back door installed into a computer once the GhostWalkers had uncovered a tie to Whitney. Zara could easily use that back door to get into all of Chandler's computers, talk to them and take every one of their secrets.

"Barry became aggressive, sir. It happens to me. I can't help it sometimes, no matter how hard I try not to. He told Chandler. I think Barry genuinely wanted help for everyone. I did too. I wanted that woman here. I thought if she could help all of us, maybe we'd be all right." Kingsley looked down at his boots and shook his head.

"I want you to take me to the pilot immediately," Joe said.

"He didn't tell us anything," Kingsley said. "No matter what

Chandler ordered done to him. He wouldn't tell us where he was supposed to take her or what she could do for everyone. He wouldn't say anything but his name and rank. He acted like a prisoner of war." There was grudging respect in his voice.

Kingsley stepped out of line and began walking toward a smaller building to the left of the main building. "This way, sir."

Joe followed Kingsley, with Ezekiel, Mordichai and Draden in step behind Joe. Rubin watched them go.

I'll be checking on those sitting on the lawn, Diego, so don't freak out on me.

Diego shot him a glare. *That isn't in the plan.*

It is now. They aren't looking too good. Wyatt, tell the others "at ease" and let's take a look at them.

"At ease. We're doctors. We're going to be assessing all of you, asking a few questions. Answer honestly. Don't try to be heroes. That doesn't get you anywhere in this situation," Wyatt said.

Rubin stepped out from between the men guarding him and strode straight to the man he thought looked in the worst shape. He was sitting on the grass, alert but curled into himself. He had a yellowish tinge to his skin and orange in his eyes, indicating his liver wasn't functioning properly.

"You feeling extremely fatigued?"

"Yes, sir," the soldier acknowledged.

His uniform indicated he was Army, a member of Green Berets. "Your name?" Rubin knelt in the grass beside the soldier, ignoring the horror on the man's face.

"Sergeant Major Brick Zion, sir. I can stand."

"You can lie down right where you are. I'm going to examine you the way GhostWalkers are often examined. You're going to feel heat. I want you to remain very still while I do this. I need to see what's going on with you." Rubin's voice was low but stern, expecting no arguments. He was wearing his uniform, declaring he was a colonel in the Air Force. He had stated he was a GhostWalker. No one was going to quarrel with a thing he said.

"Yes, sir."

Wyatt came up on the other side of the downed man. All the men watched with great interest as Rubin and Wyatt extended their hands, palms down over the sergeant major's body and began moving them over him, a scant inch from him. Anyone could see the light bursting from Wyatt's palms. It was much more difficult to see the light coming from under Rubin's.

The two men exchanged a long look. *Liver's in bad shape. He's leaking too much blood,* Wyatt said. *Can you save him?*

Rubin nodded. *He's not nearly as bad as the squirrel men. I think Jonquille could do this one on her own. I won't let her yet, she's not ready, but she could if we were in trouble. He's serious, and we need to get to him immediately, but it's not an intricate operation. Let's move on to the next one.*

Wyatt nodded.

"All right, Sergeant Major. You're going to need surgery, but you should be fine. You'll have to be transfused and your liver looks like hell. Drinking is out for you from now on, so if you really like the taste, you might want to make a resolution to decide you don't like it after all. You get me?"

"Yes, sir."

For the first time Brick Zion looked hopeful. His friends broke into grins. One started to say something, but at the last minute, stopped himself.

Rubin and Wyatt moved to the next man seated in the grass. Just observing him for a moment, Rubin realized this man was having trouble breathing and doing his best to conceal it. He caught the man's hand and looked at his fingernails and then up at his lips. Was there a bluish tinge?

"Your name?"

"Chief Petty Officer Harris Ledes, sir." Every word was gasped out, his chest and belly moving in and out rapidly.

Rubin wasn't certain the best thing for the man was to lie down. "Does Chandler have a medical room? Someplace he would keep oxygen?" He looked to Jarod Barnard, the Marine from the Raider Regiment.

"Yes, sir."

"I need that now."

"Yes, sir."

"One of my men will accompany you."

"Yes, sir."

Barnard didn't seem to take offense when Malichai went with him. If the soldier noticed that Malichai was on an artificial leg, he didn't comment on it. Rubin hoped he wasn't stupid enough, or desperate enough, to try to escape or challenge Malichai. The order was clear: If anyone got out of line, they weren't to hesitate to kill them. Malichai would carry out that order, and he was fast and deadly.

"We're going to examine you, the same way we assessed Sergeant Major Zion. You'll feel heat. Just stay still and let us do this." Rubin was extremely concerned. He passed his palms over the chest area first, looking at the heart and lungs from every angle. Wyatt did the same. They examined the arteries going to the heart and up into the neck and brain and then to the lower extremities. Rubin didn't make the mistake of letting anything show on his face.

He's a mess. He's going to have to be operated on first. We'll need to set that up right away. He'll need lines in him now, or we'll lose him,

Wyatt. Draden never misses. Get him working on him. See if any of Ryland's men can help. I'll assess the next patient while you're setting up to operate on this one. I'm calling in Jonquille. We've got Bellisia if we need blood. She can donate to anyone, although I hate using her. She has such a bad reaction to needles. Hopefully, there is enough blood on hand for all of these men and we won't have to ask her.

Harris Ledes had the same kind of damage in his body as the squirrel men Rubin and Jonquille had repaired. The body parts didn't fit because they weren't all human. How much time he had remaining was anyone's guess. Rubin had to get to work on him immediately.

"This man has to be moved to the infirmary now. Dr. Fontenot, Colonel, will be setting up for the operation. Anything he needs, get it for him," Rubin snapped.

Draden, need you back here, stat. Emergency operation. Calling in the women. Jonquille, need you now, Rubin said, moving to the third man down.

Fortunately, this man didn't look as if he was going to die any moment. He made a halfhearted attempt to give Rubin a smile and glanced up at Diego, Rubin's ever-present shadow.

"I'm not so bad, sir. Master Sergeant Kevin Morris, sir." He coughed, covering his mouth with his arm. When he took his arm away there was a tinge of pink around his lips.

Rubin sighed. "Are you having problems breathing?"

Morris hesitated. "Sometimes. Lying down."

Rubin passed his hands over the man's chest just as there was a small stir among the men, telling him the women had arrived. Zara was already in the building. Bellisia, Jonquille and Cayenne came up behind him. All three women looked sweet and innocent enough, but all three were deadly.

Rubin, we need you now. Double-time it, Joe's voice blasted in his mind.

That shocked him. Joe had to know he was setting up for several important operations, operations that were time sensitive. That meant whatever he was going to find was even more pressing.

"Jonquille, finish assessing this patient and then lay out what we'll need in the operating room for the others. We're running out of time with Chief Petty Officer Harris Ledes. You may have to start without me. You've already done two of these before, so no worries, and you have access to my memories."

Are you out of your mind? She had the presence of mind not to say it aloud where all the men could hear her, especially the patient she was kneeling down to take his place beside.

No choice, Lightning Bug. Wyatt's with you. You'll do fine. "Leaving you in good hands, Master Sergeant." Rubin turned and sprinted in the direction Kingsley had led Joe. Diego followed him.

Ezekiel met them halfway to show them through the maze of stairwells and doors to the basement where the pilot was being held.

"Kingsley said they called him Swamp Man. Everyone did."

Rubin's gut knotted. He didn't know why, maybe the warning note in Ezekiel's voice. "Who is it, Zeke? Someone we know?"

"Wyatt's brother," Ezekiel whispered, as if saying it aloud would somehow make him overheard. Wyatt's psychic gifts were powerful. The last thing they needed was for him to lose his mind while they were trying to save so many lives. "His brother Roch. I don't know what the hell he's doing here. He's in bad shape, Rubin, but you have to save his life. You don't, Wyatt will bring down this compound and everyone in it."

"Thanks, Zeke, don't put any pressure on me or anything." Rubin kept pace with him, matching him stride for stride. "What am I looking at?"

"I've got lines into him. Loss of blood. They beat the holy shit out of him. Organ damage. Chandler injected him with chemicals for sure. Tried to get him to talk. He was enhanced as well. I think Chandler went at him a second time, this time on his own, without a surgical team. Really messed him up. I don't know if you can fix him."

Rubin drew in a sharp breath. "I might need Jonquille. If I do, we'll lose the Navy SEAL, Chief Petty Officer Ledes. I can't be in two places at one time, and neither can she, Zeke. Wyatt and Joe can maybe handle the other two, keep them alive until we can get there, but no way will the SEAL make it that long."

Zeke swore under his breath as they leapt over the railing and landed at the bottom of the stairwell. Rubin followed Zeke down another narrow hallway to what appeared to be a gloomy basement without windows. The room smelled of blood and death. There were blazing lights set up. Clearly, operations had been performed in this room. There were bloodstains on the floor.

A man lay on a thin, boardlike gurney, a mop of thick black hair a stark contrast to the white cloth beneath his head. His face looked mostly gray, with bruises around his sunken eyes, nose and mouth, although his jaw was covered in that same jet-black hair, helping to hide any swelling. Rubin didn't wait to be told anything else. He could feel the urgency in all the men in the room.

He laid his palms over Roch's chest. He was shirtless, his body shivering uncontrollably. They had been fortunate that Draden had gone with them as protection. He could find a vein on anyone in the worst of circumstances, and he'd gotten a line into Roch.

We'll need blood fast. Get Bellisia. Hopefully, Chandler has blood on hand for the others. Get Trap working on finding that out. Diego, get behind me. Stay right behind me. This one was going to be bad. *Joe, you're going to have to be on the other side of him.*

For the first time, Joe looked helpless. "This is beyond my experience, Rubin."

"I'll tell you what to do. Get over there." *Jonquille?* He poured urgency into his voice. *Listen to me, Lightning Bug. I know you think you can't do that operation, but you have it down. Follow the map in your head. I need you here as quickly as possible. If I don't have you, I'll lose this patient, and I'm telling you, honey, we can't afford to lose him. He's too important to people we love. I need you to get that SEAL clear and then get to me. We clear?*

We're clear. No hesitation. She was a miracle, his lightning bug. He took a breath and began to unravel the mess that was the insides of Roch's body. He was a big man, built like his brothers, a lot of muscle with that same thick black hair and strong heart. That was what had saved him. That strong heart.

He was confident Jonquille could perform the actual surgeries without repercussions to her body or mind other than being exhausted. Roch was a different story. He needed actual surgery and he also had trauma to his body. There would be an exchange, which he would never allow Jonquille to do with him, not that part, but this surgery would take hours, if—and it was a big if—he could save this man.

No one talked much about the absent Fontenot brothers. They were gone. They'd left home and they were gone. One thing Rubin was certain of—they were intelligent. You had to be if you were a Fontenot. And they were strong. Very few men would have lasted with the kind of torture Chandler had inflicted on this man.

He'd been enhanced more than once. Rubin could see evidence of a recent operation. Chandler had "practiced" on Roch. He hadn't had an operating team to work with and he hadn't cared because he assumed Roch would die. The man was experimenting, determined to have his own soldiers, not understanding what was going wrong with the enhancements. Chandler was a butcher, not a doctor.

Chandler had brought in two different teams of genetic doctors to operate on soldiers and then arranged accidents so they would die before they could take home what they knew about the highly secretive GhostWalker program. He hadn't done it because he was a patriot and he was protecting his country's assets, he'd done it because he coveted his own soldiers to use as mercenaries.

Rubin knew Major General had already gathered the information on Chandler before the GhostWalkers had been sent to terminate him and anyone else deemed a threat to the United States. Any of the men Chandler had enhanced were to be saved if at all possible.

Fortunately, all the men in Rubin's unit were skilled doctors and gifted healers, whether they wanted to admit it or not. He had the feeling they would need every one of them. Rubin moved through Roch's body slowly, closing himself off to his surroundings and the sense of urgency telling him he had to move fast or he'd not only lose this patient but others as well. He would have to trust the others to do their jobs. His only concern was Roch, keeping him breathing, keeping his heart and brain functioning. This man was a Fontenot. He was Nonny's. He was Wyatt's.

He found himself breathing in and out slowly, willing Roch to breathe with him, even though a machine was breathing for his patient. Chandler had done so much damage by trying to create a modern-day Frankenstein. He had left a list of the traits he most coveted in a soldier and then tried to splice them all into Roch, ignoring what had already been done to him.

A small computer was set up in the room, presumably to show

Chandler what to do. He must have filmed the original operation and thought he could just follow along with the already complicated and errant map. Rubin was no genetics surgeon. He didn't have a clue what he was doing in that department, nor could he undo what Whitney or anyone else had done to these men or women, as Jonquille had hoped he could. For one moment he had thought it a possibility, but looking at the mess inside Roch's body, he knew his gift was this—putting back together those torn apart on battlefields or by ruthless scientists. Maybe someone else had a talent yet undiscovered that would help them all psychically, but he knew it wasn't him.

Twice he found himself staggering and dizzy. Both times, Diego caught him and lowered him into a chair, wiping his face and giving him water to drink. He kept his mind firmly in Roch's, not looking around him, not knowing who was in the room or who wasn't. He had no idea of time passing. He only knew he wasn't nearly done.

He would never have gotten as far as he had without Joe or Bellisia. The woman kept giving blood as if she had endless amounts when he knew she was very small and her little body really couldn't possibly have that much in it. And Joe, he just kept stepping up. He was an extremely talented healer, well on his way to becoming a surgeon, whether he knew it or not. He had the gift, he just hadn't unlocked it, probably with all the other gifts he had blocking it. He was the commander of their unit and had so many other problems weighing him down, it was little surprise that his talent was easing its way out of him rather than pouring out.

The second time Rubin staggered to his feet, Jonquille had joined them. She not only looked exhausted, but she felt it as well. He gave her the smaller jobs he'd been having Joe do and pushed Joe to help him with the intricate surgery that would hopefully put

Roch back together. Rubin had no idea what he would turn out like, but Zara had come in and managed to get the computer on and the video to work so he could see what the first set of surgeons had done to the pilot and how. He had Chandler's notes, his wish list of traits he wanted to endow Fontenot with. He also had the list of Roch's actual strongest psychic and physical attributes.

Sorting out the DNA was impossible, although Trap was working on that as fast as he could, but Rubin had to figure out how to make everything fit together inside the body like a giant puzzle. It all not only had to fit, but it had to work smoothly and efficiently. Once he was out of there, he didn't want it to suddenly break down, especially if he wasn't around.

Sweat trickled down his face, and he was aware of Diego wiping it away. It was annoying to be human and weak. Twice he snapped at Joe. Once at Jonquille. Neither said anything back to him, but he felt pretty low and apologized when he could force words through his dry throat. They had to be as tired as he was. They had to be thinking of Wyatt. Of Nonny. The longer this took, the less likely Roch would pull through. He was taking too long. And if he didn't sit down again soon, he was going to fall on the floor face-first.

Diego caught his swaying body and dragged him to the chair again. This time, he wasn't alone. Wyatt was on the other side of him, holding him up as well, his face a mask of emotion when Wyatt normally didn't show anything at all.

"Can't," Rubin muttered, but his throat was rebelling, closing on him. He couldn't see for some strange reason. He kept wiping his eyes, and his ears were ringing. He coughed, turning his face away.

"Drink," Diego insisted. "You don't, you're done and he's dead anyway. You're all he's got, Rubin, so take a minute and rest your brain. You're bleeding."

"I am?" He brushed at his eyes again. He was. His eyes and ears. Not a good sign. He would have forced Joe or Jonquille to stop if either of them were that far gone.

"This is your last shot," Diego said. "You don't get it this time, we're calling it."

"That's on me, brother. He's still alive. I fight for him," Rubin said softly. "He's fighting, I'm fighting." He sucked down the cold water, letting it pour down his throat. Once more he stood up over the body, this time with Diego's support on one side and Wyatt's on the other, and he began working again.

20

Lightning flashed across the sky, great forks streaking in every direction, a wild display of nature's power. Thunder roared simultaneously, shaking the ground, shaking the house so the walls seemed to dance, undulating together with the white-hot veins in the heavily laden purple clouds. The wind whipped tree branches into a frenzy of movement, making the Spanish moss dance like mysterious veils. Leaves and twigs whirled free into the air, tossed about by the unpredictable squall as it burst through the woods, first in one direction and then abruptly changing to another. Jonquille slipped her hand into Rubin's and watched as rain poured into the wide expanse of water, adding to the river and the rich ecosystem.

"You were so right about this exact location, Rubin," she whispered in awe. "It truly is beautiful and so different from one moment to the next."

Just an hour earlier, the weather was sunny and the snowy white egrets were out in full force. She was coming to love to sit on the shaded deck with Rubin, watching the birds as they patiently stalked bullfrogs and fish, shrimp and mice. She enjoyed their beauty as they moved with grace on their long stalk-like legs in the shallow water in the cool of the cypress forest just down from her new home.

She couldn't help allowing her gaze to drift over Rubin, assessing him carefully as she'd been doing the last two weeks. He was still a little pale, but she knew he was far stronger and feeling much better. He wouldn't like it if he knew she was still just as anxious about his health as she'd been when they'd had to fly him home from Chandler's property in a helicopter, with a man she didn't know attending to him because she was too exhausted to do so herself. That man had been flown in from another GhostWalker team, one from San Francisco.

She'd had to rely heavily on Paul Mangan to save the man she loved and care for him while she recovered. The GhostWalkers barely allowed her to get up the first two days and certainly didn't allow her in the room with Rubin. Diego brought her news, but he always looked grim and bleak when he told her Rubin was alive, but still not conscious.

Rubin had remained unconscious for several days, and each one of those days had been agony for Jonquille. Once she was up, she realized she wasn't alone in the endless anguish while she waited for Rubin's brain and body to heal. Diego was just as miserable and anxious as she was—if not more. She spent time with him, just going for walks without speaking, sitting beside him on Nonny's porch or holding vigil in Rubin's room when Paul would allow it.

She grew closer to Diego, feeling like a sister to him, protective and protected by him. They were already forming a family, already *had* formed a family in the short time they'd been together. The intense situation and their love for Rubin simply strengthened their bond. The GhostWalkers made it easy for Jonquille to be around them, keeping their energy down so she wasn't bombarded all the time, but the little ones sometimes made it difficult and she would have to go into the swamp and rid herself of the crackling fireworks.

Roch had also been brought to the Fontenot home, only because, like Rubin, he needed the care of a psychic surgeon and, although no one was saying so, clearly that was what Paul was. Nonny and Wyatt were rarely away from Roch. The oldest brother, Raoul "Gator" Fontenot, arrived by private plane the following day and, like Nonny and Wyatt, didn't leave Roch's side other than to check on Rubin numerous times. Jonquille liked him for that.

When Rubin finally woke and was able to sit up and have visitors, it was all Jonquille could do not to have a complete breakdown. She just sat on the bed with him and cried. Diego didn't say a word, just sat across the room looking at his brother as if Rubin *had* died. Rubin kept his arm around Jonquille and his eyes on Diego. In the end, the three of them just stayed silent that first hour's visit, other than her silly weeping, but it was intense. And she felt love in that room.

Everyone was wonderful at the Fontenot household, but there were too many people, and Jonquille was just grateful she had Rubin back and they were finally in their own home. She couldn't breathe with so many people around her. Diego brought groceries and did most of the cooking for them. He was a rock they both leaned on. She didn't want Rubin to do anything but rest and recuperate.

She realized why Diego and the others on his team watched over him so closely. He was a brilliant surgeon. He did what others couldn't do. She doubted if anyone else could have saved Roch Fontenot, or even if they would have had the strength and endurance let alone the knowledge to do so. He also had the tenacity to keep going when others would have given up. She would have given up. She knew she would have. Even after all the work Rubin had done on Roch, when she arrived and saw what a mess the man was, she thought the case was hopeless and Rubin was risking his life for nothing. Rubin's team understood what they had in him. He didn't want to be treated any differently, she could understand that as well, but he was different and he had to come to terms with that.

"Lightning Bug, stop looking at me like that." There was a trace of amusement in Rubin's voice.

"How am I looking at you?" She knew. Her heart was in her eyes. She adored him and she didn't try to hide it. Diego wasn't out on the porch to make it into a joke. They weren't in their bedroom to make it sultry and sensual. She didn't care what he thought. The sun rose and set on Rubin for her. It always would.

"I'm afraid you're going to have to get used to it, honey," she said softly. "I'm always going to look at you this way because it's the way I feel about you."

Lightning flickered across the bottoms of the purple-blue clouds roiling overhead and this time, she felt the answering jolt in her body. Her hair moved subtly, lifting toward the sky, and the little fireflies began to dance around her midsection.

"I'm going to have to walk out into the meadow until the storm passes. You stay here, Rubin," she directed and went to push up on the arms of the wooden rocking chair. The rocker had been hand-carved by the two brothers. She loved it so much. It was her favorite piece of furniture.

Rubin put his hand over hers. "Stay there, Jonquille. We can practice right here. The water, you, perfect attraction for lightning."

Trepidation seized her. Her tongue touched her lower lip.

"You're too close. So is the house. One miss and our beautiful home is toast." And so was he. Her man. Her everything. She'd come too close to losing him already. That miss was too near. How did one tell a strong man no? Her heart began to accelerate like a race car out of control. She almost started hyperventilating. "Rubin . . ."

"Lightning Bug." His thumb slid over the back of her hand in that mesmerizing and soothing slide. His voice was pure velvet. "This is what we do. We'll just sit here and play. It's relaxing. Think of it like a video game."

"I don't play video games." She tried to glare at him, but she'd found that it was impossible to glare at Rubin ever since she'd nearly lost him. "This is dangerous and you know it. That lead stroke is going to come straight for me. I don't care if the military wants a weapon and you're supposed to be helping them figure out how to develop one, I don't want to take a chance with your life." There. She'd said it and been straight to the point.

The lines in his face softened. The expression in his dark, dark eyes was suddenly unfathomable, but it made her stomach do a slow somersault.

"Think about what's going to happen when the two of us have children, Lightning Bug. Because we are going to have them. Beautiful little girls who look like fairy-tale princesses. If they attract lightning, we have to be able to direct it away from them. If they can direct it away from their siblings, they have to be taught no matter how young. That's going to be our family, and they'll learn that responsibility. We'll keep them safe and they'll keep each other safe. Settle for me now."

She wanted to. She just looked at him. Rubin. Her home. Her man. The best of the best. For a moment her vision blurred and she blinked rapidly to bring him in focus. "You don't understand, Rubin. You can't understand. I almost lost you." She whispered the dreaded secret to him. "I can't sleep. I just stay awake and stare at you while you sleep. I have to. I have to know you're alive and breathing. I understand Diego so much better, the way he can barely breathe sometimes, pacing outside our door, guarding the house while you sleep. He *has* to. We almost lost you." She blinked rapidly again to correct that troublesome blurred vision.

Lightning forked in every direction overhead. Jonquille's pale, silvery hair rose straight toward the sky as thunder roared in a violent accompaniment. Her eyes had gone nearly completely silver, and sparks rained from her fingertips, little charges racing toward the sky. The invisible channel of electrically charged air streaked straight toward Jonquille at approximately two hundred thousand miles per hour.

A powerful surge of electricity burst from Jonquille, bright, beautiful sparks of dancing lights, millions of them, like the fireflies dancing on the grasses of the Appalachian Mountains, or the fireworks exploding over the lakes on the Fourth of July. Before the two charges could meet, Rubin had already shifted the direction of the lead stroke away from the ground charge so that the cloud stroke hit a dead tree in the woods, one hollow and already soaked through. It was clear he'd chosen his target far in advance.

Little sparkles rained down on the porch as the electrical energy settled around her. The charge was building again with the storm directly overhead. She either had to jump off the porch and make a run for it, or ride it out with Rubin and practice for the sake of their nonexistent family.

Rubin was calm. Sometimes the strikes came one after another. Other times they were minutes apart. During those times, he would rub his thumb over her inner wrist, making her intensely aware of him.

"Are you the only one that can direct electrical energy like this?" Jonquille's voice shook.

"I don't know. I'm precise and fast because I work at it. I don't know if there are any other GhostWalkers working on the same things."

His voice was always so matter-of-fact. So calm. She watched the storm as it drifted away, leaving her feeling a little drained after the fifteen minutes of nail-biting fright. Rubin, however, looked as cool as ever.

"You do know that you saved Chief Petty Officer Harris Ledes's life, Jonquille. You operated on him with Wyatt assisting you, and you saved that man's life."

There was both admiration and respect in Rubin's voice, and she couldn't help feeling some pride in herself. It had been a long and exhausting job. She'd had a blueprint to work off of. His body hadn't presented the exact same problem as those in Sean's unit, but she knew what she was doing and at least was familiar with what she had to do. Wyatt was shocked and a little horrified by the mixture of parts that didn't fit. Still, he'd stuck with her and in the end, he knew so much about anatomy he'd been more of a help than the medical books she'd memorized.

"I was lucky I'd been able to work on the two in Sean's crew."

"And you saved the other one, Sergeant Major Brick Zion. You took care of the others with the healers and then helped me. You certainly shouldered more than your fair share of work, Jonquille. I'd say your gift is quite strong."

She gave him a small smile. She loved healing. It felt like such an accomplishment. As if she was actually making a contribution instead of reading about herbs or plants that could aid others. Sometimes her hands used to burn when she was around people and she hadn't been able to do anything. Now she could. Wyatt had helped her so much. Everyone had. Draden. Ezekiel. Each person who reached out to help one of the sick men that she worked on, or that they worked on with her, taught her something new. They were generous about imparting knowledge. That was the other thing: Not only did she have a family, she felt a part of something. Rubin had given her the GhostWalkers.

"Perhaps we can say it's getting there. I love that it is, Rubin. I love that I have all of this. The house. Diego. The GhostWalkers. My ability to help others through healing. What really matters to me is you. Having you."

She went to him because she didn't want him to get up and she knew that he would. Rubin was always the gentleman—unless he was the ruthless predator. She stood between his thighs and framed his face with her hands, looking into his dark eyes. Her heart turned over. This man.

"Kiss me, Lightning Bug," he murmured. "Right now. Kiss me. Sit on my lap and kiss me."

His hands urged her to straddle him. It was easy enough. She was small, and her legs fit under the wooden arms of the rocking chair. She slid her arms around his neck and lifted her face to his. She'd give him anything. Kissing was like lighting the world on fire. An explosion. Their lips came together, soft at first, just a few touches, brushing gently to set off the butterflies, and then she opened her mouth to his. The electrical charges that swirled in her body, growing hotter and more aggressive, dragged at the vast amounts of power produced in him so they came together in a fiery collision.

Sparks rained down like fire all around them. Red and orange. Gold and white. The fireflies zipped like magical beings around both of them, lighting the darkening sky. But it was the fire spreading through her body, white hot and flowing like lava through her veins, that was all she could concentrate on.

Rubin's arms pulled her into him, tightened around her, strong, the way he was, protective, just like him, his mouth devouring her, taking over, feeding the lightning even more fuel, more energy, so they both went up in flames. The porch glowed with red and orange, while gold and white wound around them in wild electrical currents.

"Oh, for the love of St. Peter. Knock it off you two before you burn down the house. Seriously, Rubin, if you don't act in the least responsibly, I'm dumping both your asses in the river. *Both* of you."

Jonquille couldn't help it, she started giggling. She'd never giggled in her life. Rubin fished around for a gun. Or a knife. Any weapon at all.

"Do you not see that I'm busy?"

"I can see that you're disturbing the wildlife and the natural order of things. You want to fool around with your woman, take her in the house so we don't have some kind of nuclear explosion and I have to spend the next twelve months doing paperwork and thinking up lies to cover your asses. I like this house and mine, by the way, which would probably blow up as well if you two kept this up, so just don't."

"What makes you think you'd survive?" Rubin asked.

His voice was so dry that Jonquille pressed her forehead to his chest and laughed so hard her stomach hurt. He threaded his fingers through hers and pressed her hand to his thigh. She could see his answering laughter in his mind, but he kept his features expressionless as he faced his brother.

"I'm made up of the same DNA as you are," Diego said. "You survive an explosion, I'm going to, and that means you'll make me do the paperwork. You always bow out with some excuse, even if it's your mess. And kissing Jonquille and lighting up the swamp is definitely *your* mess."

"Is that true, Rubin?" Jonquille asked, unable to resist, kissing his chin. He had the most delicious stubble there. She nibbled at it. At him. He tasted . . . wonderful. Like love.

"Sadly, he speaks the truth. I do make him do the tedious paperwork. And if he isn't around, you will have to be prepared to do it, because I won't. As for the mess of kissing you . . ." He bunched her hair in one hand and pulled her head back, his dark eyes moving over her face.

Her heart nearly stood still at what she saw there. Stark, raw love. For her. She knew he saw the same mirrored right back at him. Then his mouth was on hers and lightning struck, white hot and perfect.

CHRISTINE FEEHAN

PIATKUS